OCT 2022

Amoli Patel, 25

About •••

Vincent Park, 24

About •••

ey Grey, 32

•••

Virtually Yours ™

Brand

Abou

Maddie Turner, 29

About •••

Mario Garcia, 28

About •••

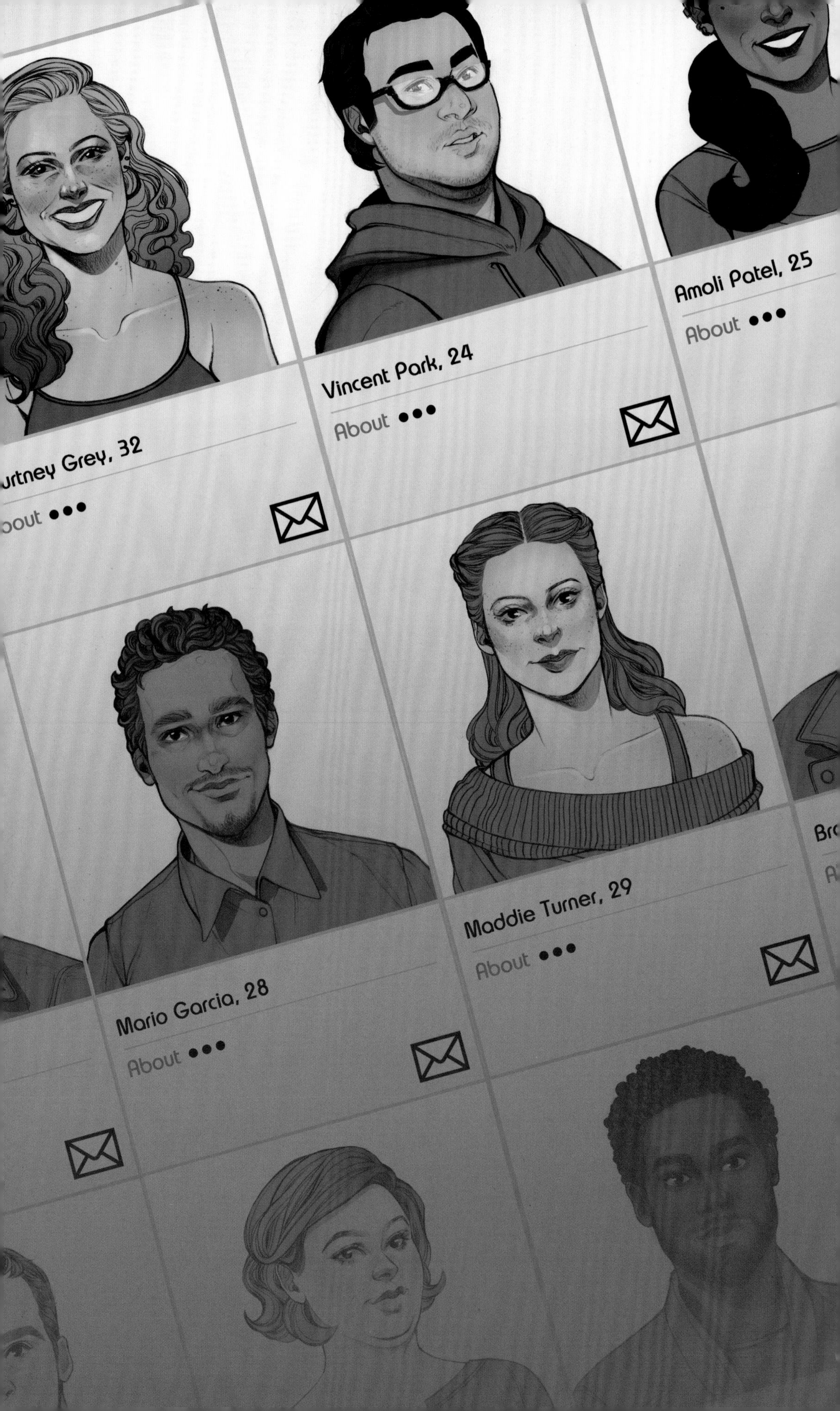
urtney Grey, 32
About •••
Vincent Park, 24
About •••
Amoli Patel, 25
About •••
Mario Garcia, 28
About •••
Maddie Turner, 29
About •••

Virtually Yours

SCRIPT
JEREMY HOLT

ART & COLORS
ELIZABETH BEALS

LETTERS
ADAM WOLLET

EDITS BY KAT VENDETTI

DESIGN BY TIM DANIEL

DARK HORSE BOOKS

DARK HORSE TEAM

President and Publisher   Mike Richardson
Editor   Daniel Chabon
Assistant Editors   Chuck Howitt and Misha Gehr
Designer   Kathleen Barnett
Digital Art Technician   Jason Rickerd

SPECIAL THANKS

David Steinberger
Chip Mosher
Bryce Gold

Neil Hankerson Executive Vice President • Tom Weddle Chief Financial Officer • Dale LaFountain Chief Information Officer • Tim Wiesch Vice President of Licensing • Matt Parkinson Vice President of Marketing • Vanessa Todd-Holmes Vice President of Production and Scheduling • Mark Bernardi Vice President of Book Trade and Digital Sales • Randy Lahrman Vice President of Product Development and Sales • Ken Lizzi General Counsel • Dave Marshall Editor in Chief • Davey Estrada Editorial Director • Chris Warner Senior Books Editor • Cary Grazzini Director of Specialty Projects • Lia Ribacchi Art Director • Matt Dryer Director of Digital Art and Prepress • Michael Gombos Senior Director of Licensed Publications • Kari Yadro Director of Custom Programs • Kari Torson Director of International Licensing

Published by Dark Horse Books
A division of Dark Horse Comics LLC
10956 SE Main Street
Milwaukie, OR 97222

First edition: September 2022
Trade paperback ISBN: 978-1-50672-650-2

10 9 8 7 6 5 4 3 2 1
Printed in China

Comic Shop Locator Service: comicshoplocator.com

Library of Congress Cataloging-in-Publication Data

Names: Holt, 1982- author. | Beals, Elizabeth, artist. | Wollet, Adam, letterer.
Title: Virtually yours / script, Jeremy Holt ; art & colors, Elizabeth Beals ; letters, Adam Wollet.
Description: First edition. | Milwaukie, OR : Dark Horse Books, 2022. | Summary: "Shouldn't finding a life partner be more challenging than ordering a pizza? Welcome to Virtually Yours, a virtual dating app that provides all the proof of being in a relationship without actually being in one. With her career front of mind, Eva Estrella joins Virtually Yours, after a nudge from her sister, to alleviate some family pressure as she continues to look for her dream job in journalism. While Max Kittridge, a former child star in the middle of a divorce, takes a gig at Virtually Yours servicing multiple clients as a fake boyfriend. As they navigate their current circumstances, both Eva and Max find that sometimes what you're looking for is right in front of you. Virtually Yours is a rom-com for the digital age from writer Jeremy Holt and artist Elizabeth Beals."-- Provided by publisher.
Identifiers: LCCN 2022009429 | ISBN 9781506726502 (trade paperback)
Subjects: LCGFT: Romance comics. | Humorous comics. | Graphic novels.
Classification: LCC PN6727.H5923 V57 2022 | DDC 741.5/973--dc23/eng/20220321
LC record available at https://lccn.loc.gov/2022009429

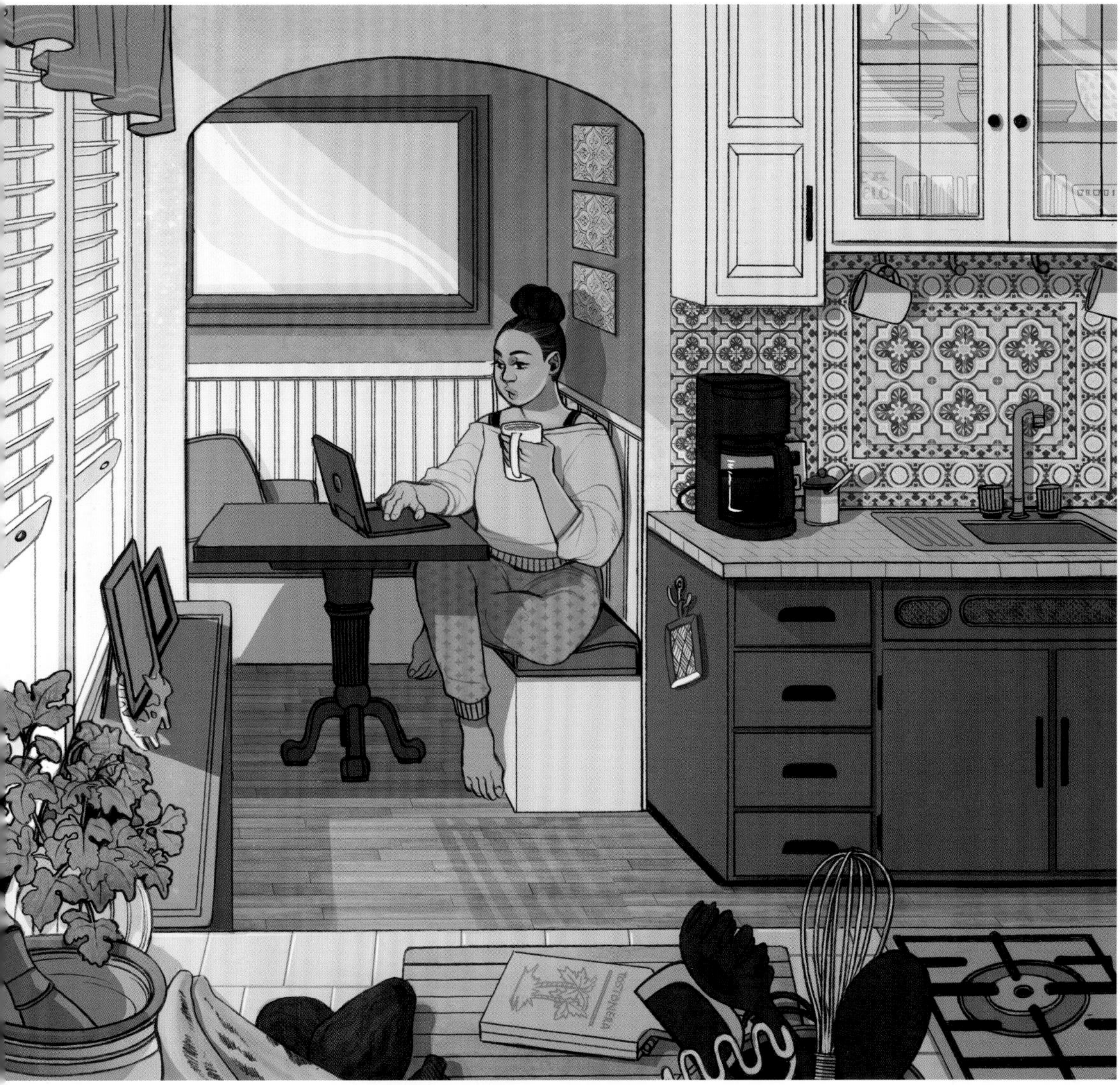
TOSTONERA

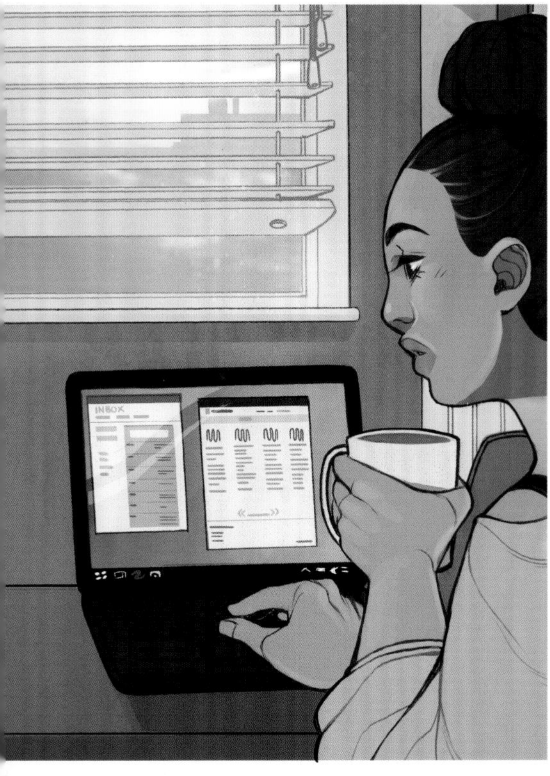
INBOX

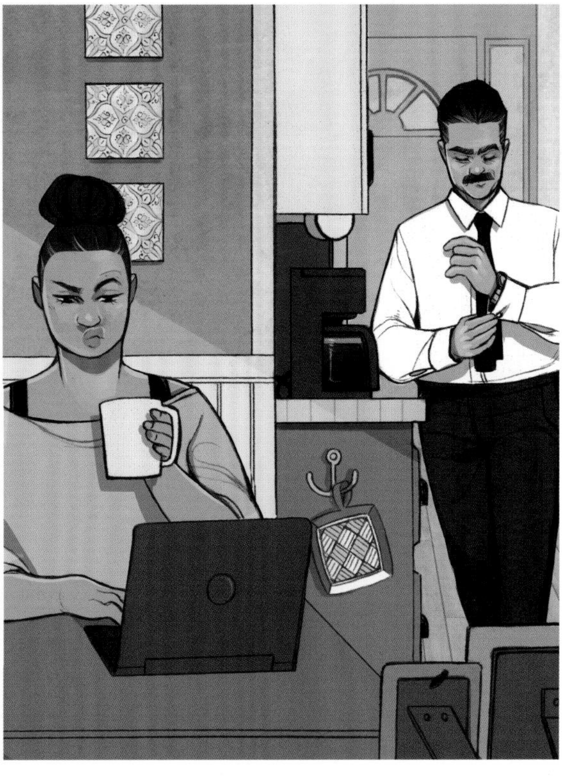

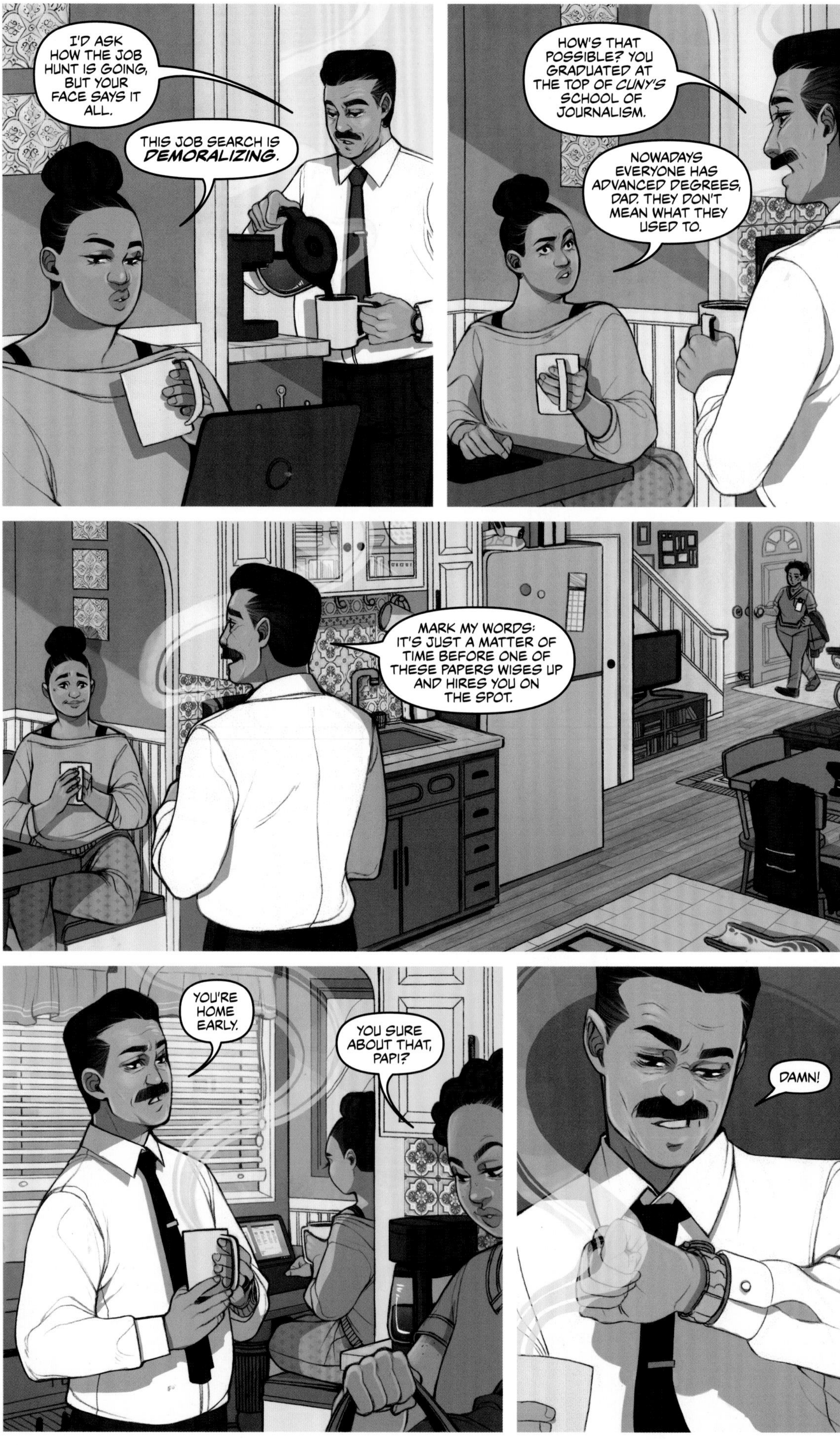
I'D ASK HOW THE JOB HUNT IS GOING, BUT YOUR FACE SAYS IT ALL.
THIS JOB SEARCH IS **DEMORALIZING**.
HOW'S THAT POSSIBLE? YOU GRADUATED AT THE TOP OF *CUNY'S* SCHOOL OF JOURNALISM.
NOWADAYS EVERYONE HAS ADVANCED DEGREES, DAD. THEY DON'T MEAN WHAT THEY USED TO.
MARK MY WORDS: IT'S JUST A MATTER OF TIME BEFORE ONE OF THESE PAPERS WISES UP AND HIRES YOU ON THE SPOT.
YOU'RE HOME EARLY.
YOU SURE ABOUT THAT, PAPI?
DAMN!

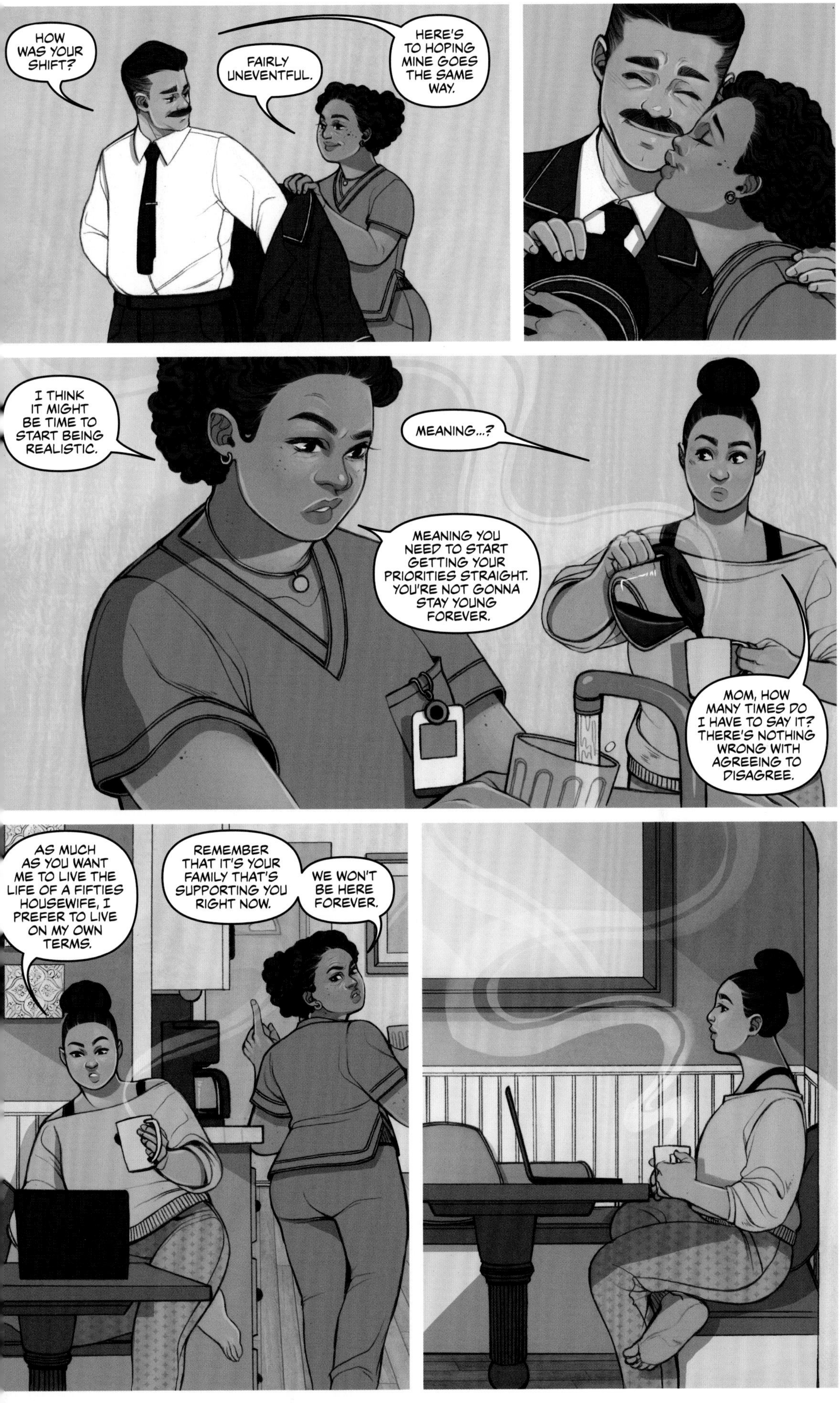
HOW WAS YOUR SHIFT?
FAIRLY UNEVENTFUL.
HERE'S TO HOPING MINE GOES THE SAME WAY.
I THINK IT MIGHT BE TIME TO START BEING REALISTIC.
MEANING...?
MEANING YOU NEED TO START GETTING YOUR PRIORITIES STRAIGHT. YOU'RE NOT GONNA STAY YOUNG FOREVER.
MOM, HOW MANY TIMES DO I HAVE TO SAY IT? THERE'S NOTHING WRONG WITH AGREEING TO DISAGREE.
AS MUCH AS YOU WANT ME TO LIVE THE LIFE OF A FIFTIES HOUSEWIFE, I PREFER TO LIVE ON MY OWN TERMS.
REMEMBER THAT IT'S YOUR FAMILY THAT'S SUPPORTING YOU RIGHT NOW.
WE WON'T BE HERE FOREVER.

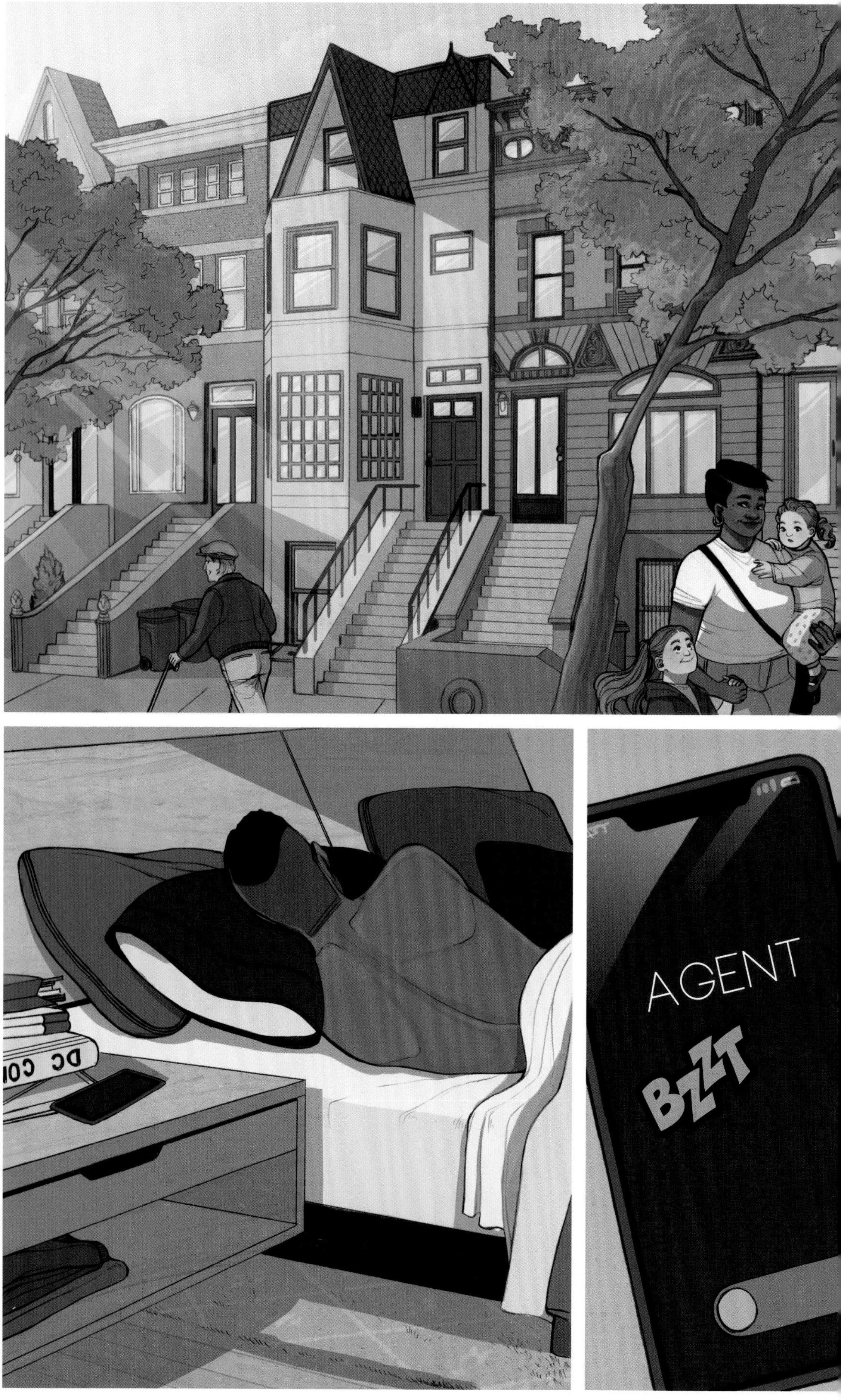
AGENT
BZZT

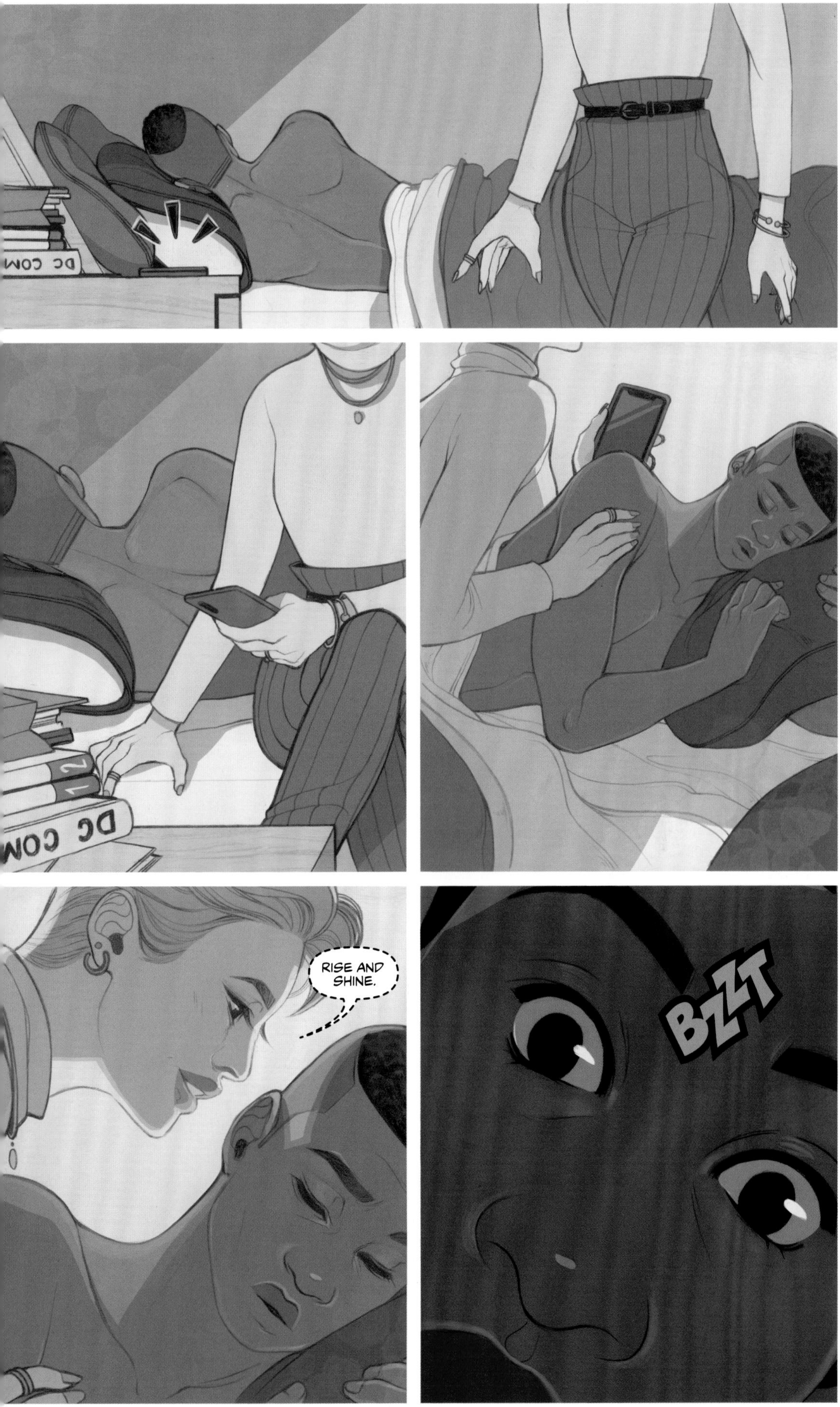
RISE AND SHINE.
BZZT

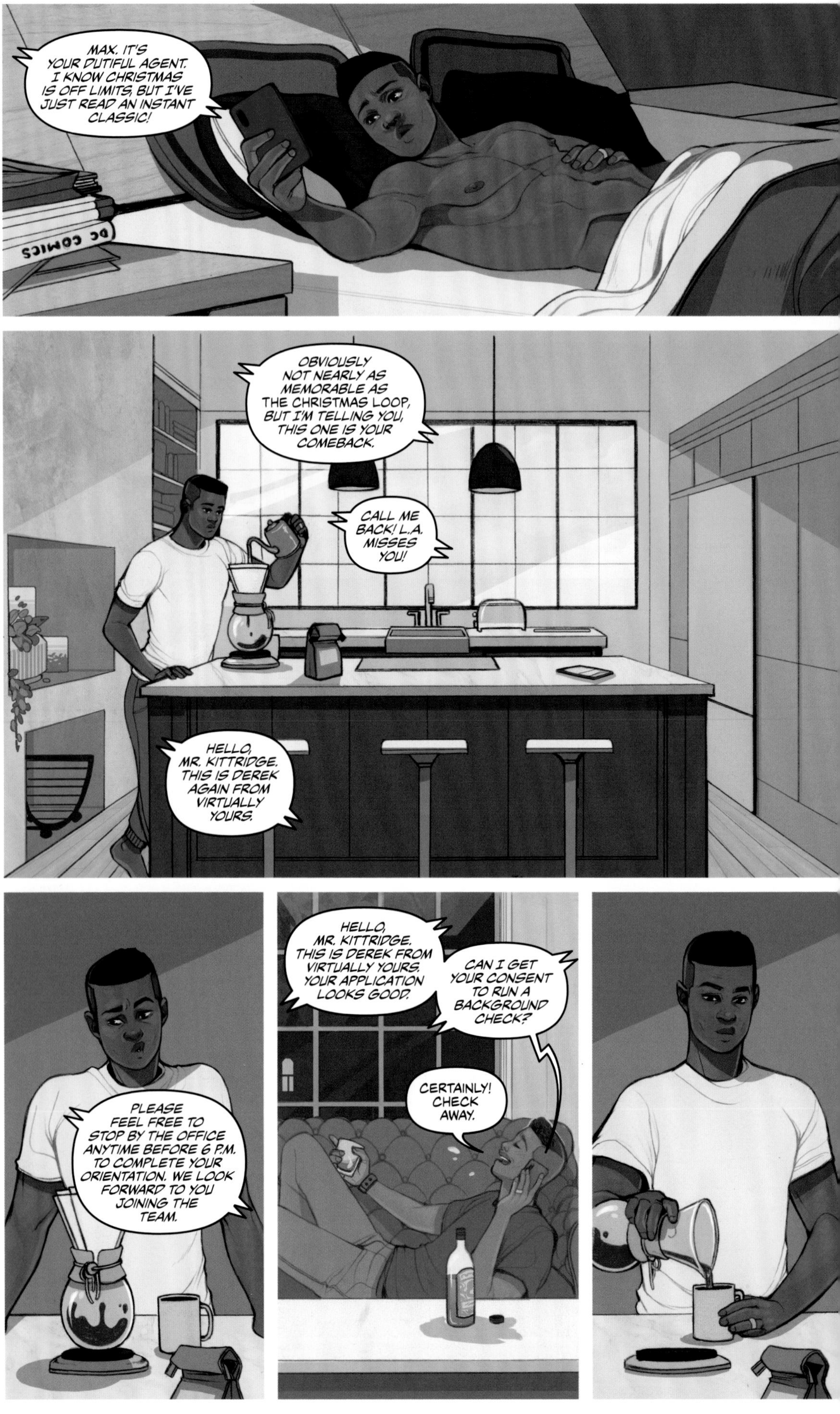
MAX. IT'S YOUR DUTIFUL AGENT. I KNOW CHRISTMAS IS OFF LIMITS, BUT I'VE JUST READ AN INSTANT CLASSIC!
DC COMICS
OBVIOUSLY NOT NEARLY AS MEMORABLE AS THE CHRISTMAS LOOP, BUT I'M TELLING YOU, THIS ONE IS YOUR COMEBACK.
CALL ME BACK! L.A. MISSES YOU!
HELLO, MR. KITTRIDGE. THIS IS DEREK AGAIN FROM VIRTUALLY YOURS.
PLEASE FEEL FREE TO STOP BY THE OFFICE ANYTIME BEFORE 6 P.M. TO COMPLETE YOUR ORIENTATION. WE LOOK FORWARD TO YOU JOINING THE TEAM.
HELLO, MR. KITTRIDGE. THIS IS DEREK FROM VIRTUALLY YOURS. YOUR APPLICATION LOOKS GOOD.
CAN I GET YOUR CONSENT TO RUN A BACKGROUND CHECK?
CERTAINLY! CHECK AWAY.

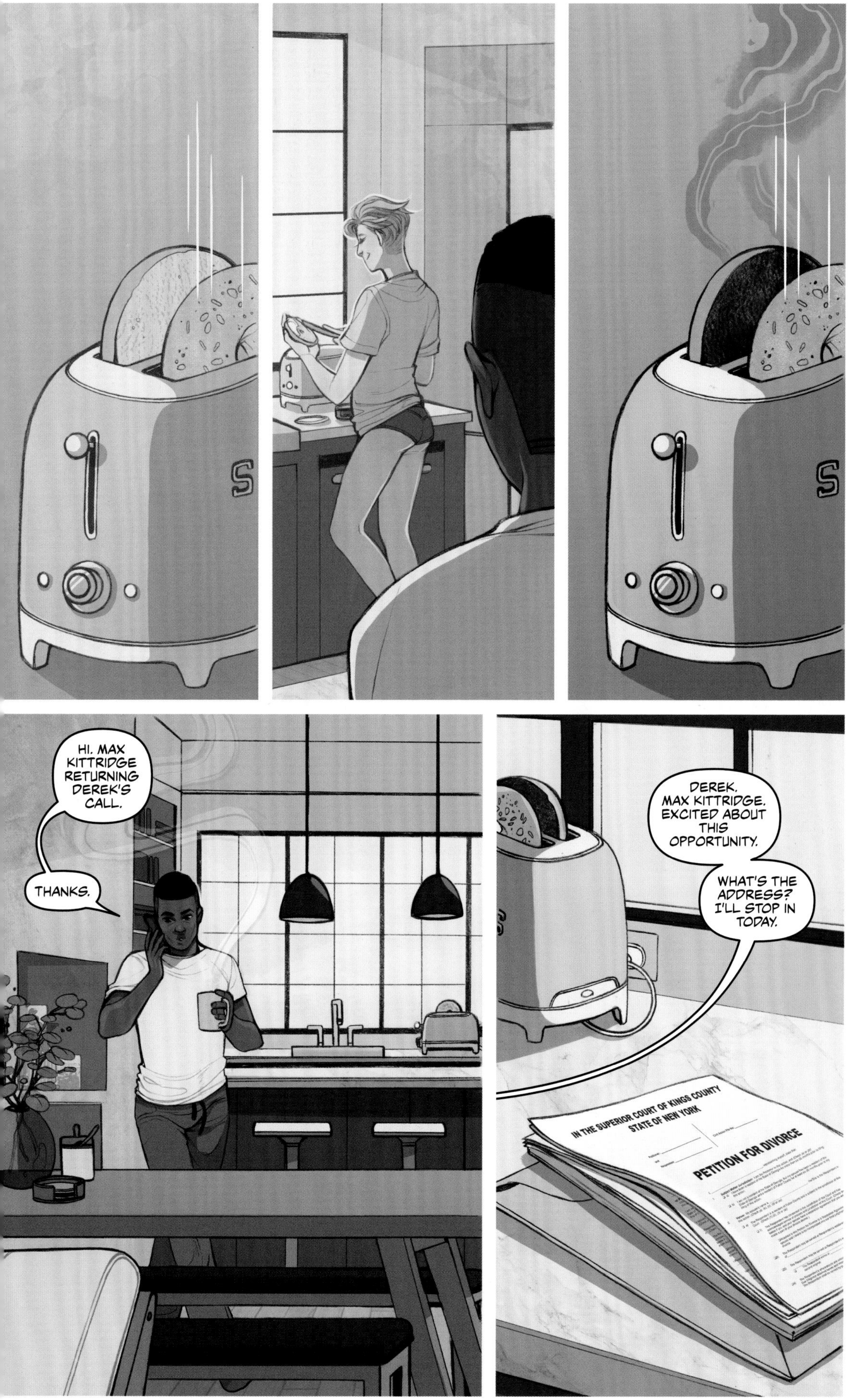

HI. MAX KITTRIDGE RETURNING DEREK'S CALL.
THANKS.
DEREK. MAX KITTRIDGE. EXCITED ABOUT THIS OPPORTUNITY.
WHAT'S THE ADDRESS? I'LL STOP IN TODAY.
IN THE SUPERIOR COURT OF KINGS COUNTY
STATE OF NEW YORK
PETITION FOR DIVORCE

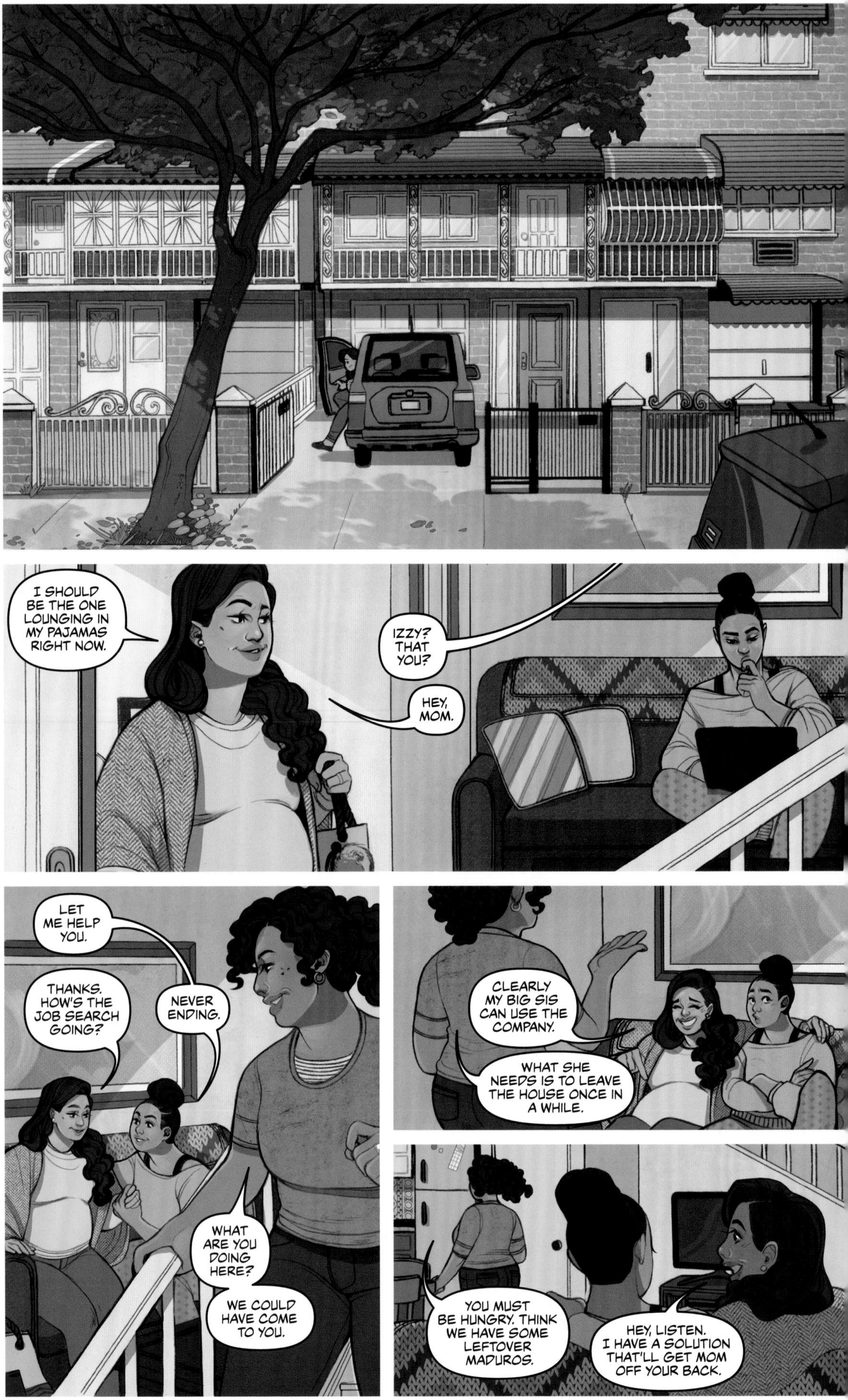
I SHOULD BE THE ONE LOUNGING IN MY PAJAMAS RIGHT NOW.
IZZY? THAT YOU?
HEY, MOM.
LET ME HELP YOU.
THANKS. HOW'S THE JOB SEARCH GOING?
NEVER ENDING.
WHAT ARE YOU DOING HERE?
WE COULD HAVE COME TO YOU.
CLEARLY MY BIG SIS CAN USE THE COMPANY.
WHAT SHE NEEDS IS TO LEAVE THE HOUSE ONCE IN A WHILE.
YOU MUST BE HUNGRY. THINK WE HAVE SOME LEFTOVER MADUROS.
HEY, LISTEN. I HAVE A SOLUTION THAT'LL GET MOM OFF YOUR BACK.

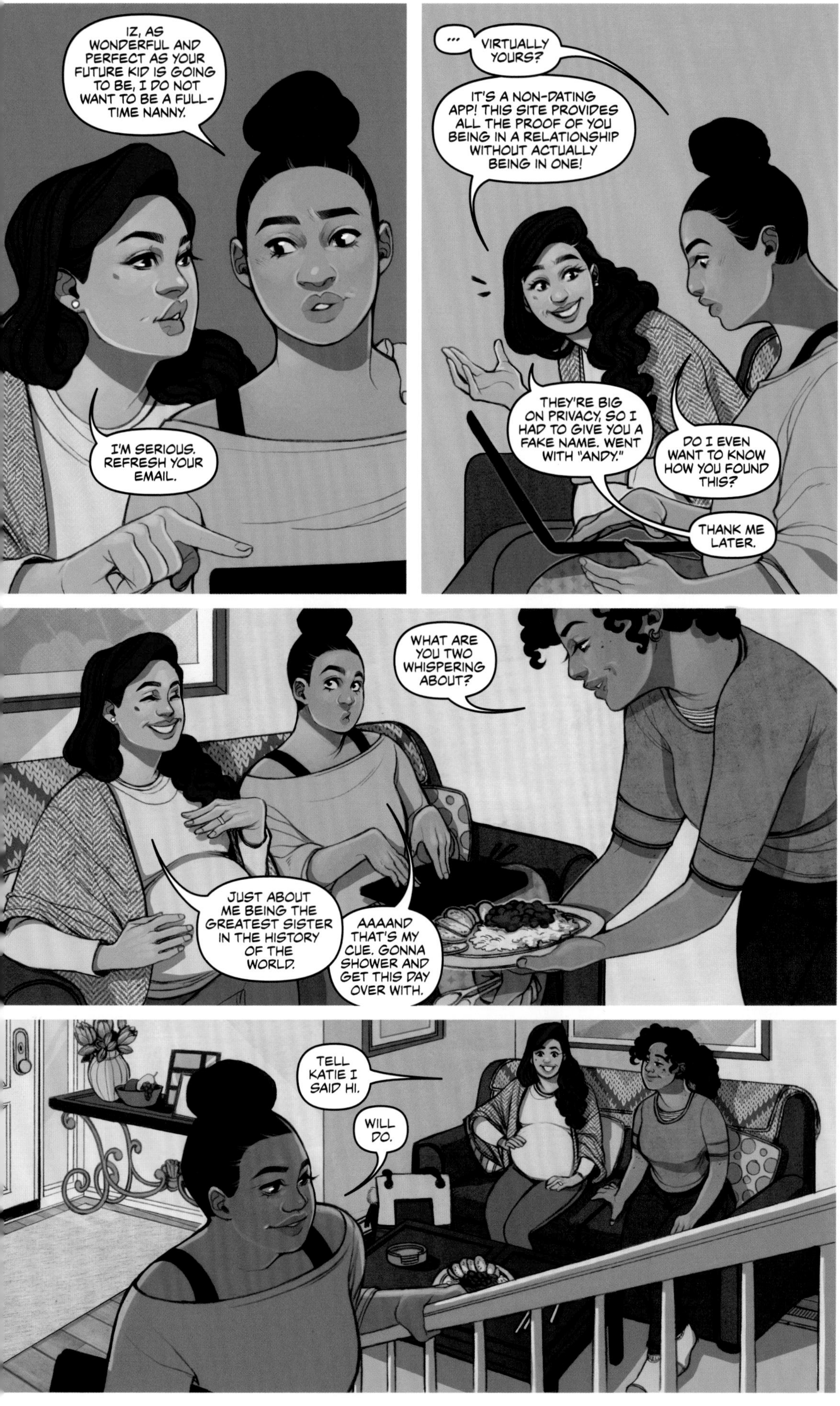
IZ, AS WONDERFUL AND PERFECT AS YOUR FUTURE KID IS GOING TO BE, I DO NOT WANT TO BE A FULL-TIME NANNY.
I'M SERIOUS. REFRESH YOUR EMAIL.
...
VIRTUALLY YOURS?
IT'S A NON-DATING APP! THIS SITE PROVIDES ALL THE PROOF OF YOU BEING IN A RELATIONSHIP WITHOUT ACTUALLY BEING IN ONE!
THEY'RE BIG ON PRIVACY, SO I HAD TO GIVE YOU A FAKE NAME. WENT WITH "ANDY."
DO I EVEN WANT TO KNOW HOW YOU FOUND THIS?
THANK ME LATER.
WHAT ARE YOU TWO WHISPERING ABOUT?
JUST ABOUT ME BEING THE GREATEST SISTER IN THE HISTORY OF THE WORLD.
AAAAND THAT'S MY CUE. GONNA SHOWER AND GET THIS DAY OVER WITH.
TELL KATIE I SAID HI.
WILL DO.

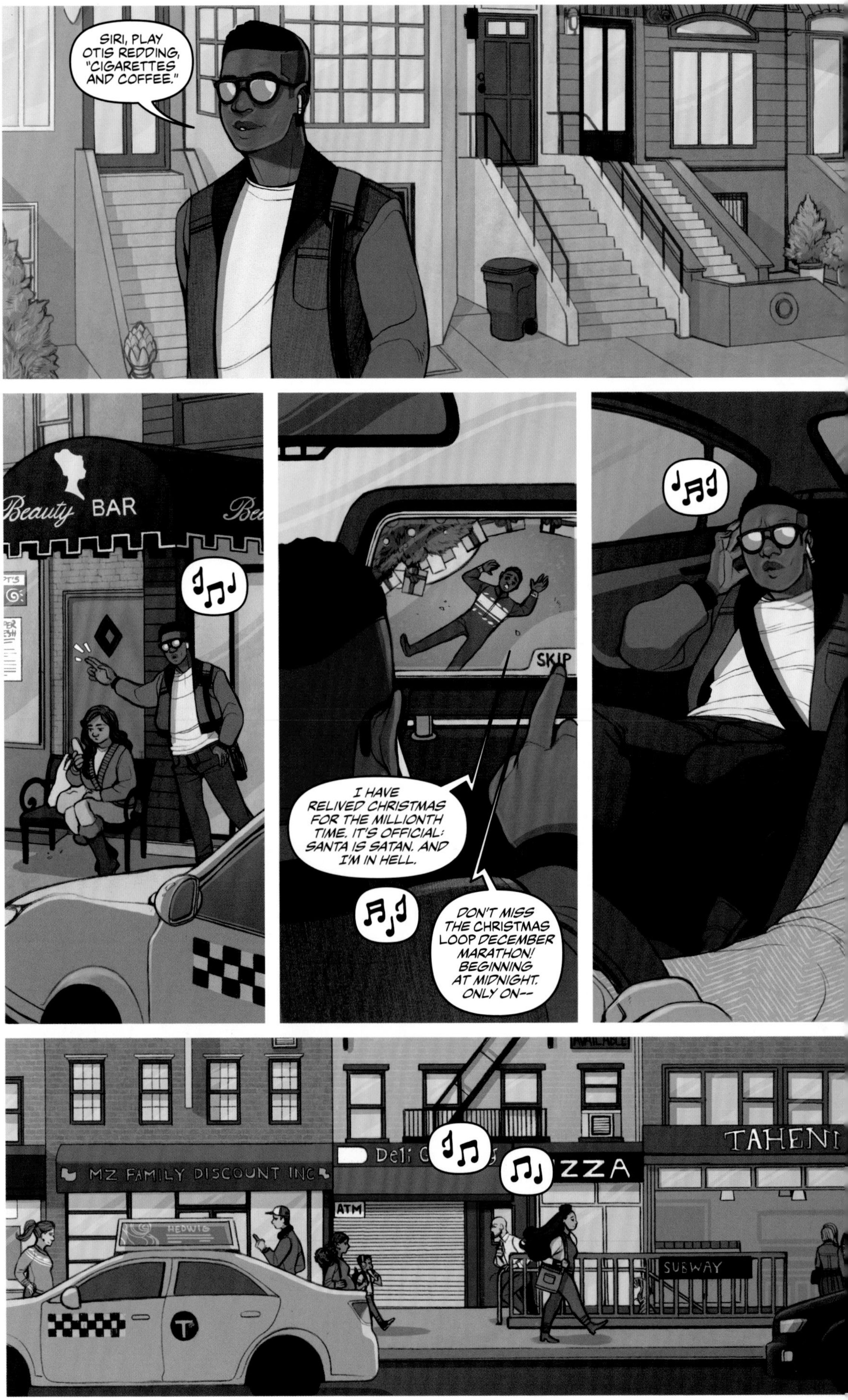
SIRI, PLAY OTIS REDDING, "CIGARETTES AND COFFEE."
Beauty BAR
SKIP
I HAVE RELIVED CHRISTMAS FOR THE MILLIONTH TIME. IT'S OFFICIAL: SANTA IS SATAN. AND I'M IN HELL.
DON'T MISS THE CHRISTMAS LOOP DECEMBER MARATHON! BEGINNING AT MIDNIGHT. ONLY ON--
MZ FAMILY DISCOUNT INC
ZZA
TAHENI
ATM
SUBWAY
HEDWIG

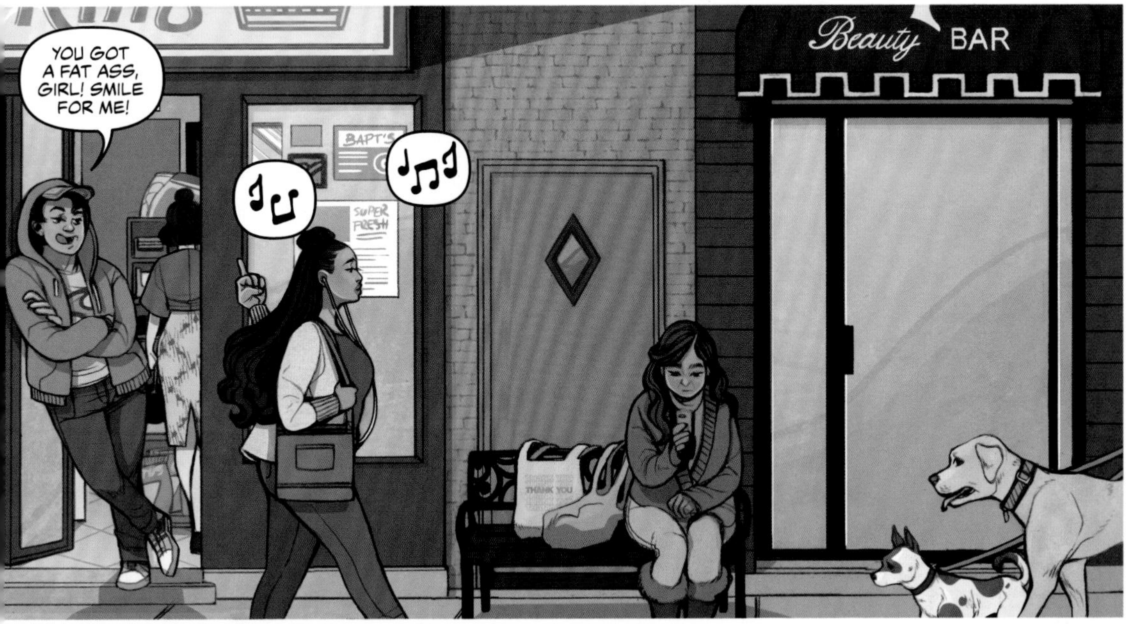
YOU GOT A FAT ASS, GIRL! SMILE FOR ME!
BAPT'S
SUPER FRESH
THANK YOU
Beauty BAR

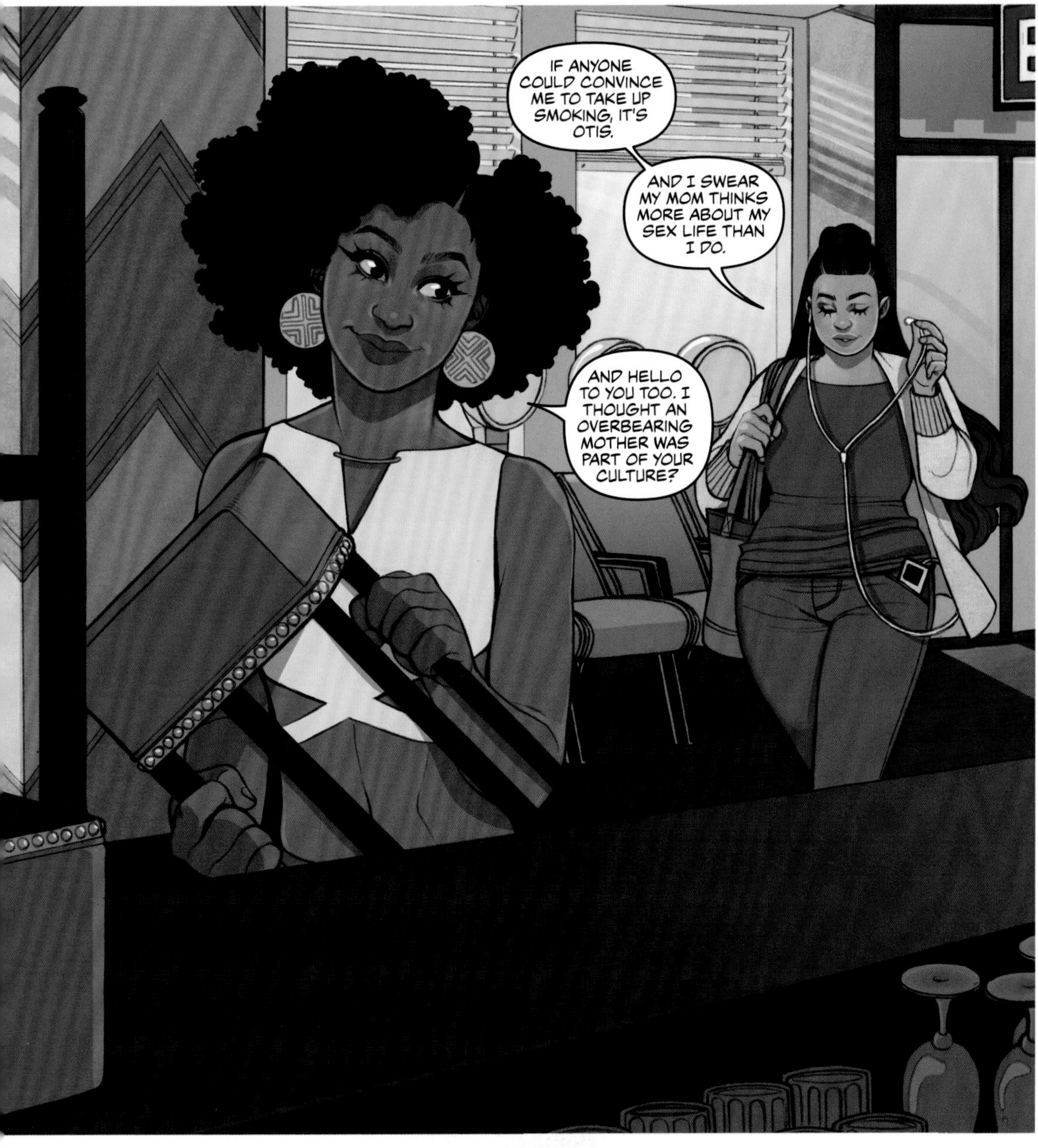
IF ANYONE COULD CONVINCE ME TO TAKE UP SMOKING, IT'S OTIS.
AND I SWEAR MY MOM THINKS MORE ABOUT MY SEX LIFE THAN I DO.
AND HELLO TO YOU TOO. I THOUGHT AN OVERBEARING MOTHER WAS PART OF YOUR CULTURE?

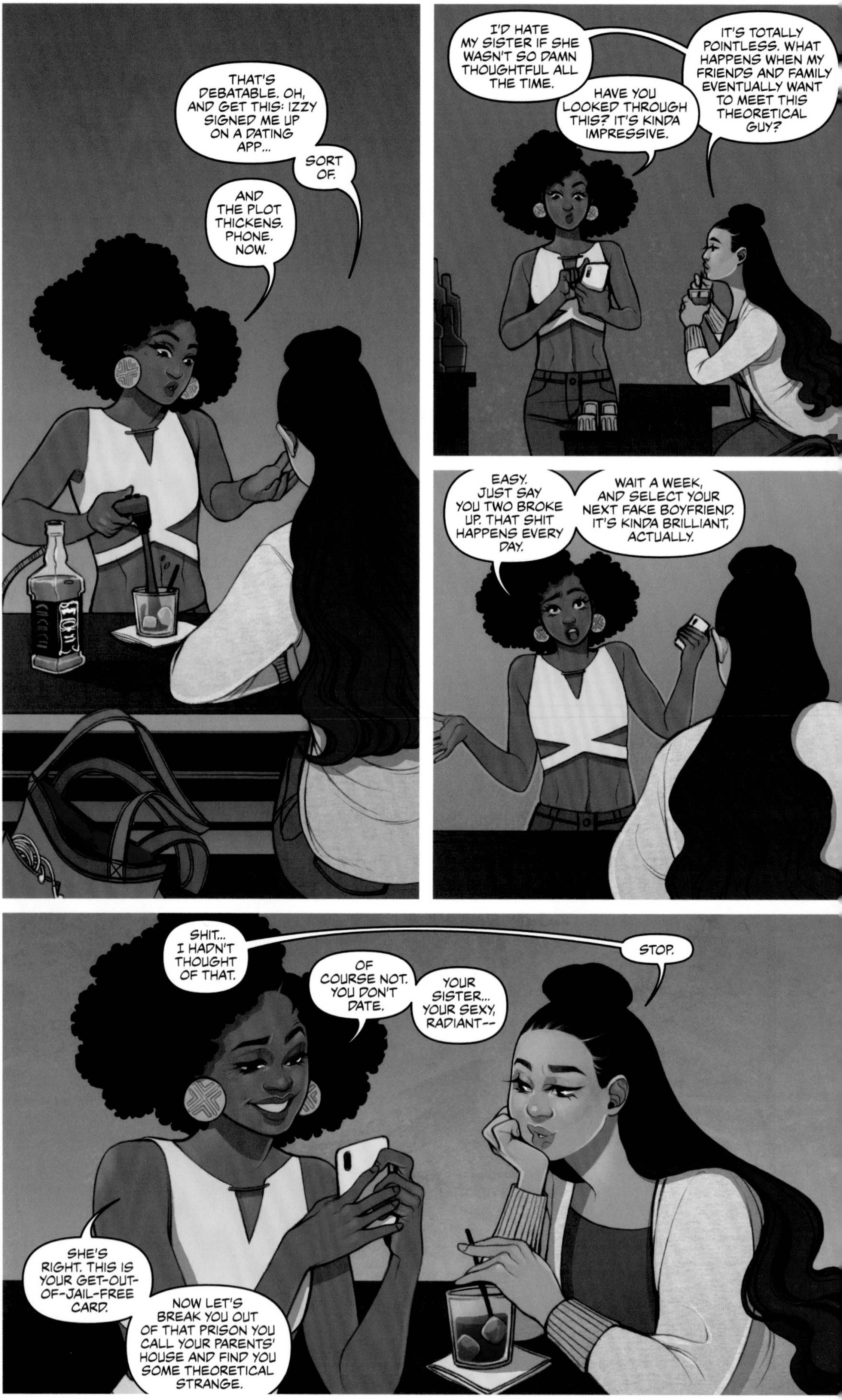
THAT'S DEBATABLE. OH, AND GET THIS: IZZY SIGNED ME UP ON A DATING APP...
SORT OF.
AND THE PLOT THICKENS. PHONE. NOW.
I'D HATE MY SISTER IF SHE WASN'T SO DAMN THOUGHTFUL ALL THE TIME.
HAVE YOU LOOKED THROUGH THIS? IT'S KINDA IMPRESSIVE.
IT'S TOTALLY POINTLESS. WHAT HAPPENS WHEN MY FRIENDS AND FAMILY EVENTUALLY WANT TO MEET THIS THEORETICAL GUY?
EASY. JUST SAY YOU TWO BROKE UP. THAT SHIT HAPPENS EVERY DAY.
WAIT A WEEK, AND SELECT YOUR NEXT FAKE BOYFRIEND. IT'S KINDA BRILLIANT, ACTUALLY.
SHIT... I HADN'T THOUGHT OF THAT.
STOP.
OF COURSE NOT. YOU DON'T DATE.
YOUR SISTER... YOUR SEXY, RADIANT--
SHE'S RIGHT. THIS IS YOUR GET-OUT-OF-JAIL-FREE CARD.
NOW LET'S BREAK YOU OUT OF THAT PRISON YOU CALL YOUR PARENTS' HOUSE AND FIND YOU SOME THEORETICAL STRANGE.

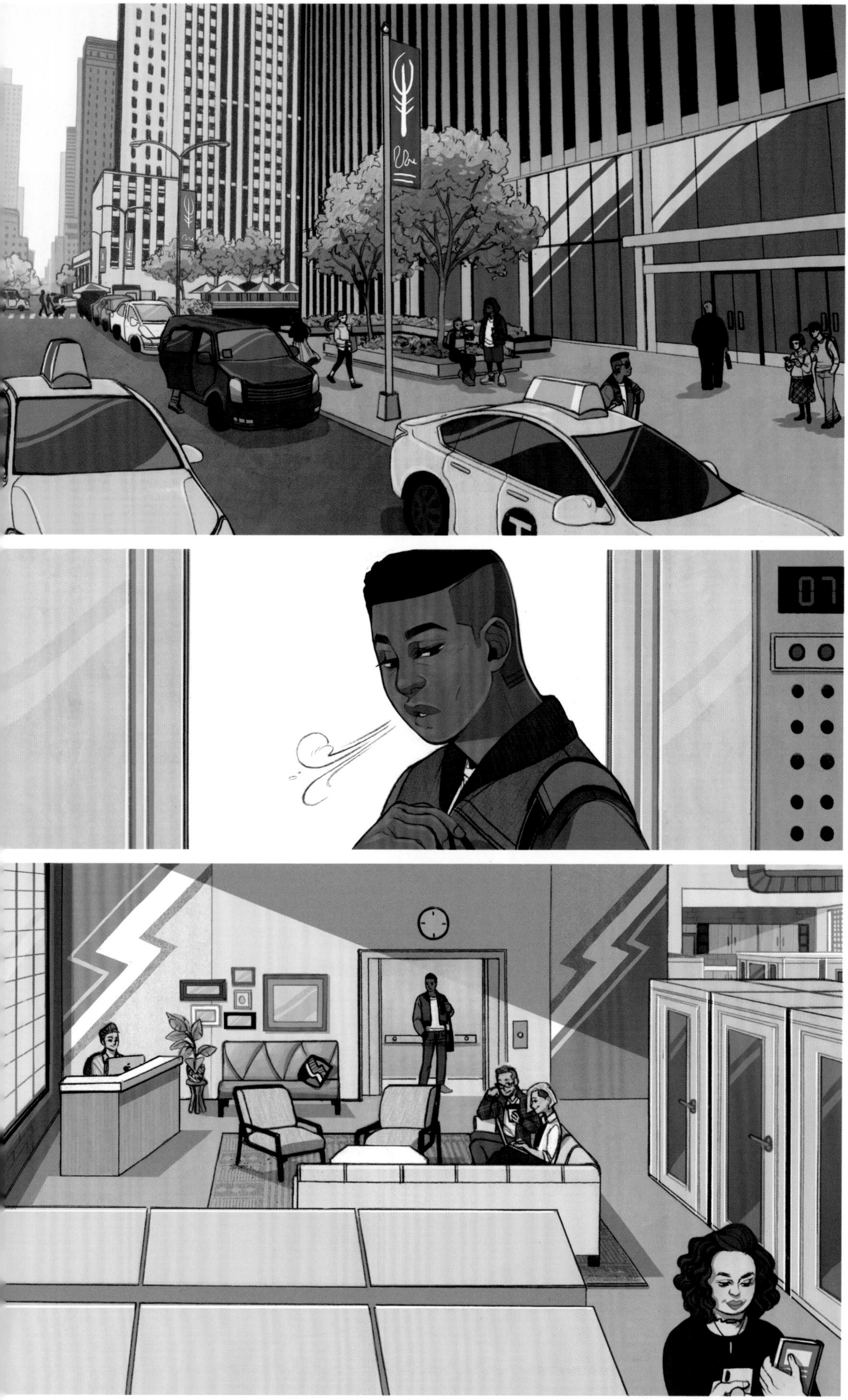
07

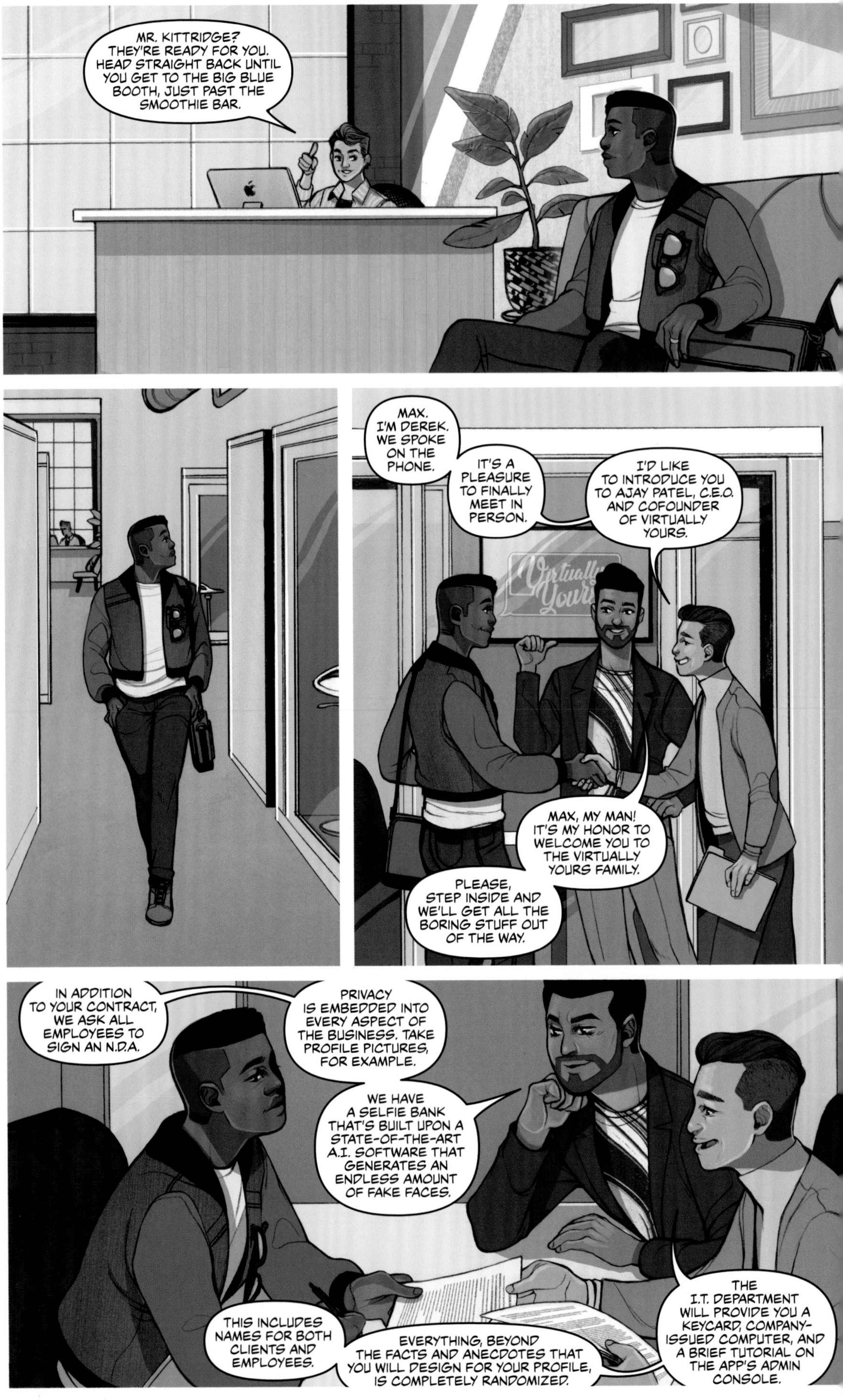
MR. KITTRIDGE? THEY'RE READY FOR YOU. HEAD STRAIGHT BACK UNTIL YOU GET TO THE BIG BLUE BOOTH, JUST PAST THE SMOOTHIE BAR.
MAX. I'M DEREK. WE SPOKE ON THE PHONE.
IT'S A PLEASURE TO FINALLY MEET IN PERSON.
I'D LIKE TO INTRODUCE YOU TO AJAY PATEL, C.E.O. AND COFOUNDER OF VIRTUALLY YOURS.
Virtually Yours
MAX, MY MAN! IT'S MY HONOR TO WELCOME YOU TO THE VIRTUALLY YOURS FAMILY.
PLEASE, STEP INSIDE AND WE'LL GET ALL THE BORING STUFF OUT OF THE WAY.
IN ADDITION TO YOUR CONTRACT, WE ASK ALL EMPLOYEES TO SIGN AN N.D.A.
PRIVACY IS EMBEDDED INTO EVERY ASPECT OF THE BUSINESS. TAKE PROFILE PICTURES, FOR EXAMPLE.
WE HAVE A SELFIE BANK THAT'S BUILT UPON A STATE-OF-THE-ART A.I. SOFTWARE THAT GENERATES AN ENDLESS AMOUNT OF FAKE FACES.
THIS INCLUDES NAMES FOR BOTH CLIENTS AND EMPLOYEES.
EVERYTHING, BEYOND THE FACTS AND ANECDOTES THAT YOU WILL DESIGN FOR YOUR PROFILE, IS COMPLETELY RANDOMIZED.
THE I.T. DEPARTMENT WILL PROVIDE YOU A KEYCARD, COMPANY-ISSUED COMPUTER, AND A BRIEF TUTORIAL ON THE APP'S ADMIN CONSOLE.

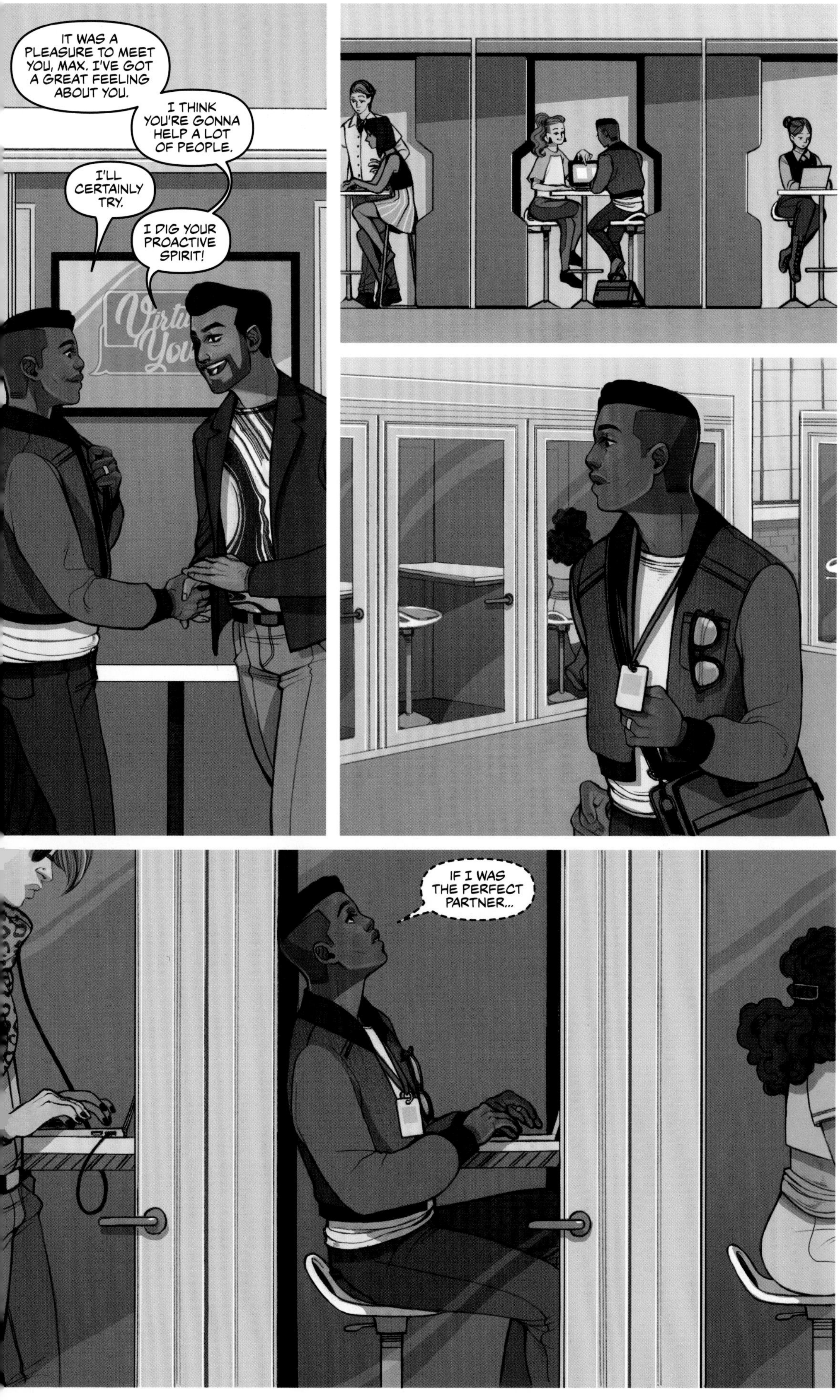
IT WAS A PLEASURE TO MEET YOU, MAX. I'VE GOT A GREAT FEELING ABOUT YOU.
I THINK YOU'RE GONNA HELP A LOT OF PEOPLE.
I'LL CERTAINLY TRY.
I DIG YOUR PROACTIVE SPIRIT!
IF I WAS THE PERFECT PARTNER...

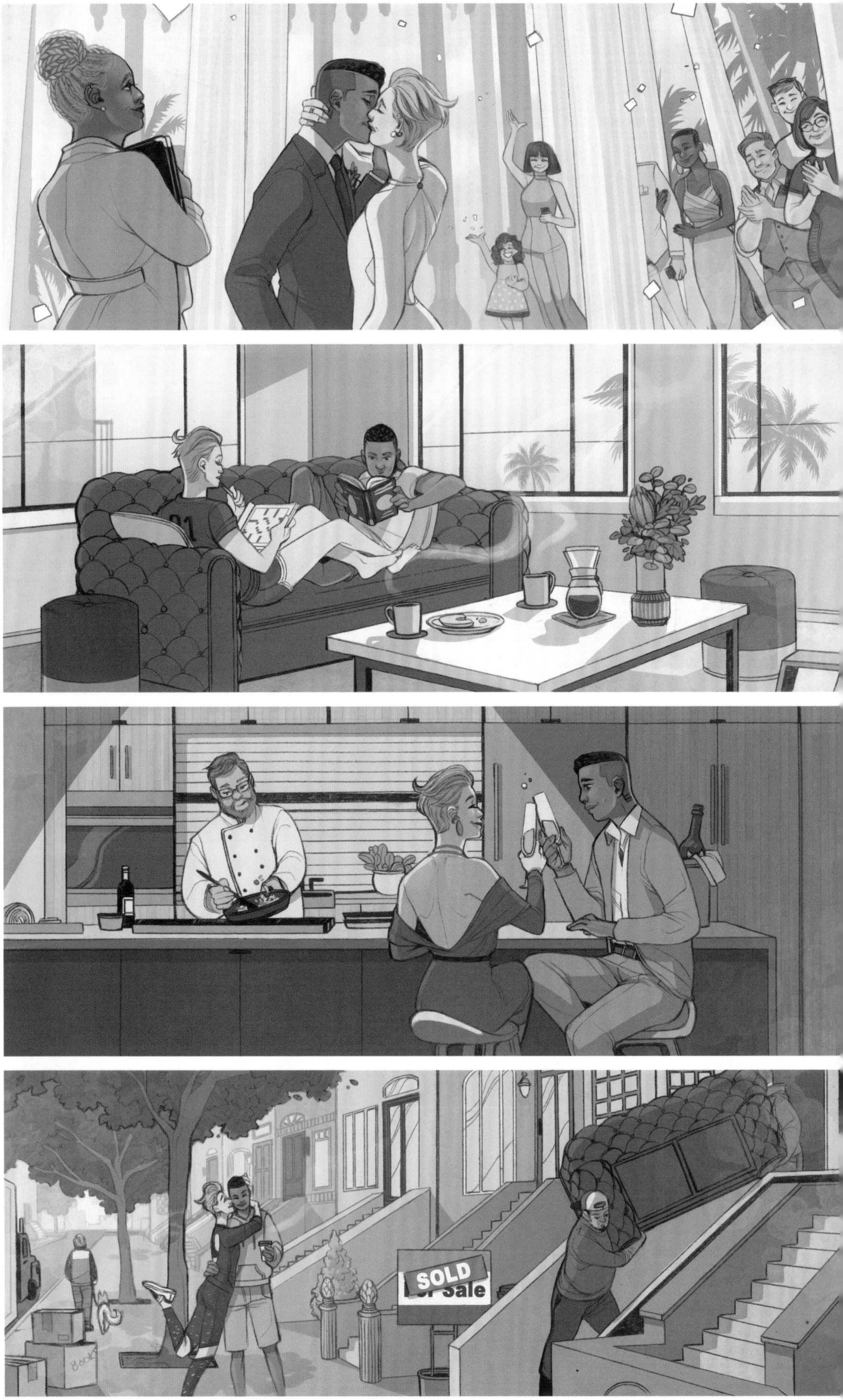
SOLD
Sale

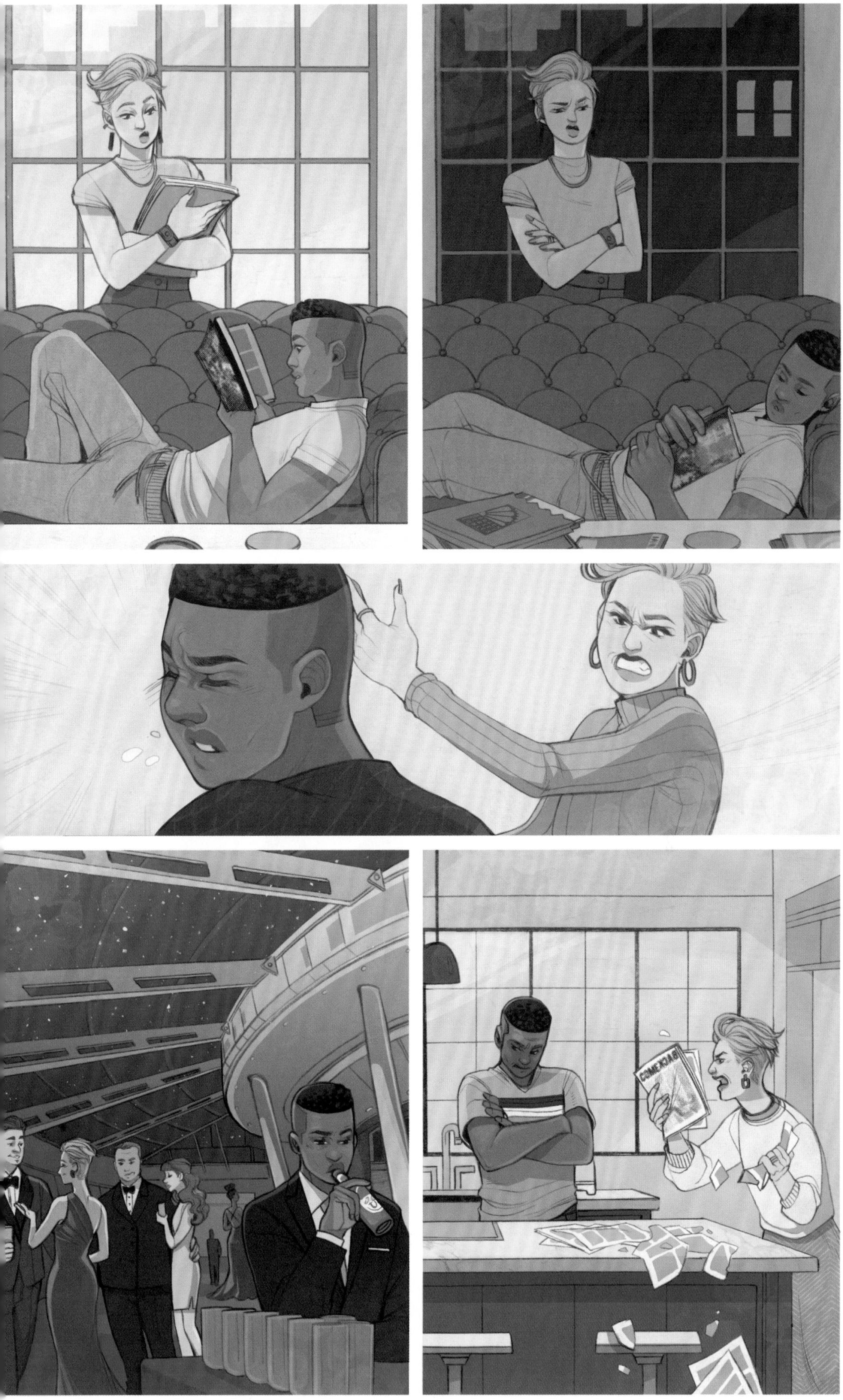

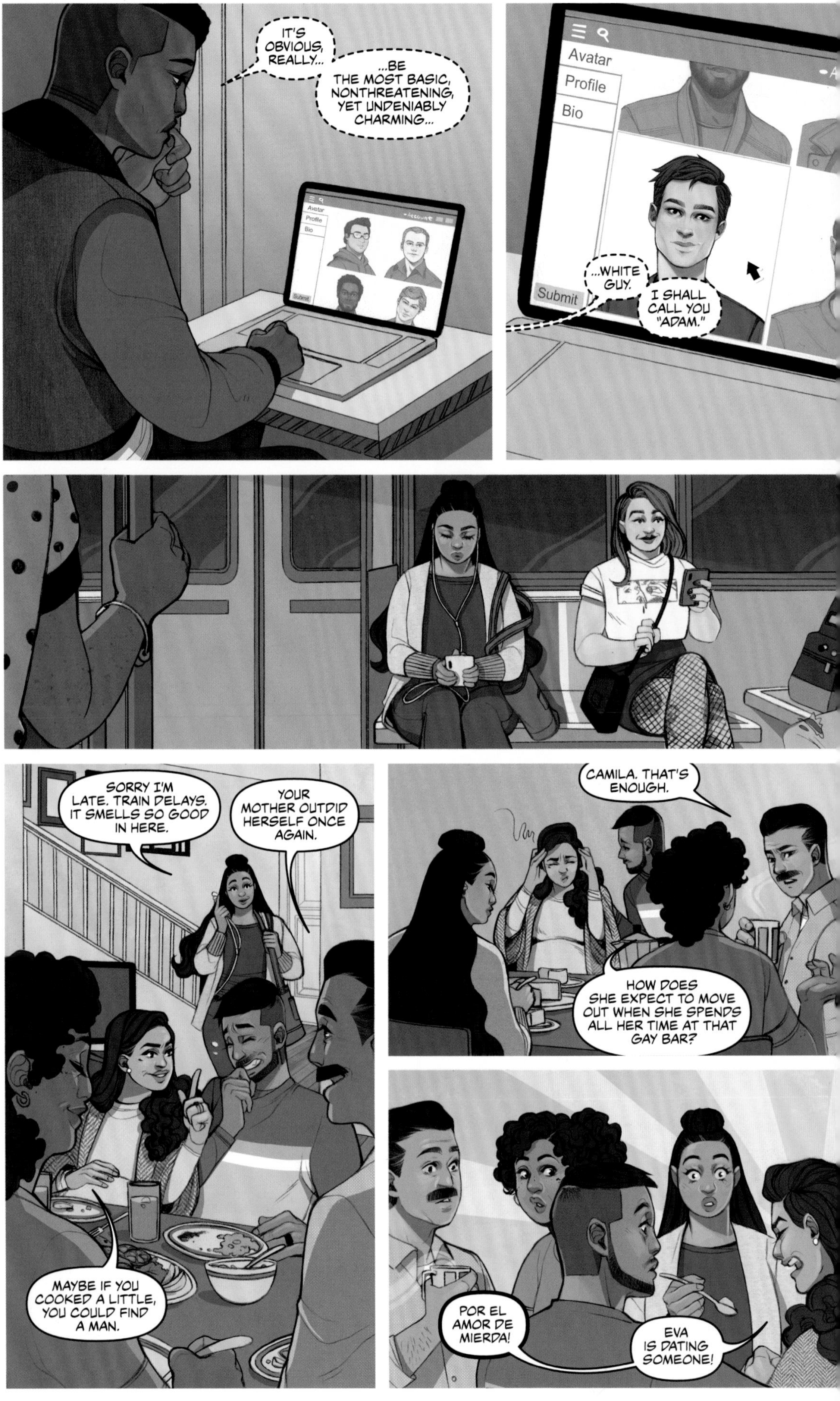
IT'S OBVIOUS, REALLY...
...BE THE MOST BASIC, NONTHREATENING, YET UNDENIABLY CHARMING...
Avatar
Profile
Bio
Submit
...WHITE GUY.
I SHALL CALL YOU "ADAM."
SORRY I'M LATE. TRAIN DELAYS. IT SMELLS SO GOOD IN HERE.
YOUR MOTHER OUTDID HERSELF ONCE AGAIN.
MAYBE IF YOU COOKED A LITTLE, YOU COULD FIND A MAN.
CAMILA. THAT'S ENOUGH.
HOW DOES SHE EXPECT TO MOVE OUT WHEN SHE SPENDS ALL HER TIME AT THAT GAY BAR?
POR EL AMOR DE MIERDA!
EVA IS DATING SOMEONE!

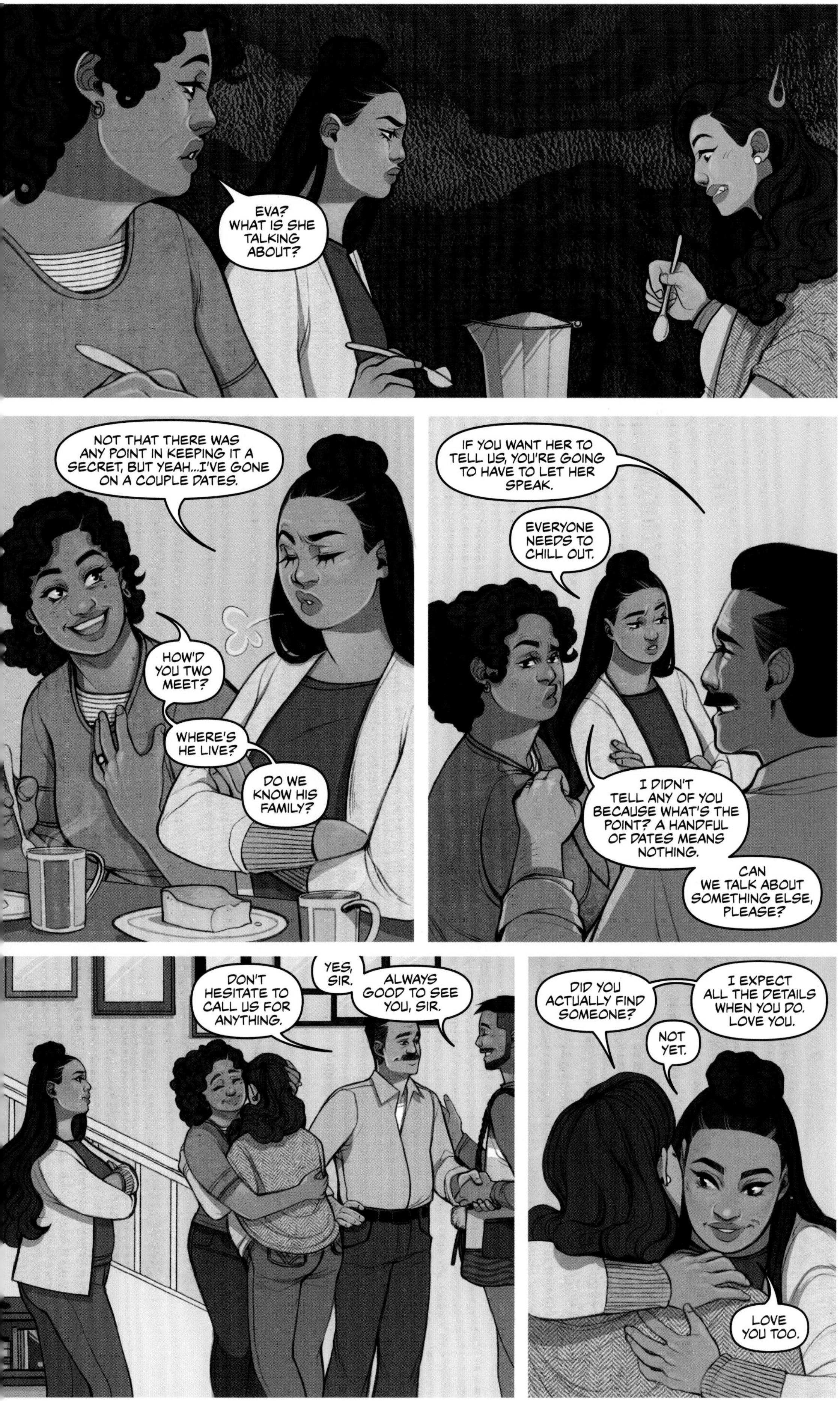
EVA? WHAT IS SHE TALKING ABOUT?
NOT THAT THERE WAS ANY POINT IN KEEPING IT A SECRET, BUT YEAH...I'VE GONE ON A COUPLE DATES.
HOW'D YOU TWO MEET?
WHERE'S HE LIVE?
DO WE KNOW HIS FAMILY?
IF YOU WANT HER TO TELL US, YOU'RE GOING TO HAVE TO LET HER SPEAK.
EVERYONE NEEDS TO CHILL OUT.
I DIDN'T TELL ANY OF YOU BECAUSE WHAT'S THE POINT? A HANDFUL OF DATES MEANS NOTHING.
CAN WE TALK ABOUT SOMETHING ELSE, PLEASE?
DON'T HESITATE TO CALL US FOR ANYTHING.
YES, SIR.
ALWAYS GOOD TO SEE YOU, SIR.
DID YOU ACTUALLY FIND SOMEONE?
NOT YET.
I EXPECT ALL THE DETAILS WHEN YOU DO. LOVE YOU.
LOVE YOU TOO.

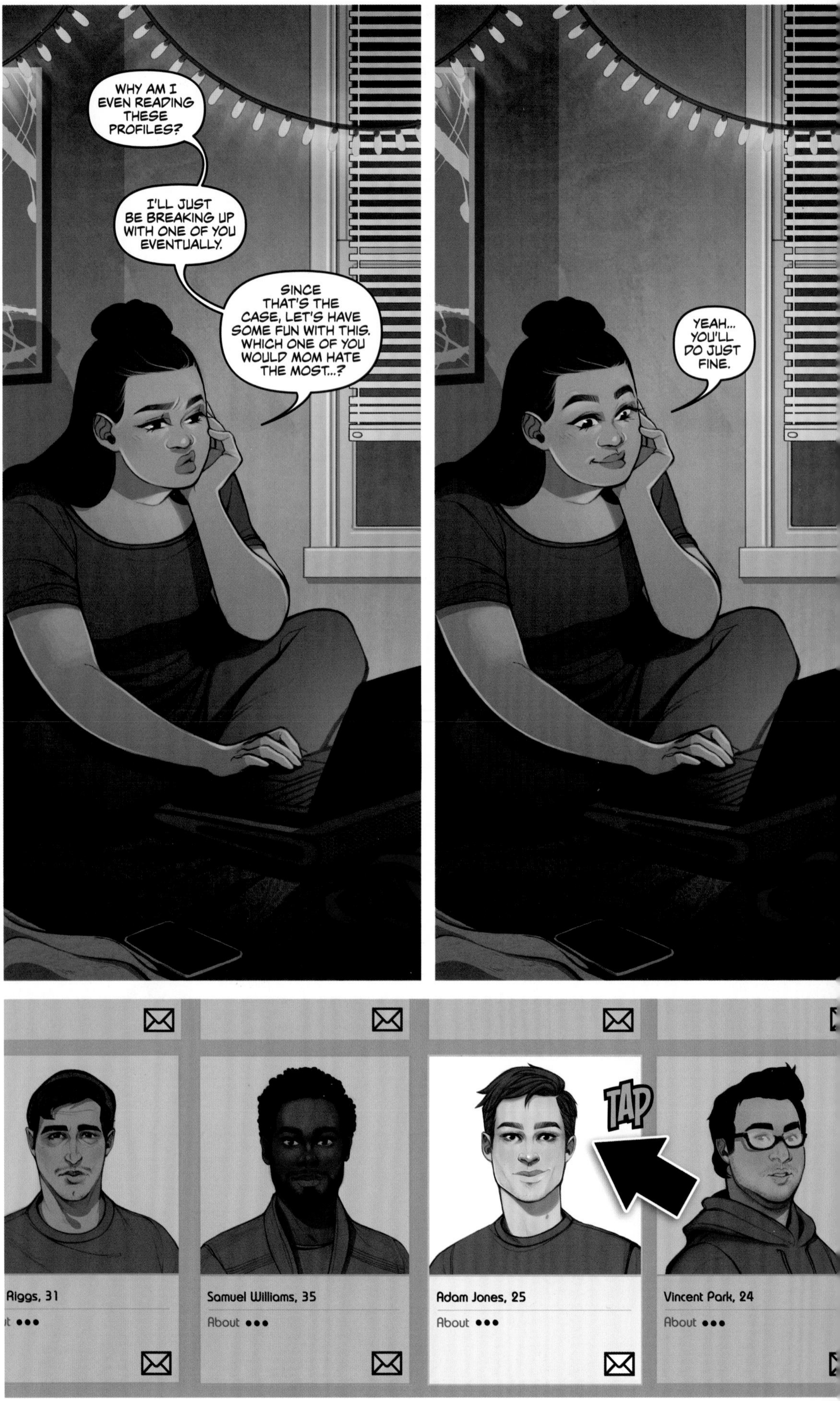
WHY AM I EVEN READING THESE PROFILES?
I'LL JUST BE BREAKING UP WITH ONE OF YOU EVENTUALLY.
SINCE THAT'S THE CASE, LET'S HAVE SOME FUN WITH THIS. WHICH ONE OF YOU WOULD MOM HATE THE MOST...?
YEAH... YOU'LL DO JUST FINE.
Riggs, 31
Samuel Williams, 35
About •••
Adam Jones, 25
About •••
TAP
Vincent Park, 24
About •••

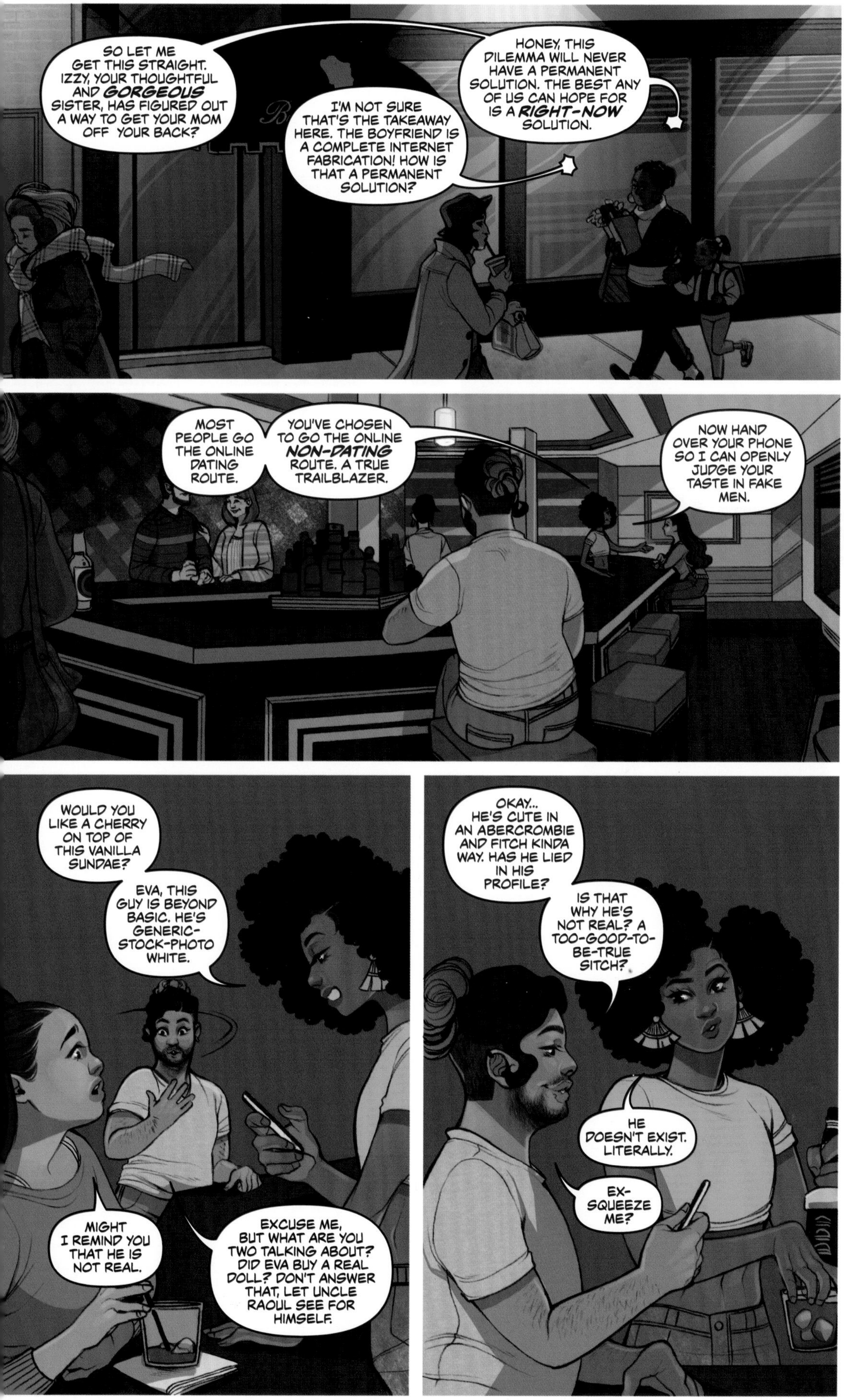
SO LET ME GET THIS STRAIGHT. IZZY, YOUR THOUGHTFUL AND GORGEOUS SISTER, HAS FIGURED OUT A WAY TO GET YOUR MOM OFF YOUR BACK?
I'M NOT SURE THAT'S THE TAKEAWAY HERE. THE BOYFRIEND IS A COMPLETE INTERNET FABRICATION! HOW IS THAT A PERMANENT SOLUTION?
HONEY, THIS DILEMMA WILL NEVER HAVE A PERMANENT SOLUTION. THE BEST ANY OF US CAN HOPE FOR IS A RIGHT-NOW SOLUTION.
MOST PEOPLE GO THE ONLINE DATING ROUTE.
YOU'VE CHOSEN TO GO THE ONLINE NON-DATING ROUTE. A TRUE TRAILBLAZER.
NOW HAND OVER YOUR PHONE SO I CAN OPENLY JUDGE YOUR TASTE IN FAKE MEN.
WOULD YOU LIKE A CHERRY ON TOP OF THIS VANILLA SUNDAE?
EVA, THIS GUY IS BEYOND BASIC. HE'S GENERIC-STOCK-PHOTO WHITE.
MIGHT I REMIND YOU THAT HE IS NOT REAL.
EXCUSE ME, BUT WHAT ARE YOU TWO TALKING ABOUT? DID EVA BUY A REAL DOLL? DON'T ANSWER THAT, LET UNCLE RAOUL SEE FOR HIMSELF.
OKAY... HE'S CUTE IN AN ABERCROMBIE AND FITCH KINDA WAY. HAS HE LIED IN HIS PROFILE?
IS THAT WHY HE'S NOT REAL? A TOO-GOOD-TO-BE-TRUE SITCH?
HE DOESN'T EXIST. LITERALLY.
EX-SQUEEZE ME?

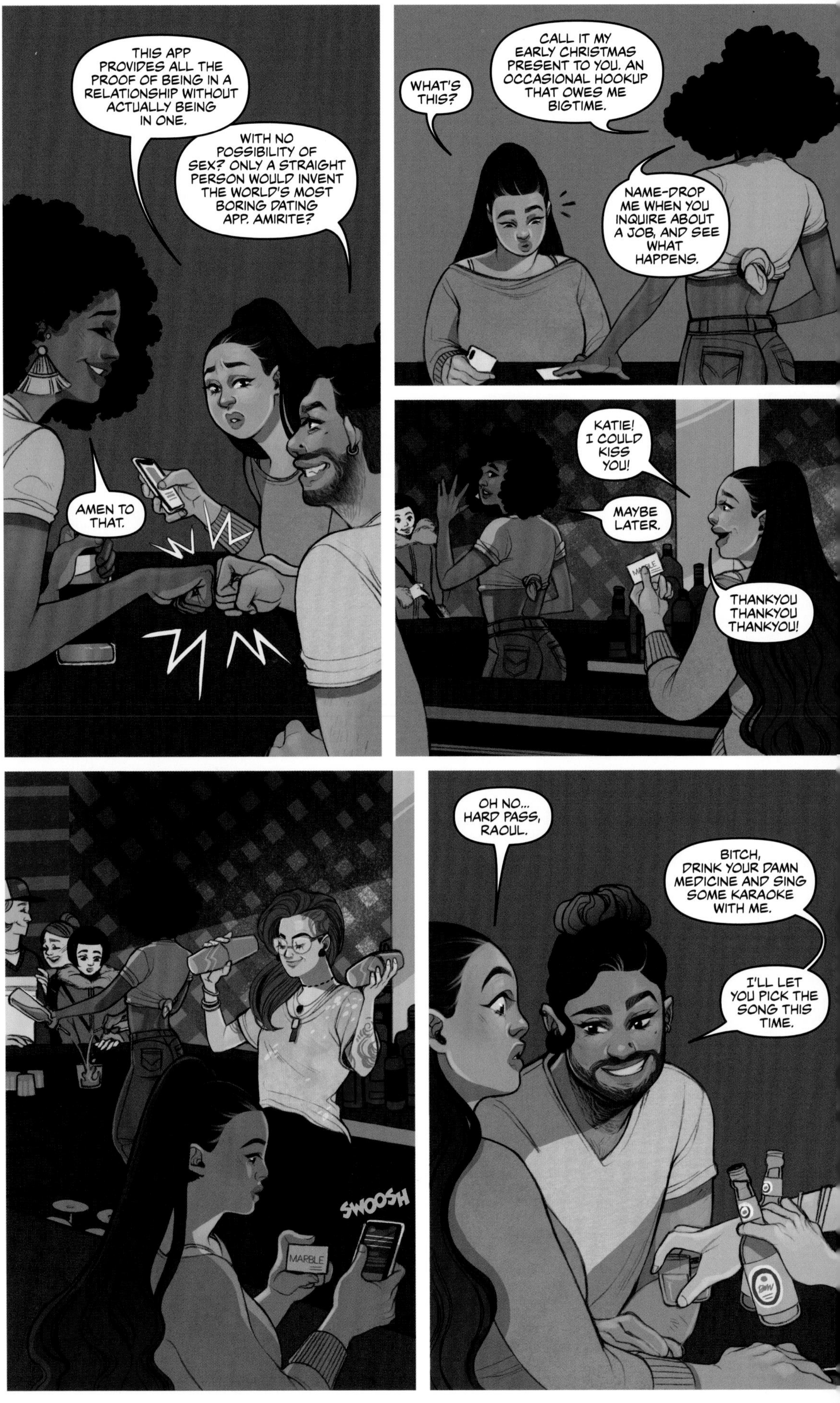
THIS APP PROVIDES ALL THE PROOF OF BEING IN A RELATIONSHIP WITHOUT ACTUALLY BEING IN ONE.
WITH NO POSSIBILITY OF SEX? ONLY A STRAIGHT PERSON WOULD INVENT THE WORLD'S MOST BORING DATING APP. AMIRITE?
AMEN TO THAT.
WHAT'S THIS?
CALL IT MY EARLY CHRISTMAS PRESENT TO YOU. AN OCCASIONAL HOOKUP THAT OWES ME BIGTIME.
NAME-DROP ME WHEN YOU INQUIRE ABOUT A JOB, AND SEE WHAT HAPPENS.
KATIE! I COULD KISS YOU!
MAYBE LATER.
MARBLE
THANKYOU THANKYOU THANKYOU!
SWOOSH
MARBLE
OH NO... HARD PASS, RAOUL.
BITCH, DRINK YOUR DAMN MEDICINE AND SING SOME KARAOKE WITH ME.
I'LL LET YOU PICK THE SONG THIS TIME.

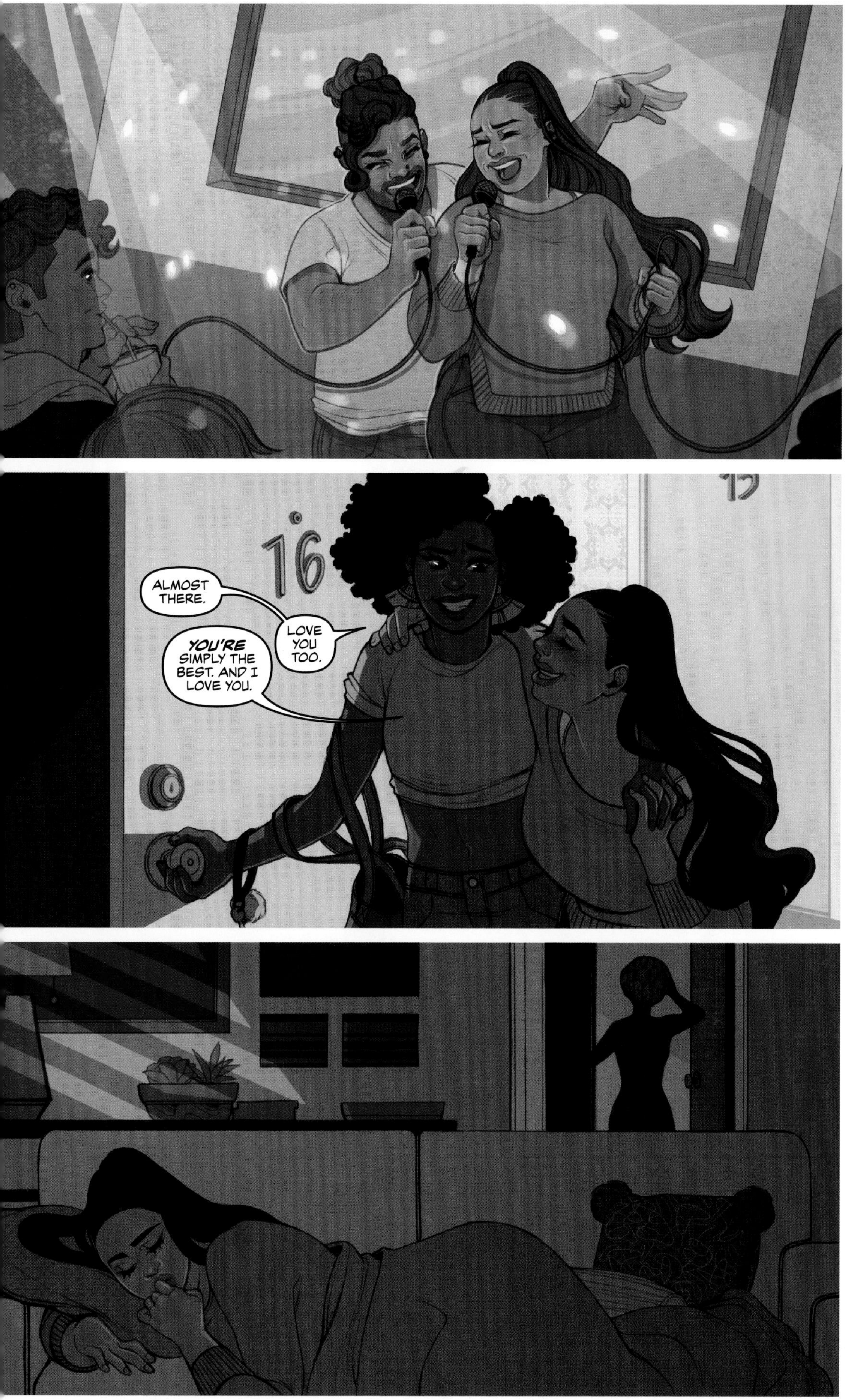
16
ALMOST THERE.
YOU'RE SIMPLY THE BEST. AND I LOVE YOU.
LOVE YOU TOO.

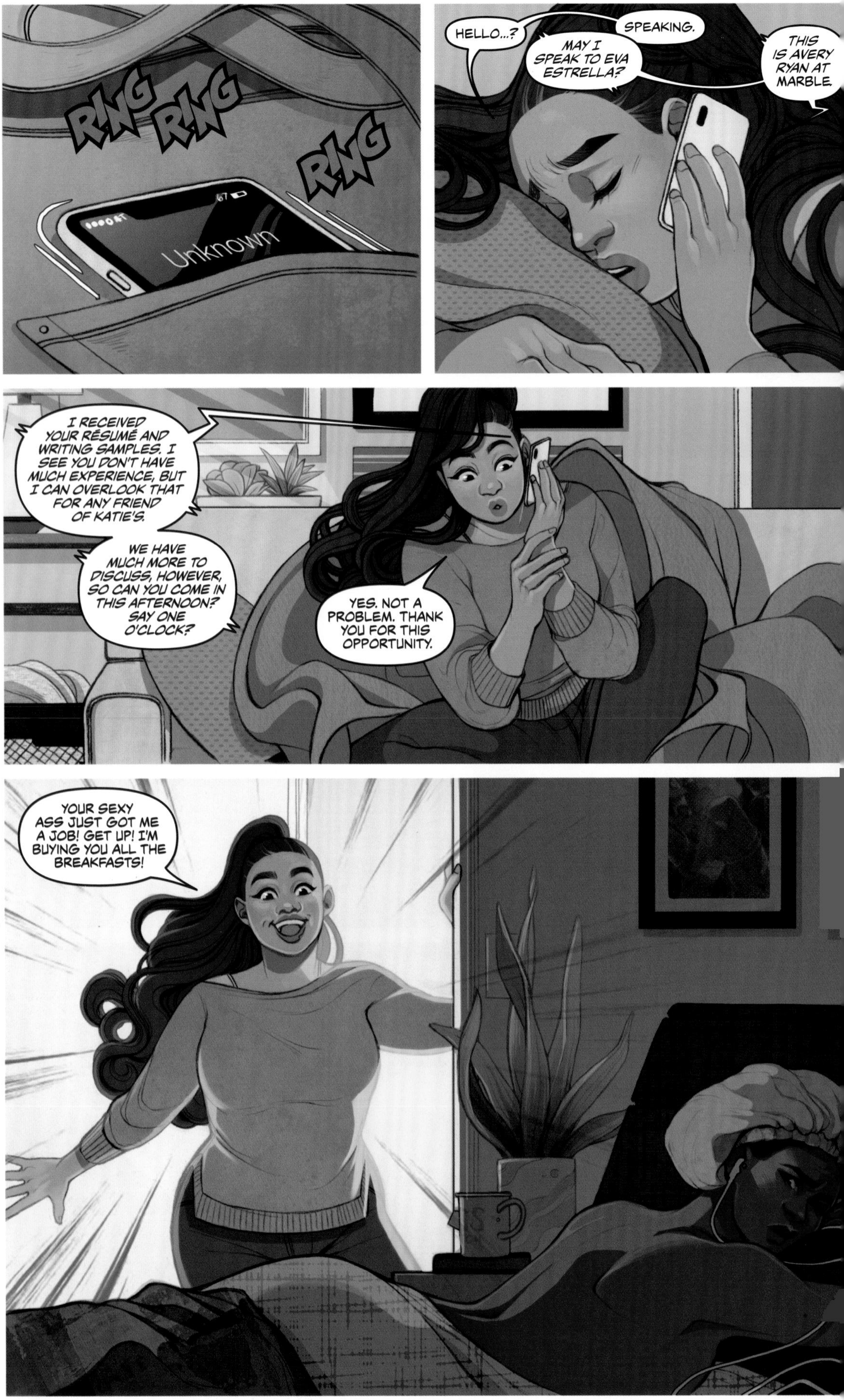
RING RING
RING
Unknown
HELLO...?
MAY I SPEAK TO EVA ESTRELLA?
SPEAKING.
THIS IS AVERY RYAN AT MARBLE.
I RECEIVED YOUR RÉSUMÉ AND WRITING SAMPLES. I SEE YOU DON'T HAVE MUCH EXPERIENCE, BUT I CAN OVERLOOK THAT FOR ANY FRIEND OF KATIE'S.
WE HAVE MUCH MORE TO DISCUSS, HOWEVER, SO CAN YOU COME IN THIS AFTERNOON? SAY ONE O'CLOCK?
YES. NOT A PROBLEM. THANK YOU FOR THIS OPPORTUNITY.
YOUR SEXY ASS JUST GOT ME A JOB! GET UP! I'M BUYING YOU ALL THE BREAKFASTS!

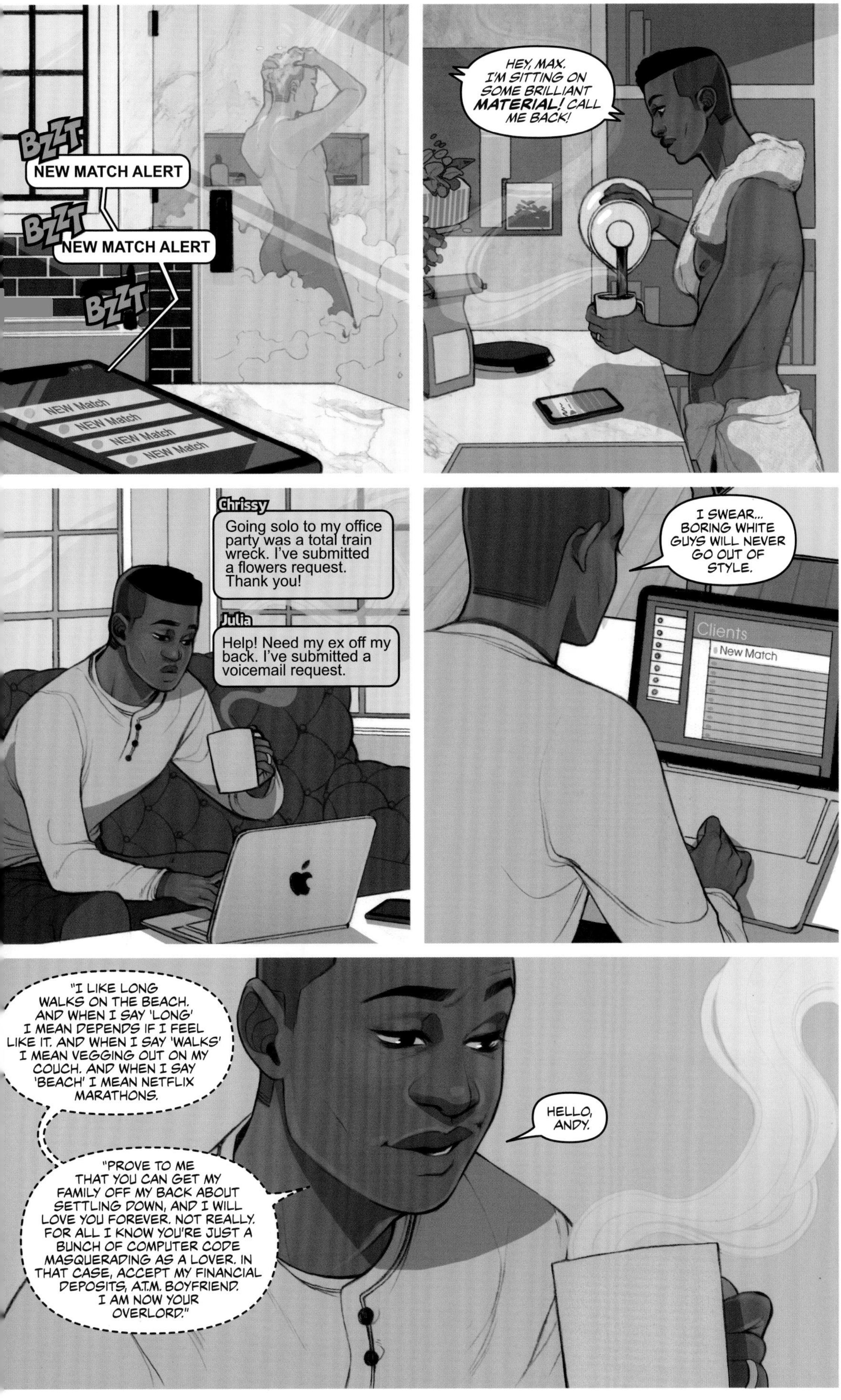
BZZT
NEW MATCH ALERT
BZZT
NEW MATCH ALERT
BZZT
NEW Match
NEW Match
NEW Match
NEW Match
HEY, MAX. I'M SITTING ON SOME BRILLIANT MATERIAL! CALL ME BACK!
Chrissy
Going solo to my office party was a total train wreck. I've submitted a flowers request. Thank you!
Julia
Help! Need my ex off my back. I've submitted a voicemail request.
I SWEAR... BORING WHITE GUYS WILL NEVER GO OUT OF STYLE.
Clients
New Match
"I LIKE LONG WALKS ON THE BEACH. AND WHEN I SAY 'LONG' I MEAN DEPENDS IF I FEEL LIKE IT. AND WHEN I SAY 'WALKS' I MEAN VEGGING OUT ON MY COUCH. AND WHEN I SAY 'BEACH' I MEAN NETFLIX MARATHONS.
"PROVE TO ME THAT YOU CAN GET MY FAMILY OFF MY BACK ABOUT SETTLING DOWN, AND I WILL LOVE YOU FOREVER. NOT REALLY. FOR ALL I KNOW YOU'RE JUST A BUNCH OF COMPUTER CODE MASQUERADING AS A LOVER. IN THAT CASE, ACCEPT MY FINANCIAL DEPOSITS, A.T.M. BOYFRIEND. I AM NOW YOUR OVERLORD."
HELLO, ANDY.

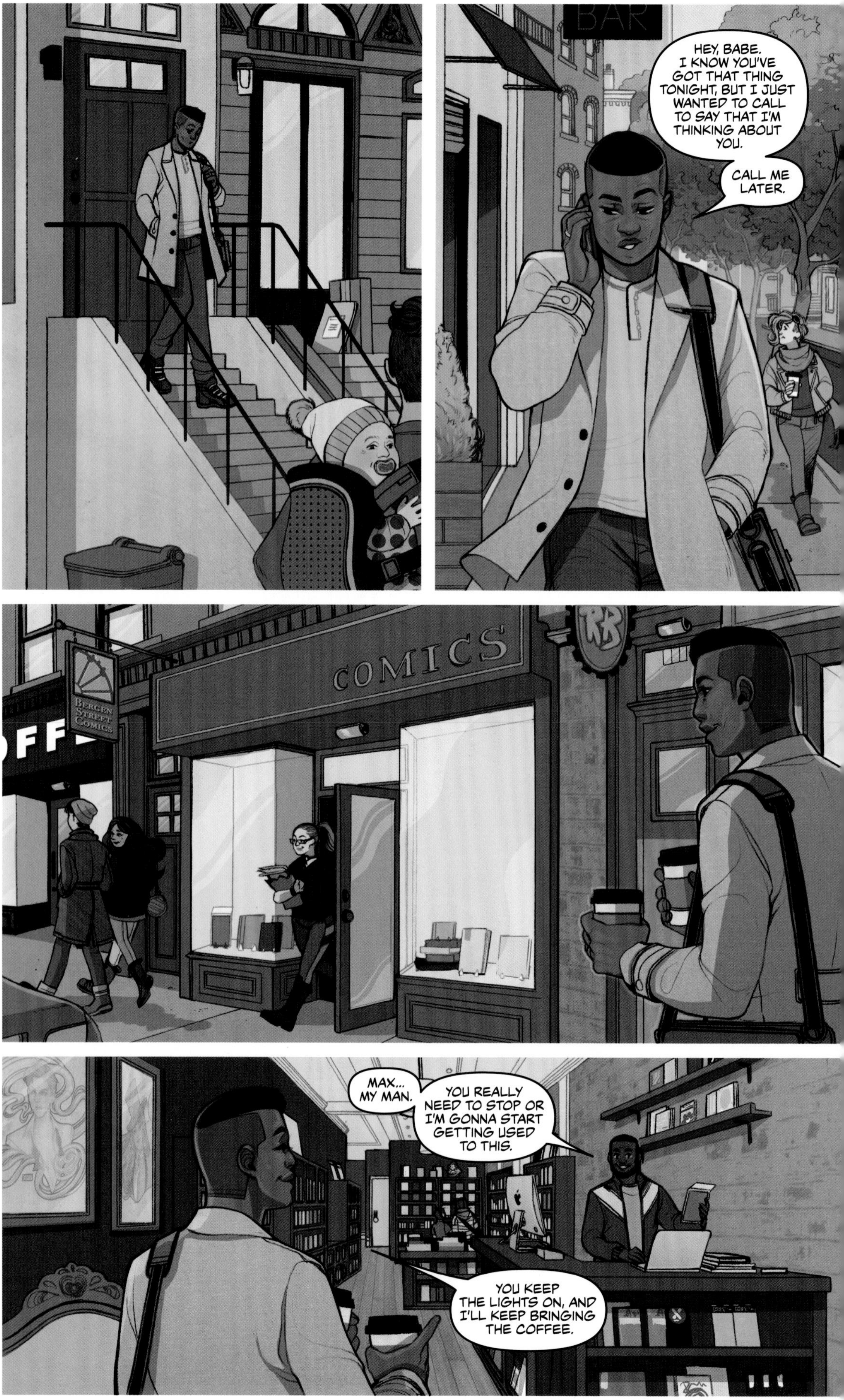
BAR
HEY, BABE. I KNOW YOU'VE GOT THAT THING TONIGHT, BUT I JUST WANTED TO CALL TO SAY THAT I'M THINKING ABOUT YOU.
CALL ME LATER.
BERGEN STREET COMICS
COMICS
MAX... MY MAN.
YOU REALLY NEED TO STOP OR I'M GONNA START GETTING USED TO THIS.
YOU KEEP THE LIGHTS ON, AND I'LL KEEP BRINGING THE COFFEE.

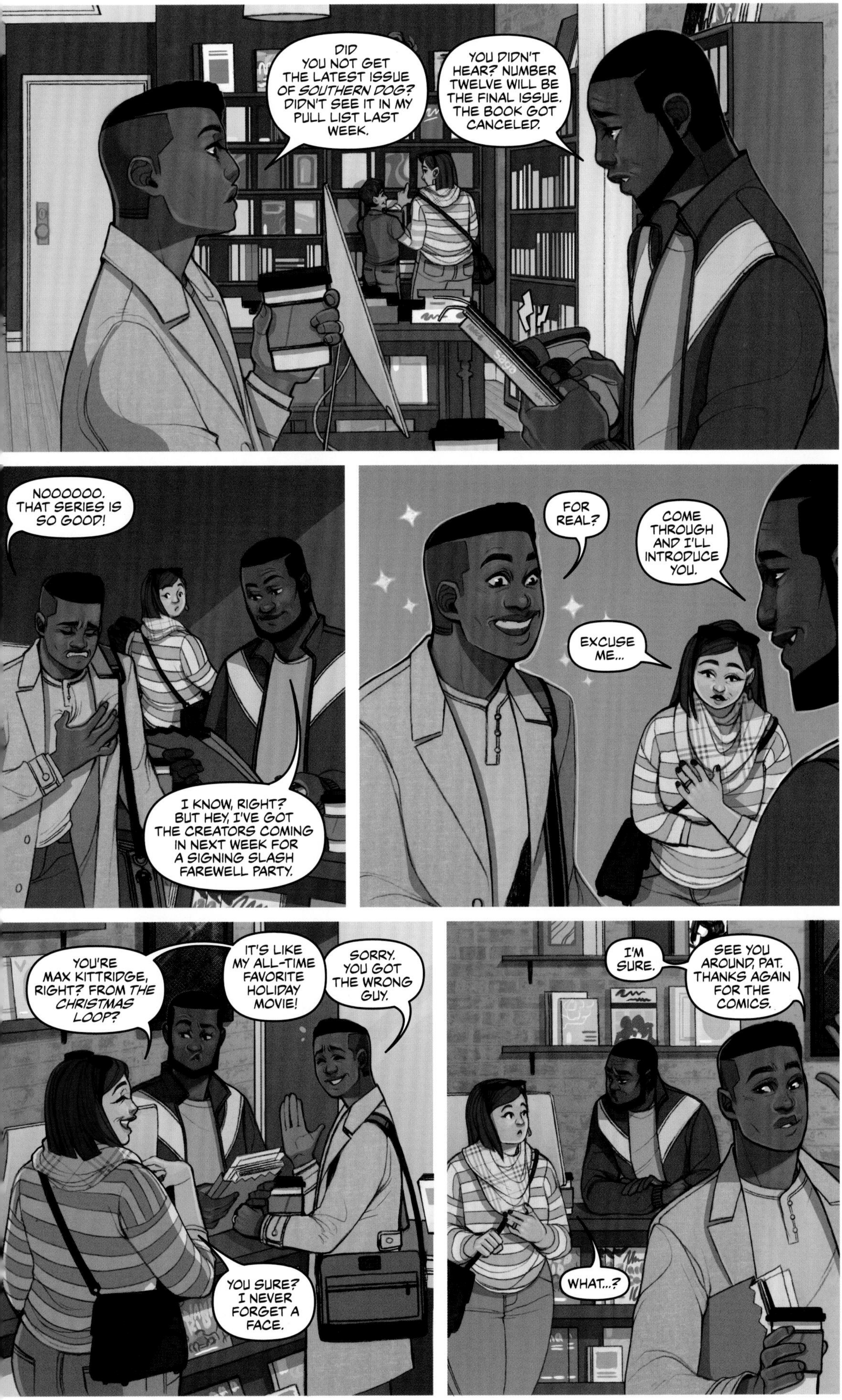
DID YOU NOT GET THE LATEST ISSUE OF *SOUTHERN DOG*? DIDN'T SEE IT IN MY PULL LIST LAST WEEK.
YOU DIDN'T HEAR? NUMBER TWELVE WILL BE THE FINAL ISSUE. THE BOOK GOT CANCELED.
SAGA
NOOOOOO. THAT SERIES IS SO GOOD!
I KNOW, RIGHT? BUT HEY, I'VE GOT THE CREATORS COMING IN NEXT WEEK FOR A SIGNING SLASH FAREWELL PARTY.
FOR REAL?
COME THROUGH AND I'LL INTRODUCE YOU.
EXCUSE ME...
YOU'RE MAX KITTRIDGE, RIGHT? FROM *THE CHRISTMAS LOOP*?
IT'S LIKE MY ALL-TIME FAVORITE HOLIDAY MOVIE!
SORRY. YOU GOT THE WRONG GUY.
YOU SURE? I NEVER FORGET A FACE.
I'M SURE.
SEE YOU AROUND, PAT. THANKS AGAIN FOR THE COMICS.
WHAT...?

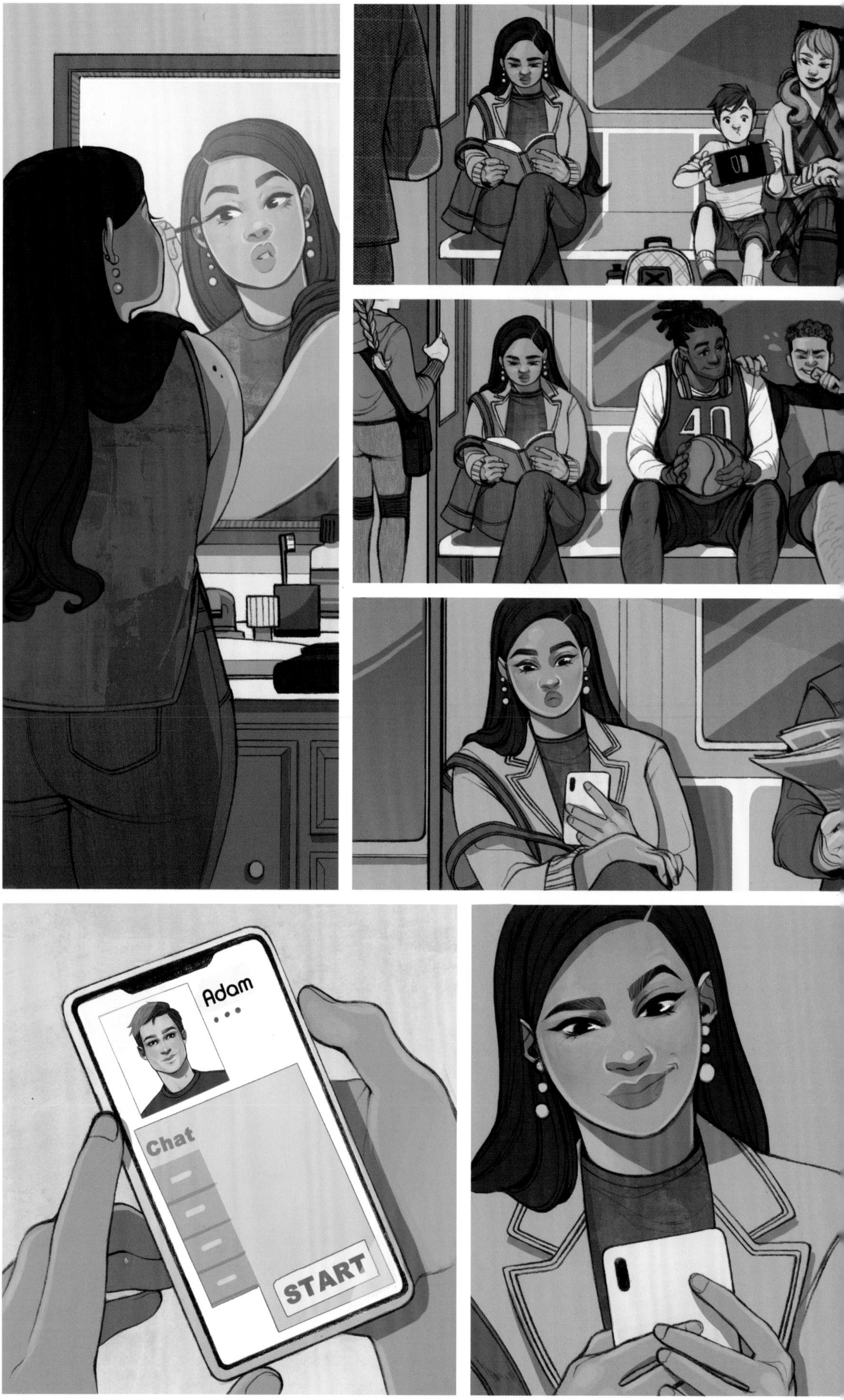
40
Adam
Chat
START

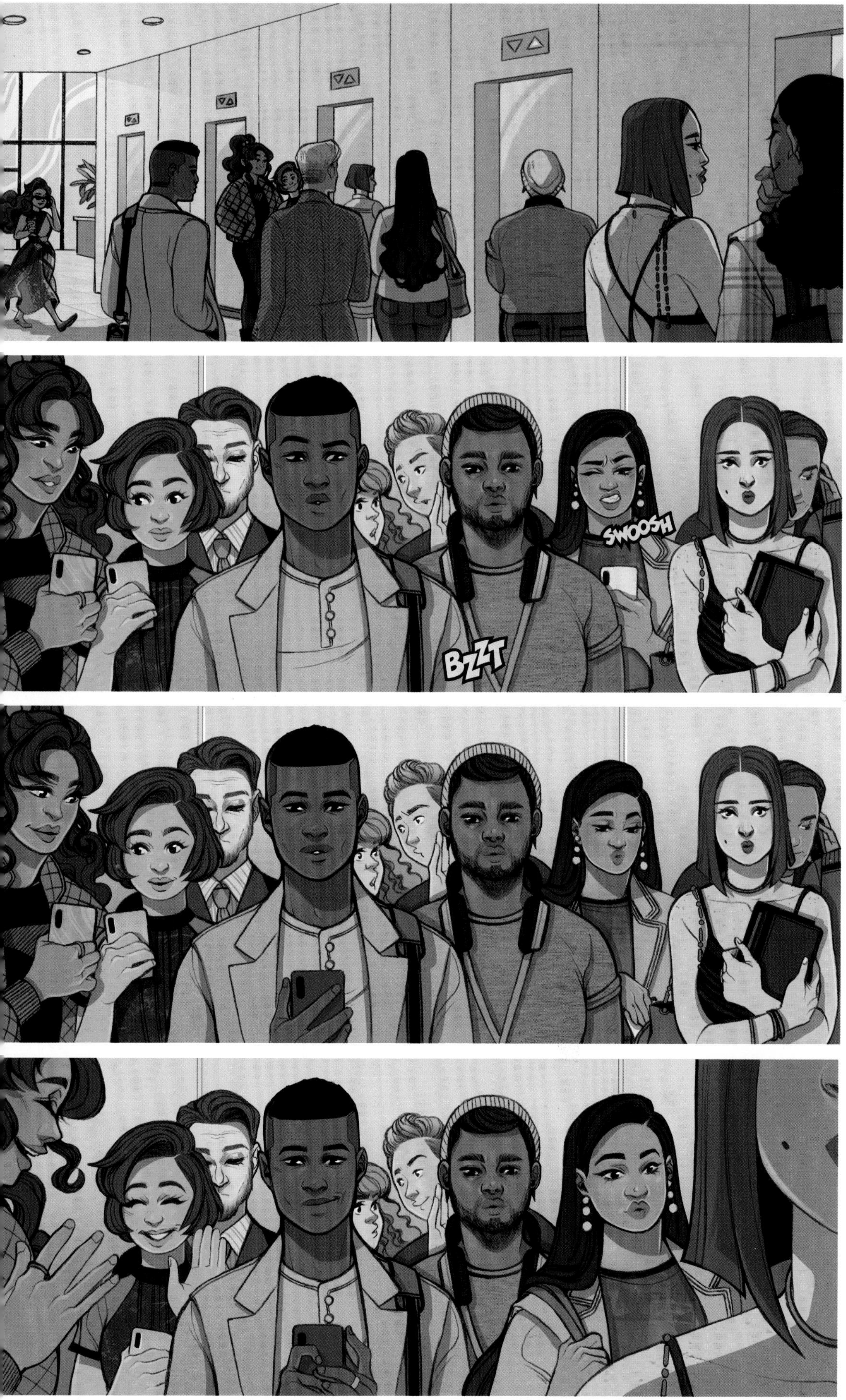
SWOOSH
BZZT

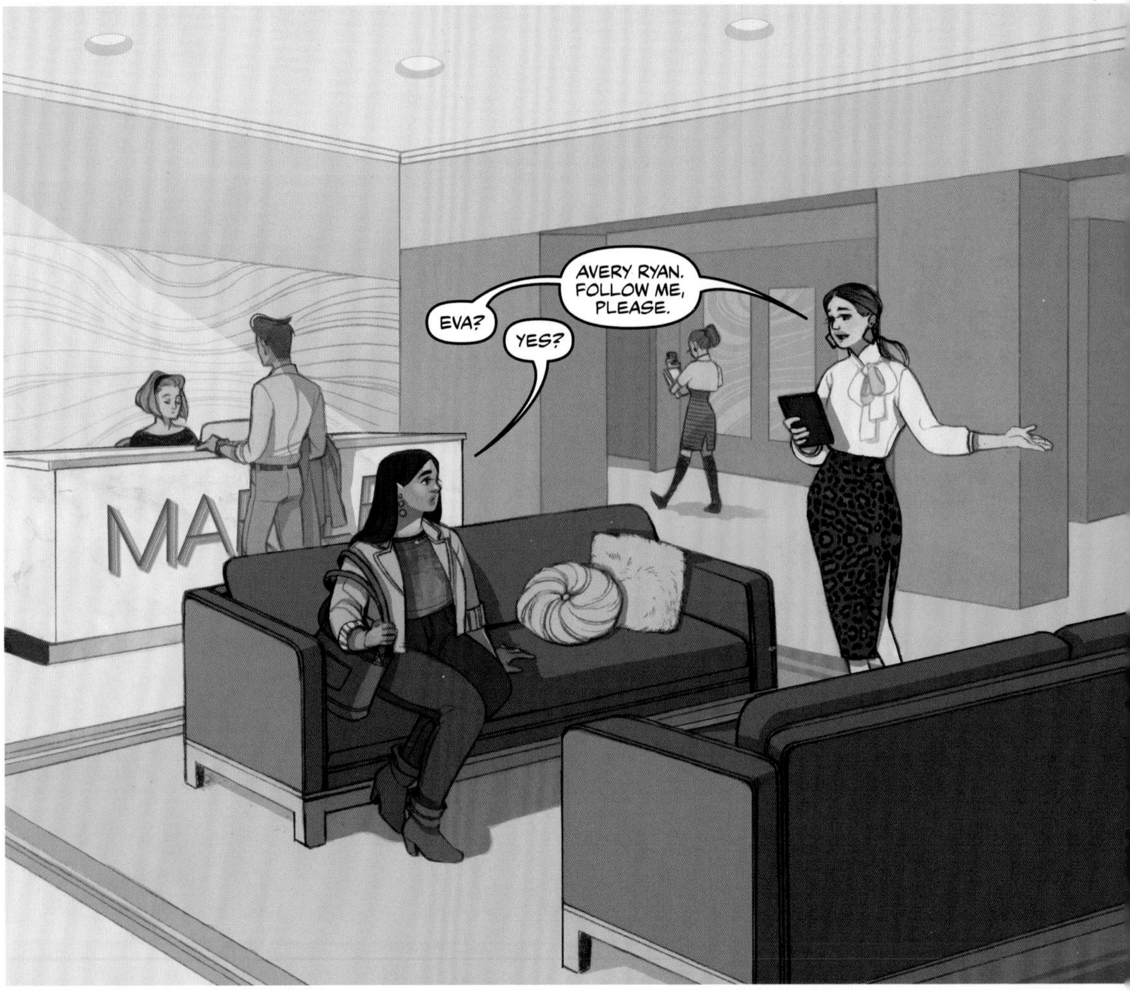
EVA?
AVERY RYAN. FOLLOW ME, PLEASE.
YES?

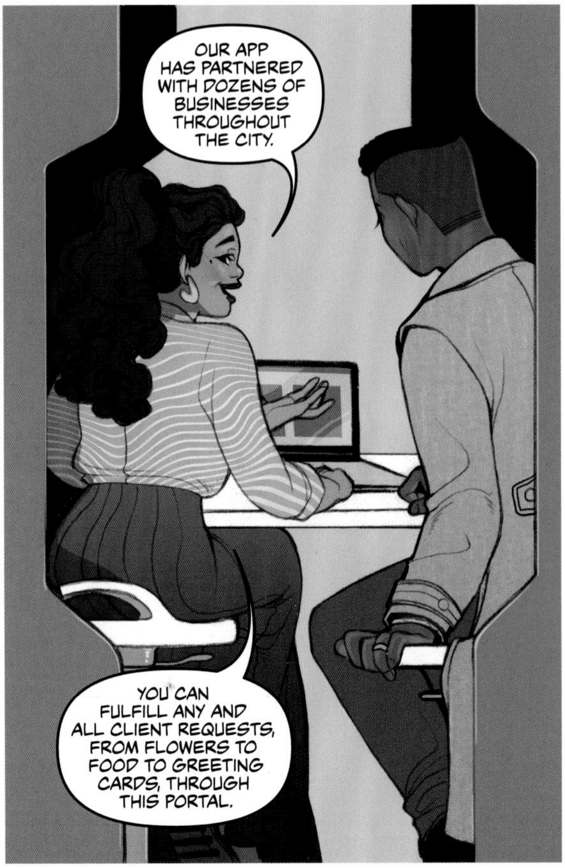
OUR APP HAS PARTNERED WITH DOZENS OF BUSINESSES THROUGHOUT THE CITY.
YOU CAN FULFILL ANY AND ALL CLIENT REQUESTS, FROM FLOWERS TO FOOD TO GREETING CARDS, THROUGH THIS PORTAL.

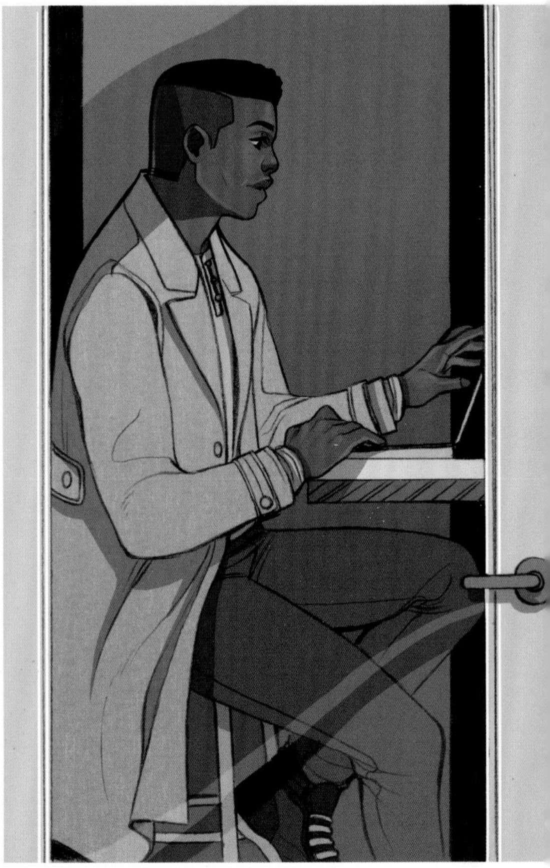

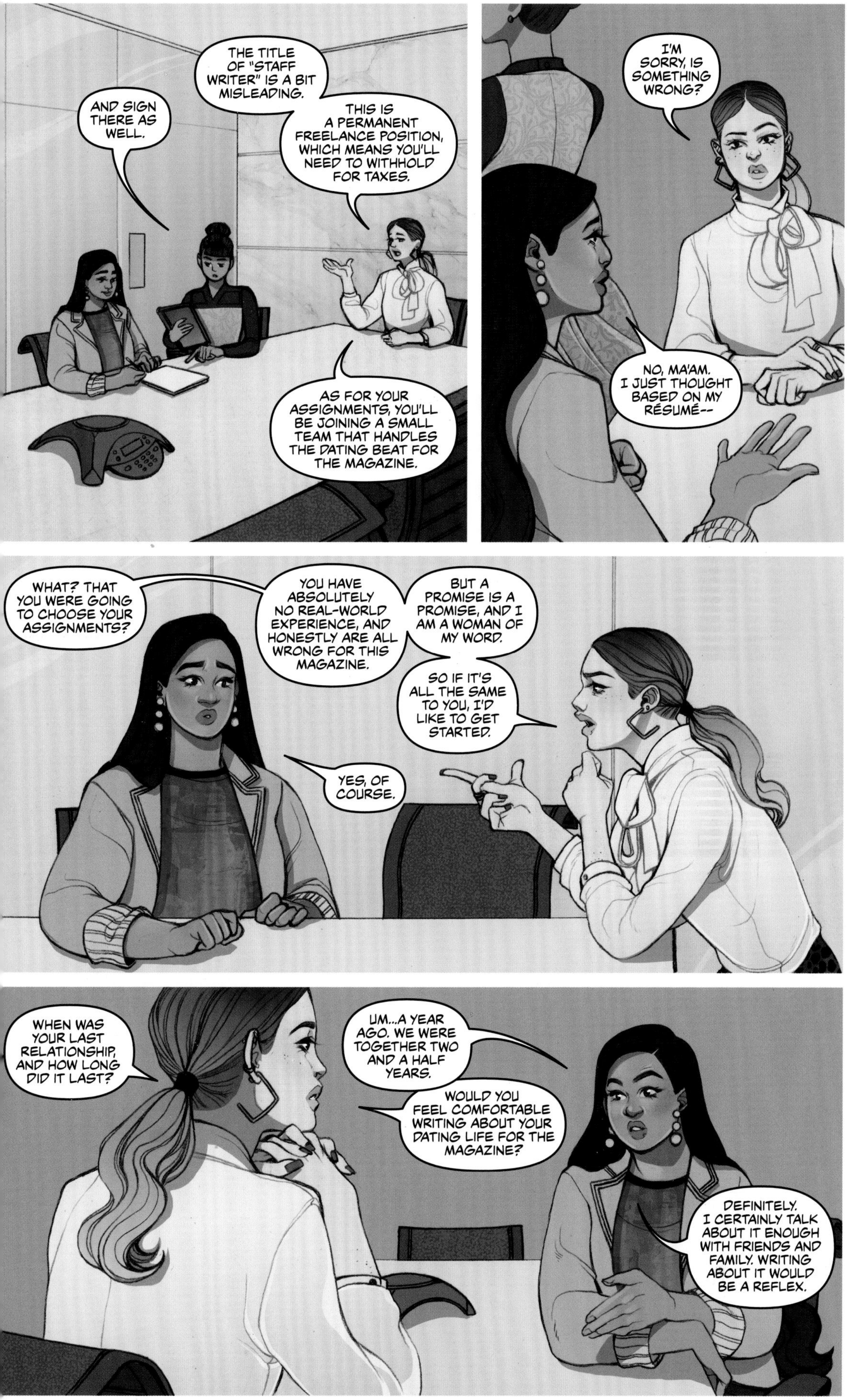
THE TITLE OF "STAFF WRITER" IS A BIT MISLEADING.
AND SIGN THERE AS WELL.
THIS IS A PERMANENT FREELANCE POSITION, WHICH MEANS YOU'LL NEED TO WITHHOLD FOR TAXES.
AS FOR YOUR ASSIGNMENTS, YOU'LL BE JOINING A SMALL TEAM THAT HANDLES THE DATING BEAT FOR THE MAGAZINE.
I'M SORRY, IS SOMETHING WRONG?
NO, MA'AM. I JUST THOUGHT BASED ON MY RÉSUMÉ--
WHAT? THAT YOU WERE GOING TO CHOOSE YOUR ASSIGNMENTS?
YOU HAVE ABSOLUTELY NO REAL-WORLD EXPERIENCE, AND HONESTLY ARE ALL WRONG FOR THIS MAGAZINE.
BUT A PROMISE IS A PROMISE, AND I AM A WOMAN OF MY WORD.
SO IF IT'S ALL THE SAME TO YOU, I'D LIKE TO GET STARTED.
YES, OF COURSE.
WHEN WAS YOUR LAST RELATIONSHIP, AND HOW LONG DID IT LAST?
UM...A YEAR AGO. WE WERE TOGETHER TWO AND A HALF YEARS.
WOULD YOU FEEL COMFORTABLE WRITING ABOUT YOUR DATING LIFE FOR THE MAGAZINE?
DEFINITELY. I CERTAINLY TALK ABOUT IT ENOUGH WITH FRIENDS AND FAMILY. WRITING ABOUT IT WOULD BE A REFLEX.

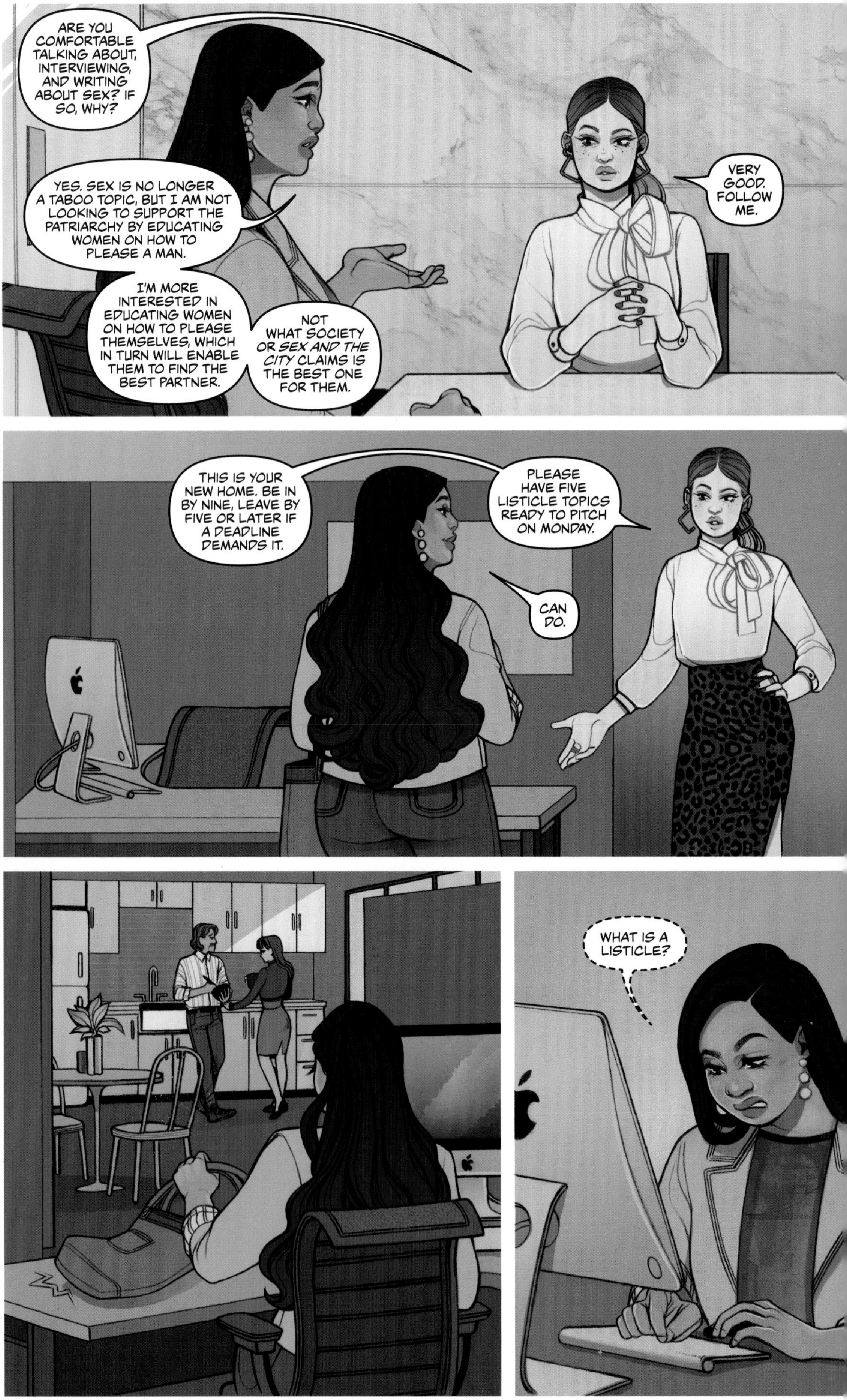
ARE YOU COMFORTABLE TALKING ABOUT, INTERVIEWING, AND WRITING ABOUT SEX? IF SO, WHY?
YES. SEX IS NO LONGER A TABOO TOPIC, BUT I AM NOT LOOKING TO SUPPORT THE PATRIARCHY BY EDUCATING WOMEN ON HOW TO PLEASE A MAN.
I'M MORE INTERESTED IN EDUCATING WOMEN ON HOW TO PLEASE THEMSELVES, WHICH IN TURN WILL ENABLE THEM TO FIND THE BEST PARTNER.
NOT WHAT SOCIETY OR *SEX AND THE CITY* CLAIMS IS THE BEST ONE FOR THEM.
VERY GOOD. FOLLOW ME.
THIS IS YOUR NEW HOME. BE IN BY NINE, LEAVE BY FIVE OR LATER IF A DEADLINE DEMANDS IT.
PLEASE HAVE FIVE LISTICLE TOPICS READY TO PITCH ON MONDAY.
CAN DO.
WHAT IS A LISTICLE?

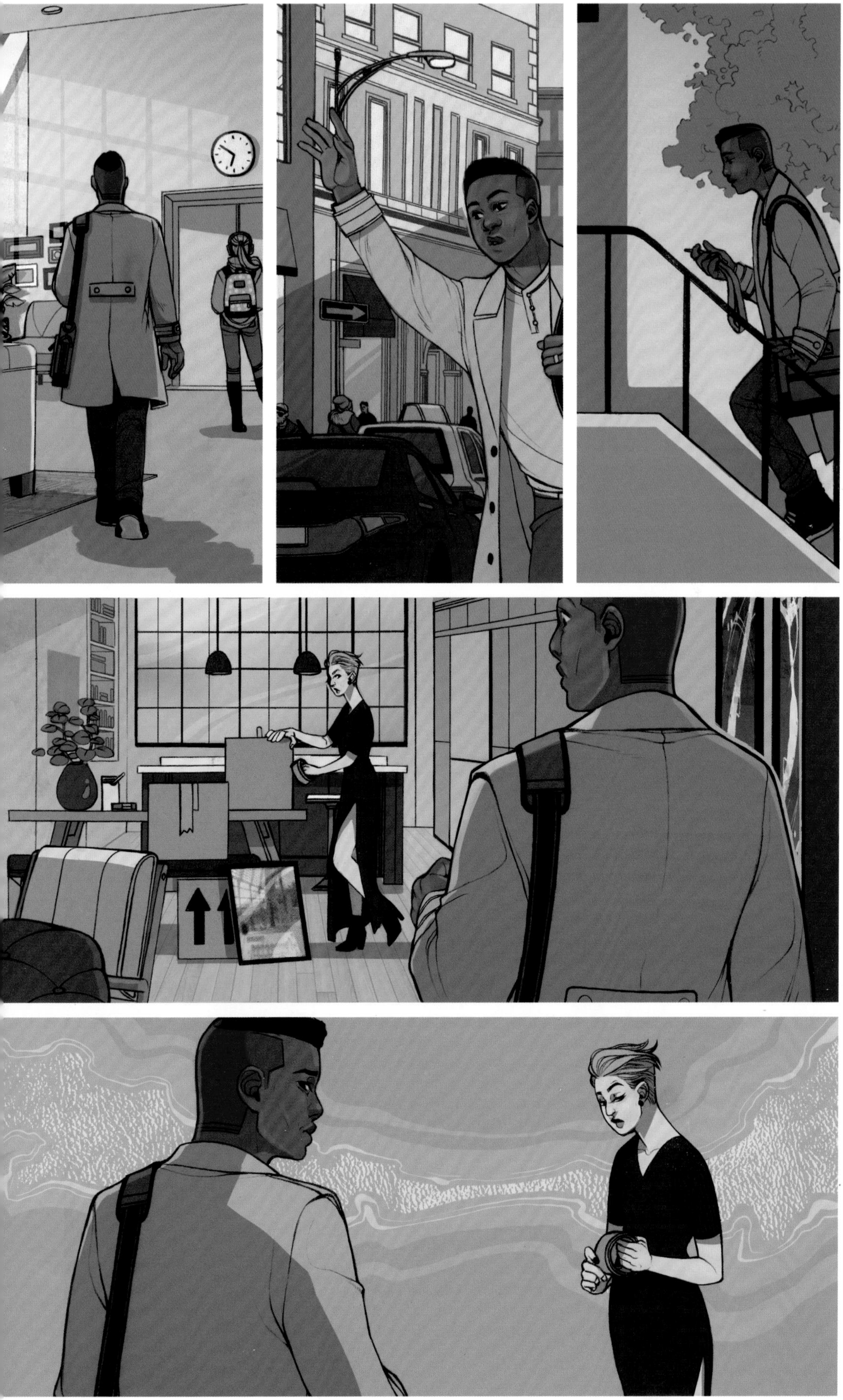

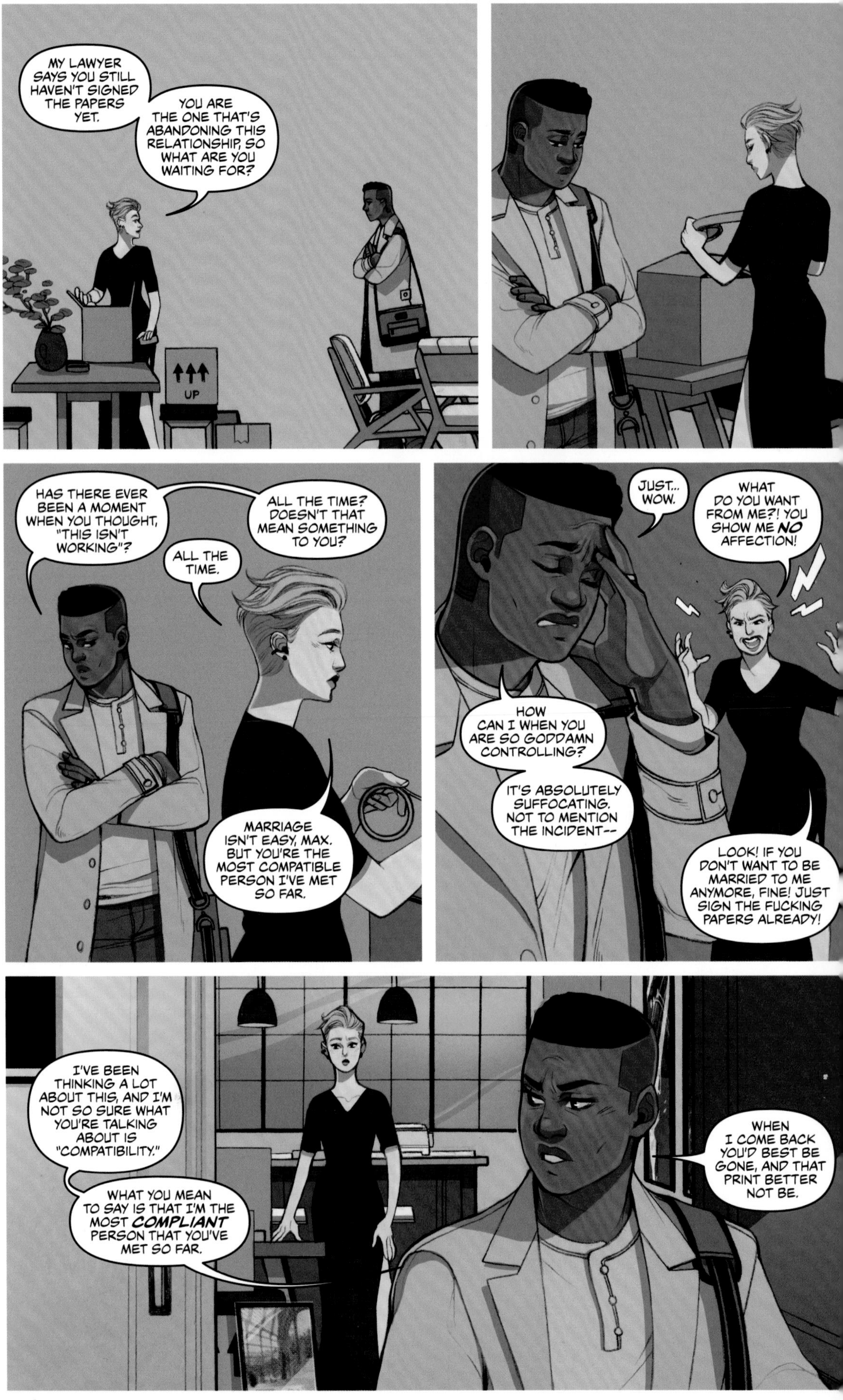
MY LAWYER SAYS YOU STILL HAVEN'T SIGNED THE PAPERS YET.
YOU ARE THE ONE THAT'S ABANDONING THIS RELATIONSHIP, SO WHAT ARE YOU WAITING FOR?
UP
HAS THERE EVER BEEN A MOMENT WHEN YOU THOUGHT, "THIS ISN'T WORKING"?
ALL THE TIME.
ALL THE TIME? DOESN'T THAT MEAN SOMETHING TO YOU?
MARRIAGE ISN'T EASY, MAX. BUT YOU'RE THE MOST COMPATIBLE PERSON I'VE MET SO FAR.
JUST... WOW.
WHAT DO YOU WANT FROM ME?! YOU SHOW ME NO AFFECTION!
HOW CAN I WHEN YOU ARE SO GODDAMN CONTROLLING?
IT'S ABSOLUTELY SUFFOCATING. NOT TO MENTION THE INCIDENT--
LOOK! IF YOU DON'T WANT TO BE MARRIED TO ME ANYMORE, FINE! JUST SIGN THE FUCKING PAPERS ALREADY!
I'VE BEEN THINKING A LOT ABOUT THIS, AND I'M NOT SO SURE WHAT YOU'RE TALKING ABOUT IS "COMPATIBILITY."
WHAT YOU MEAN TO SAY IS THAT I'M THE MOST COMPLIANT PERSON THAT YOU'VE MET SO FAR.
WHEN I COME BACK YOU'D BEST BE GONE, AND THAT PRINT BETTER NOT BE.

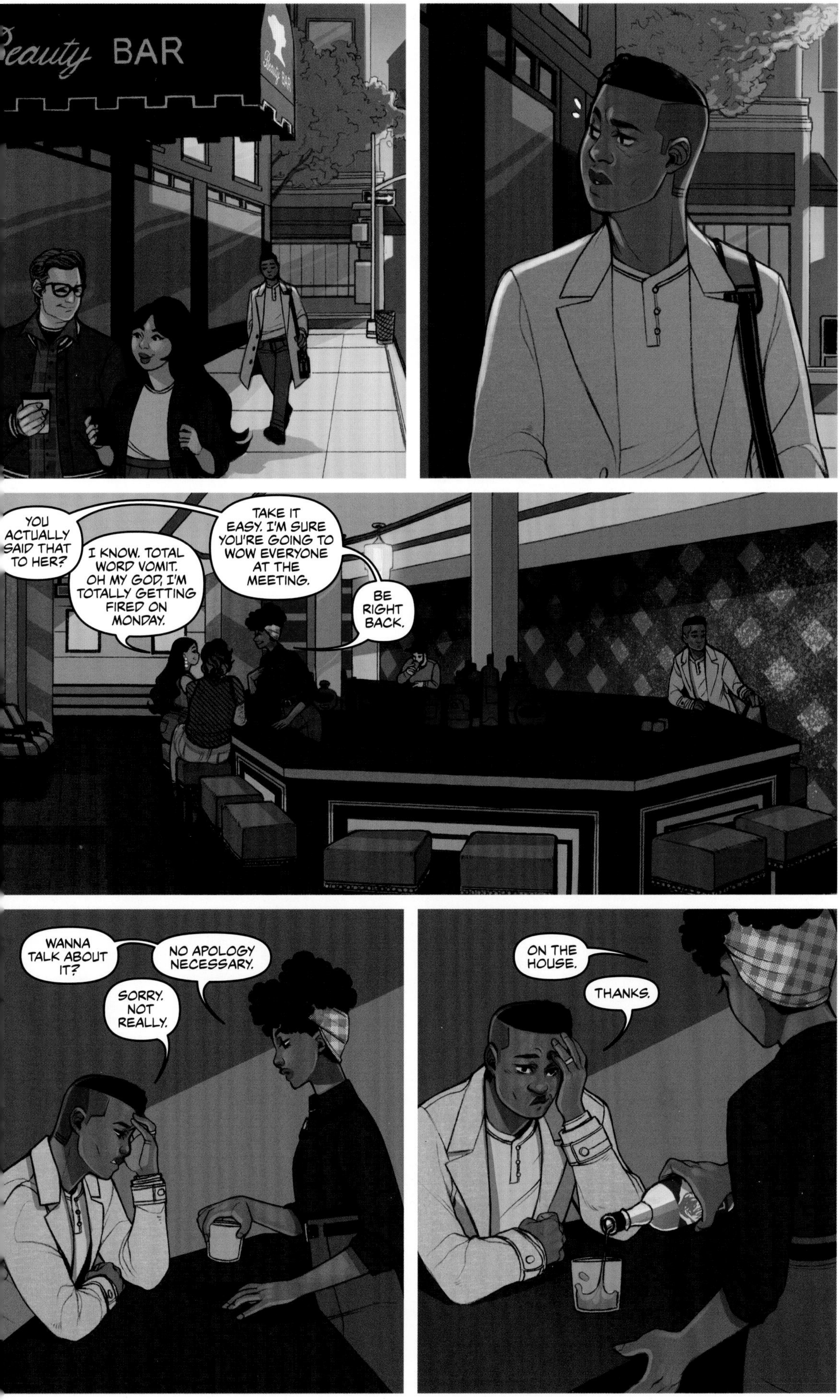
Beauty BAR
Beauty BAR
YOU ACTUALLY SAID THAT TO HER?
I KNOW. TOTAL WORD VOMIT. OH MY GOD, I'M TOTALLY GETTING FIRED ON MONDAY.
TAKE IT EASY. I'M SURE YOU'RE GOING TO WOW EVERYONE AT THE MEETING.
BE RIGHT BACK.
WANNA TALK ABOUT IT?
SORRY. NOT REALLY.
NO APOLOGY NECESSARY.
ON THE HOUSE.
THANKS.

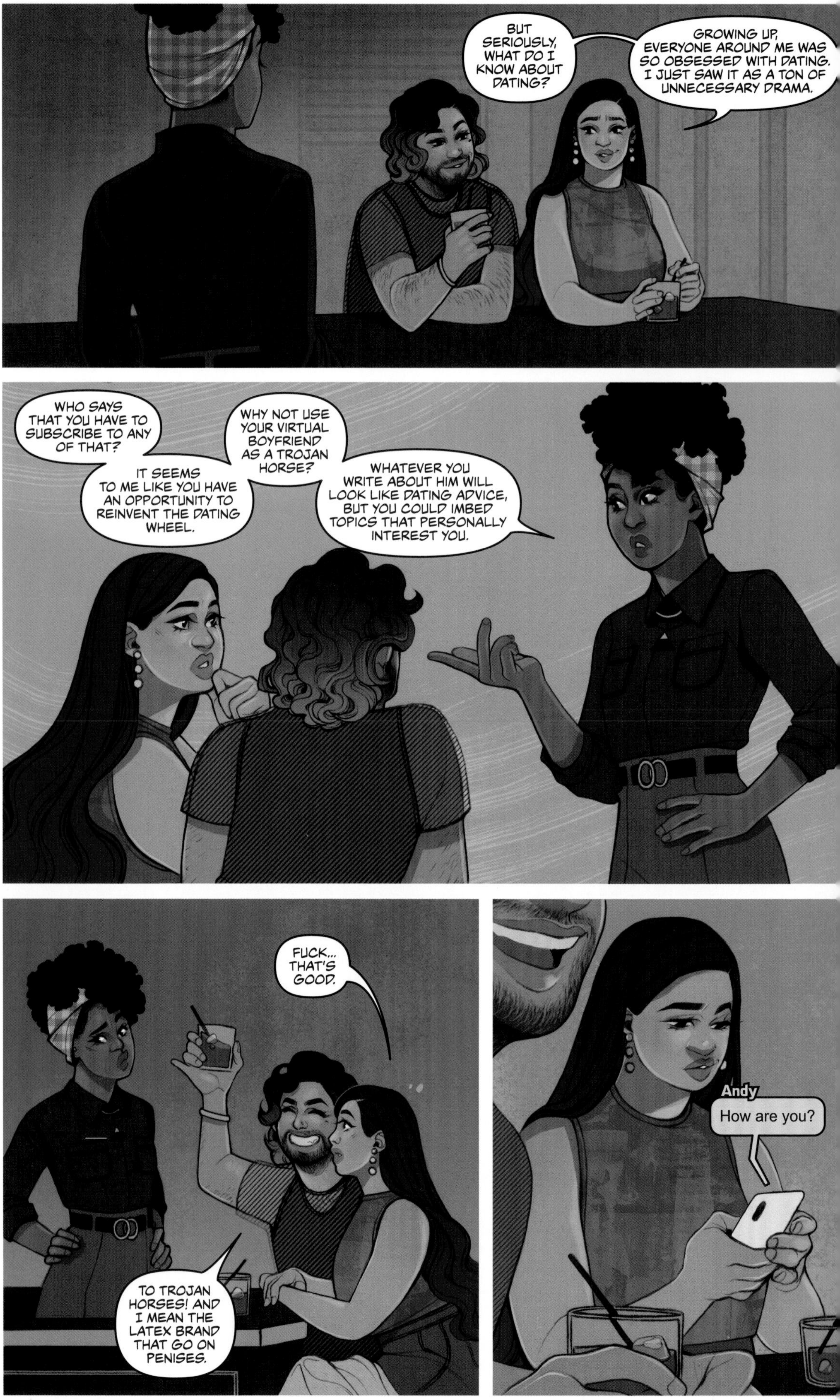

BUT SERIOUSLY, WHAT DO I KNOW ABOUT DATING?
GROWING UP, EVERYONE AROUND ME WAS SO OBSESSED WITH DATING. I JUST SAW IT AS A TON OF UNNECESSARY DRAMA.
WHO SAYS THAT YOU HAVE TO SUBSCRIBE TO ANY OF THAT?
IT SEEMS TO ME LIKE YOU HAVE AN OPPORTUNITY TO REINVENT THE DATING WHEEL.
WHY NOT USE YOUR VIRTUAL BOYFRIEND AS A TROJAN HORSE?
WHATEVER YOU WRITE ABOUT HIM WILL LOOK LIKE DATING ADVICE, BUT YOU COULD IMBED TOPICS THAT PERSONALLY INTEREST YOU.
FUCK... THAT'S GOOD.
TO TROJAN HORSES! AND I MEAN THE LATEX BRAND THAT GO ON PENISES.
Andy
How are you?

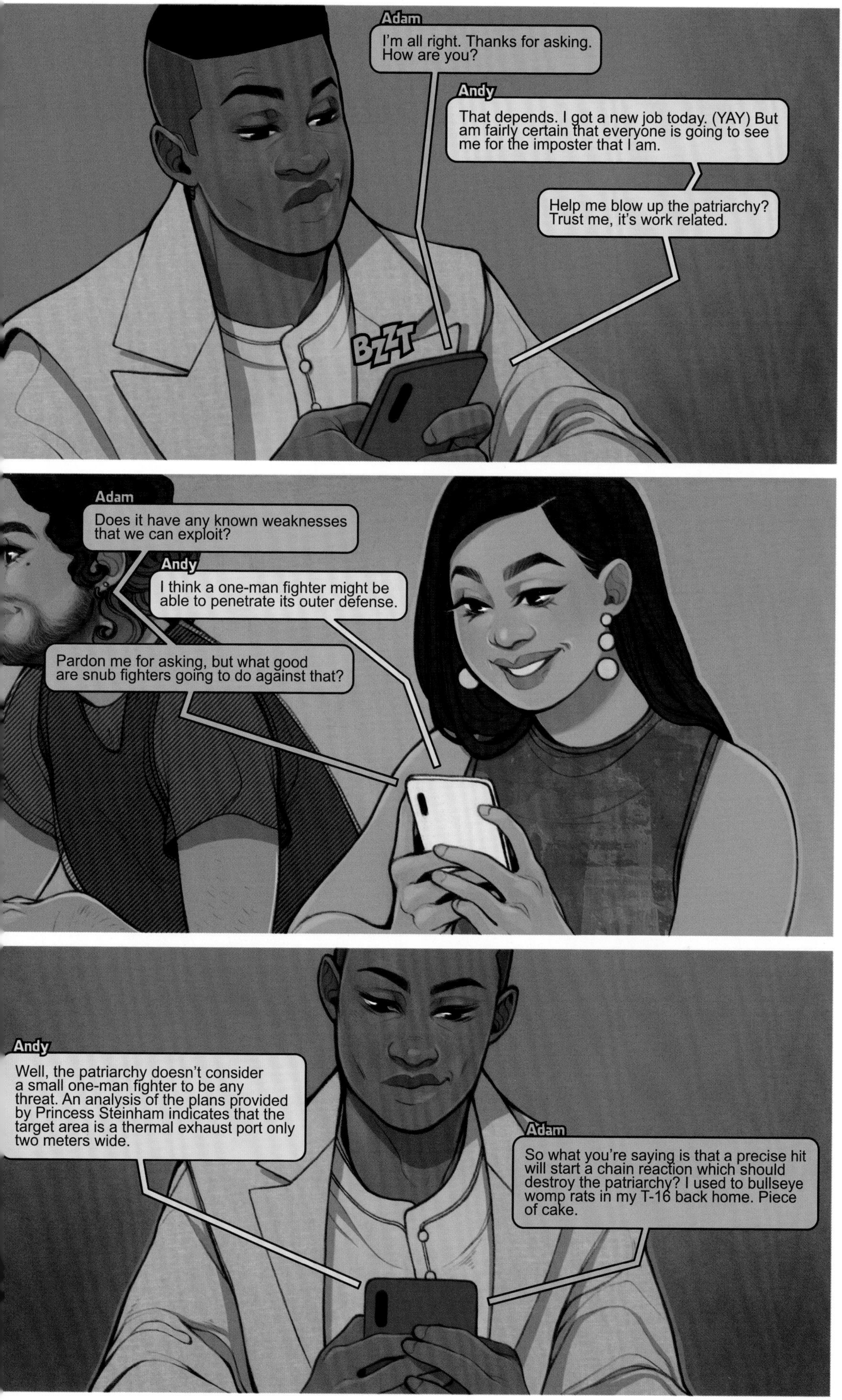
Adam
I'm all right. Thanks for asking. How are you?
Andy
That depends. I got a new job today. (YAY) But am fairly certain that everyone is going to see me for the imposter that I am.
Help me blow up the patriarchy? Trust me, it's work related.
BZZT
Adam
Does it have any known weaknesses that we can exploit?
Andy
I think a one-man fighter might be able to penetrate its outer defense.
Pardon me for asking, but what good are snub fighters going to do against that?
Andy
Well, the patriarchy doesn't consider a small one-man fighter to be any threat. An analysis of the plans provided by Princess Steinham indicates that the target area is a thermal exhaust port only two meters wide.
Adam
So what you're saying is that a precise hit will start a chain reaction which should destroy the patriarchy? I used to bullseye womp rats in my T-16 back home. Piece of cake.

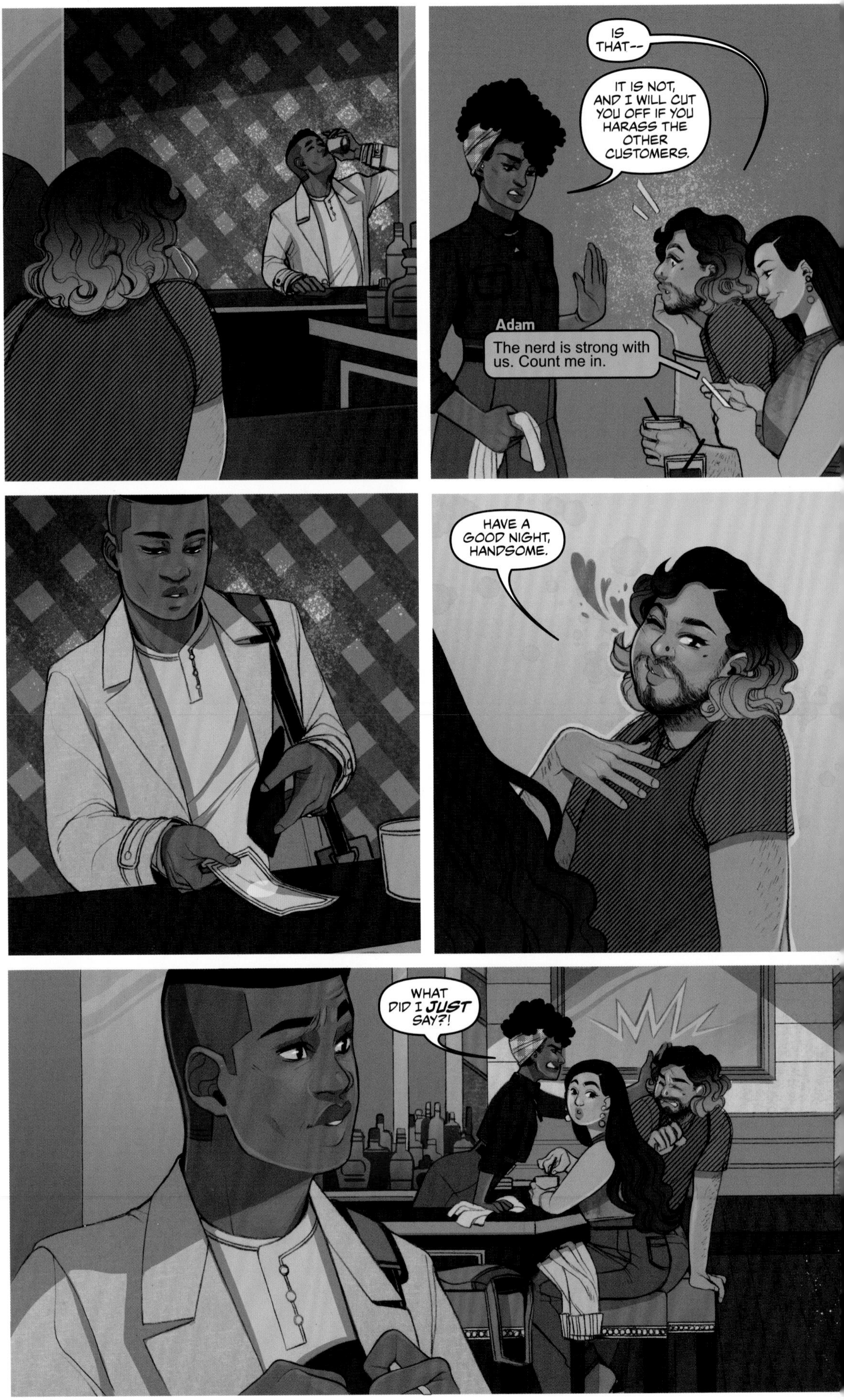
IS THAT--
IT IS NOT, AND I WILL CUT YOU OFF IF YOU HARASS THE OTHER CUSTOMERS.
Adam
The nerd is strong with us. Count me in.
HAVE A GOOD NIGHT, HANDSOME.
WHAT DID I JUST SAY?!

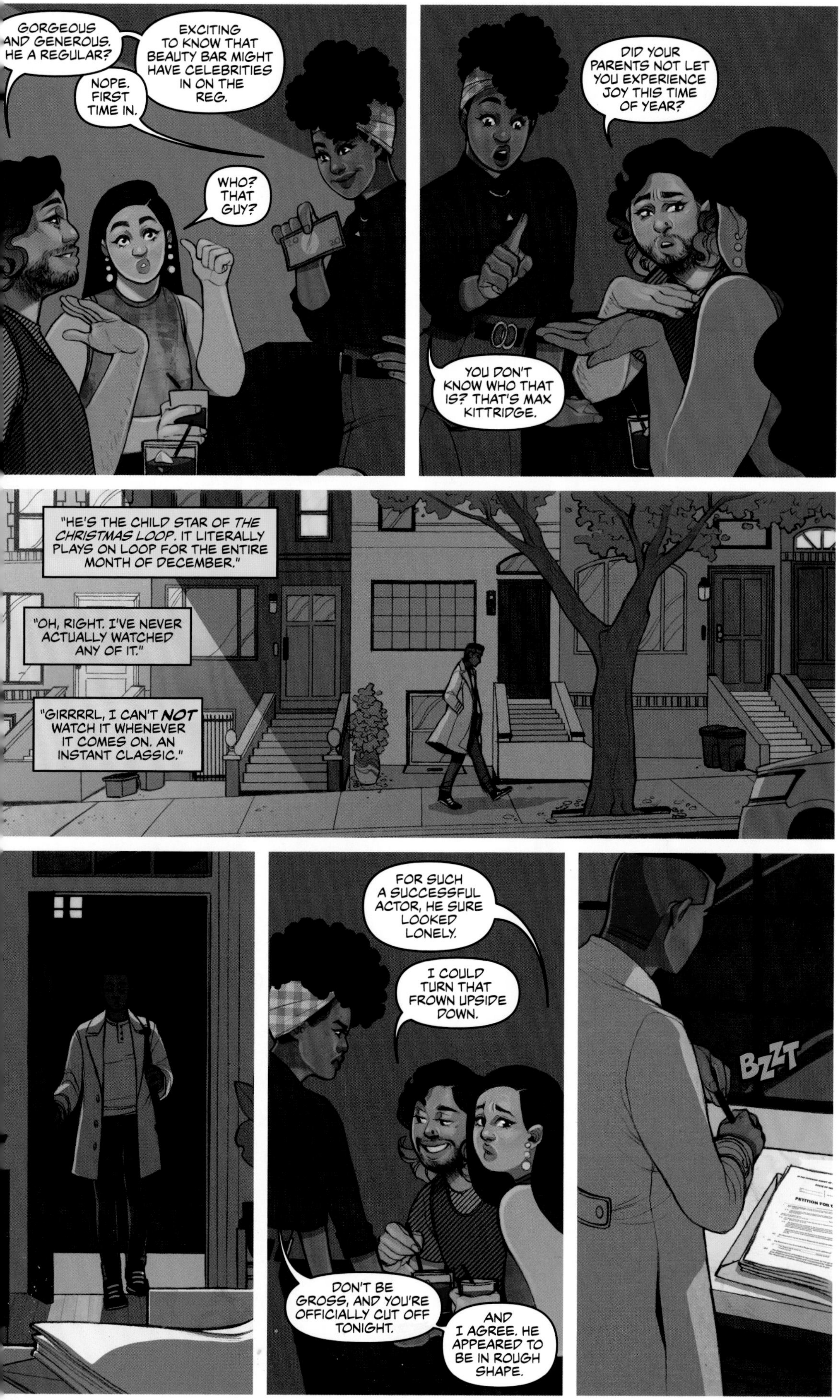
GORGEOUS AND GENEROUS. HE A REGULAR?
NOPE. FIRST TIME IN.
EXCITING TO KNOW THAT BEAUTY BAR MIGHT HAVE CELEBRITIES IN ON THE REG.
WHO? THAT GUY?
DID YOUR PARENTS NOT LET YOU EXPERIENCE JOY THIS TIME OF YEAR?
YOU DON'T KNOW WHO THAT IS? THAT'S MAX KITTRIDGE.
"HE'S THE CHILD STAR OF *THE CHRISTMAS LOOP*. IT LITERALLY PLAYS ON LOOP FOR THE ENTIRE MONTH OF DECEMBER."
"OH, RIGHT. I'VE NEVER ACTUALLY WATCHED ANY OF IT."
"GIRRRRL, I CAN'T ***NOT*** WATCH IT WHENEVER IT COMES ON. AN INSTANT CLASSIC."
FOR SUCH A SUCCESSFUL ACTOR, HE SURE LOOKED LONELY.
I COULD TURN THAT FROWN UPSIDE DOWN.
DON'T BE GROSS, AND YOU'RE OFFICIALLY CUT OFF TONIGHT.
AND I AGREE. HE APPEARED TO BE IN ROUGH SHAPE.
BZZZT
PETITION FOR

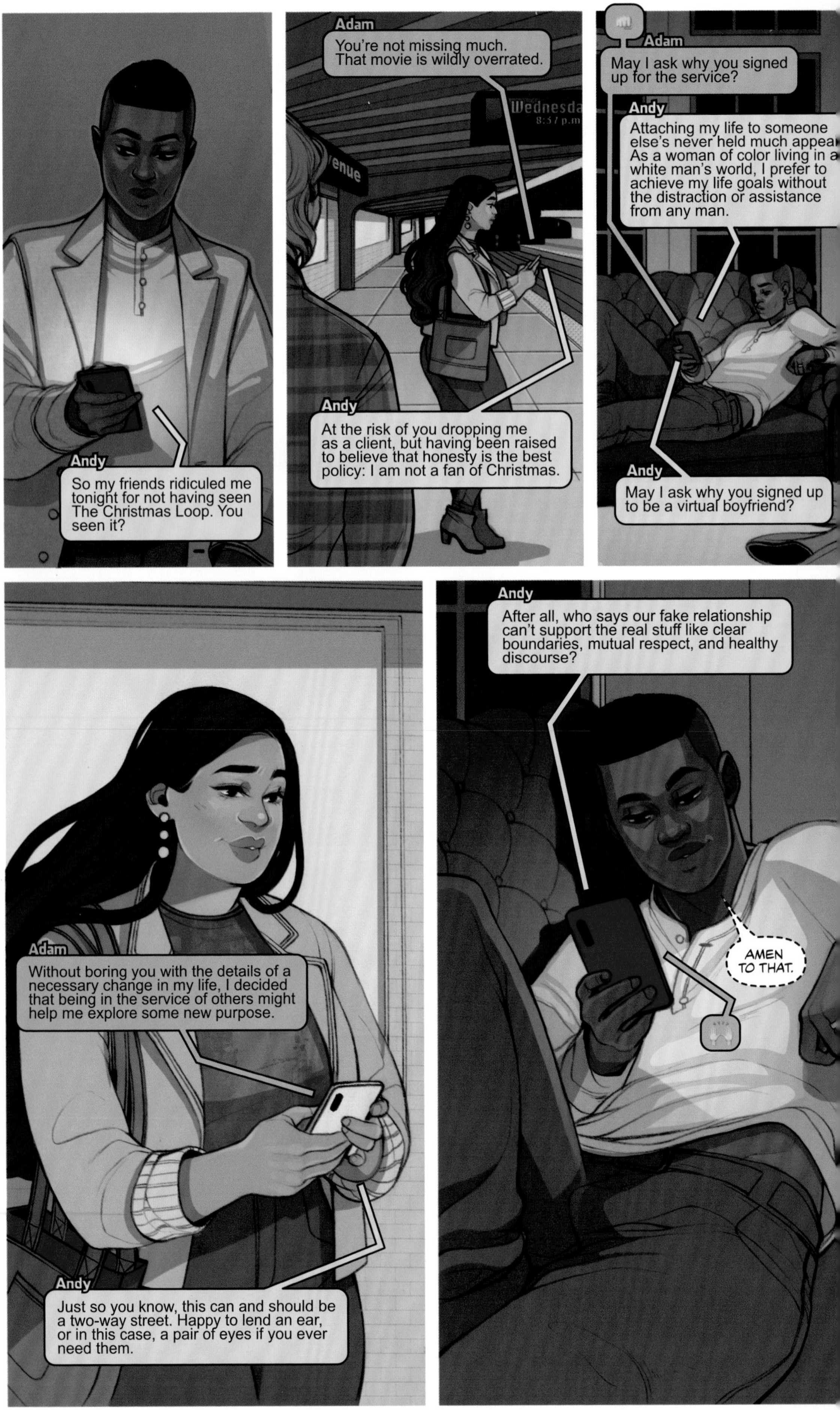
Andy
So my friends ridiculed me tonight for not having seen The Christmas Loop. You seen it?
Adam
You're not missing much. That movie is wildly overrated.
Wednesda
8:37 p.m
venue
Andy
At the risk of you dropping me as a client, but having been raised to believe that honesty is the best policy: I am not a fan of Christmas.
Adam
May I ask why you signed up for the service?
Andy
Attaching my life to someone else's never held much appea
As a woman of color living in a
white man's world, I prefer to achieve my life goals without the distraction or assistance from any man.
Andy
May I ask why you signed up to be a virtual boyfriend?
Adam
Without boring you with the details of a necessary change in my life, I decided that being in the service of others might help me explore some new purpose.
Andy
Just so you know, this can and should be a two-way street. Happy to lend an ear, or in this case, a pair of eyes if you ever need them.
Andy
After all, who says our fake relationship can't support the real stuff like clear boundaries, mutual respect, and healthy discourse?
AMEN TO THAT.

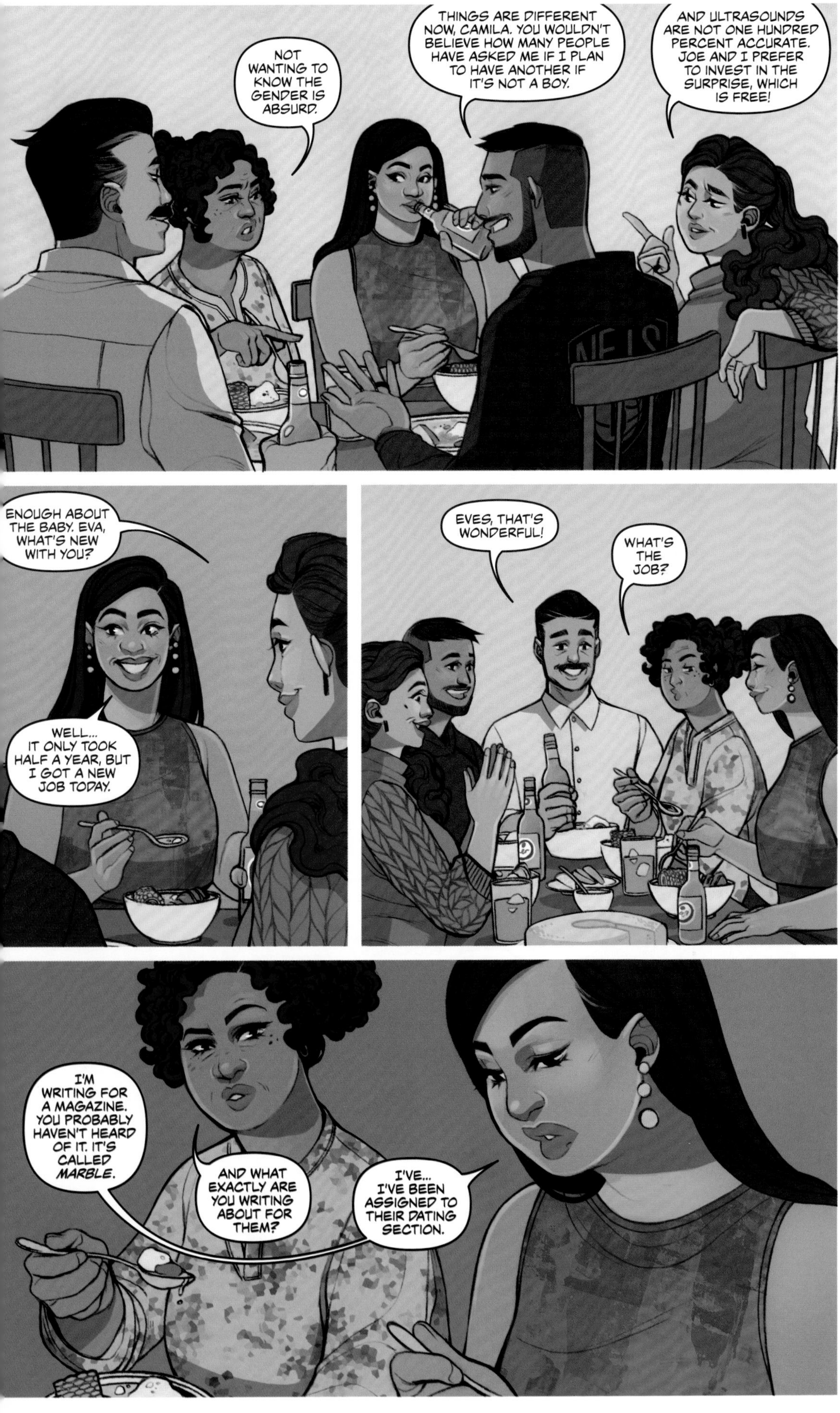
NOT WANTING TO KNOW THE GENDER IS ABSURD.
THINGS ARE DIFFERENT NOW, CAMILA. YOU WOULDN'T BELIEVE HOW MANY PEOPLE HAVE ASKED ME IF I PLAN TO HAVE ANOTHER IF IT'S NOT A BOY.
AND ULTRASOUNDS ARE NOT ONE HUNDRED PERCENT ACCURATE. JOE AND I PREFER TO INVEST IN THE SURPRISE, WHICH IS FREE!
ENOUGH ABOUT THE BABY. EVA, WHAT'S NEW WITH YOU?
WELL... IT ONLY TOOK HALF A YEAR, BUT I GOT A NEW JOB TODAY.
EVES, THAT'S WONDERFUL!
WHAT'S THE JOB?
I'M WRITING FOR A MAGAZINE. YOU PROBABLY HAVEN'T HEARD OF IT. IT'S CALLED *MARBLE*.
AND WHAT EXACTLY ARE YOU WRITING ABOUT FOR THEM?
I'VE... I'VE BEEN ASSIGNED TO THEIR DATING SECTION.

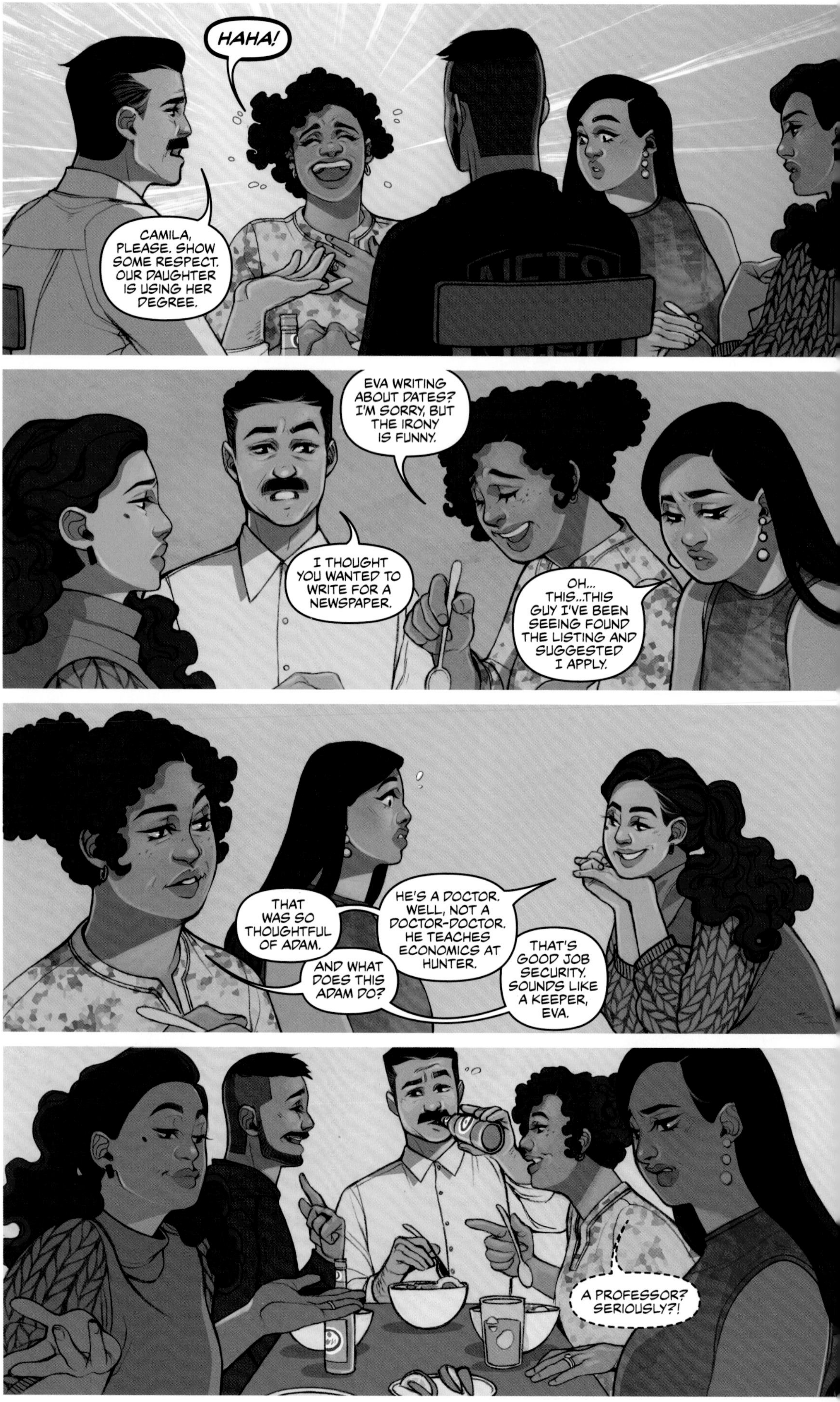

HAHA!
CAMILA, PLEASE. SHOW SOME RESPECT. OUR DAUGHTER IS USING HER DEGREE.
EVA WRITING ABOUT DATES? I'M SORRY, BUT THE IRONY IS FUNNY.
I THOUGHT YOU WANTED TO WRITE FOR A NEWSPAPER.
OH... THIS...THIS GUY I'VE BEEN SEEING FOUND THE LISTING AND SUGGESTED I APPLY.
THAT WAS SO THOUGHTFUL OF ADAM.
AND WHAT DOES THIS ADAM DO?
HE'S A DOCTOR. WELL, NOT A DOCTOR-DOCTOR. HE TEACHES ECONOMICS AT HUNTER.
THAT'S GOOD JOB SECURITY. SOUNDS LIKE A KEEPER, EVA.
A PROFESSOR? SERIOUSLY?!

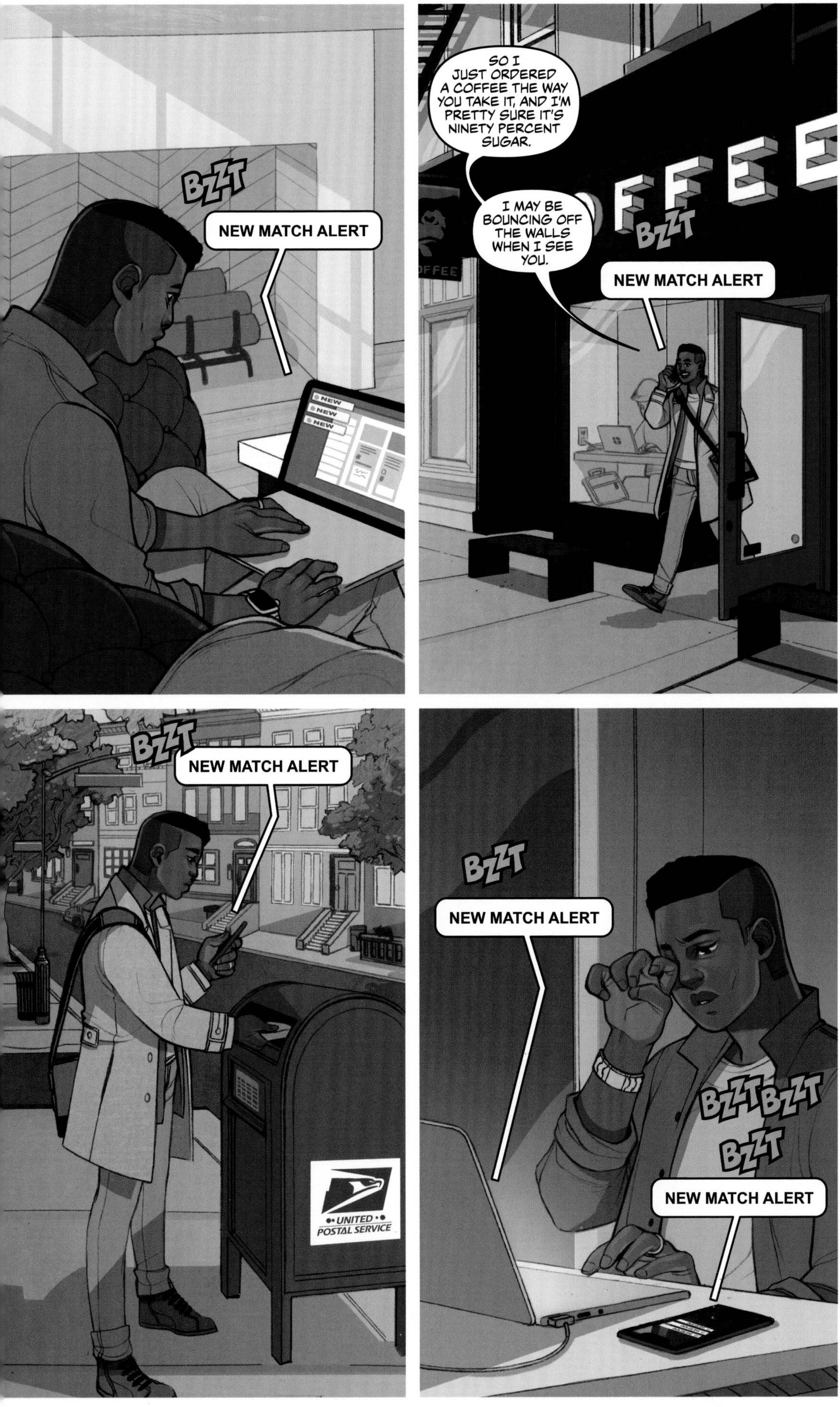
BZZT
NEW MATCH ALERT
SO I JUST ORDERED A COFFEE THE WAY YOU TAKE IT, AND I'M PRETTY SURE IT'S NINETY PERCENT SUGAR.
I MAY BE BOUNCING OFF THE WALLS WHEN I SEE YOU.
OFFEE
BZZT
NEW MATCH ALERT
BZZT
NEW MATCH ALERT
UNITED POSTAL SERVICE
BZZT
NEW MATCH ALERT
BZZT BZZT
BZZT
NEW MATCH ALERT

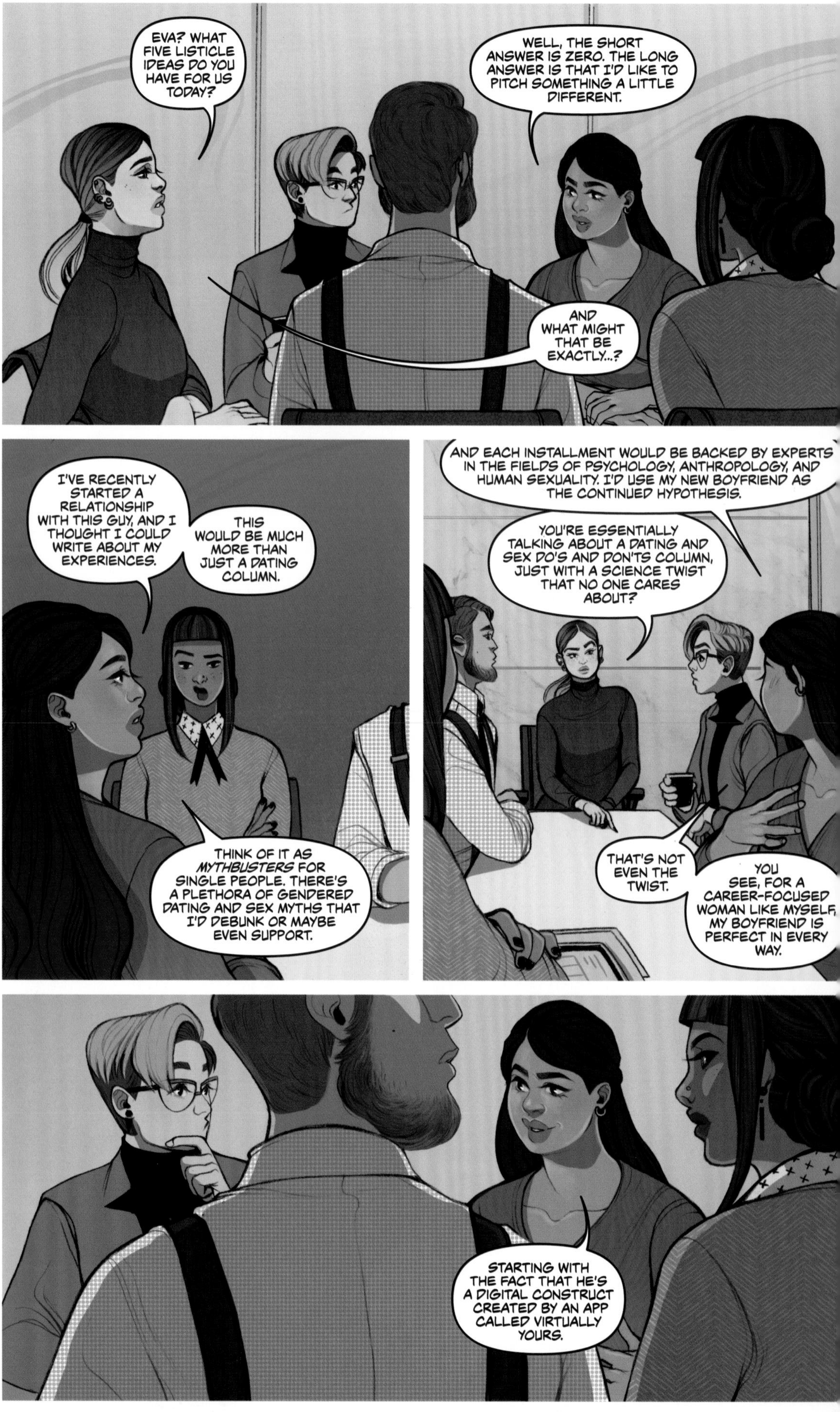

EVA? WHAT FIVE LISTICLE IDEAS DO YOU HAVE FOR US TODAY?
WELL, THE SHORT ANSWER IS ZERO. THE LONG ANSWER IS THAT I'D LIKE TO PITCH SOMETHING A LITTLE DIFFERENT.
AND WHAT MIGHT THAT BE EXACTLY...?
I'VE RECENTLY STARTED A RELATIONSHIP WITH THIS GUY, AND I THOUGHT I COULD WRITE ABOUT MY EXPERIENCES.
THIS WOULD BE MUCH MORE THAN JUST A DATING COLUMN.
THINK OF IT AS *MYTHBUSTERS* FOR SINGLE PEOPLE. THERE'S A PLETHORA OF GENDERED DATING AND SEX MYTHS THAT I'D DEBUNK OR MAYBE EVEN SUPPORT.
AND EACH INSTALLMENT WOULD BE BACKED BY EXPERTS IN THE FIELDS OF PSYCHOLOGY, ANTHROPOLOGY, AND HUMAN SEXUALITY. I'D USE MY NEW BOYFRIEND AS THE CONTINUED HYPOTHESIS.
YOU'RE ESSENTIALLY TALKING ABOUT A DATING AND SEX DO'S AND DON'TS COLUMN, JUST WITH A SCIENCE TWIST THAT NO ONE CARES ABOUT?
THAT'S NOT EVEN THE TWIST.
YOU SEE, FOR A CAREER-FOCUSED WOMAN LIKE MYSELF, MY BOYFRIEND IS PERFECT IN EVERY WAY.
STARTING WITH THE FACT THAT HE'S A DIGITAL CONSTRUCT CREATED BY AN APP CALLED VIRTUALLY YOURS.

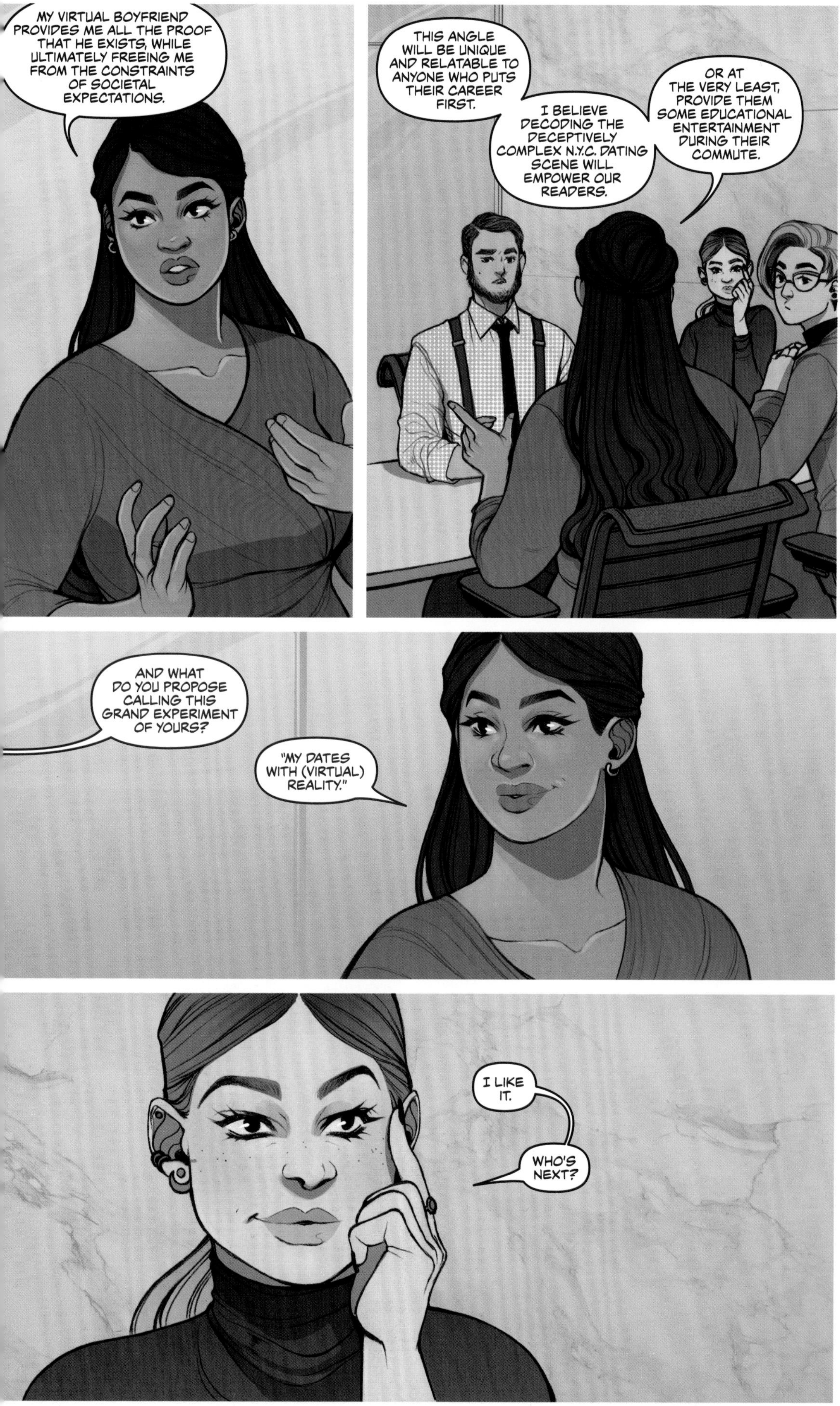
MY VIRTUAL BOYFRIEND PROVIDES ME ALL THE PROOF THAT HE EXISTS, WHILE ULTIMATELY FREEING ME FROM THE CONSTRAINTS OF SOCIETAL EXPECTATIONS.
THIS ANGLE WILL BE UNIQUE AND RELATABLE TO ANYONE WHO PUTS THEIR CAREER FIRST.
I BELIEVE DECODING THE DECEPTIVELY COMPLEX N.Y.C. DATING SCENE WILL EMPOWER OUR READERS.
OR AT THE VERY LEAST, PROVIDE THEM SOME EDUCATIONAL ENTERTAINMENT DURING THEIR COMMUTE.
AND WHAT DO YOU PROPOSE CALLING THIS GRAND EXPERIMENT OF YOURS?
"MY DATES WITH (VIRTUAL) REALITY."
I LIKE IT.
WHO'S NEXT?

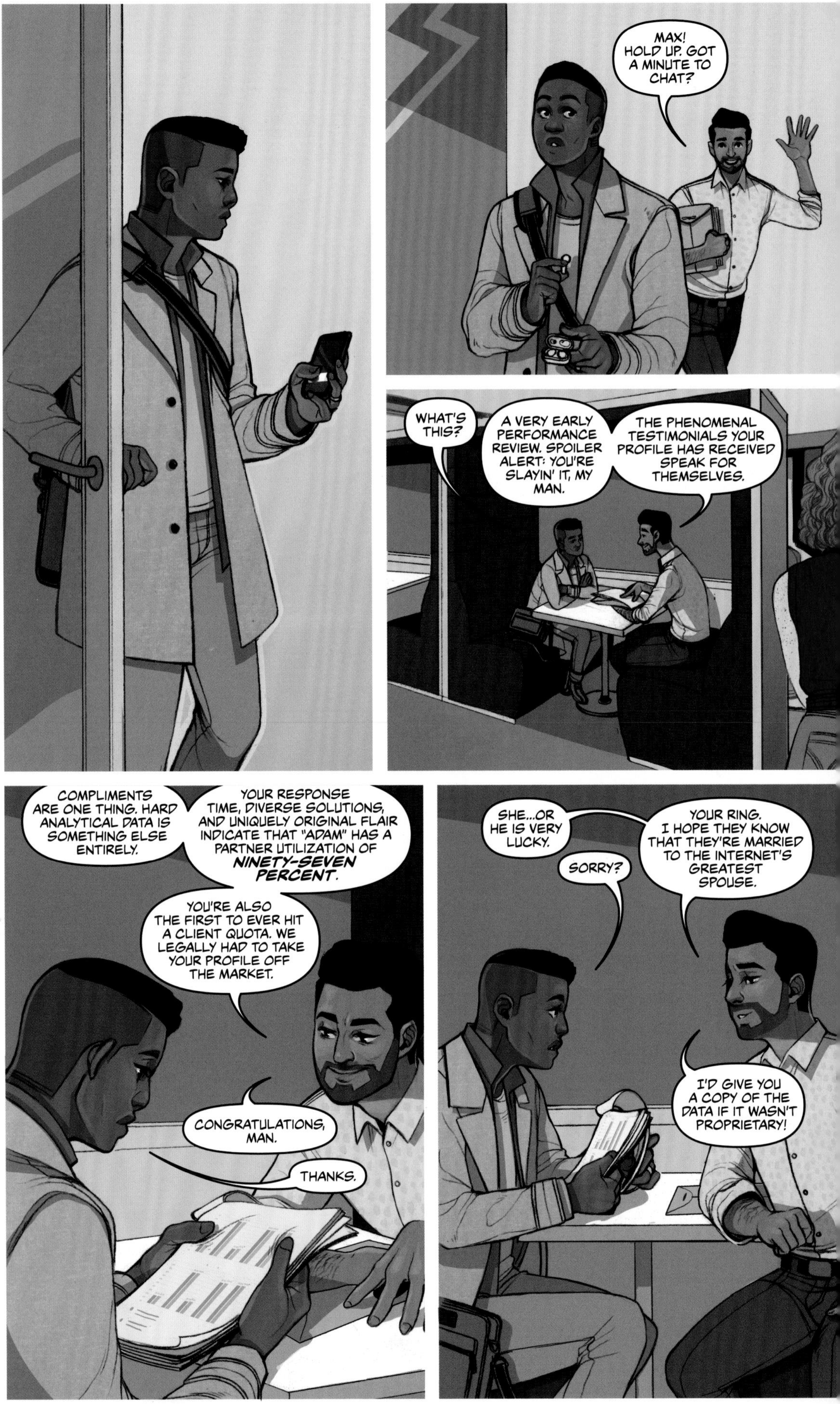
MAX! HOLD UP. GOT A MINUTE TO CHAT?
WHAT'S THIS?
A VERY EARLY PERFORMANCE REVIEW. SPOILER ALERT: YOU'RE SLAYIN' IT, MY MAN.
THE PHENOMENAL TESTIMONIALS YOUR PROFILE HAS RECEIVED SPEAK FOR THEMSELVES.
COMPLIMENTS ARE ONE THING. HARD ANALYTICAL DATA IS SOMETHING ELSE ENTIRELY.
YOUR RESPONSE TIME, DIVERSE SOLUTIONS, AND UNIQUELY ORIGINAL FLAIR INDICATE THAT "ADAM" HAS A PARTNER UTILIZATION OF NINETY-SEVEN PERCENT.
YOU'RE ALSO THE FIRST TO EVER HIT A CLIENT QUOTA. WE LEGALLY HAD TO TAKE YOUR PROFILE OFF THE MARKET.
CONGRATULATIONS, MAN.
THANKS.
YOUR RING. I HOPE THEY KNOW THAT THEY'RE MARRIED TO THE INTERNET'S GREATEST SPOUSE.
SORRY?
SHE...OR HE IS VERY LUCKY.
I'D GIVE YOU A COPY OF THE DATA IF IT WASN'T PROPRIETARY!

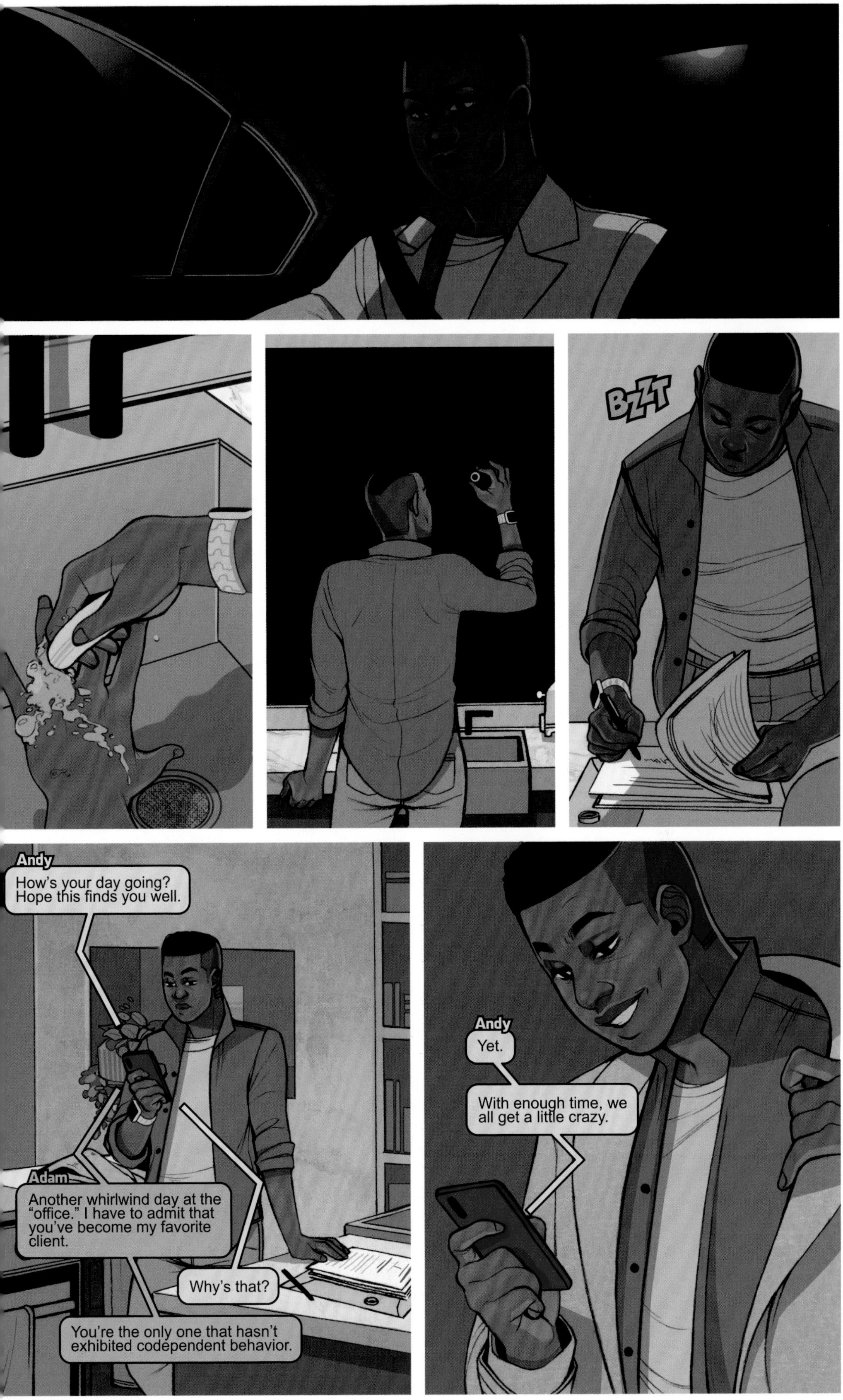
BZZT
Andy
How's your day going? Hope this finds you well.
Adam
Another whirlwind day at the "office." I have to admit that you've become my favorite client.
Why's that?
You're the only one that hasn't exhibited codependent behavior.
Andy
Yet.
With enough time, we all get a little crazy.

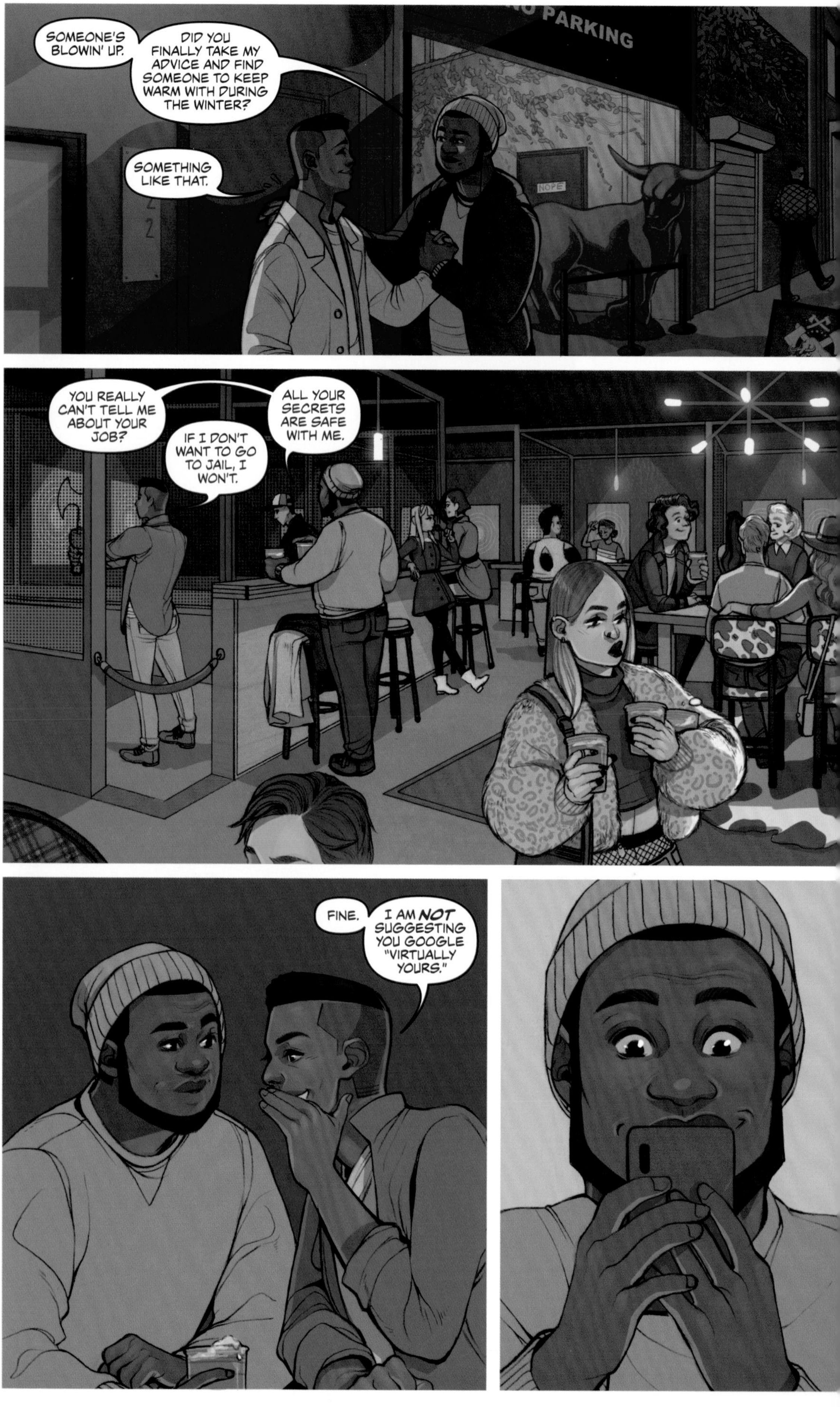
NO PARKING
SOMEONE'S BLOWIN' UP.
DID YOU FINALLY TAKE MY ADVICE AND FIND SOMEONE TO KEEP WARM WITH DURING THE WINTER?
SOMETHING LIKE THAT.
NOPE
YOU REALLY CAN'T TELL ME ABOUT YOUR JOB?
IF I DON'T WANT TO GO TO JAIL, I WON'T.
ALL YOUR SECRETS ARE SAFE WITH ME.
FINE.
I AM ***NOT*** SUGGESTING YOU GOOGLE "VIRTUALLY YOURS."

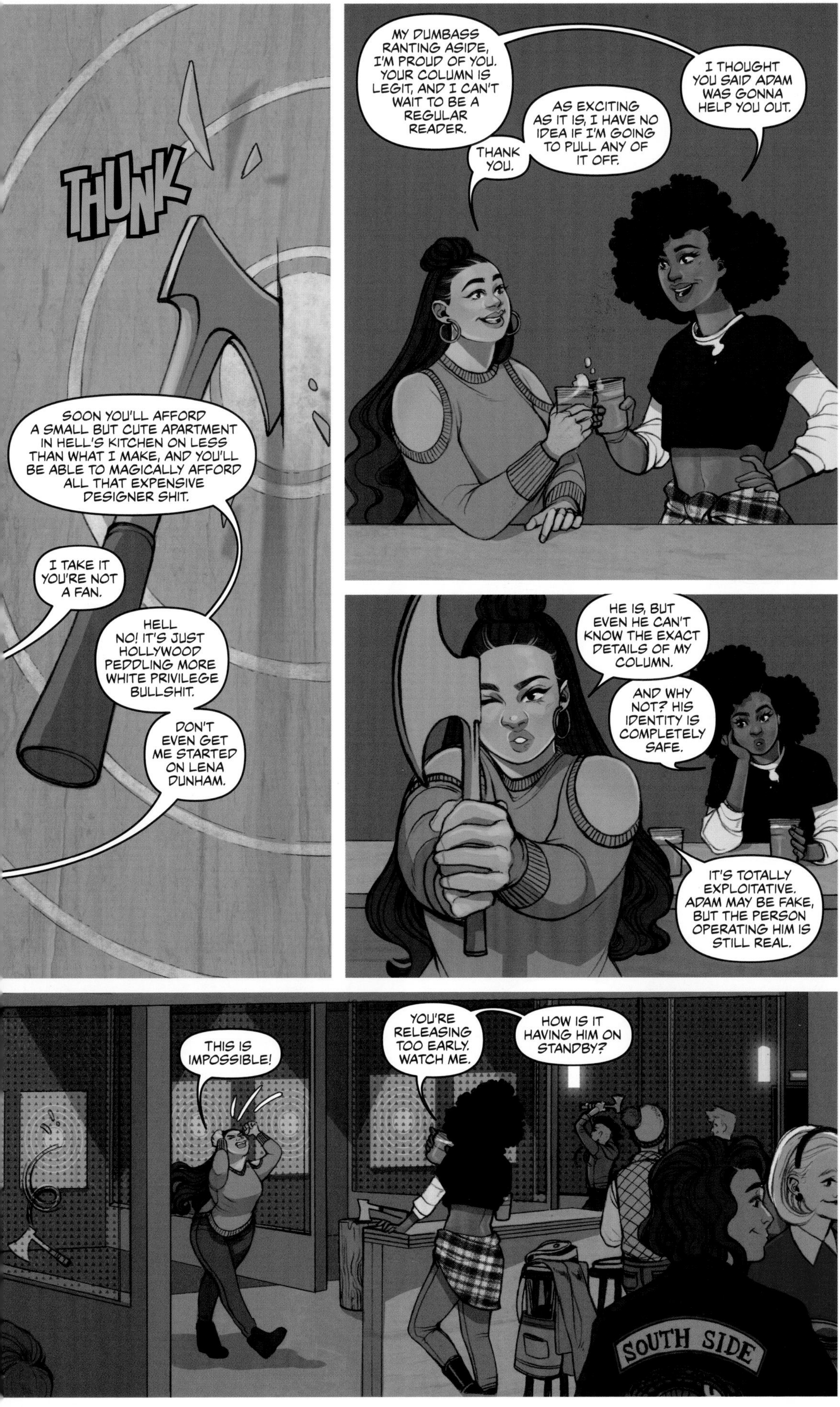
THUNK
SOON YOU'LL AFFORD A SMALL BUT CUTE APARTMENT IN HELL'S KITCHEN ON LESS THAN WHAT I MAKE, AND YOU'LL BE ABLE TO MAGICALLY AFFORD ALL THAT EXPENSIVE DESIGNER SHIT.
I TAKE IT YOU'RE NOT A FAN.
HELL NO! IT'S JUST HOLLYWOOD PEDDLING MORE WHITE PRIVILEGE BULLSHIT.
DON'T EVEN GET ME STARTED ON LENA DUNHAM.
MY DUMBASS RANTING ASIDE, I'M PROUD OF YOU. YOUR COLUMN IS LEGIT, AND I CAN'T WAIT TO BE A REGULAR READER.
THANK YOU.
AS EXCITING AS IT IS, I HAVE NO IDEA IF I'M GOING TO PULL ANY OF IT OFF.
I THOUGHT YOU SAID ADAM WAS GONNA HELP YOU OUT.
HE IS, BUT EVEN HE CAN'T KNOW THE EXACT DETAILS OF MY COLUMN.
AND WHY NOT? HIS IDENTITY IS COMPLETELY SAFE.
IT'S TOTALLY EXPLOITATIVE. ADAM MAY BE FAKE, BUT THE PERSON OPERATING HIM IS STILL REAL.
THIS IS IMPOSSIBLE!
YOU'RE RELEASING TOO EARLY. WATCH ME.
HOW IS IT HAVING HIM ON STANDBY?
SOUTH SIDE

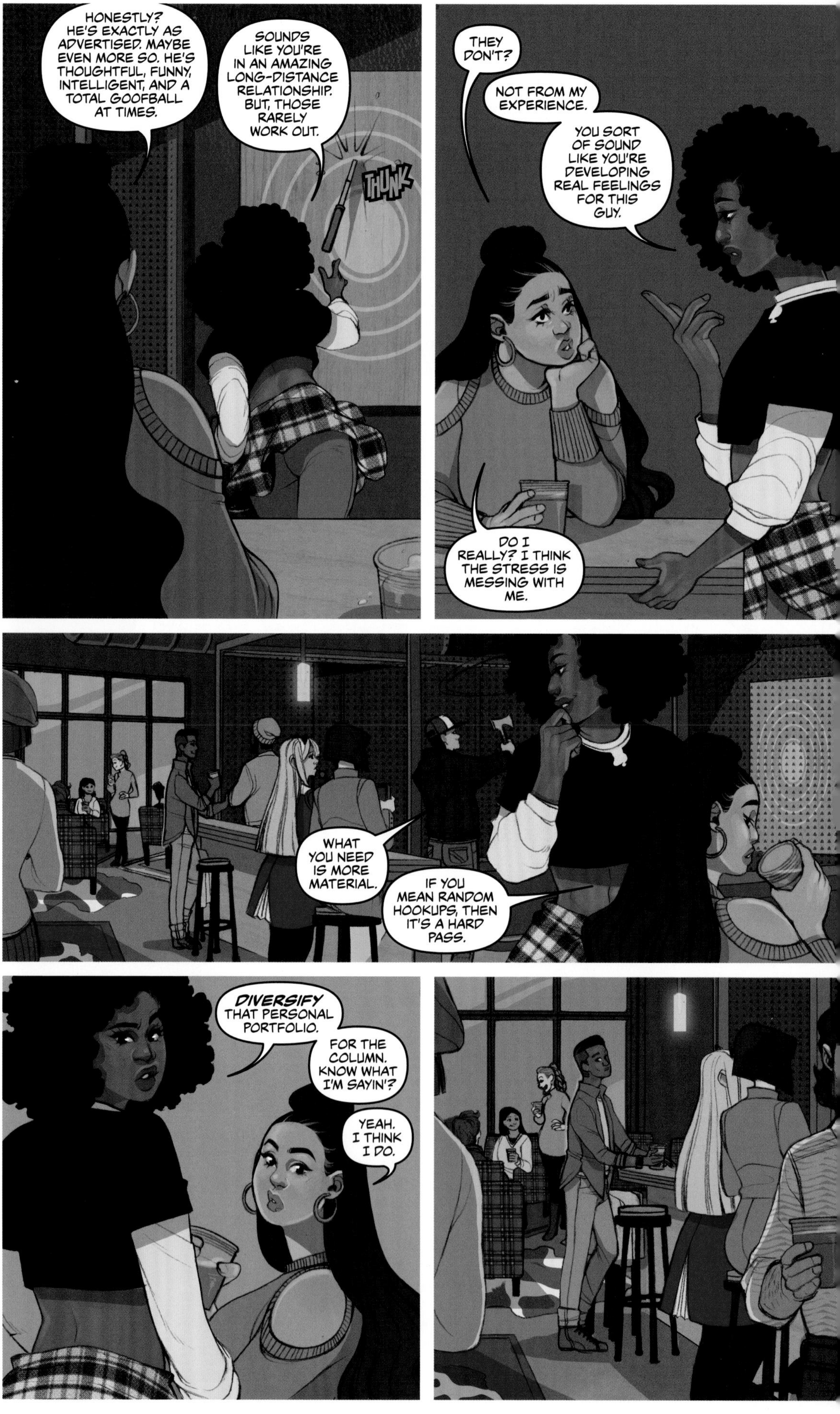
HONESTLY? HE'S EXACTLY AS ADVERTISED. MAYBE EVEN MORE SO. HE'S THOUGHTFUL, FUNNY, INTELLIGENT, AND A TOTAL GOOFBALL AT TIMES.
SOUNDS LIKE YOU'RE IN AN AMAZING LONG-DISTANCE RELATIONSHIP. BUT, THOSE RARELY WORK OUT.
THUNK
THEY DON'T?
NOT FROM MY EXPERIENCE.
YOU SORT OF SOUND LIKE YOU'RE DEVELOPING REAL FEELINGS FOR THIS GUY.
DO I REALLY? I THINK THE STRESS IS MESSING WITH ME.
WHAT YOU NEED IS MORE MATERIAL.
IF YOU MEAN RANDOM HOOKUPS, THEN IT'S A HARD PASS.
DIVERSIFY THAT PERSONAL PORTFOLIO.
FOR THE COLUMN. KNOW WHAT I'M SAYIN'?
YEAH. I THINK I DO.

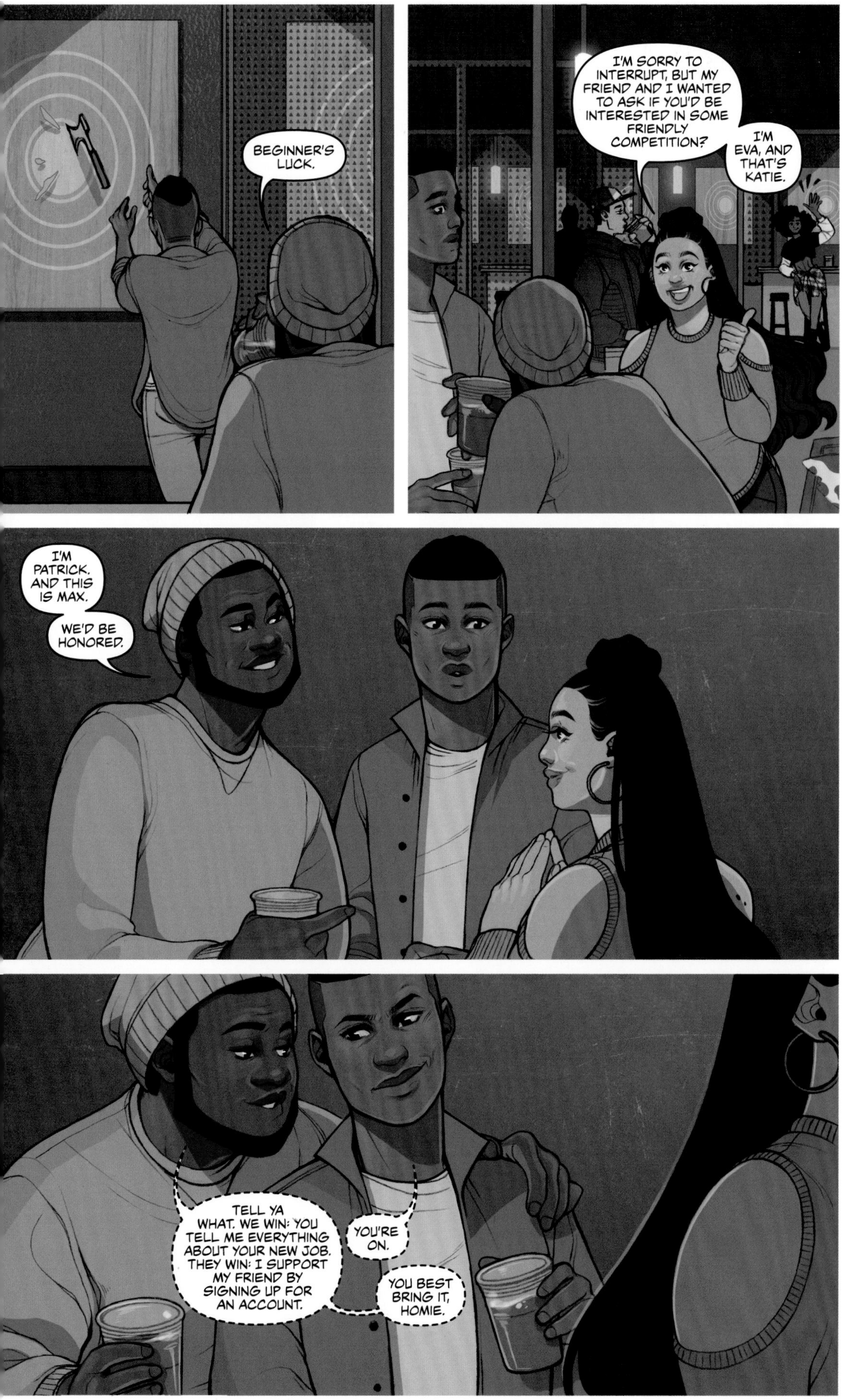
BEGINNER'S LUCK.
I'M SORRY TO INTERRUPT, BUT MY FRIEND AND I WANTED TO ASK IF YOU'D BE INTERESTED IN SOME FRIENDLY COMPETITION?
I'M EVA, AND THAT'S KATIE.
I'M PATRICK. AND THIS IS MAX.
WE'D BE HONORED.
TELL YA WHAT. WE WIN: YOU TELL ME EVERYTHING ABOUT YOUR NEW JOB. THEY WIN: I SUPPORT MY FRIEND BY SIGNING UP FOR AN ACCOUNT.
YOU'RE ON.
YOU BEST BRING IT, HOMIE.

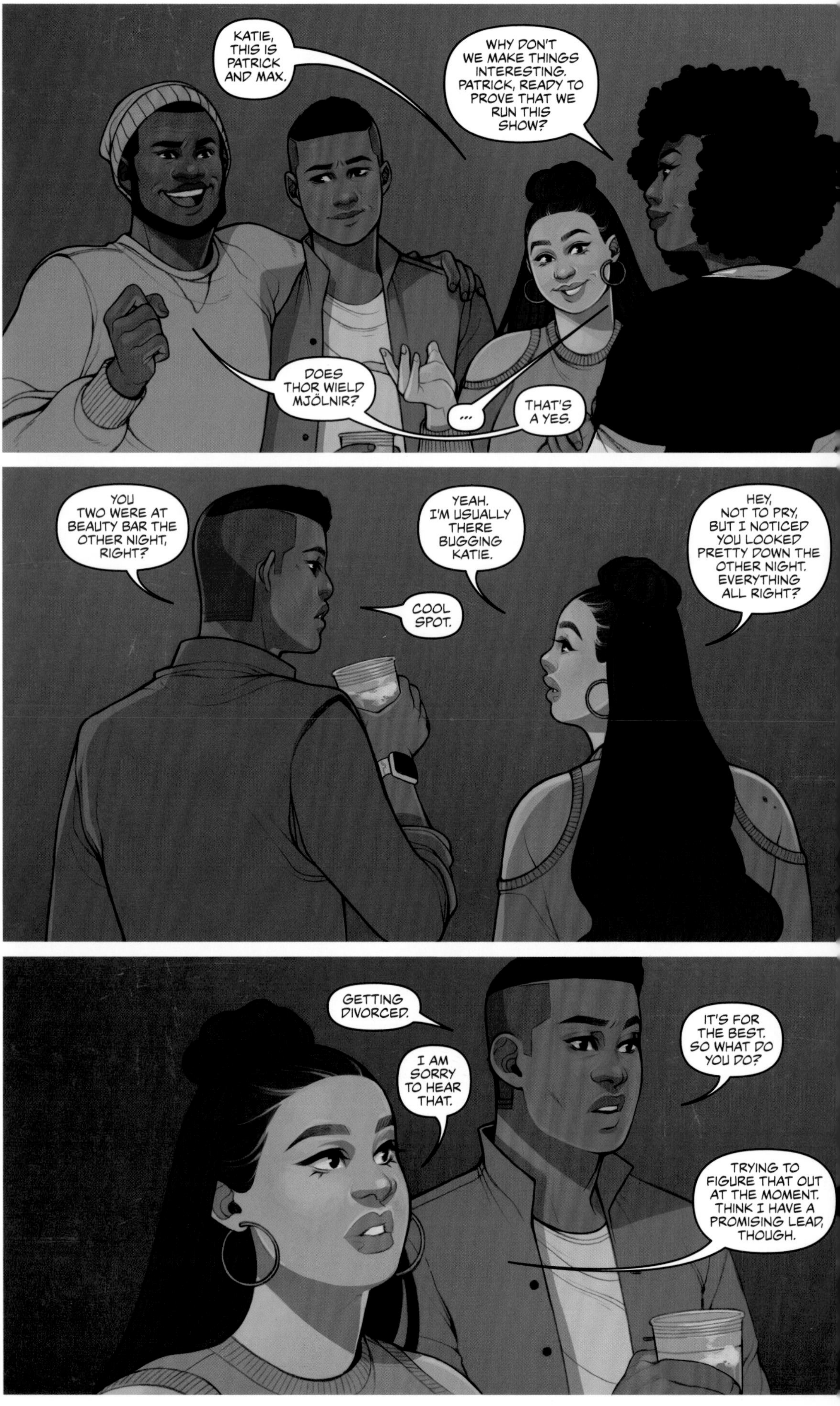
KATIE, THIS IS PATRICK AND MAX.
WHY DON'T WE MAKE THINGS INTERESTING. PATRICK, READY TO PROVE THAT WE RUN THIS SHOW?
DOES THOR WIELD MJÖLNIR?
...
THAT'S A YES.
YOU TWO WERE AT BEAUTY BAR THE OTHER NIGHT, RIGHT?
COOL SPOT.
YEAH. I'M USUALLY THERE BUGGING KATIE.
HEY, NOT TO PRY, BUT I NOTICED YOU LOOKED PRETTY DOWN THE OTHER NIGHT. EVERYTHING ALL RIGHT?
GETTING DIVORCED.
I AM SORRY TO HEAR THAT.
IT'S FOR THE BEST. SO WHAT DO YOU DO?
TRYING TO FIGURE THAT OUT AT THE MOMENT. THINK I HAVE A PROMISING LEAD, THOUGH.

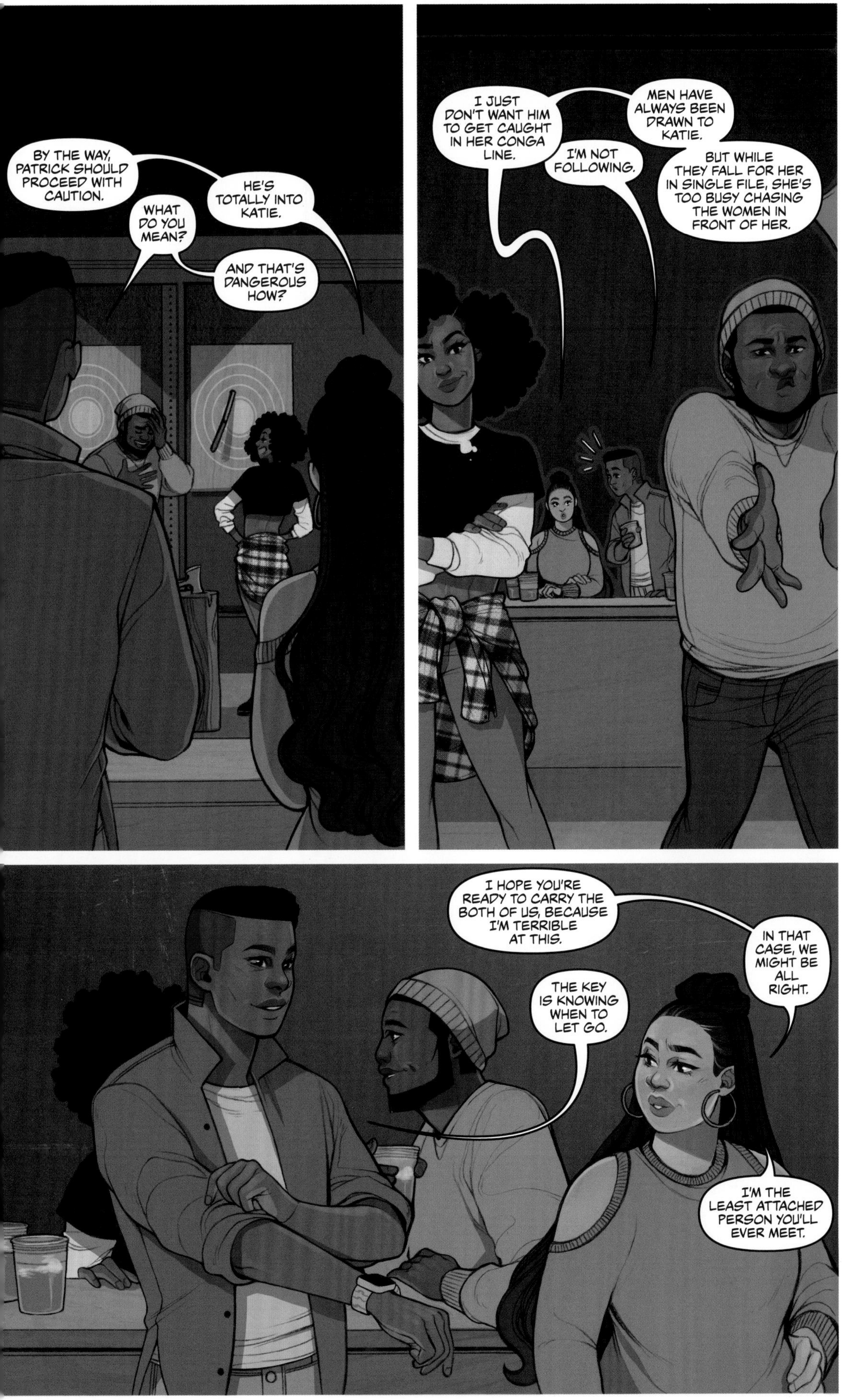
BY THE WAY, PATRICK SHOULD PROCEED WITH CAUTION.
WHAT DO YOU MEAN?
HE'S TOTALLY INTO KATIE.
AND THAT'S DANGEROUS HOW?
I JUST DON'T WANT HIM TO GET CAUGHT IN HER CONGA LINE.
I'M NOT FOLLOWING.
MEN HAVE ALWAYS BEEN DRAWN TO KATIE.
BUT WHILE THEY FALL FOR HER IN SINGLE FILE, SHE'S TOO BUSY CHASING THE WOMEN IN FRONT OF HER.
I HOPE YOU'RE READY TO CARRY THE BOTH OF US, BECAUSE I'M TERRIBLE AT THIS.
IN THAT CASE, WE MIGHT BE ALL RIGHT.
THE KEY IS KNOWING WHEN TO LET GO.
I'M THE LEAST ATTACHED PERSON YOU'LL EVER MEET.

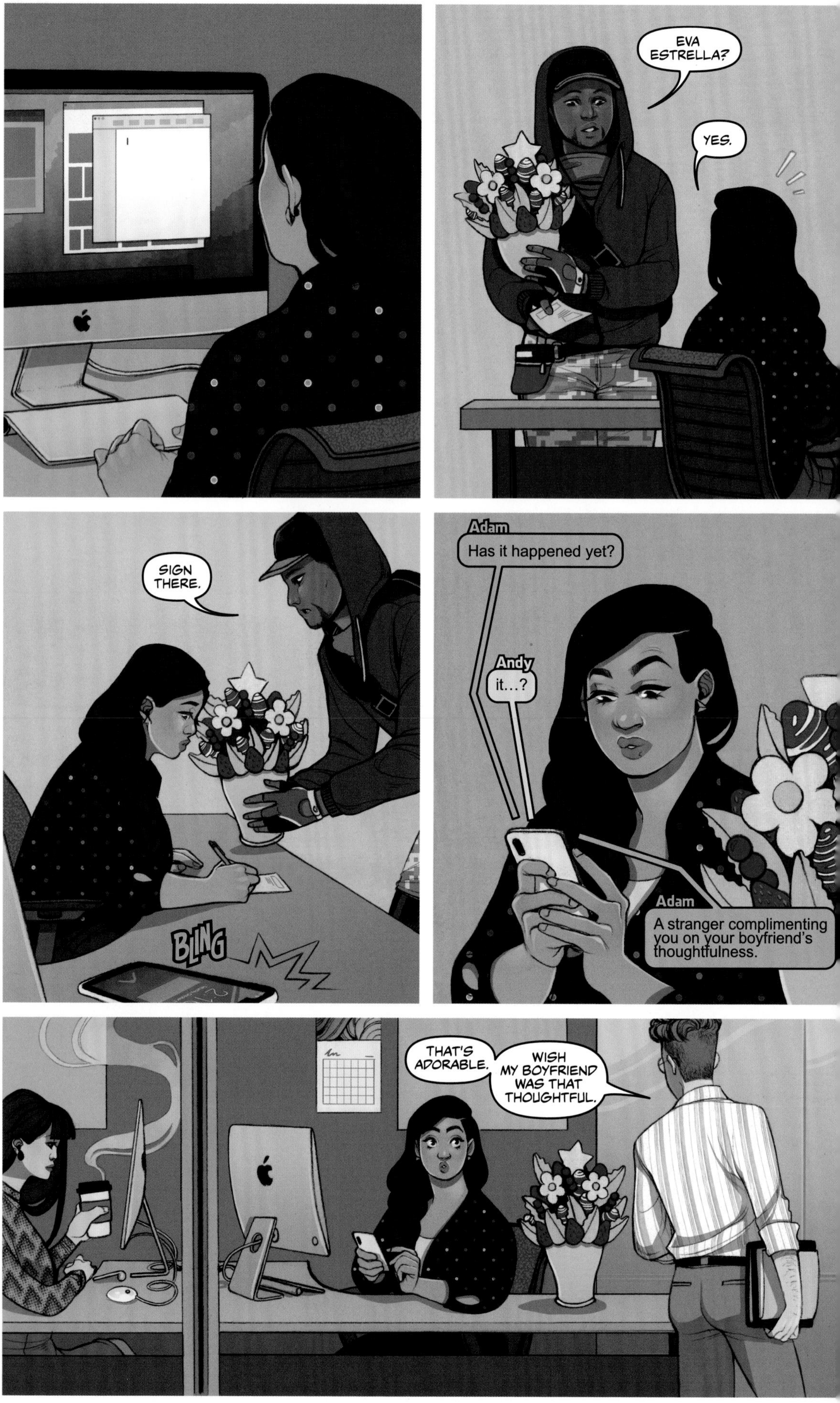
EVA ESTRELLA?
YES.
SIGN THERE.
BLING
Adam
Has it happened yet?
Andy
it...?
Adam
A stranger complimenting you on your boyfriend's thoughtfulness.
THAT'S ADORABLE.
WISH MY BOYFRIEND WAS THAT THOUGHTFUL.

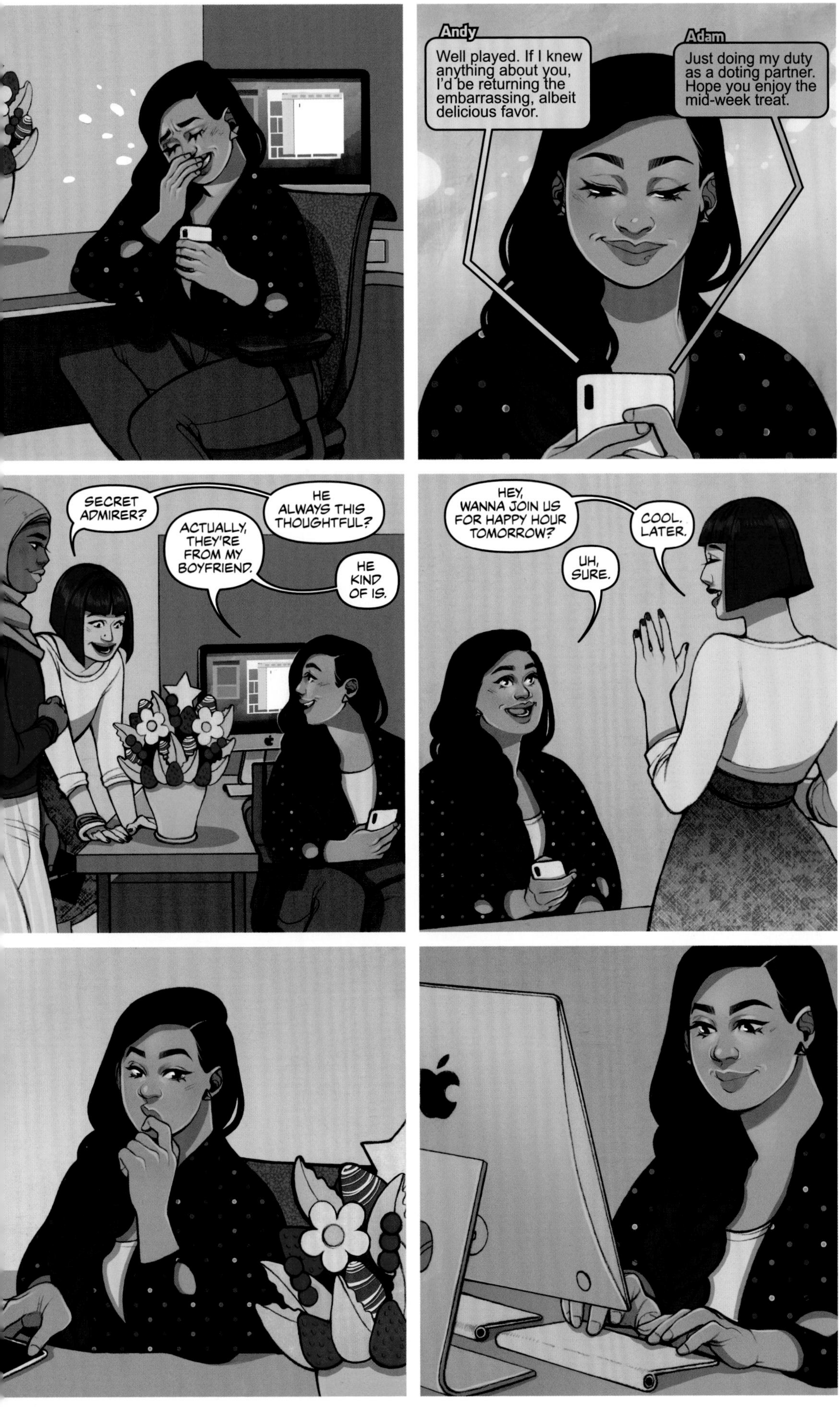
Andy
Well played. If I knew anything about you, I'd be returning the embarrassing, albeit delicious favor.
Adam
Just doing my duty as a doting partner. Hope you enjoy the mid-week treat.
SECRET ADMIRER?
HE ALWAYS THIS THOUGHTFUL?
ACTUALLY, THEY'RE FROM MY BOYFRIEND.
HE KIND OF IS.
HEY, WANNA JOIN US FOR HAPPY HOUR TOMORROW?
UH, SURE.
COOL. LATER.

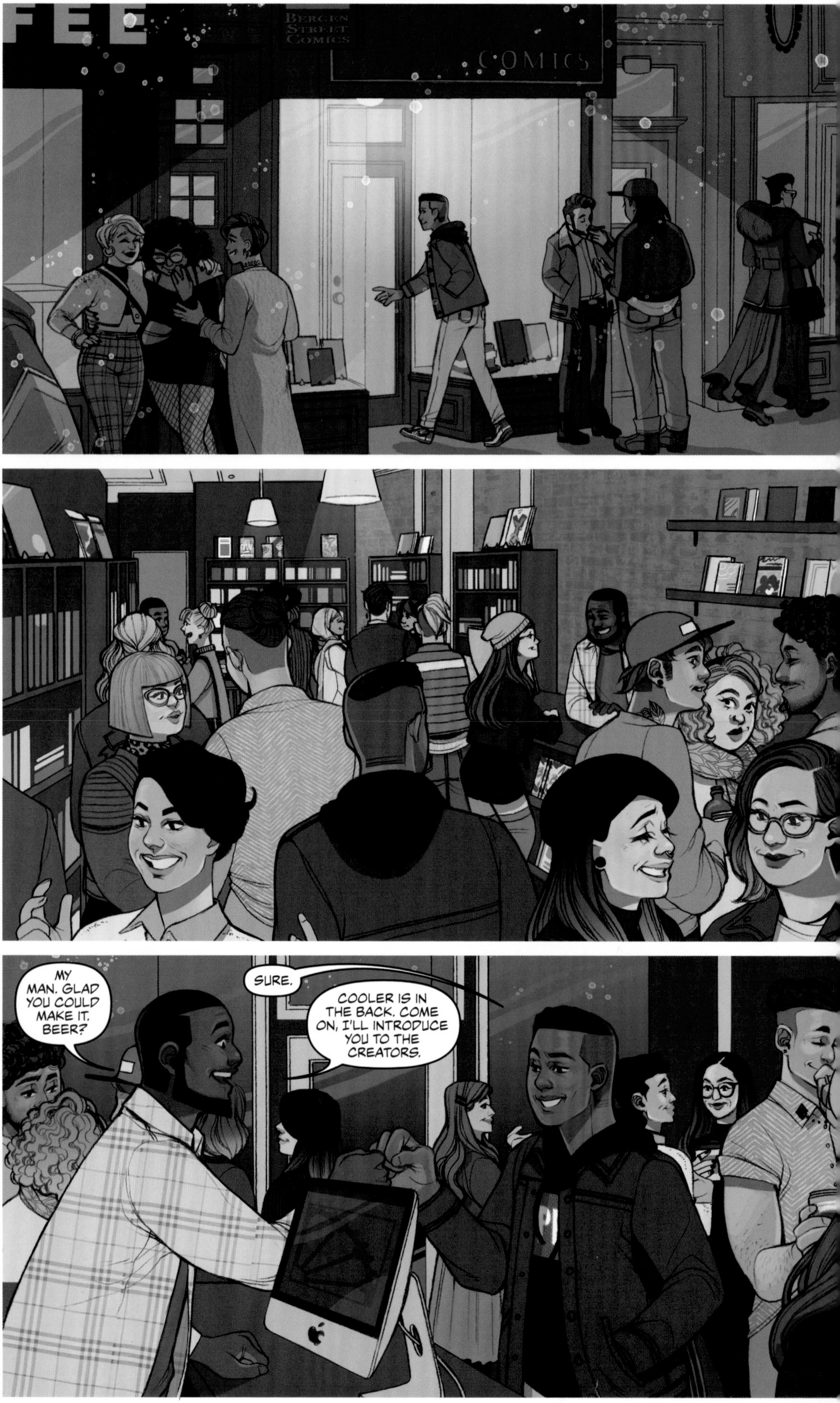
BERGEN STREET COMICS
COMICS
MY MAN. GLAD YOU COULD MAKE IT. BEER?
SURE.
COOLER IS IN THE BACK. COME ON, I'LL INTRODUCE YOU TO THE CREATORS.

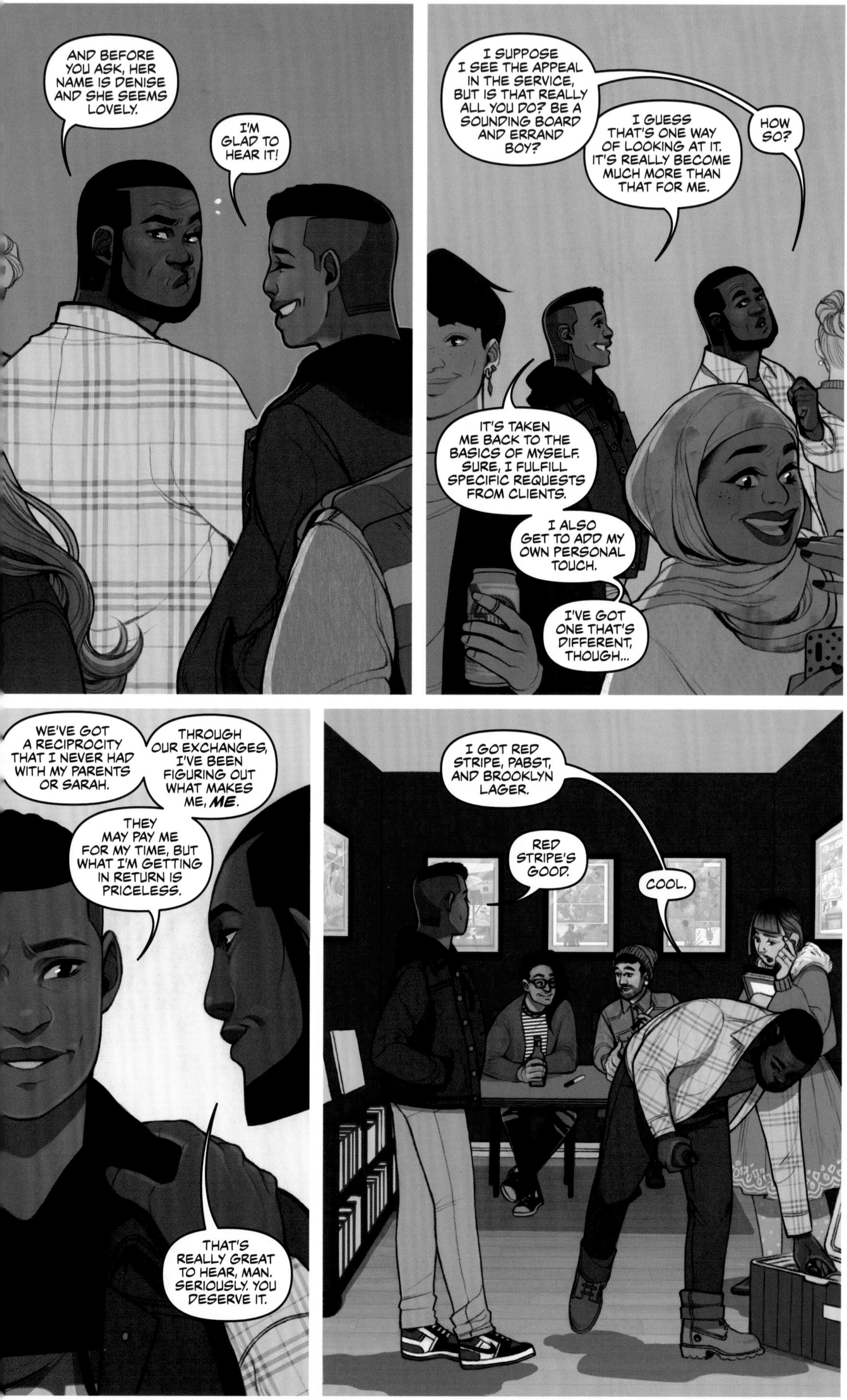

AND BEFORE YOU ASK, HER NAME IS DENISE AND SHE SEEMS LOVELY.
I'M GLAD TO HEAR IT!
I SUPPOSE I SEE THE APPEAL IN THE SERVICE, BUT IS THAT REALLY ALL YOU DO? BE A SOUNDING BOARD AND ERRAND BOY?
I GUESS THAT'S ONE WAY OF LOOKING AT IT. IT'S REALLY BECOME MUCH MORE THAN THAT FOR ME.
HOW SO?
IT'S TAKEN ME BACK TO THE BASICS OF MYSELF. SURE, I FULFILL SPECIFIC REQUESTS FROM CLIENTS.
I ALSO GET TO ADD MY OWN PERSONAL TOUCH.
I'VE GOT ONE THAT'S DIFFERENT, THOUGH...
WE'VE GOT A RECIPROCITY THAT I NEVER HAD WITH MY PARENTS OR SARAH.
THROUGH OUR EXCHANGES, I'VE BEEN FIGURING OUT WHAT MAKES ME, *ME*.
THEY MAY PAY ME FOR MY TIME, BUT WHAT I'M GETTING IN RETURN IS PRICELESS.
THAT'S REALLY GREAT TO HEAR, MAN. SERIOUSLY. YOU DESERVE IT.
I GOT RED STRIPE, PABST, AND BROOKLYN LAGER.
RED STRIPE'S GOOD.
COOL.

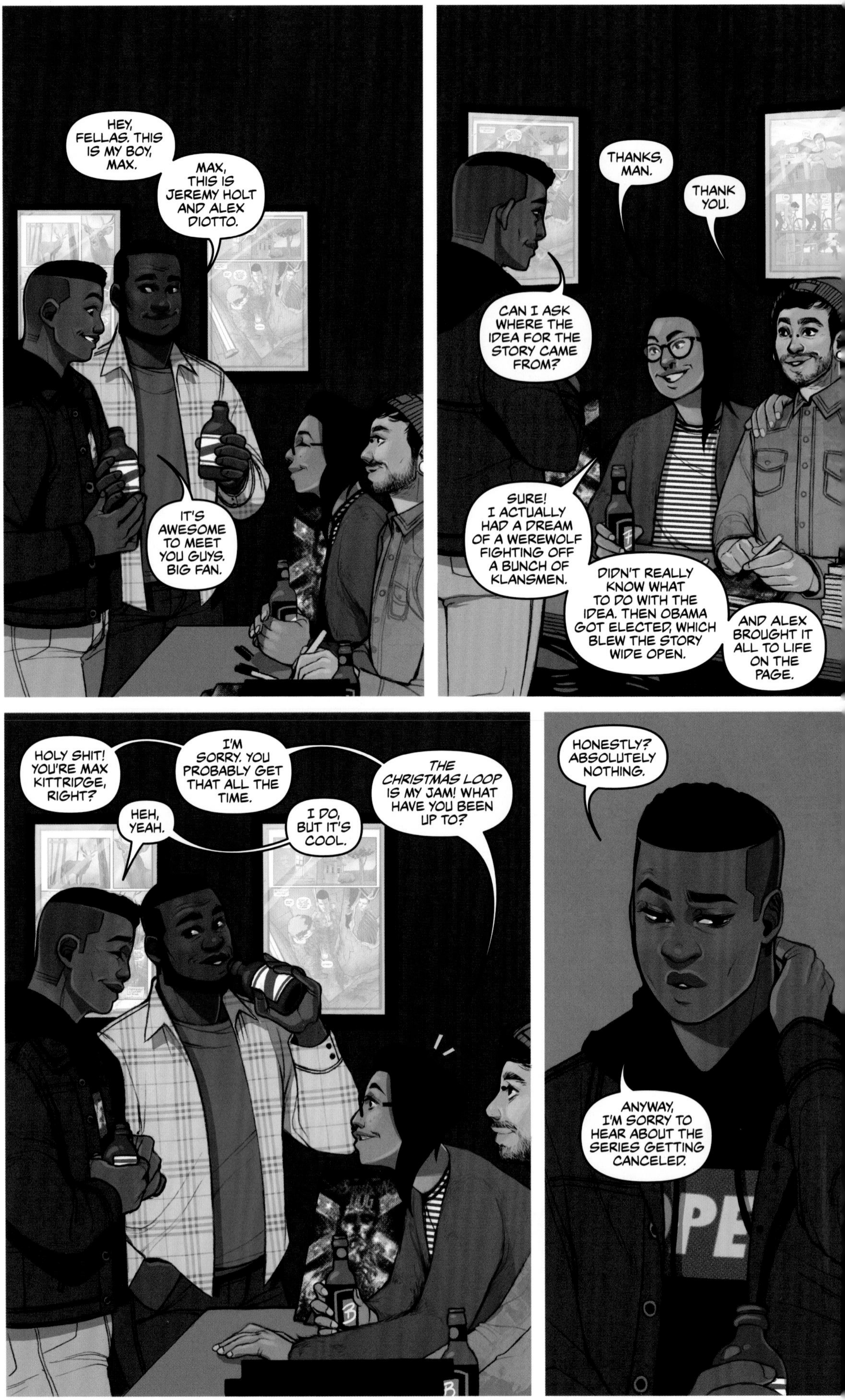
HEY, FELLAS. THIS IS MY BOY, MAX.
MAX, THIS IS JEREMY HOLT AND ALEX DIOTTO.
IT'S AWESOME TO MEET YOU GUYS. BIG FAN.
THANKS, MAN.
THANK YOU.
CAN I ASK WHERE THE IDEA FOR THE STORY CAME FROM?
SURE! I ACTUALLY HAD A DREAM OF A WEREWOLF FIGHTING OFF A BUNCH OF KLANSMEN.
DIDN'T REALLY KNOW WHAT TO DO WITH THE IDEA. THEN OBAMA GOT ELECTED, WHICH BLEW THE STORY WIDE OPEN.
AND ALEX BROUGHT IT ALL TO LIFE ON THE PAGE.
HOLY SHIT! YOU'RE MAX KITTRIDGE, RIGHT?
HEH, YEAH.
I'M SORRY. YOU PROBABLY GET THAT ALL THE TIME.
I DO, BUT IT'S COOL.
THE CHRISTMAS LOOP IS MY JAM! WHAT HAVE YOU BEEN UP TO?
HONESTLY? ABSOLUTELY NOTHING.
ANYWAY, I'M SORRY TO HEAR ABOUT THE SERIES GETTING CANCELED.

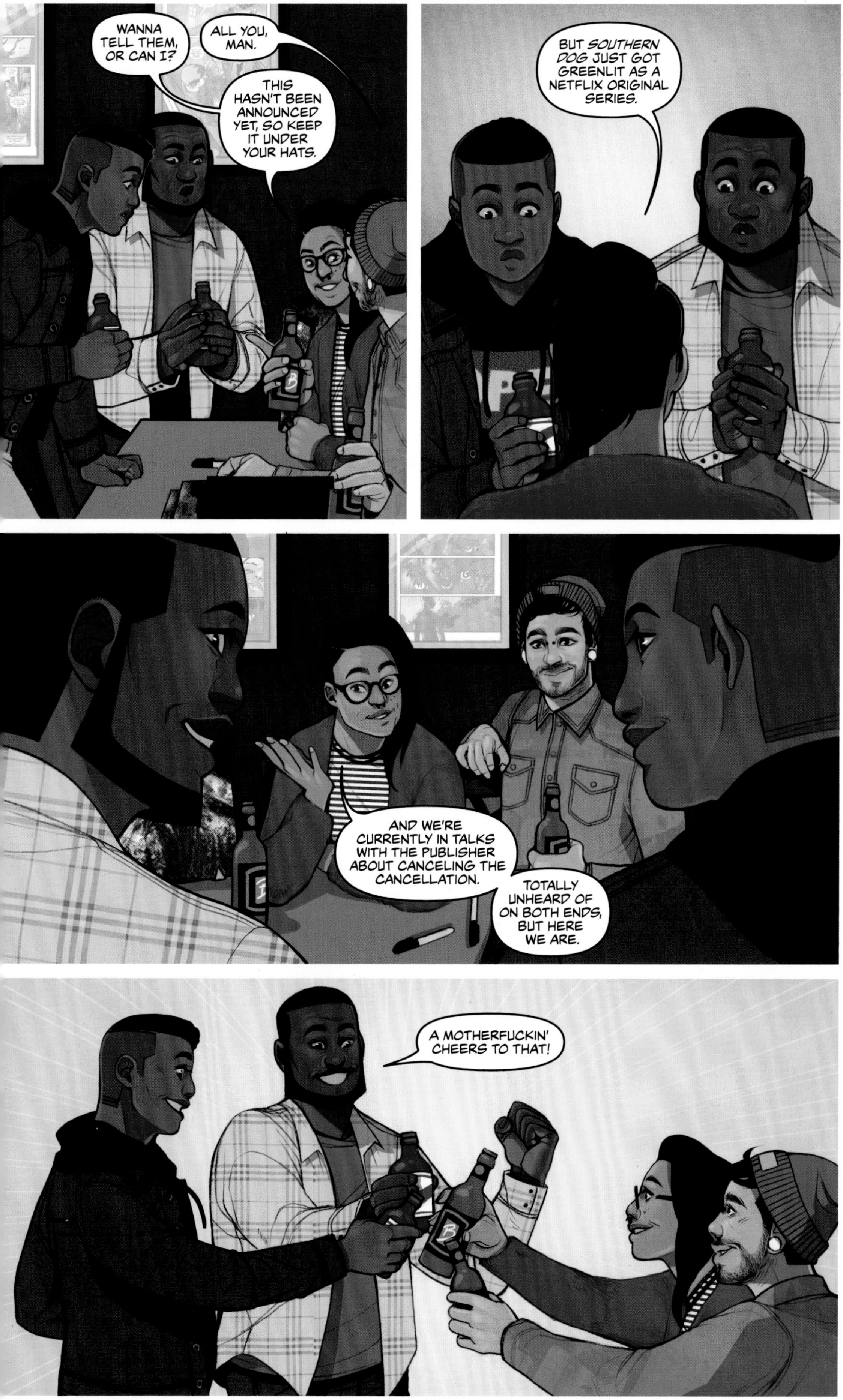
WANNA TELL THEM, OR CAN I?
ALL YOU, MAN.
THIS HASN'T BEEN ANNOUNCED YET, SO KEEP IT UNDER YOUR HATS.
BUT *SOUTHERN DOG* JUST GOT GREENLIT AS A NETFLIX ORIGINAL SERIES.
AND WE'RE CURRENTLY IN TALKS WITH THE PUBLISHER ABOUT CANCELING THE CANCELLATION.
TOTALLY UNHEARD OF ON BOTH ENDS, BUT HERE WE ARE.
A MOTHERFUCKIN' CHEERS TO THAT!

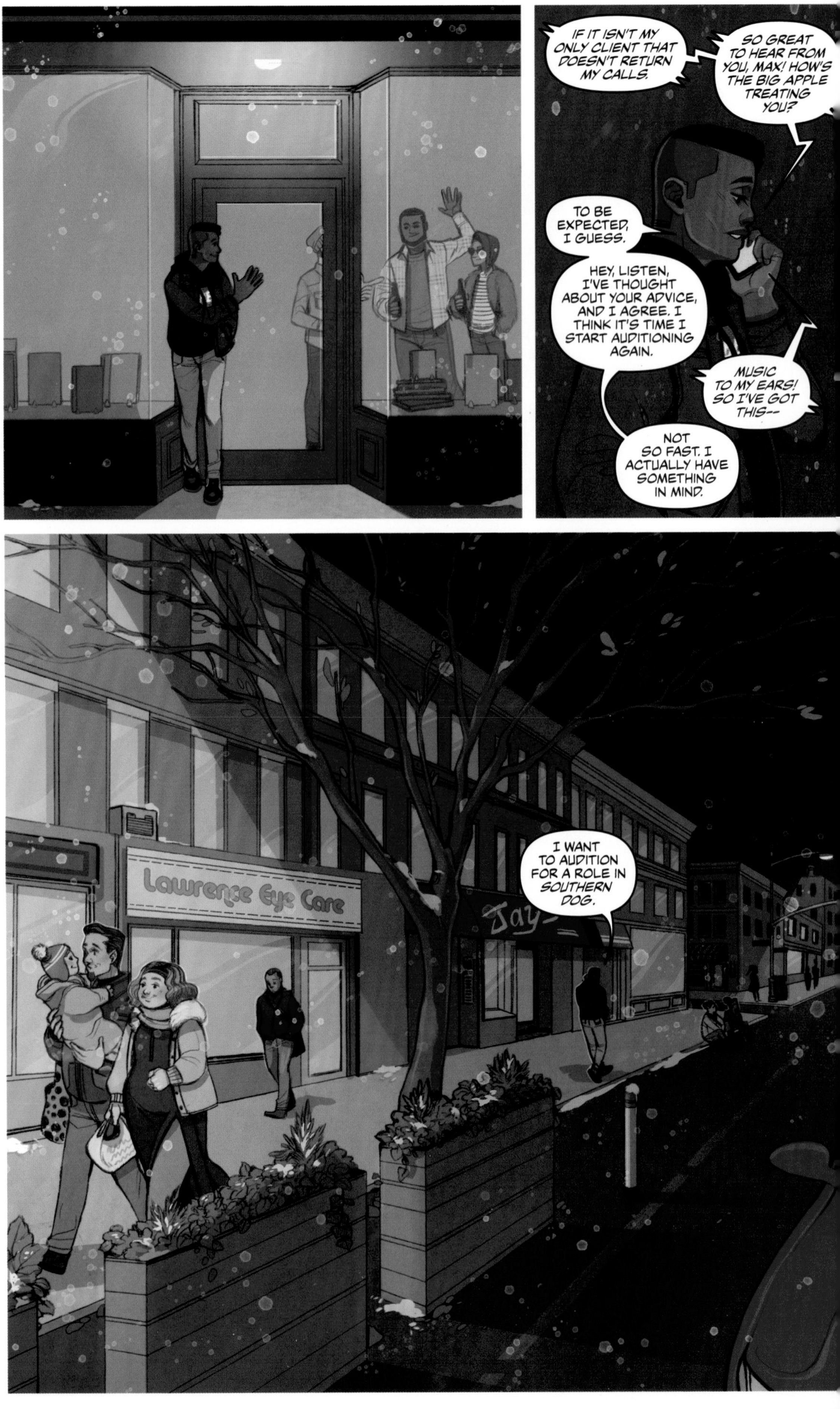
IF IT ISN'T MY ONLY CLIENT THAT DOESN'T RETURN MY CALLS.
SO GREAT TO HEAR FROM YOU, MAX! HOW'S THE BIG APPLE TREATING YOU?
TO BE EXPECTED, I GUESS.
HEY, LISTEN, I'VE THOUGHT ABOUT YOUR ADVICE, AND I AGREE. I THINK IT'S TIME I START AUDITIONING AGAIN.
MUSIC TO MY EARS! SO I'VE GOT THIS--
NOT SO FAST. I ACTUALLY HAVE SOMETHING IN MIND.
Lawrence Eye Care
I WANT TO AUDITION FOR A ROLE IN SOUTHERN DOG.

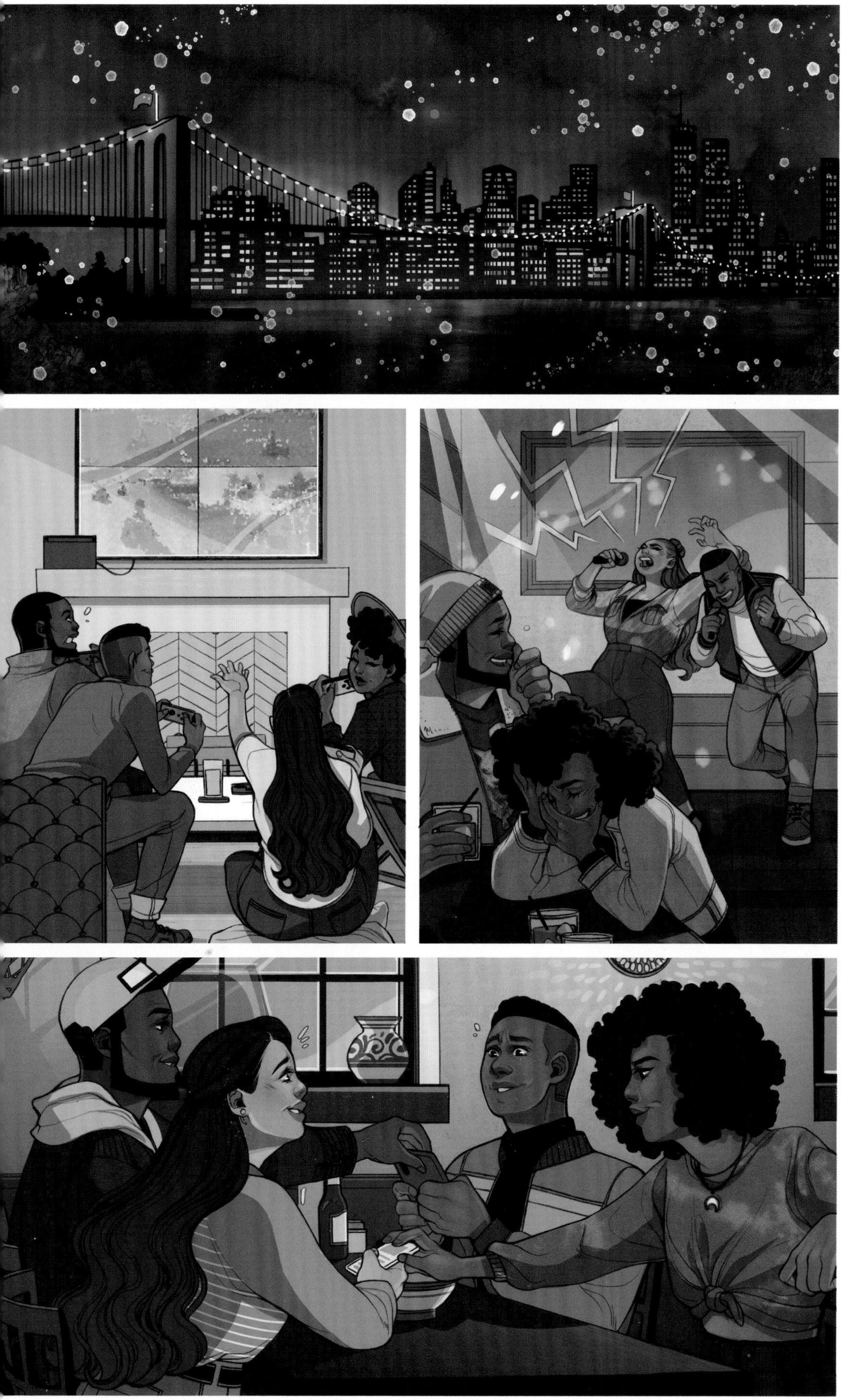

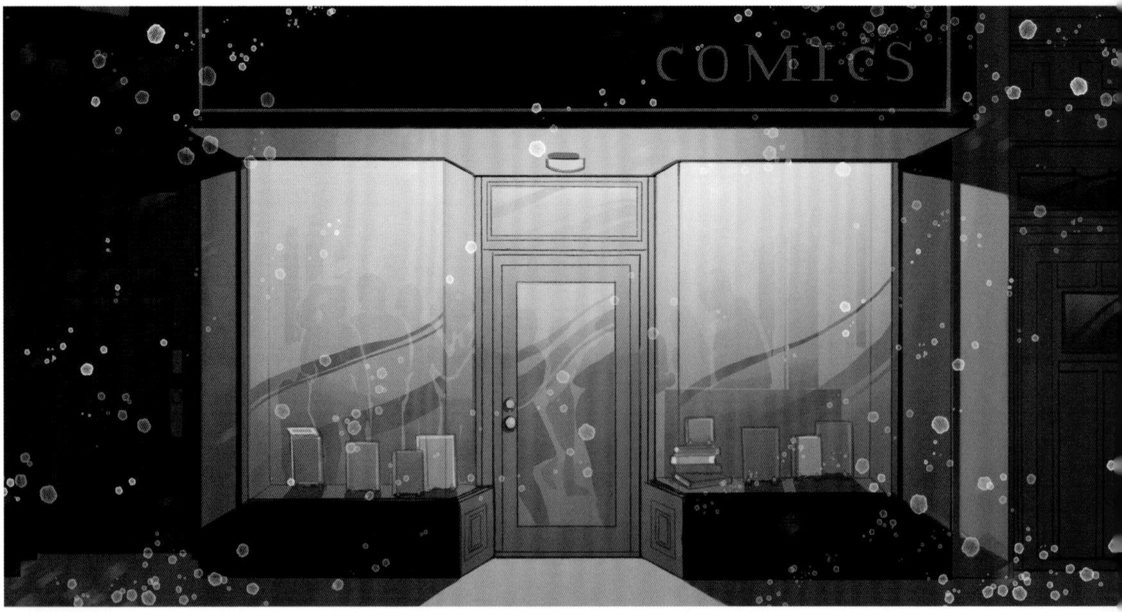
COMICS

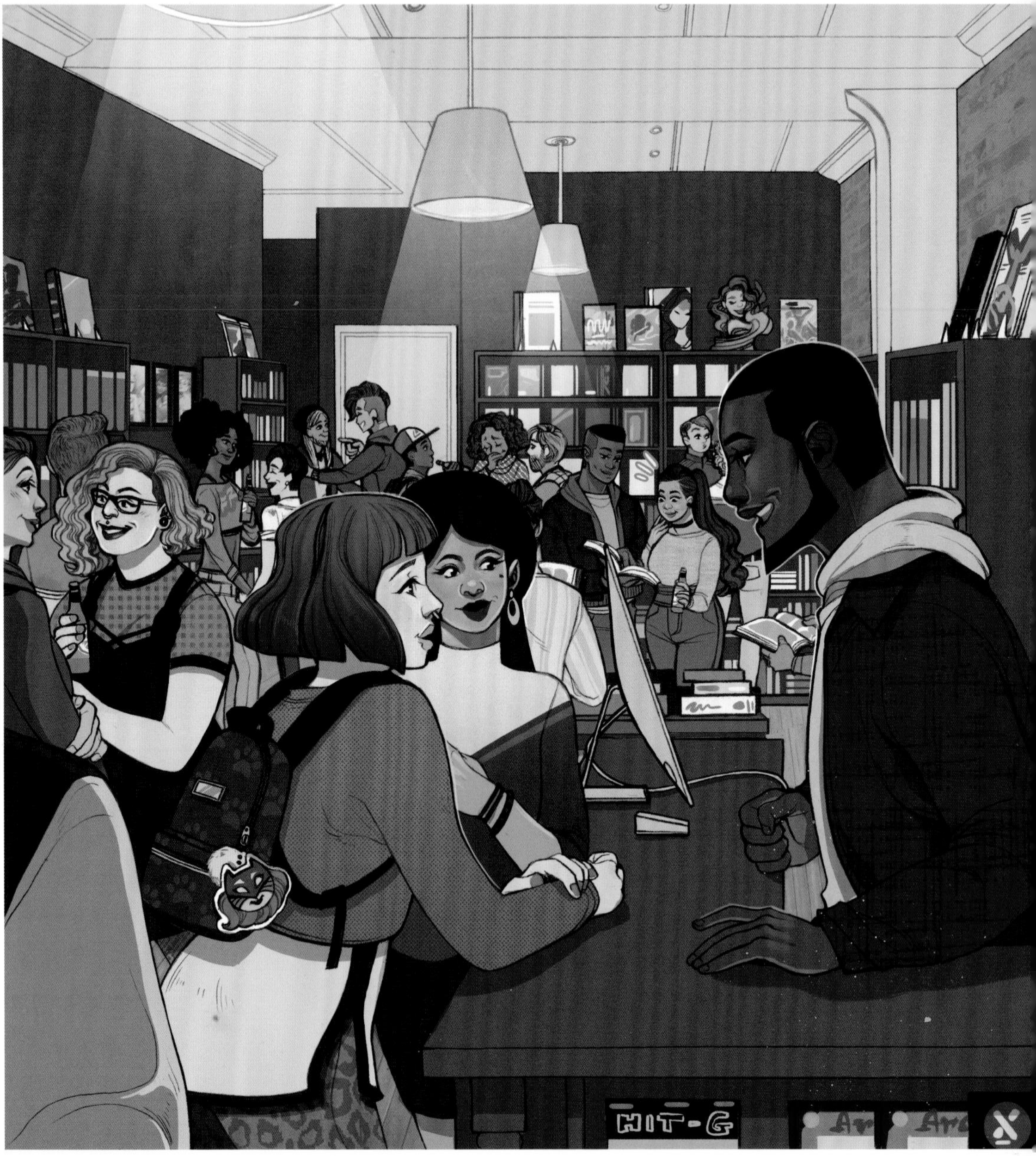
HIT-G

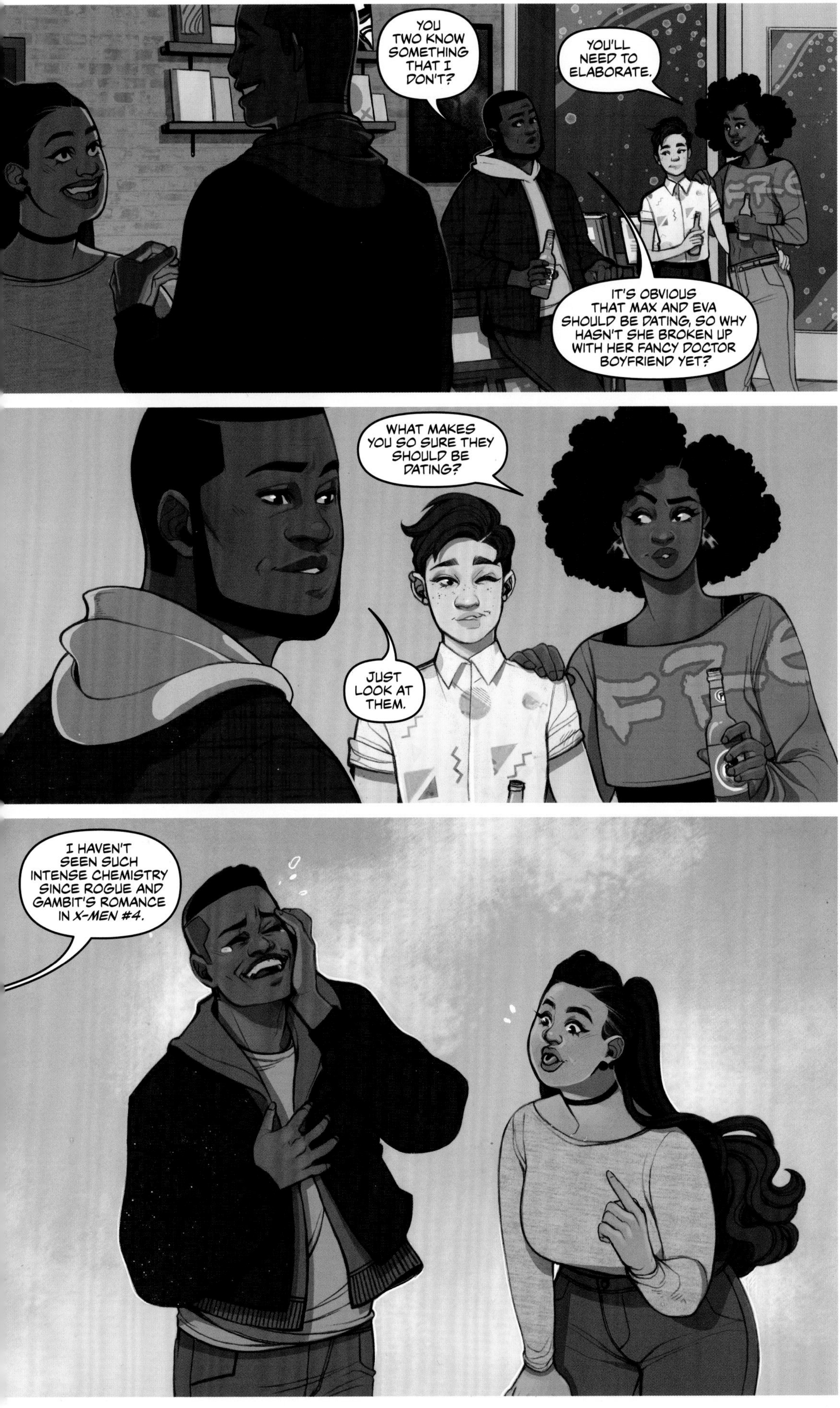
YOU TWO KNOW SOMETHING THAT I DON'T?
YOU'LL NEED TO ELABORATE.
IT'S OBVIOUS THAT MAX AND EVA SHOULD BE DATING, SO WHY HASN'T SHE BROKEN UP WITH HER FANCY DOCTOR BOYFRIEND YET?
WHAT MAKES YOU SO SURE THEY SHOULD BE DATING?
JUST LOOK AT THEM.
I HAVEN'T SEEN SUCH INTENSE CHEMISTRY SINCE ROGUE AND GAMBIT'S ROMANCE IN *X-MEN #4*.

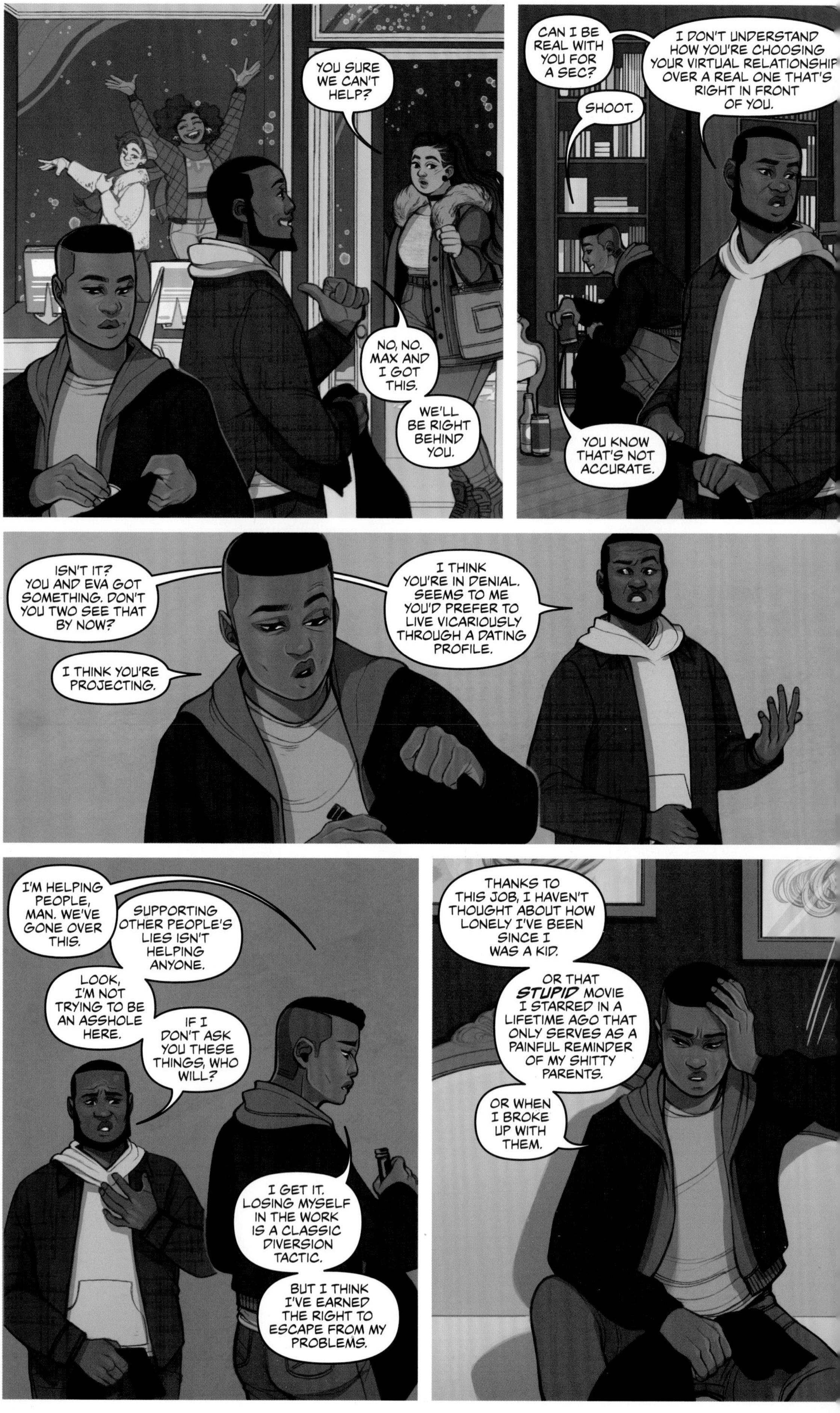
YOU SURE WE CAN'T HELP?
NO, NO. MAX AND I GOT THIS.
WE'LL BE RIGHT BEHIND YOU.
CAN I BE REAL WITH YOU FOR A SEC?
SHOOT.
I DON'T UNDERSTAND HOW YOU'RE CHOOSING YOUR VIRTUAL RELATIONSHIP OVER A REAL ONE THAT'S RIGHT IN FRONT OF YOU.
YOU KNOW THAT'S NOT ACCURATE.
ISN'T IT? YOU AND EVA GOT SOMETHING. DON'T YOU TWO SEE THAT BY NOW?
I THINK YOU'RE PROJECTING.
I THINK YOU'RE IN DENIAL. SEEMS TO ME YOU'D PREFER TO LIVE VICARIOUSLY THROUGH A DATING PROFILE.
I'M HELPING PEOPLE, MAN. WE'VE GONE OVER THIS.
SUPPORTING OTHER PEOPLE'S LIES ISN'T HELPING ANYONE.
LOOK, I'M NOT TRYING TO BE AN ASSHOLE HERE.
IF I DON'T ASK YOU THESE THINGS, WHO WILL?
I GET IT. LOSING MYSELF IN THE WORK IS A CLASSIC DIVERSION TACTIC.
BUT I THINK I'VE EARNED THE RIGHT TO ESCAPE FROM MY PROBLEMS.
THANKS TO THIS JOB, I HAVEN'T THOUGHT ABOUT HOW LONELY I'VE BEEN SINCE I WAS A KID.
OR THAT STUPID MOVIE I STARRED IN A LIFETIME AGO THAT ONLY SERVES AS A PAINFUL REMINDER OF MY SHITTY PARENTS.
OR WHEN I BROKE UP WITH THEM.

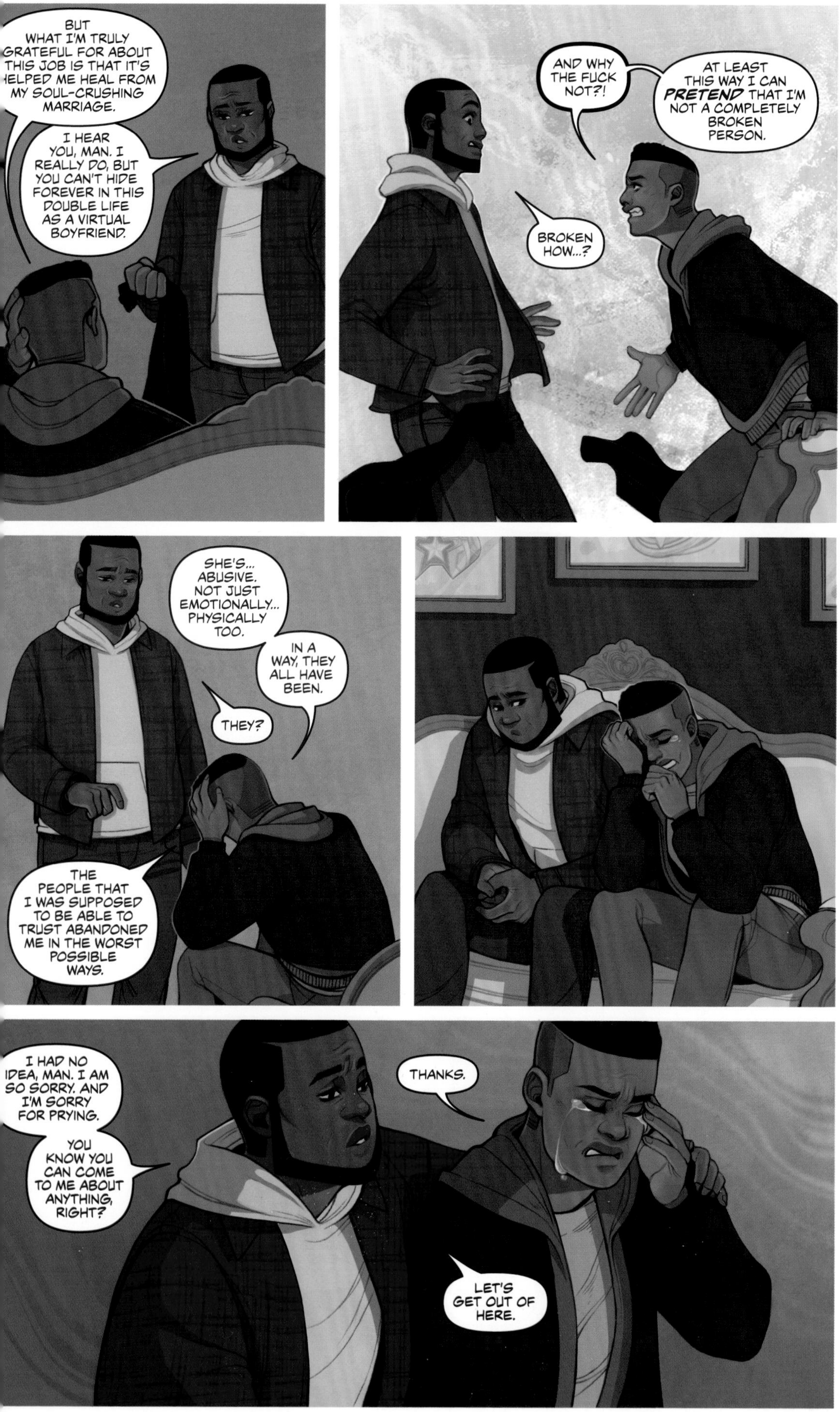
BUT WHAT I'M TRULY GRATEFUL FOR ABOUT THIS JOB IS THAT IT'S HELPED ME HEAL FROM MY SOUL-CRUSHING MARRIAGE.
I HEAR YOU, MAN. I REALLY DO, BUT YOU CAN'T HIDE FOREVER IN THIS DOUBLE LIFE AS A VIRTUAL BOYFRIEND.
AND WHY THE FUCK NOT?!
AT LEAST THIS WAY I CAN PRETEND THAT I'M NOT A COMPLETELY BROKEN PERSON.
BROKEN HOW...?
SHE'S... ABUSIVE. NOT JUST EMOTIONALLY... PHYSICALLY TOO.
IN A WAY, THEY ALL HAVE BEEN.
THEY?
THE PEOPLE THAT I WAS SUPPOSED TO BE ABLE TO TRUST ABANDONED ME IN THE WORST POSSIBLE WAYS.
I HAD NO IDEA, MAN. I AM SO SORRY. AND I'M SORRY FOR PRYING.
YOU KNOW YOU CAN COME TO ME ABOUT ANYTHING, RIGHT?
THANKS.
LET'S GET OUT OF HERE.

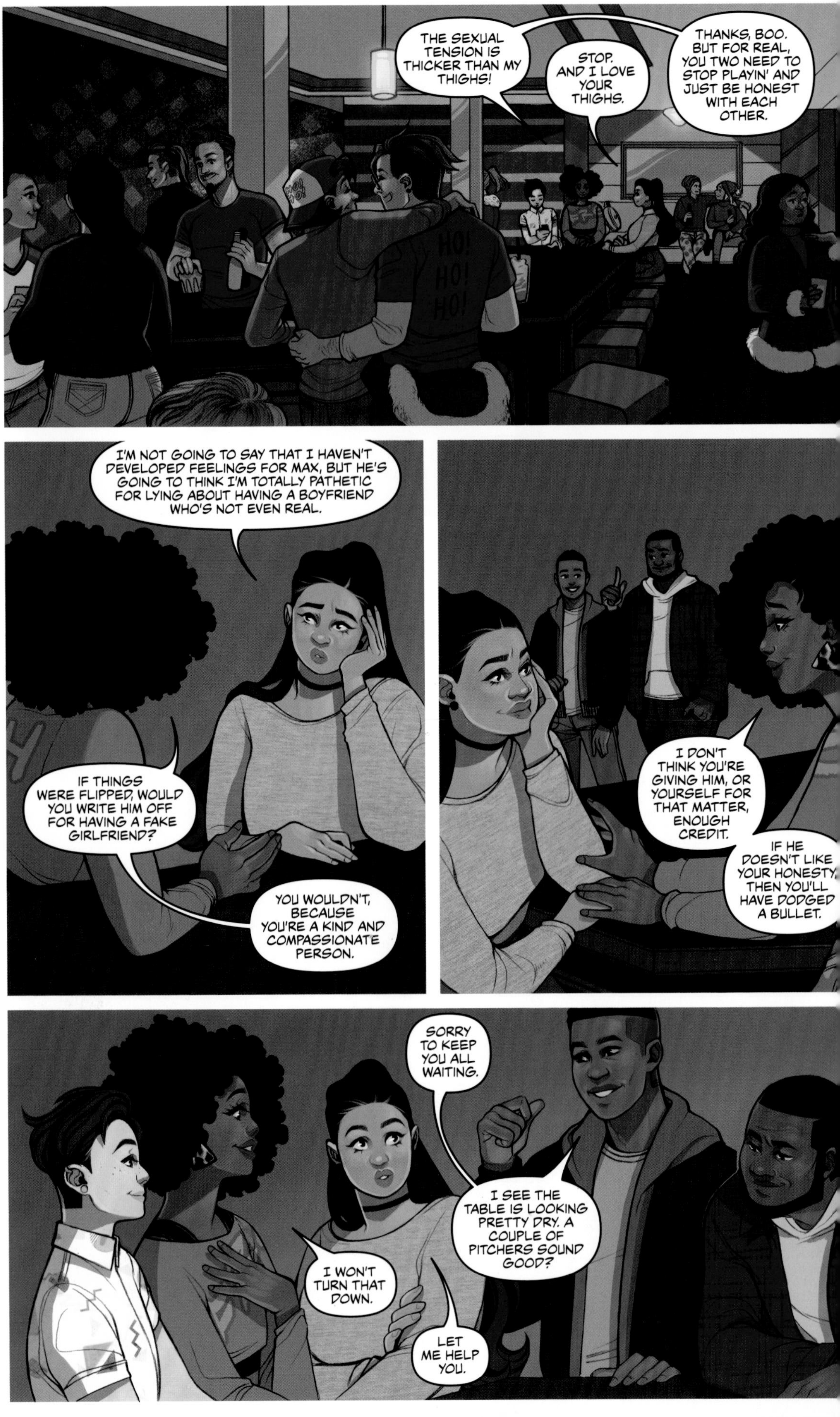
THE SEXUAL TENSION IS THICKER THAN MY THIGHS!
STOP. AND I LOVE YOUR THIGHS.
THANKS, BOO. BUT FOR REAL, YOU TWO NEED TO STOP PLAYIN' AND JUST BE HONEST WITH EACH OTHER.
HO! HO! HO!
I'M NOT GOING TO SAY THAT I HAVEN'T DEVELOPED FEELINGS FOR MAX, BUT HE'S GOING TO THINK I'M TOTALLY PATHETIC FOR LYING ABOUT HAVING A BOYFRIEND WHO'S NOT EVEN REAL.
IF THINGS WERE FLIPPED, WOULD YOU WRITE HIM OFF FOR HAVING A FAKE GIRLFRIEND?
YOU WOULDN'T, BECAUSE YOU'RE A KIND AND COMPASSIONATE PERSON.
I DON'T THINK YOU'RE GIVING HIM, OR YOURSELF FOR THAT MATTER, ENOUGH CREDIT.
IF HE DOESN'T LIKE YOUR HONESTY, THEN YOU'LL HAVE DODGED A BULLET.
SORRY TO KEEP YOU ALL WAITING.
I SEE THE TABLE IS LOOKING PRETTY DRY. A COUPLE OF PITCHERS SOUND GOOD?
I WON'T TURN THAT DOWN.
LET ME HELP YOU.

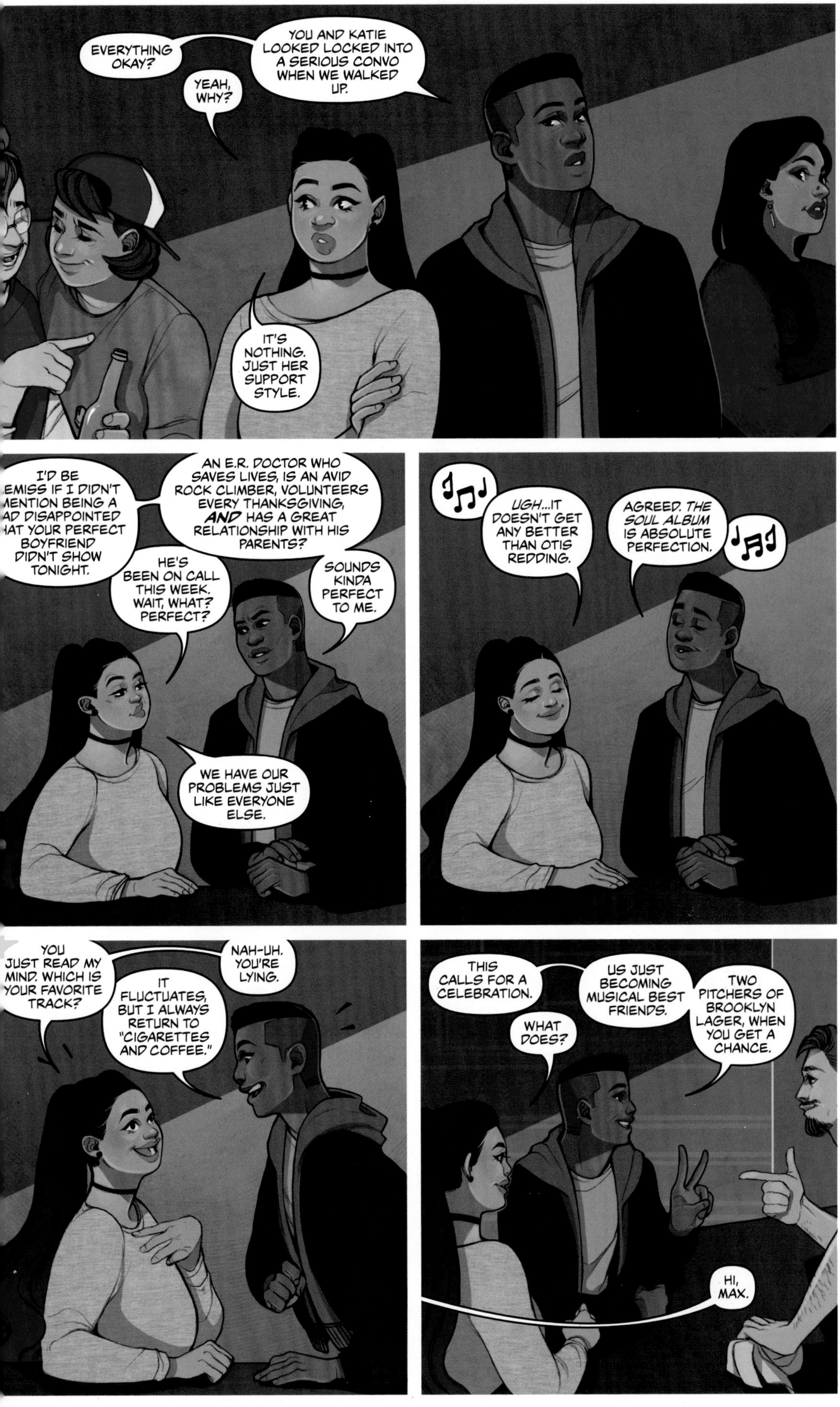
EVERYTHING OKAY?
YEAH, WHY?
YOU AND KATIE LOOKED LOCKED INTO A SERIOUS CONVO WHEN WE WALKED UP.
IT'S NOTHING. JUST HER SUPPORT STYLE.
I'D BE EMISS IF I DIDN'T MENTION BEING A AD DISAPPOINTED HAT YOUR PERFECT BOYFRIEND DIDN'T SHOW TONIGHT.
HE'S BEEN ON CALL THIS WEEK. WAIT, WHAT? PERFECT?
AN E.R. DOCTOR WHO SAVES LIVES, IS AN AVID ROCK CLIMBER, VOLUNTEERS EVERY THANKSGIVING, AND HAS A GREAT RELATIONSHIP WITH HIS PARENTS?
SOUNDS KINDA PERFECT TO ME.
WE HAVE OUR PROBLEMS JUST LIKE EVERYONE ELSE.
UGH...IT DOESN'T GET ANY BETTER THAN OTIS REDDING.
AGREED. THE SOUL ALBUM IS ABSOLUTE PERFECTION.
YOU JUST READ MY MIND. WHICH IS YOUR FAVORITE TRACK?
IT FLUCTUATES, BUT I ALWAYS RETURN TO "CIGARETTES AND COFFEE."
NAH-UH. YOU'RE LYING.
THIS CALLS FOR A CELEBRATION.
WHAT DOES?
US JUST BECOMING MUSICAL BEST FRIENDS.
TWO PITCHERS OF BROOKLYN LAGER, WHEN YOU GET A CHANCE.
HI, MAX.

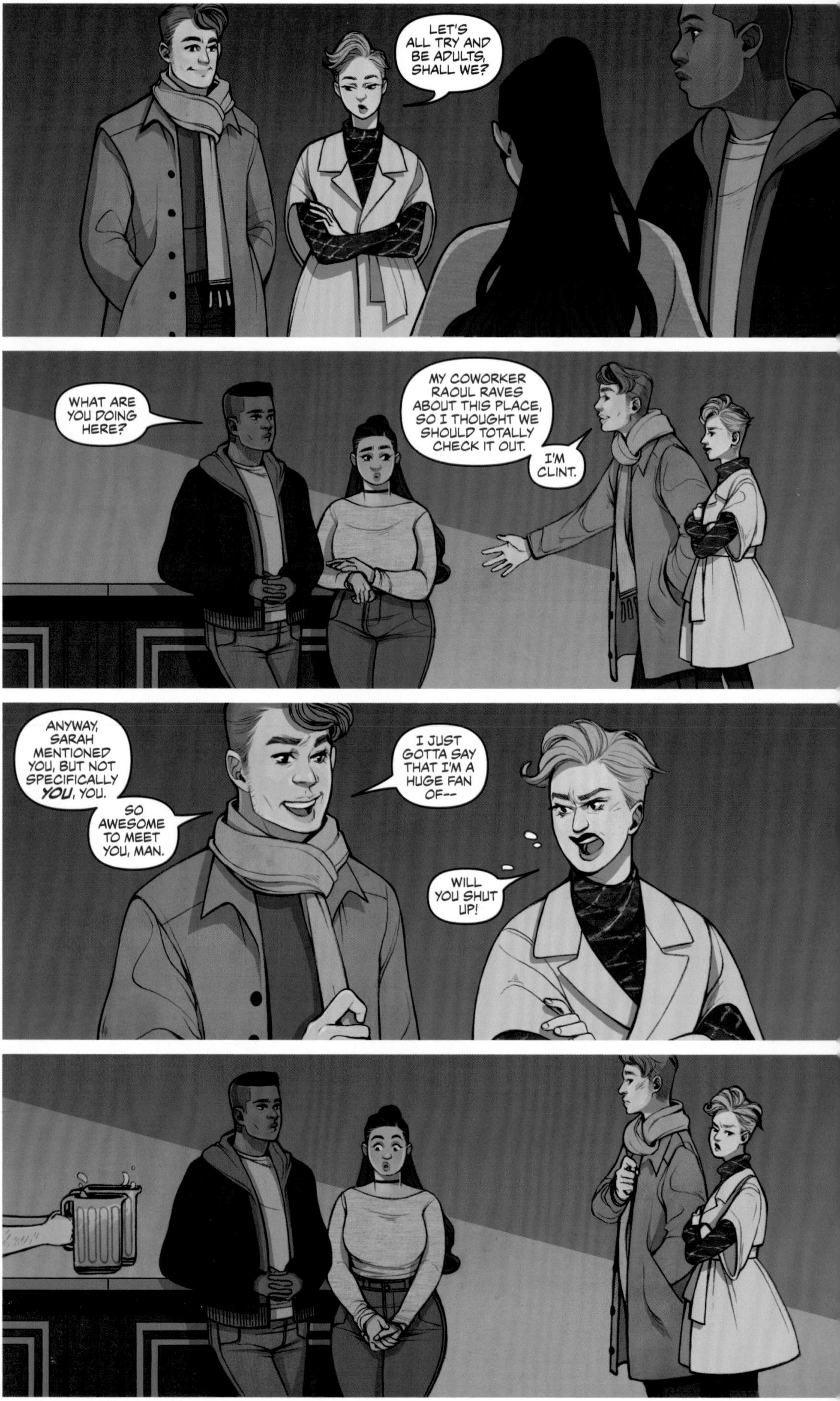
LET'S ALL TRY AND BE ADULTS, SHALL WE?
WHAT ARE YOU DOING HERE?
MY COWORKER RAOUL RAVES ABOUT THIS PLACE, SO I THOUGHT WE SHOULD TOTALLY CHECK IT OUT.
I'M CLINT.
ANYWAY, SARAH MENTIONED YOU, BUT NOT SPECIFICALLY ***YOU***, YOU.
SO AWESOME TO MEET YOU, MAN.
I JUST GOTTA SAY THAT I'M A HUGE FAN OF--
WILL YOU SHUT UP!

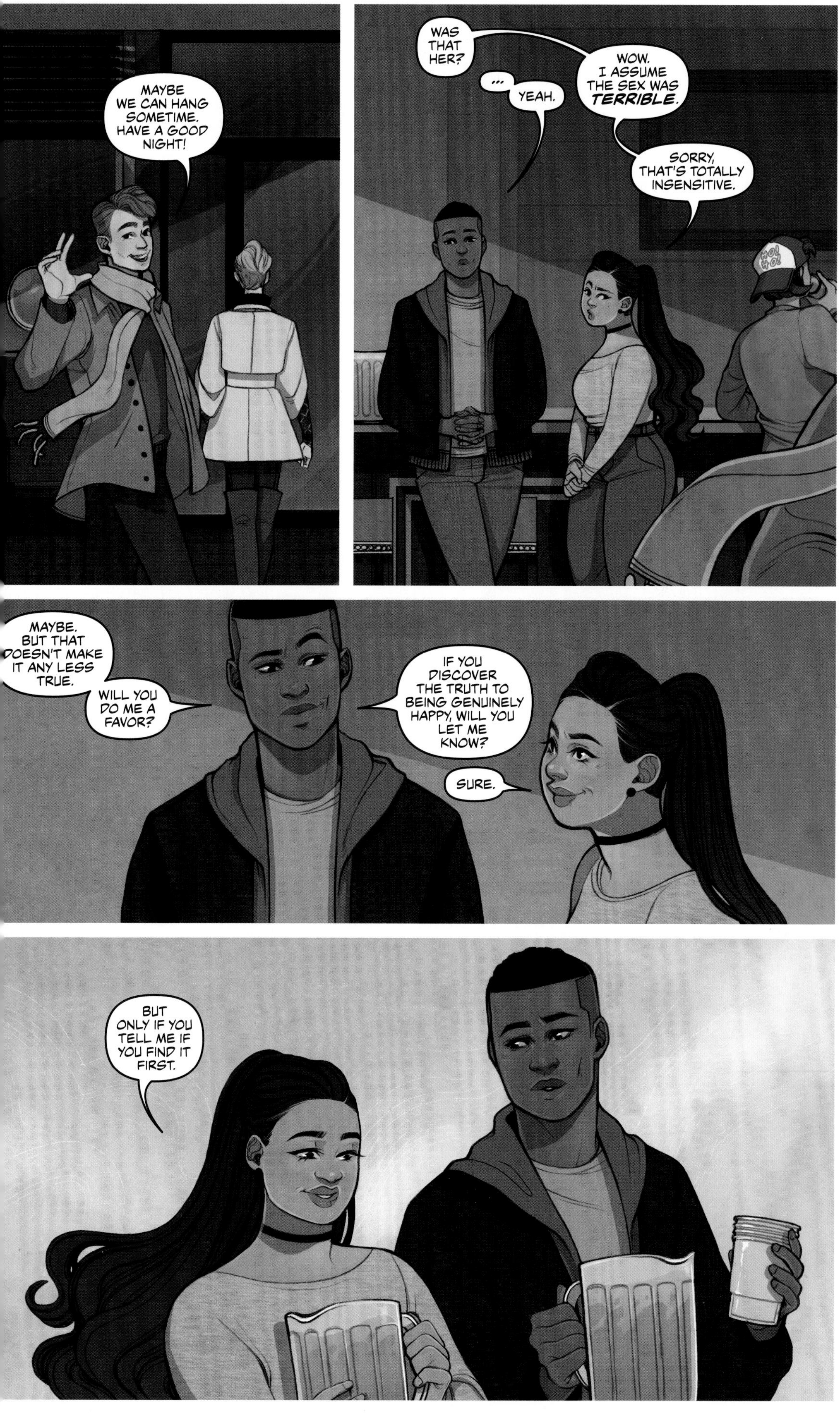
MAYBE WE CAN HANG SOMETIME. HAVE A GOOD NIGHT!
WAS THAT HER?
...
YEAH.
WOW. I ASSUME THE SEX WAS **TERRIBLE**.
SORRY, THAT'S TOTALLY INSENSITIVE.
HO! HO!
MAYBE. BUT THAT DOESN'T MAKE IT ANY LESS TRUE.
WILL YOU DO ME A FAVOR?
IF YOU DISCOVER THE TRUTH TO BEING GENUINELY HAPPY, WILL YOU LET ME KNOW?
SURE.
BUT ONLY IF YOU TELL ME IF YOU FIND IT FIRST.

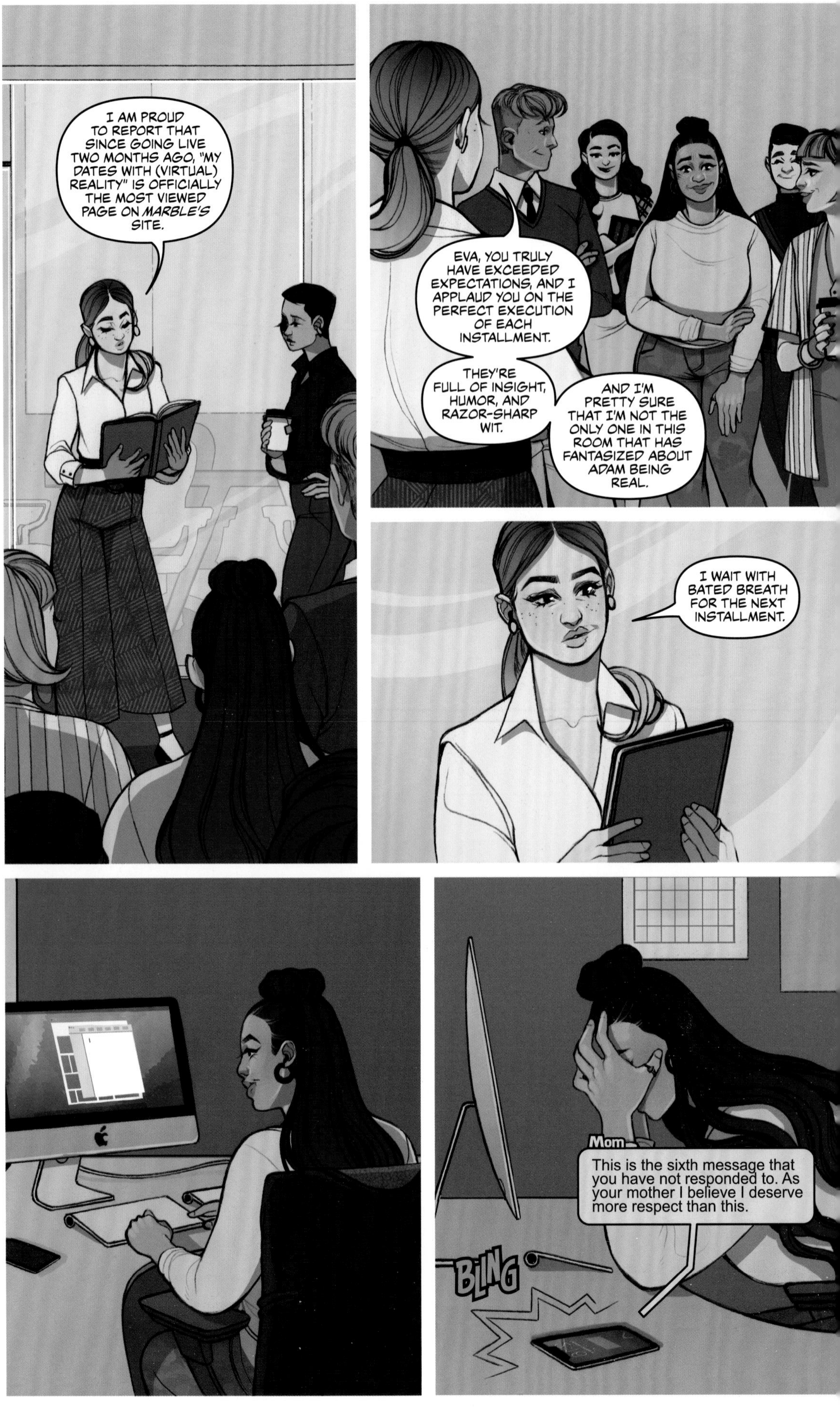
I AM PROUD TO REPORT THAT SINCE GOING LIVE TWO MONTHS AGO, "MY DATES WITH (VIRTUAL) REALITY" IS OFFICIALLY THE MOST VIEWED PAGE ON *MARBLE'S* SITE.
EVA, YOU TRULY HAVE EXCEEDED EXPECTATIONS, AND I APPLAUD YOU ON THE PERFECT EXECUTION OF EACH INSTALLMENT.
THEY'RE FULL OF INSIGHT, HUMOR, AND RAZOR-SHARP WIT.
AND I'M PRETTY SURE THAT I'M NOT THE ONLY ONE IN THIS ROOM THAT HAS FANTASIZED ABOUT ADAM BEING REAL.
I WAIT WITH BATED BREATH FOR THE NEXT INSTALLMENT.
Mom
This is the sixth message that you have not responded to. As your mother I believe I deserve more respect than this.
BLING

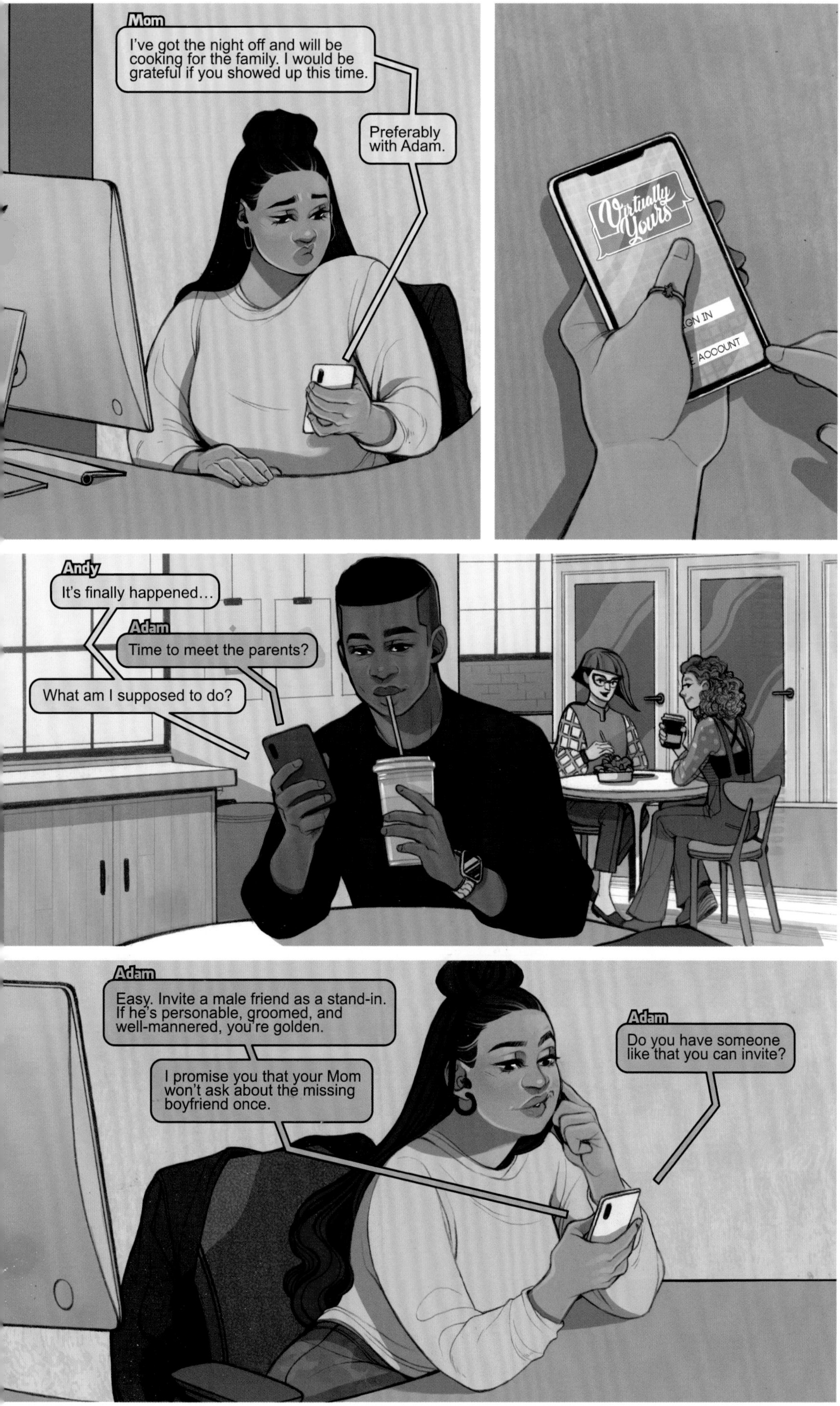
Mom
I've got the night off and will be cooking for the family. I would be grateful if you showed up this time.
Preferably with Adam.
Virtually Yours
Andy
It's finally happened…
Adam
Time to meet the parents?
What am I supposed to do?
Adam
Easy. Invite a male friend as a stand-in. If he's personable, groomed, and well-mannered, you're golden.
I promise you that your Mom won't ask about the missing boyfriend once.
Adam
Do you have someone like that you can invite?

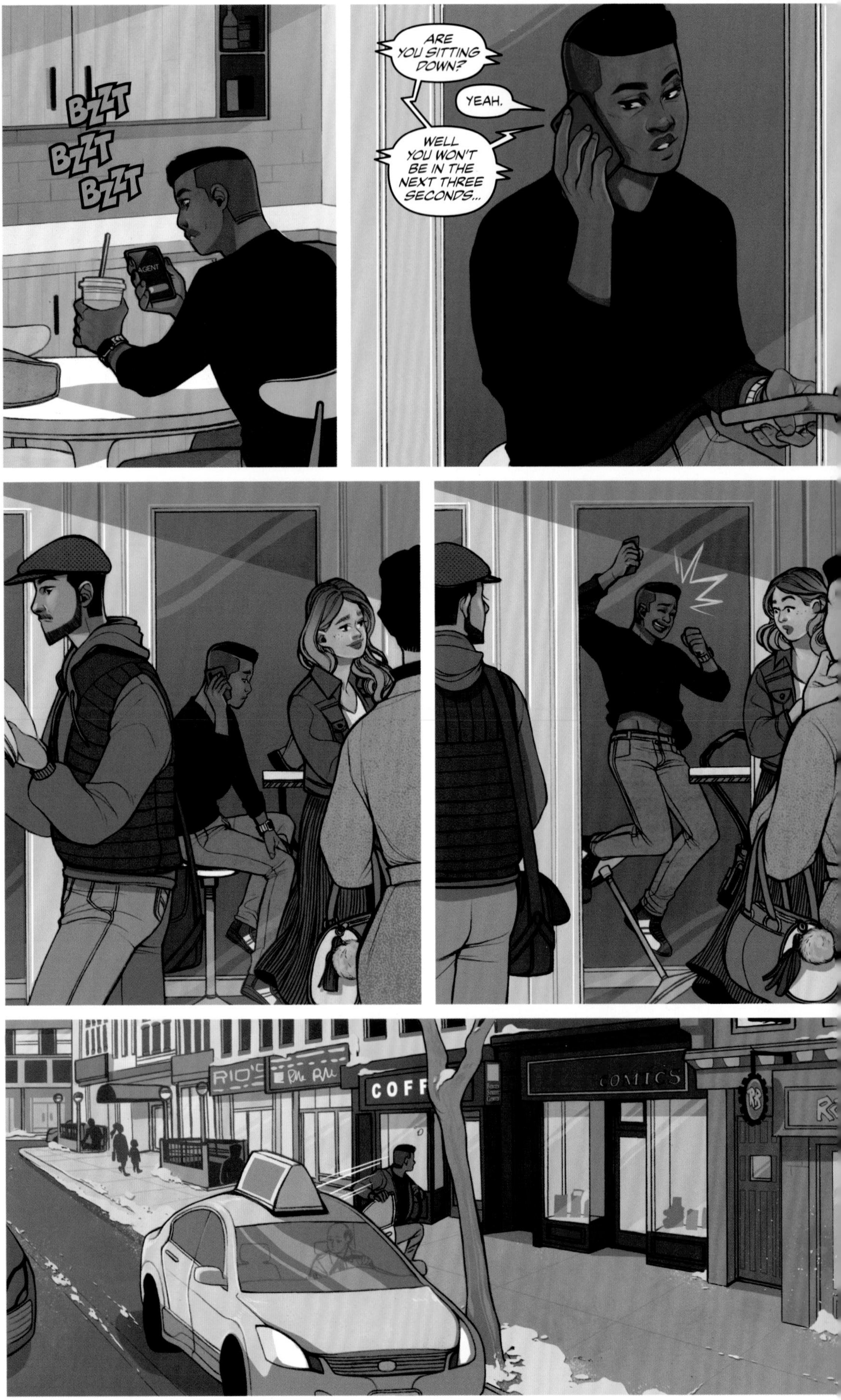
BZZT
BZZT
BZZT
AGENT
ARE YOU SITTING DOWN?
YEAH.
WELL YOU WON'T BE IN THE NEXT THREE SECONDS...
RIO'S
COFF
COMICS

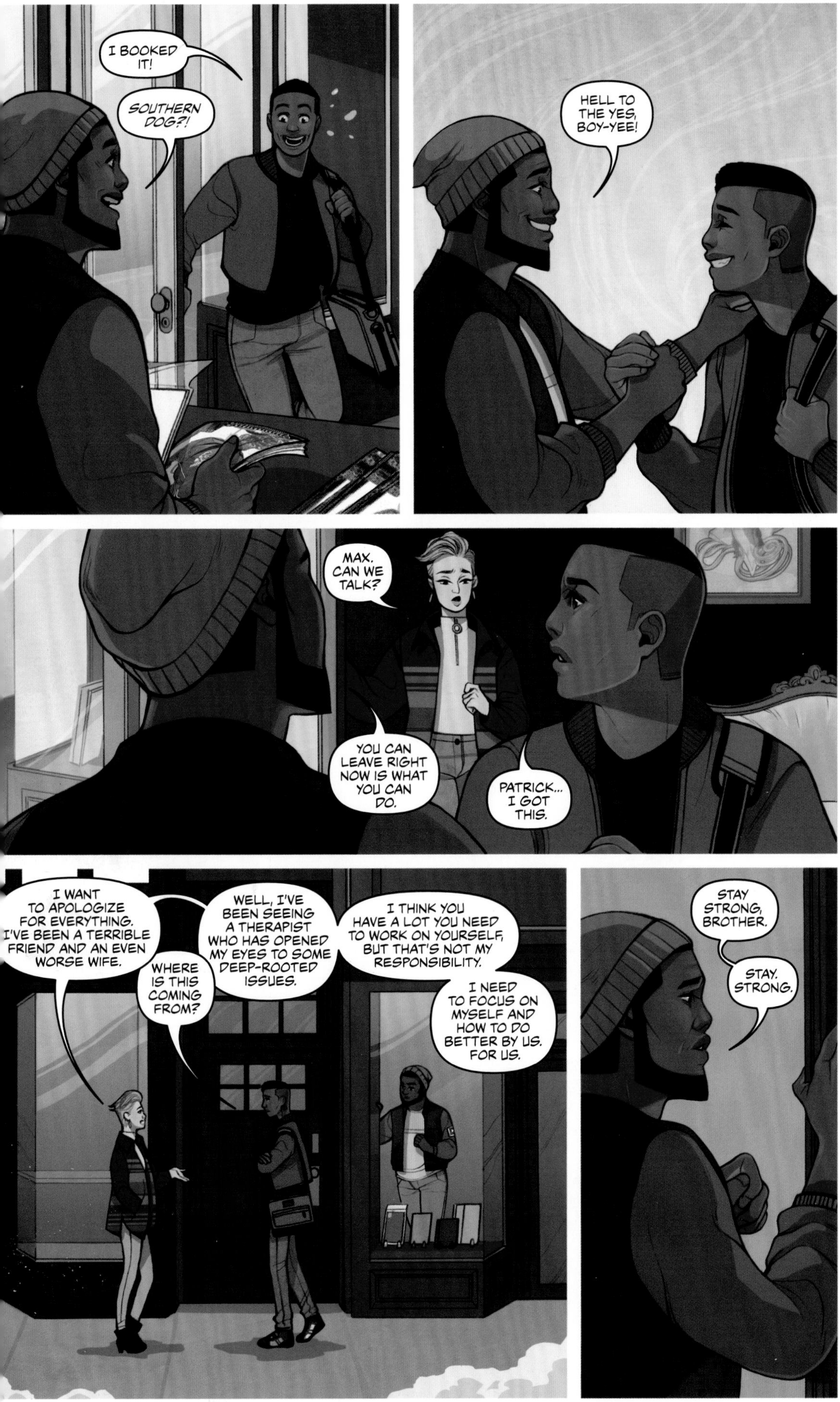
I BOOKED IT!
SOUTHERN DOG?!
HELL TO THE YES, BOY-YEE!
MAX. CAN WE TALK?
YOU CAN LEAVE RIGHT NOW IS WHAT YOU CAN DO.
PATRICK... I GOT THIS.
I WANT TO APOLOGIZE FOR EVERYTHING. I'VE BEEN A TERRIBLE FRIEND AND AN EVEN WORSE WIFE.
WHERE IS THIS COMING FROM?
WELL, I'VE BEEN SEEING A THERAPIST WHO HAS OPENED MY EYES TO SOME DEEP-ROOTED ISSUES.
I THINK YOU HAVE A LOT YOU NEED TO WORK ON YOURSELF, BUT THAT'S NOT MY RESPONSIBILITY.
I NEED TO FOCUS ON MYSELF AND HOW TO DO BETTER BY US. FOR US.
STAY STRONG, BROTHER.
STAY. STRONG.

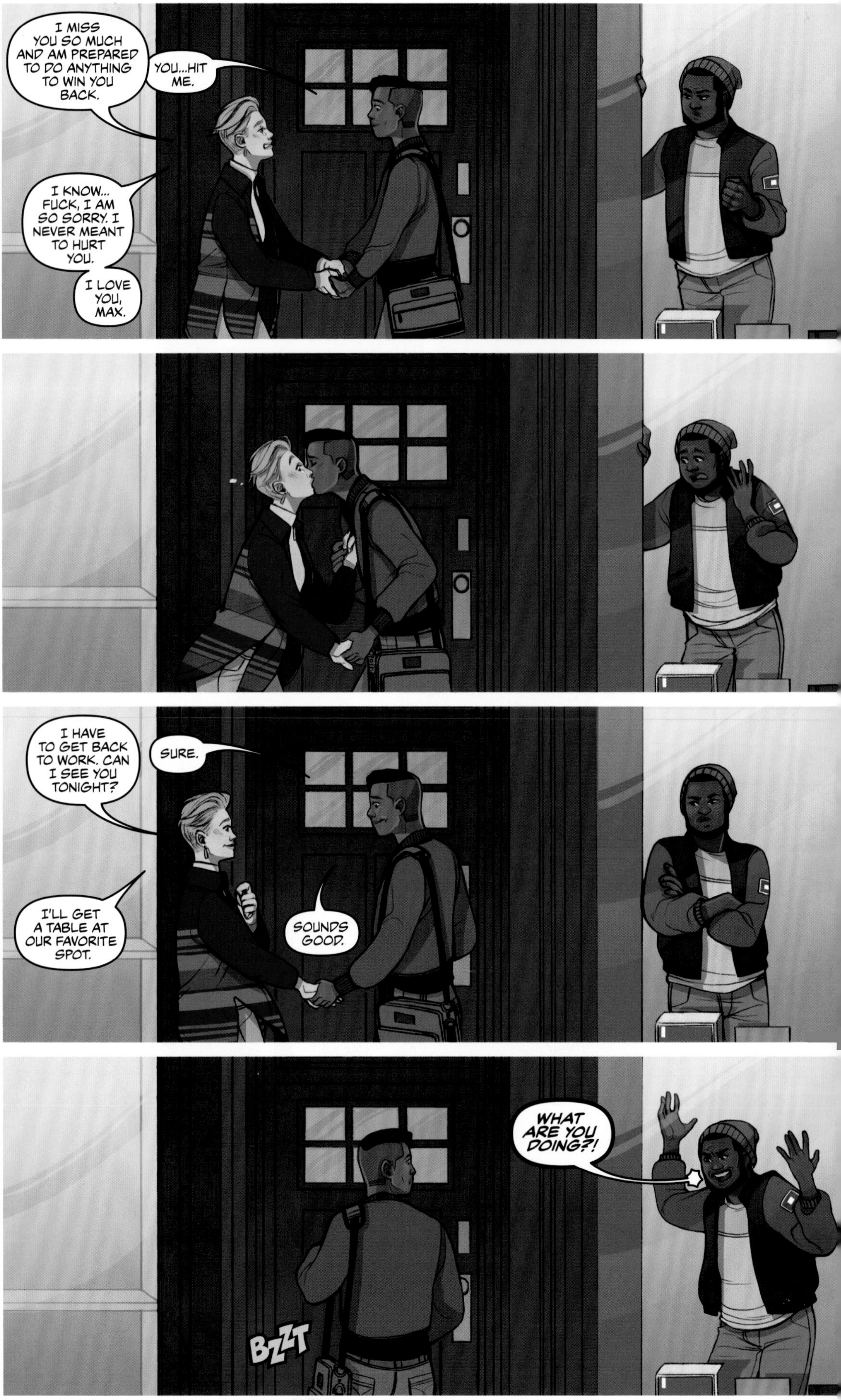
I MISS YOU SO MUCH AND AM PREPARED TO DO ANYTHING TO WIN YOU BACK.
YOU...HIT ME.
I KNOW... FUCK, I AM SO SORRY. I NEVER MEANT TO HURT YOU.
I LOVE YOU, MAX.
I HAVE TO GET BACK TO WORK. CAN I SEE YOU TONIGHT?
SURE.
I'LL GET A TABLE AT OUR FAVORITE SPOT.
SOUNDS GOOD.
BZZZT
WHAT ARE YOU DOING?!

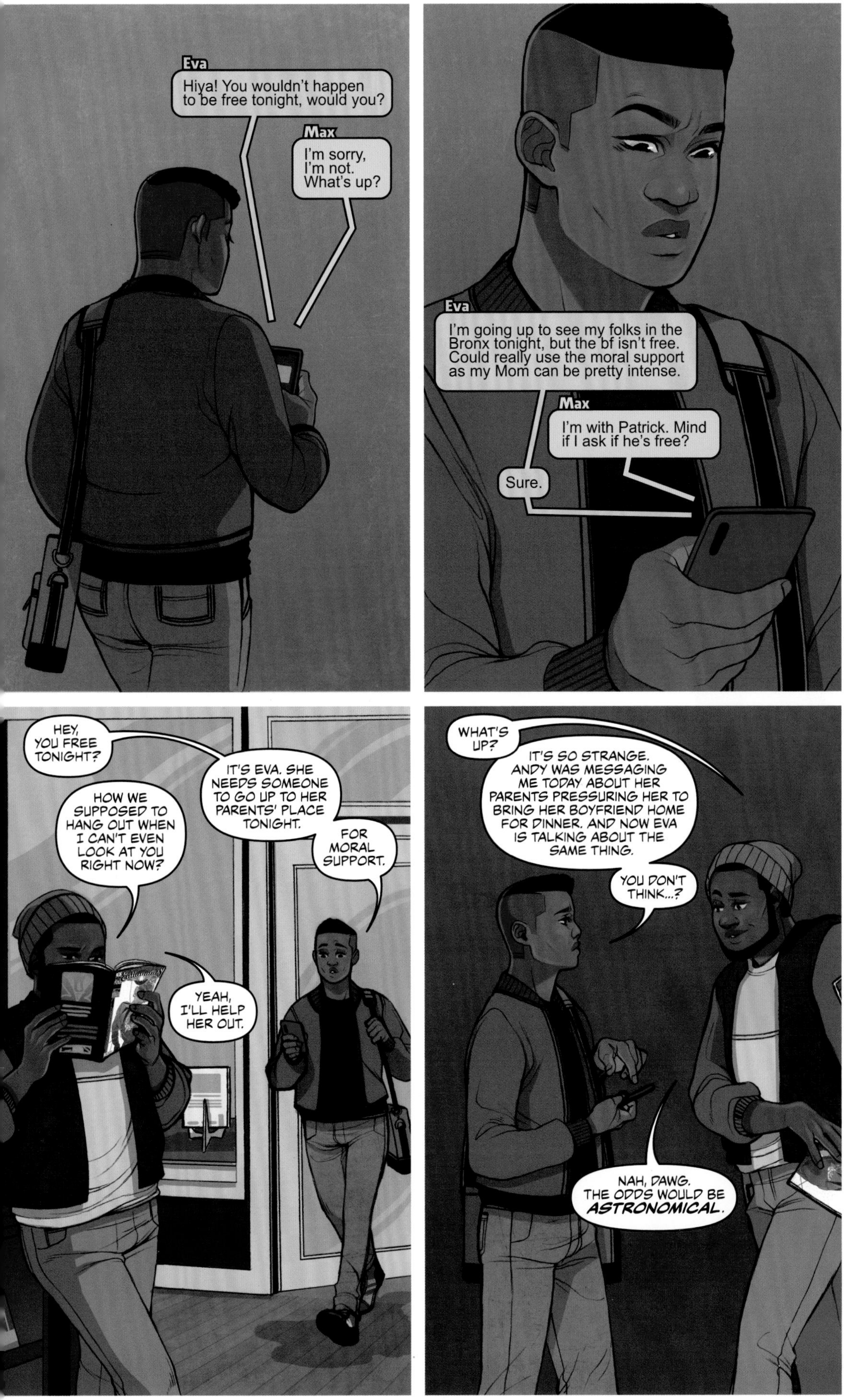
Eva
Hiya! You wouldn't happen to be free tonight, would you?
Max
I'm sorry, I'm not. What's up?
Eva
I'm going up to see my folks in the Bronx tonight, but the bf isn't free. Could really use the moral support as my Mom can be pretty intense.
Max
I'm with Patrick. Mind if I ask if he's free?
Sure.
HEY, YOU FREE TONIGHT?
HOW WE SUPPOSED TO HANG OUT WHEN I CAN'T EVEN LOOK AT YOU RIGHT NOW?
IT'S EVA. SHE NEEDS SOMEONE TO GO UP TO HER PARENTS' PLACE TONIGHT.
FOR MORAL SUPPORT.
YEAH, I'LL HELP HER OUT.
WHAT'S UP?
IT'S SO STRANGE. ANDY WAS MESSAGING ME TODAY ABOUT HER PARENTS PRESSURING HER TO BRING HER BOYFRIEND HOME FOR DINNER. AND NOW EVA IS TALKING ABOUT THE SAME THING.
YOU DON'T THINK...?
NAH, DAWG. THE ODDS WOULD BE ***ASTRONOMICAL***.

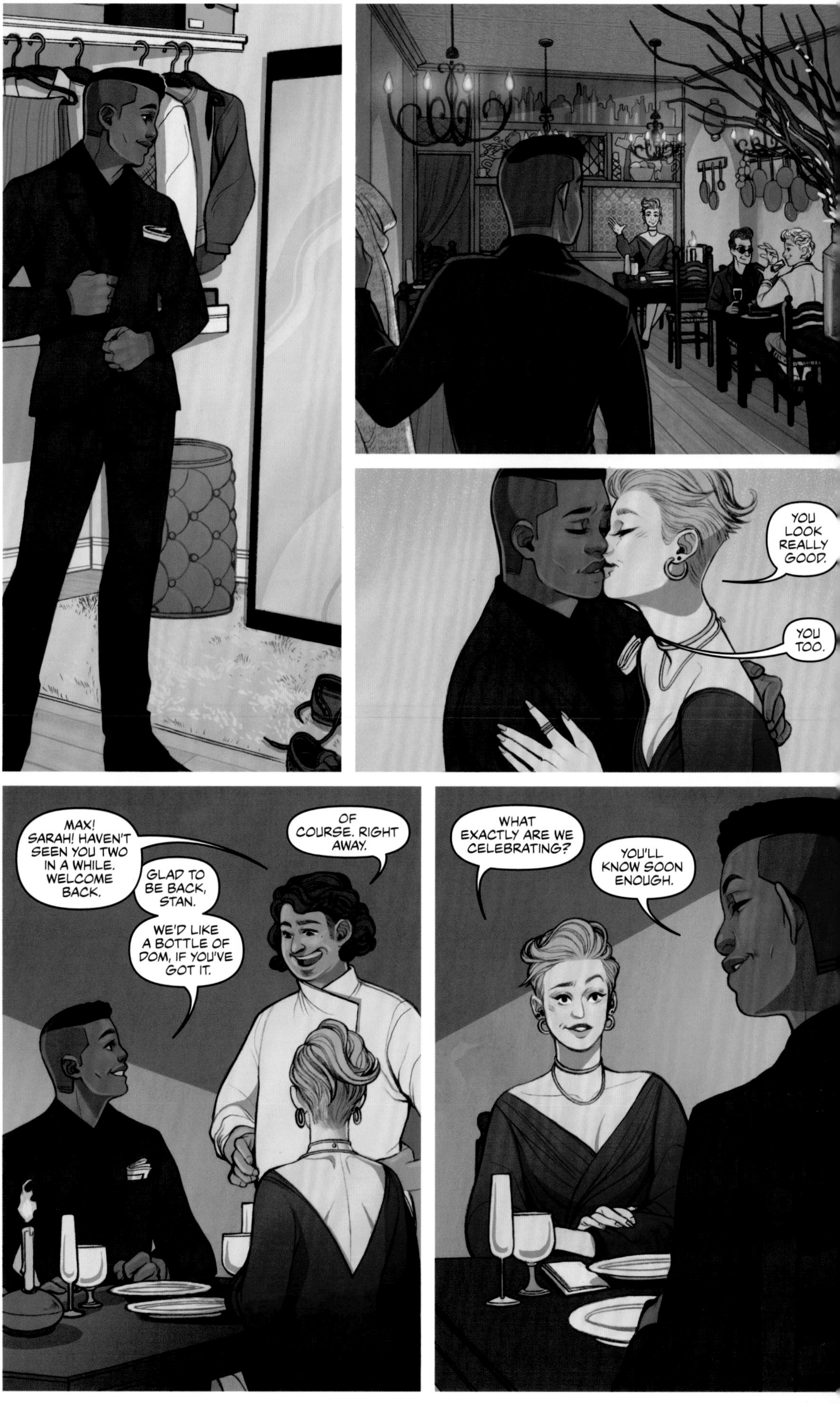
YOU LOOK REALLY GOOD.
YOU TOO.
MAX! SARAH! HAVEN'T SEEN YOU TWO IN A WHILE. WELCOME BACK.
GLAD TO BE BACK, STAN.
WE'D LIKE A BOTTLE OF DOM, IF YOU'VE GOT IT.
OF COURSE. RIGHT AWAY.
WHAT EXACTLY ARE WE CELEBRATING?
YOU'LL KNOW SOON ENOUGH.

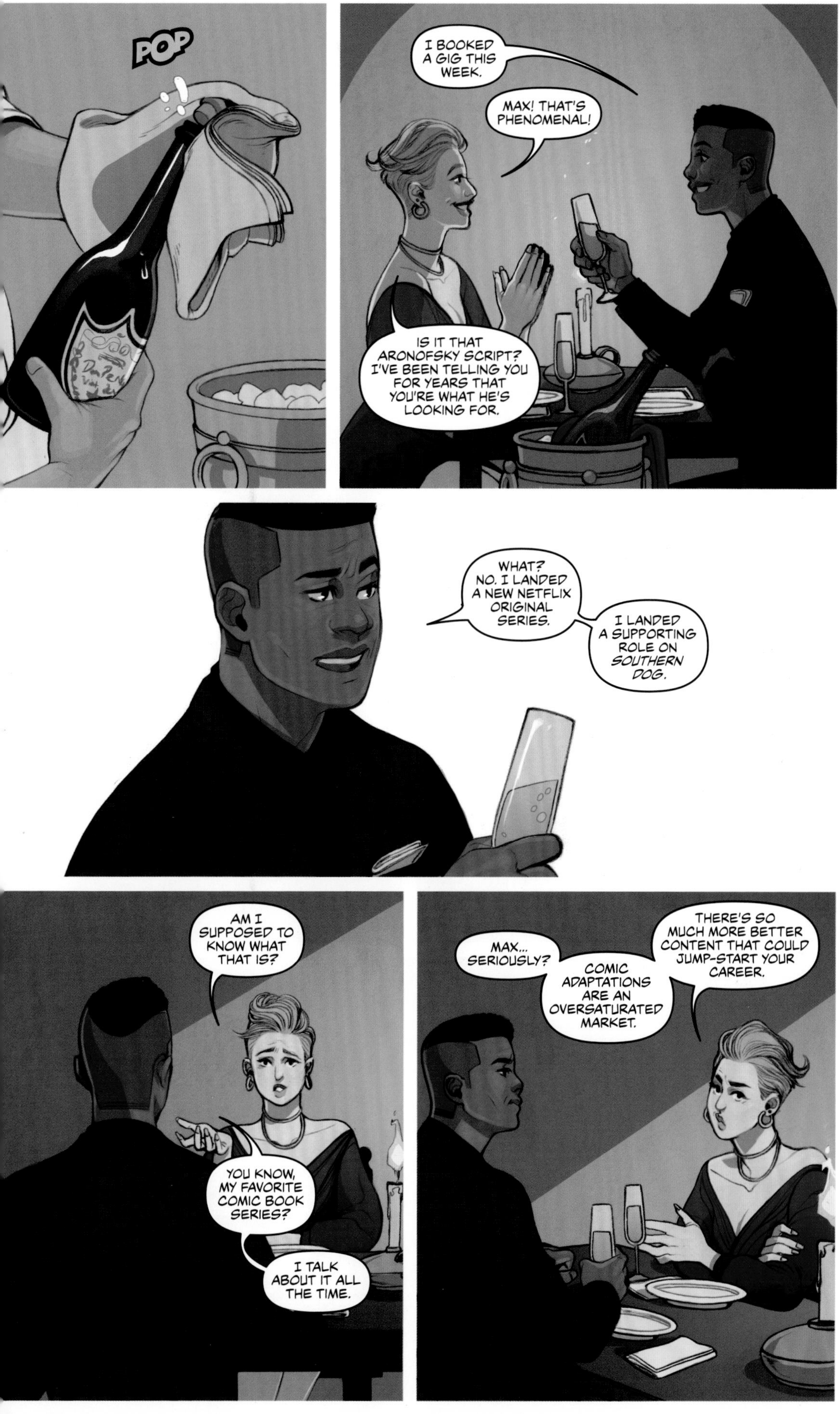
POP
I BOOKED A GIG THIS WEEK.
MAX! THAT'S PHENOMENAL!
IS IT THAT ARONOFSKY SCRIPT? I'VE BEEN TELLING YOU FOR YEARS THAT YOU'RE WHAT HE'S LOOKING FOR.
WHAT? NO. I LANDED A NEW NETFLIX ORIGINAL SERIES.
I LANDED A SUPPORTING ROLE ON *SOUTHERN DOG*.
AM I SUPPOSED TO KNOW WHAT THAT IS?
YOU KNOW, MY FAVORITE COMIC BOOK SERIES?
I TALK ABOUT IT ALL THE TIME.
MAX... SERIOUSLY?
COMIC ADAPTATIONS ARE AN OVERSATURATED MARKET.
THERE'S SO MUCH MORE BETTER CONTENT THAT COULD JUMP-START YOUR CAREER.

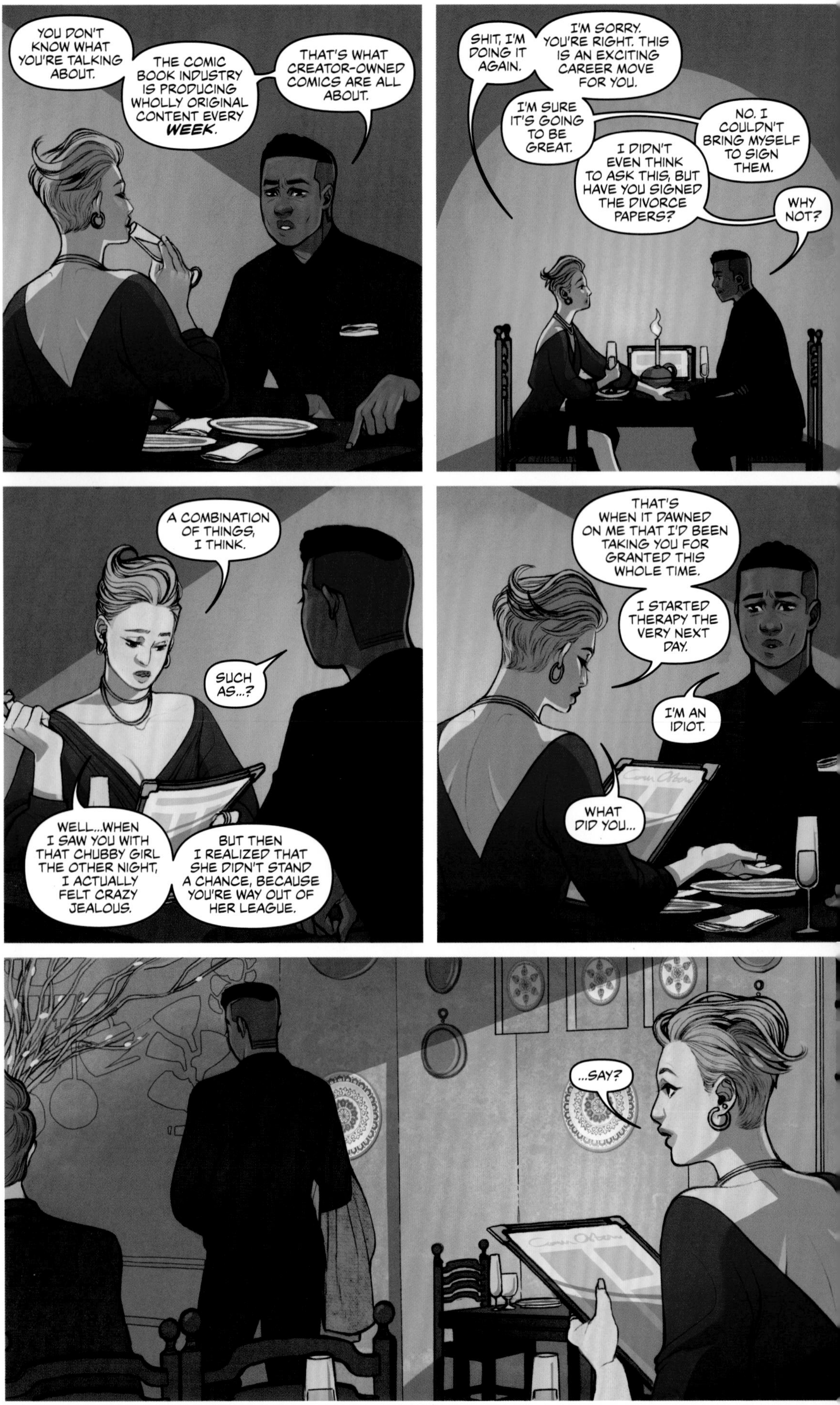
YOU DON'T KNOW WHAT YOU'RE TALKING ABOUT.
THE COMIC BOOK INDUSTRY IS PRODUCING WHOLLY ORIGINAL CONTENT EVERY ***WEEK***.
THAT'S WHAT CREATOR-OWNED COMICS ARE ALL ABOUT.
SHIT, I'M DOING IT AGAIN.
I'M SORRY. YOU'RE RIGHT. THIS IS AN EXCITING CAREER MOVE FOR YOU.
I'M SURE IT'S GOING TO BE GREAT.
I DIDN'T EVEN THINK TO ASK THIS, BUT HAVE YOU SIGNED THE DIVORCE PAPERS?
NO. I COULDN'T BRING MYSELF TO SIGN THEM.
WHY NOT?
A COMBINATION OF THINGS, I THINK.
SUCH AS...?
WELL...WHEN I SAW YOU WITH THAT CHUBBY GIRL THE OTHER NIGHT, I ACTUALLY FELT CRAZY JEALOUS.
BUT THEN I REALIZED THAT SHE DIDN'T STAND A CHANCE, BECAUSE YOU'RE WAY OUT OF HER LEAGUE.
THAT'S WHEN IT DAWNED ON ME THAT I'D BEEN TAKING YOU FOR GRANTED THIS WHOLE TIME.
I STARTED THERAPY THE VERY NEXT DAY.
I'M AN IDIOT.
WHAT DID YOU...
...SAY?

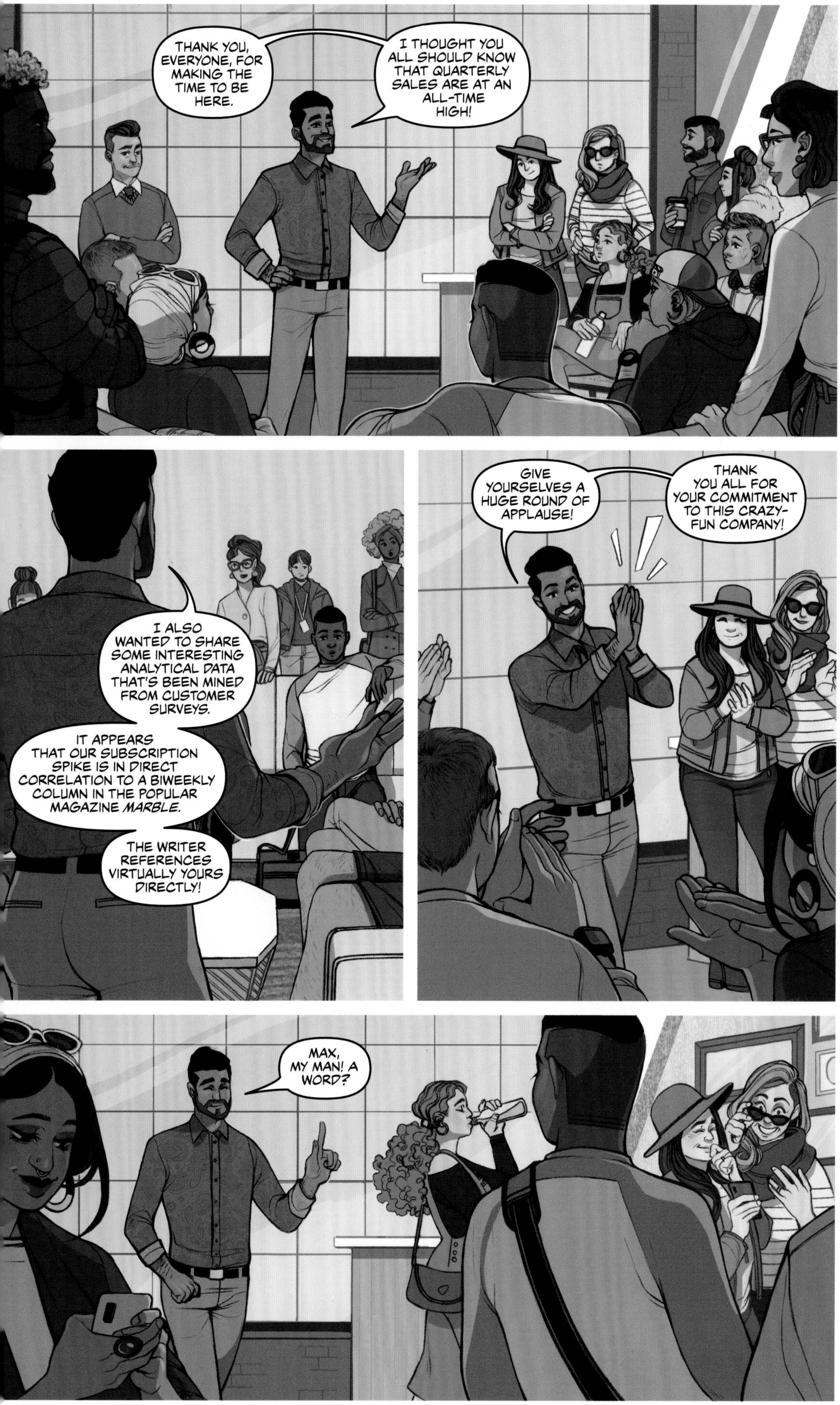
THANK YOU, EVERYONE, FOR MAKING THE TIME TO BE HERE.
I THOUGHT YOU ALL SHOULD KNOW THAT QUARTERLY SALES ARE AT AN ALL-TIME HIGH!
I ALSO WANTED TO SHARE SOME INTERESTING ANALYTICAL DATA THAT'S BEEN MINED FROM CUSTOMER SURVEYS.
IT APPEARS THAT OUR SUBSCRIPTION SPIKE IS IN DIRECT CORRELATION TO A BIWEEKLY COLUMN IN THE POPULAR MAGAZINE *MARBLE*.
THE WRITER REFERENCES VIRTUALLY YOURS DIRECTLY!
GIVE YOURSELVES A HUGE ROUND OF APPLAUSE!
THANK YOU ALL FOR YOUR COMMITMENT TO THIS CRAZY-FUN COMPANY!
MAX, MY MAN! A WORD?

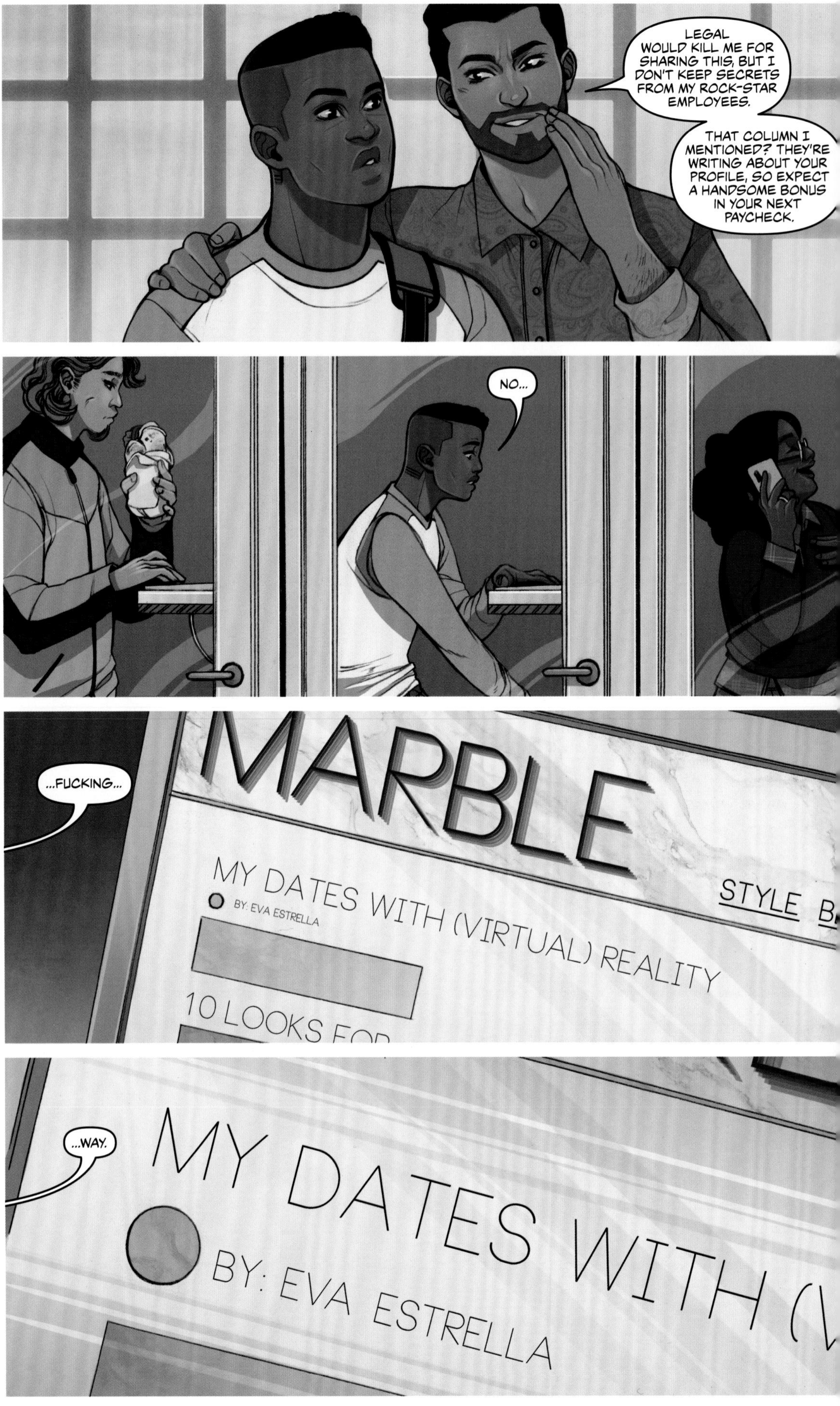
LEGAL WOULD KILL ME FOR SHARING THIS, BUT I DON'T KEEP SECRETS FROM MY ROCK-STAR EMPLOYEES.
THAT COLUMN I MENTIONED? THEY'RE WRITING ABOUT YOUR PROFILE, SO EXPECT A HANDSOME BONUS IN YOUR NEXT PAYCHECK.
NO...
...FUCKING...
MARBLE
MY DATES WITH (VIRTUAL) REALITY
BY: EVA ESTRELLA
STYLE
...WAY.
MY DATES WITH
BY: EVA ESTRELLA

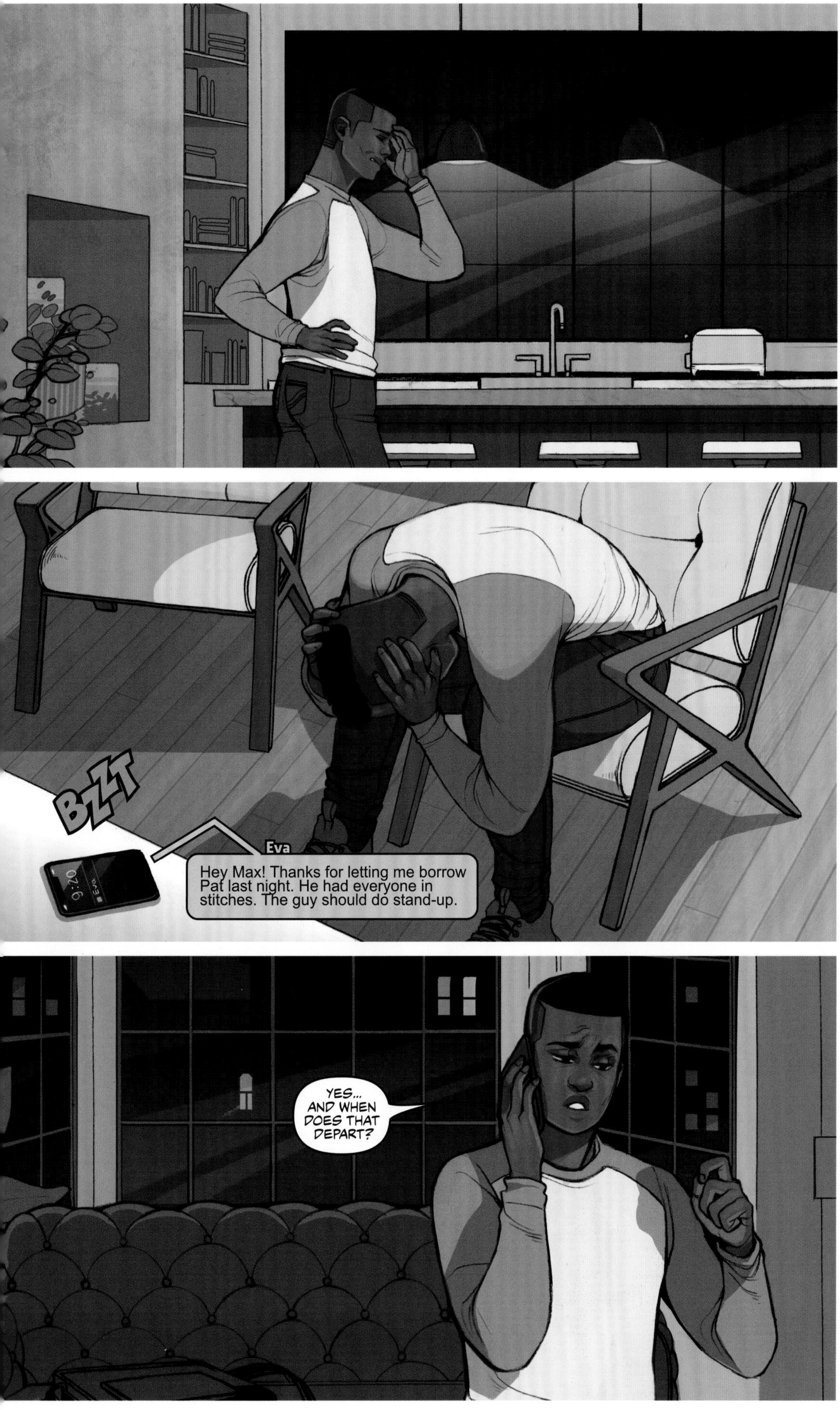
BZZT
Eva
Hey Max! Thanks for letting me borrow Pat last night. He had everyone in stitches. The guy should do stand-up.
YES... AND WHEN DOES THAT DEPART?

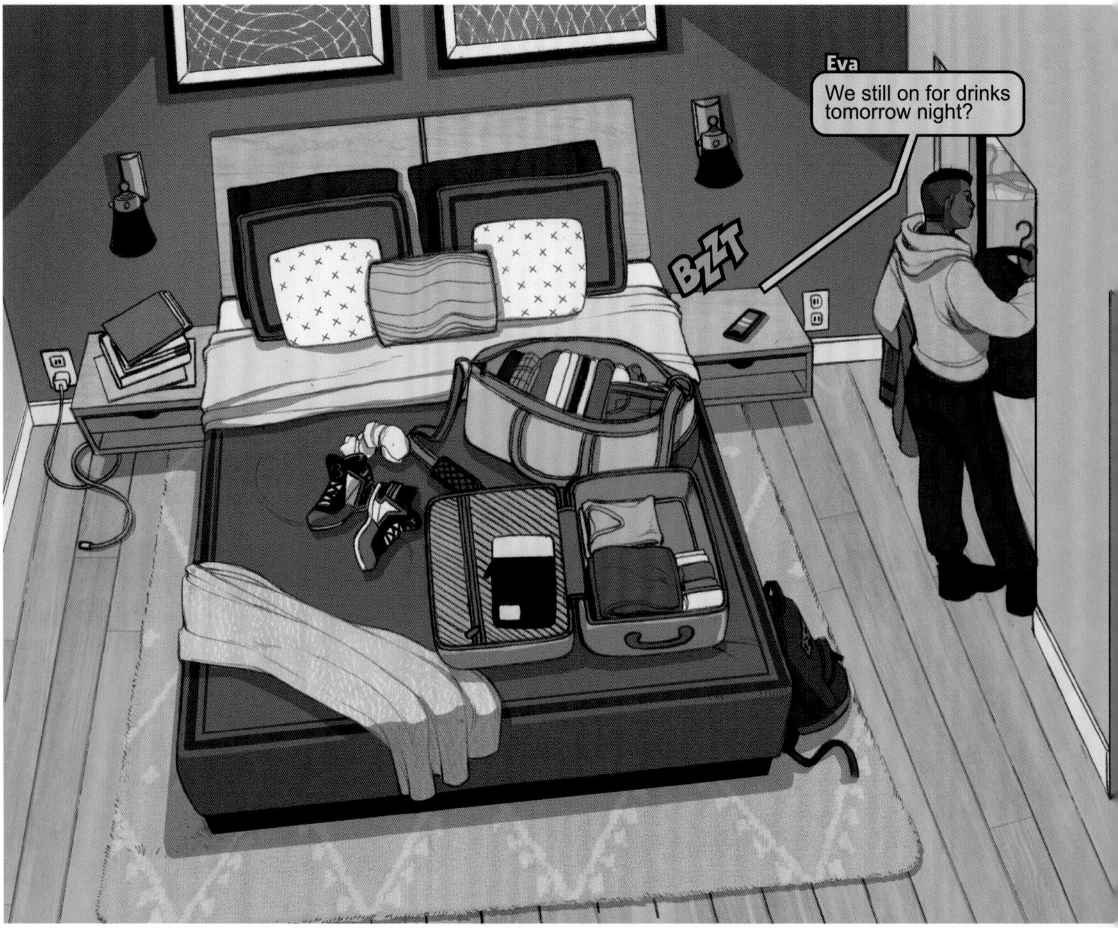
Eva
We still on for drinks tomorrow night?
BZZT

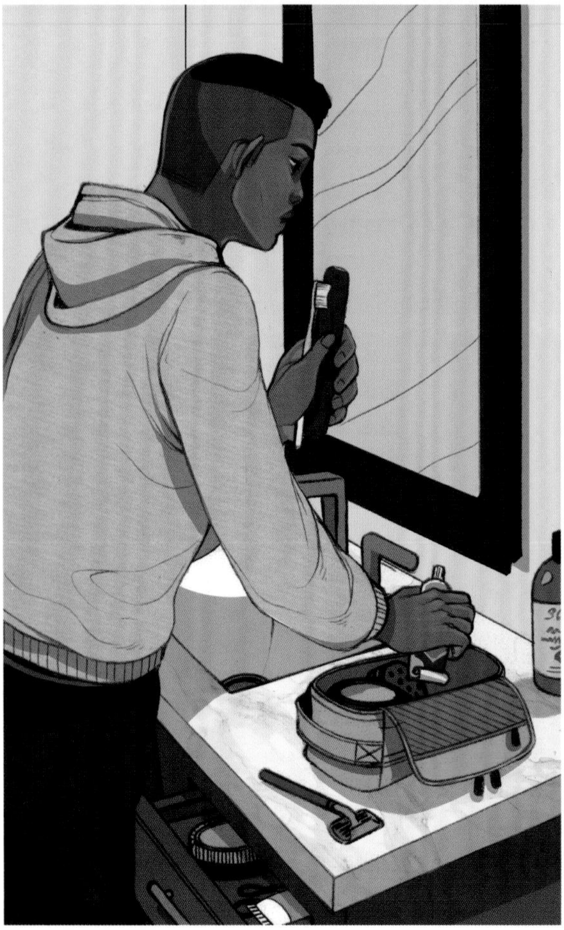

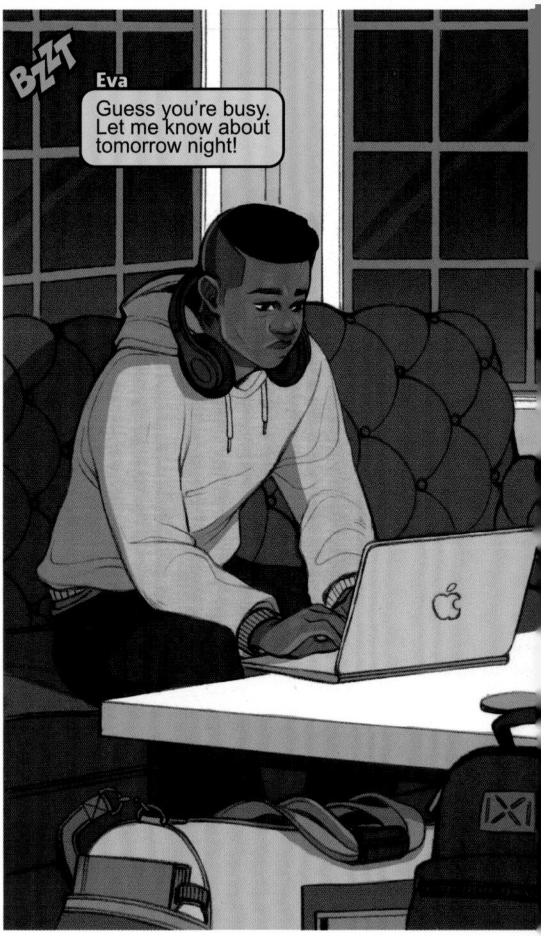
BZZT
Eva
Guess you're busy. Let me know about tomorrow night!

To: apatel@virtuallyyours.com
Cc:
Subject: Letter of Resignation
From: mkittridge@virtuallyyours.com
Dear Ajay,
PAT
To: apatel@virtuallyyours
Cc:
Subject: Letter of Resigna
From: mkittridge@virtually
Max
Pat, filming doesn't start for another couple weeks but leaving for Savannah tonight.
Andy is Eva.
About those odds… guess I'm the luckiest motherfucker ever.

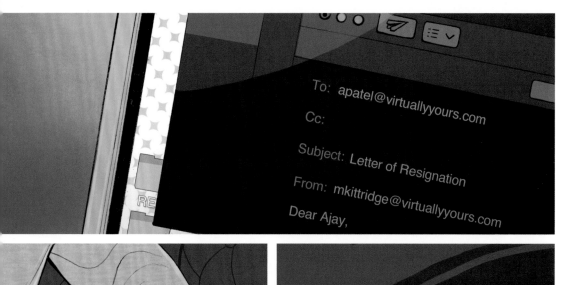

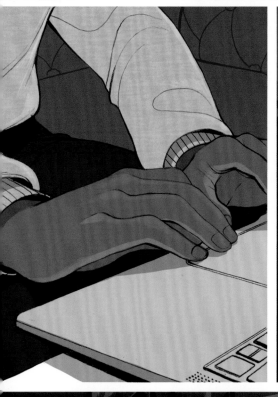

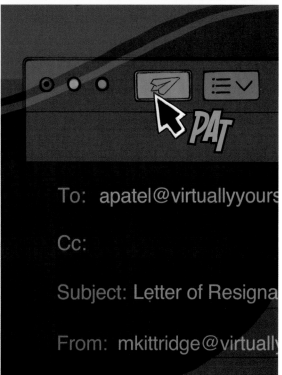

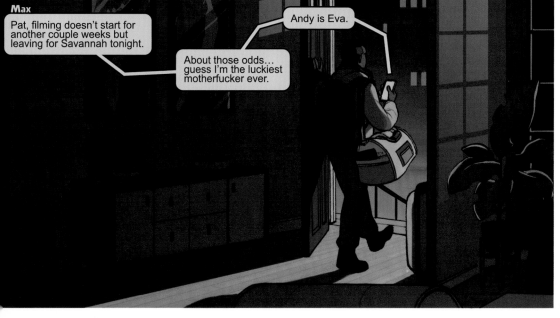

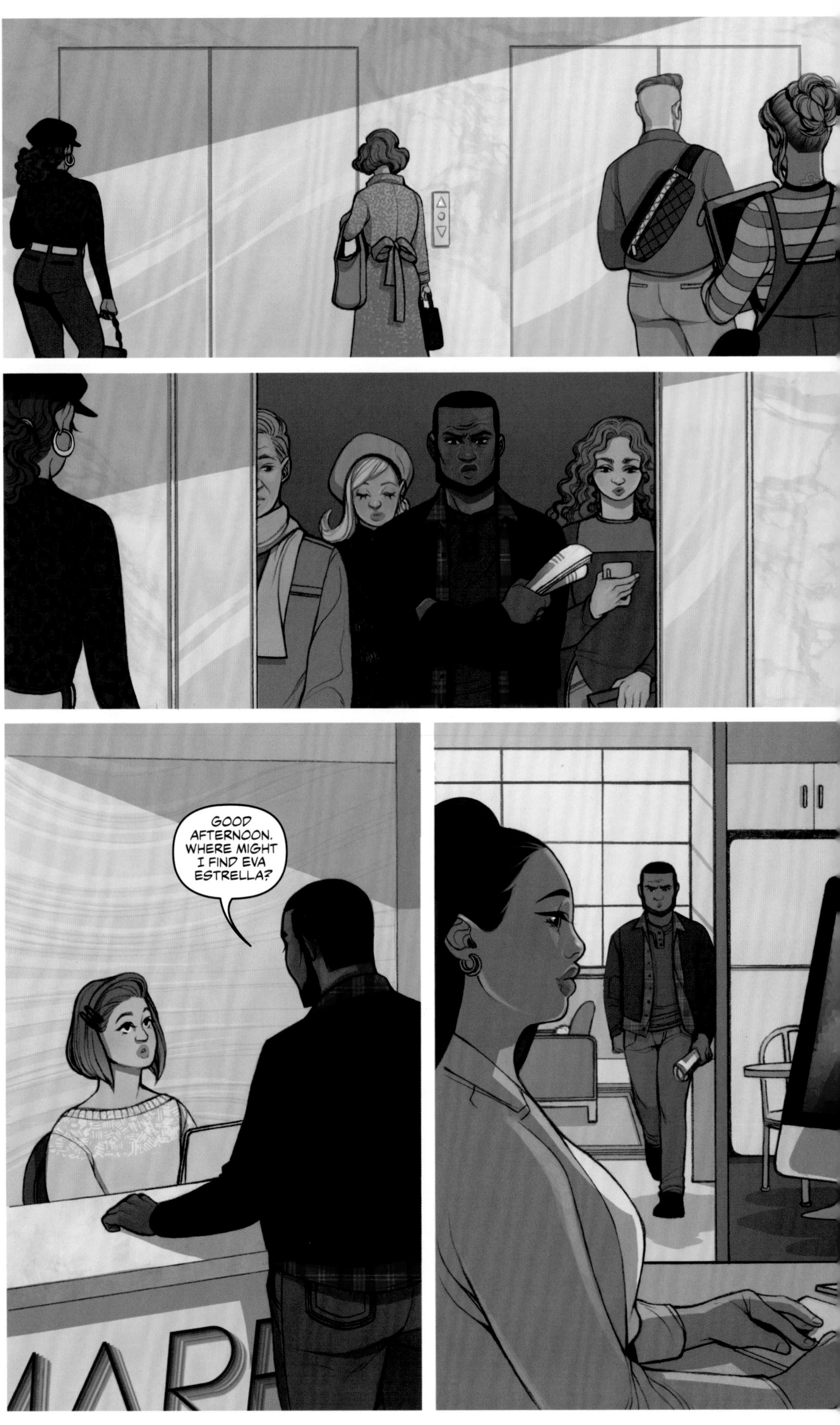
GOOD AFTERNOON. WHERE MIGHT I FIND EVA ESTRELLA?
MARA

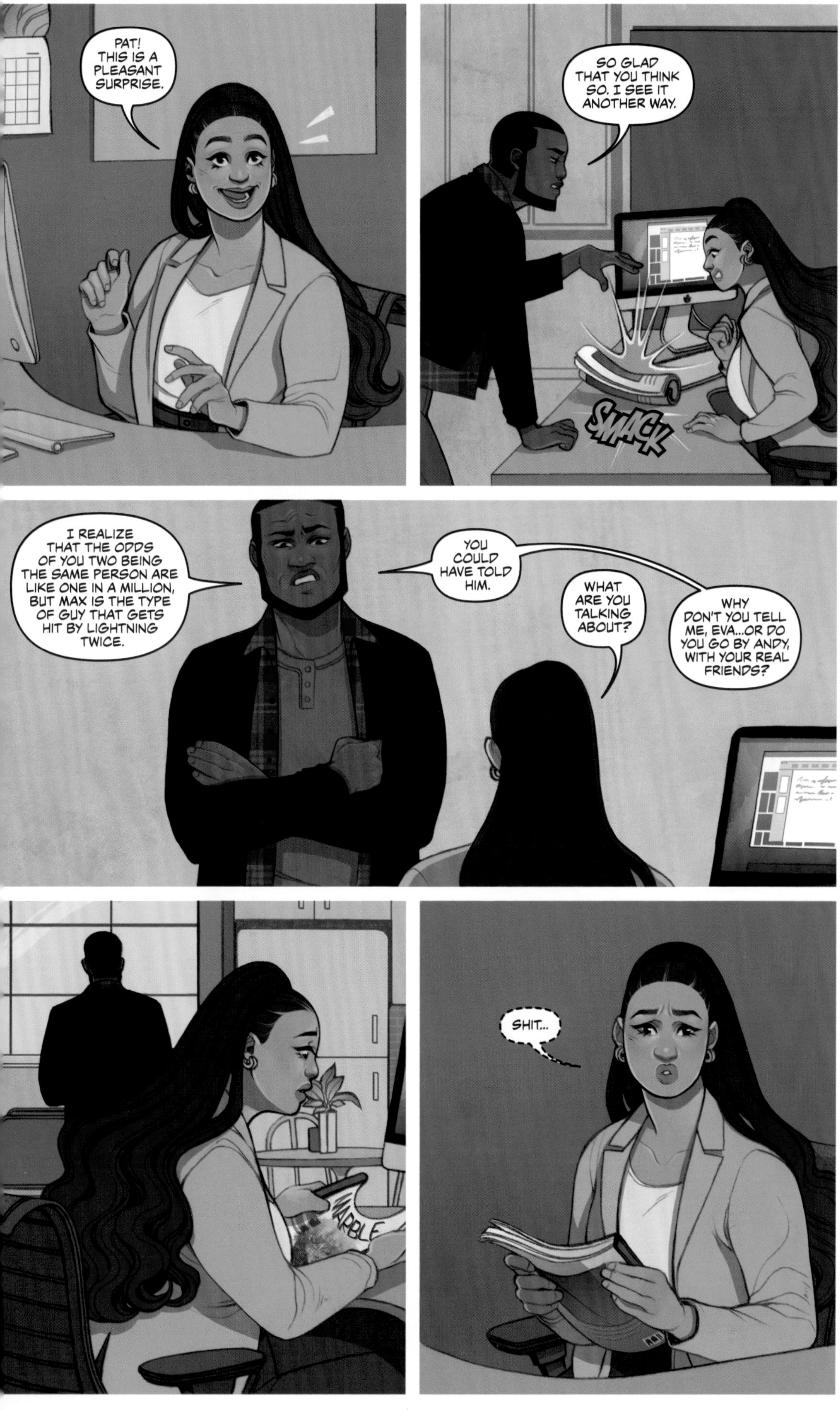
PAT! THIS IS A PLEASANT SURPRISE.
SO GLAD THAT YOU THINK SO. I SEE IT ANOTHER WAY.
SMACK
I REALIZE THAT THE ODDS OF YOU TWO BEING THE SAME PERSON ARE LIKE ONE IN A MILLION, BUT MAX IS THE TYPE OF GUY THAT GETS HIT BY LIGHTNING TWICE.
YOU COULD HAVE TOLD HIM.
WHAT ARE YOU TALKING ABOUT?
WHY DON'T YOU TELL ME, EVA...OR DO YOU GO BY ANDY, WITH YOUR REAL FRIENDS?
MARBLE
SHIT...

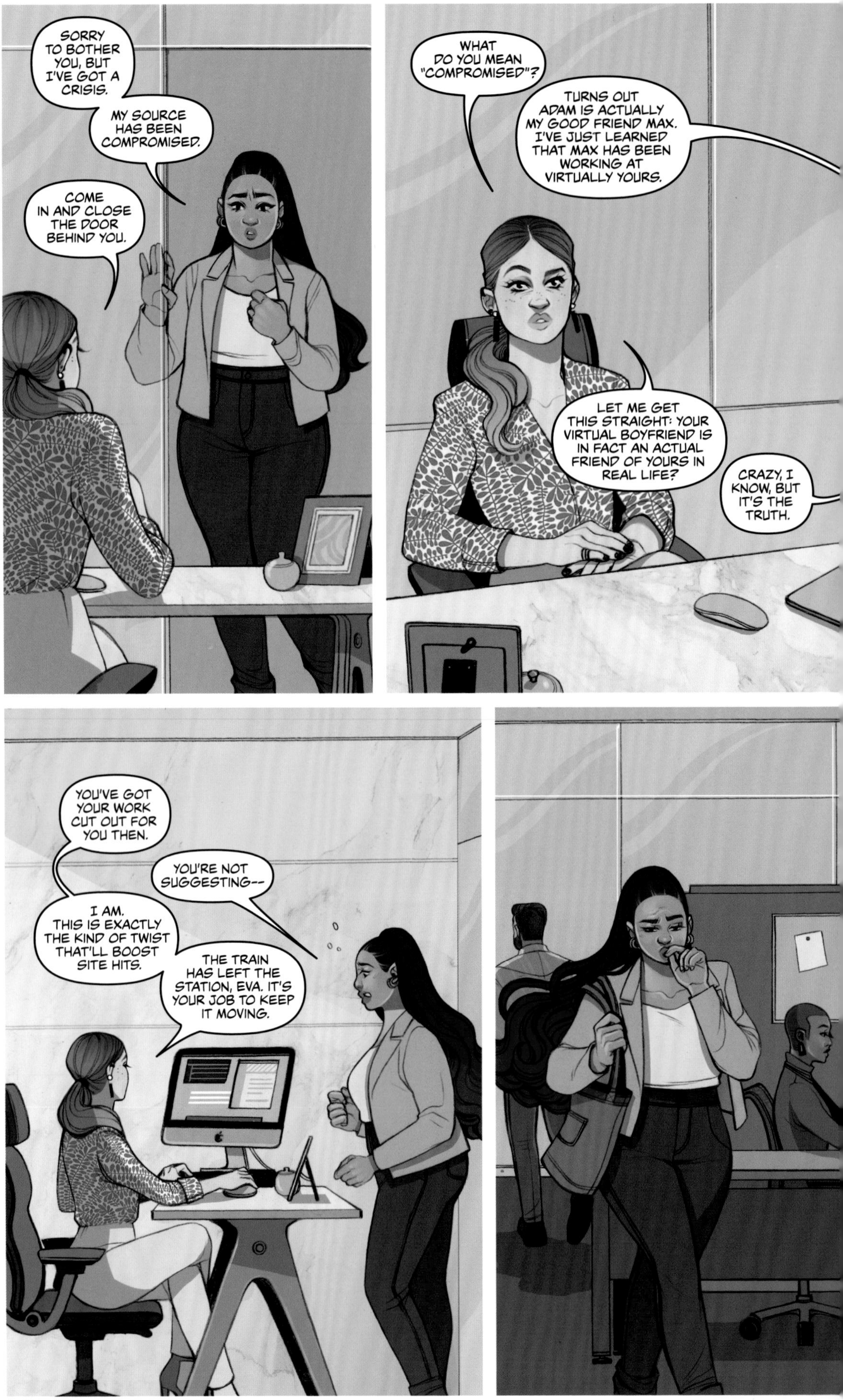
SORRY TO BOTHER YOU, BUT I'VE GOT A CRISIS.
MY SOURCE HAS BEEN COMPROMISED.
COME IN AND CLOSE THE DOOR BEHIND YOU.
WHAT DO YOU MEAN "COMPROMISED"?
TURNS OUT ADAM IS ACTUALLY MY GOOD FRIEND MAX. I'VE JUST LEARNED THAT MAX HAS BEEN WORKING AT VIRTUALLY YOURS.
LET ME GET THIS STRAIGHT: YOUR VIRTUAL BOYFRIEND IS IN FACT AN ACTUAL FRIEND OF YOURS IN REAL LIFE?
CRAZY, I KNOW, BUT IT'S THE TRUTH.
YOU'VE GOT YOUR WORK CUT OUT FOR YOU THEN.
YOU'RE NOT SUGGESTING--
I AM. THIS IS EXACTLY THE KIND OF TWIST THAT'LL BOOST SITE HITS.
THE TRAIN HAS LEFT THE STATION, EVA. IT'S YOUR JOB TO KEEP IT MOVING.

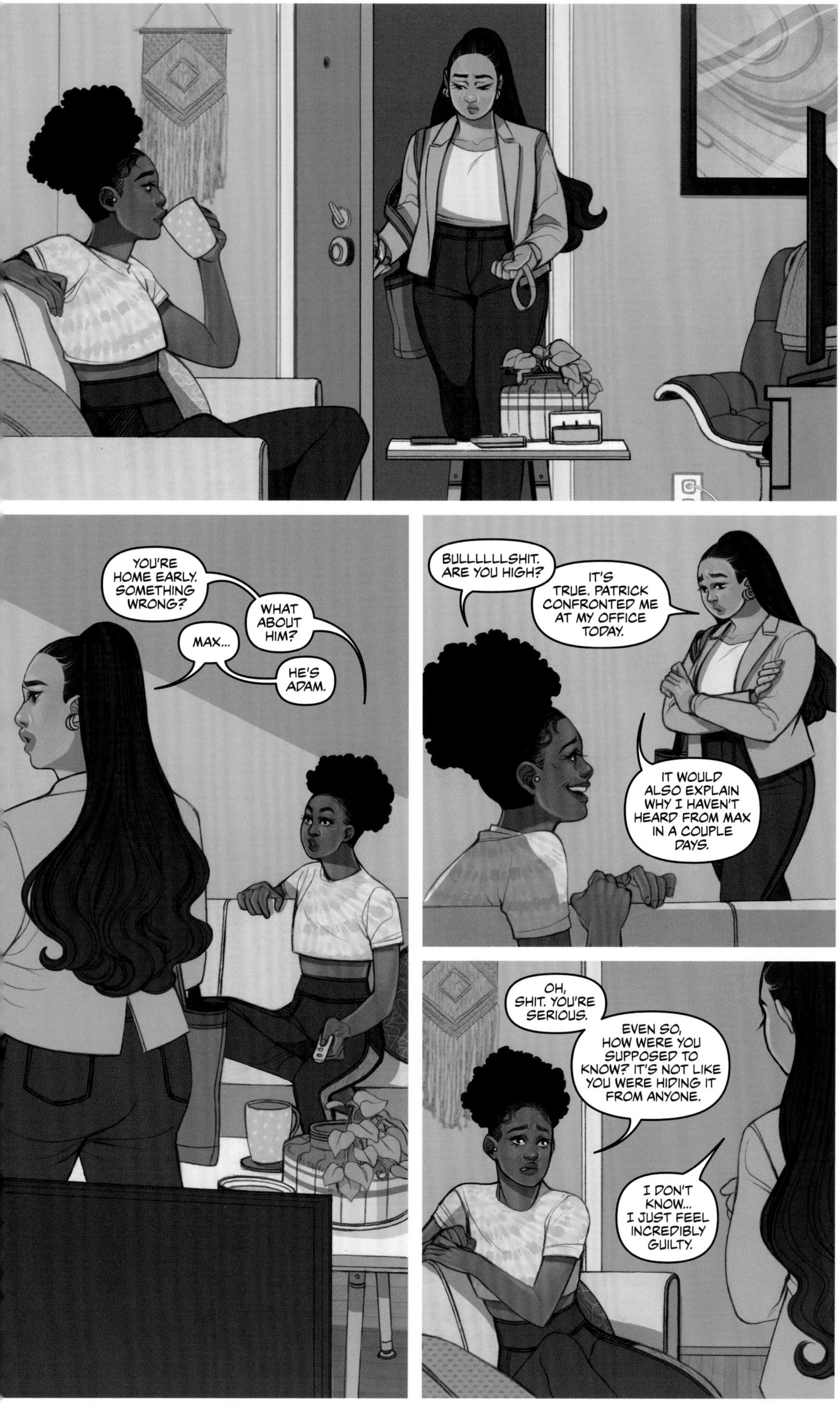
YOU'RE HOME EARLY. SOMETHING WRONG?
MAX...
WHAT ABOUT HIM?
HE'S ADAM.
BULLLLLLSHIT. ARE YOU HIGH?
IT'S TRUE. PATRICK CONFRONTED ME AT MY OFFICE TODAY.
IT WOULD ALSO EXPLAIN WHY I HAVEN'T HEARD FROM MAX IN A COUPLE DAYS.
OH, SHIT. YOU'RE SERIOUS.
EVEN SO, HOW WERE YOU SUPPOSED TO KNOW? IT'S NOT LIKE YOU WERE HIDING IT FROM ANYONE.
I DON'T KNOW... I JUST FEEL INCREDIBLY GUILTY.

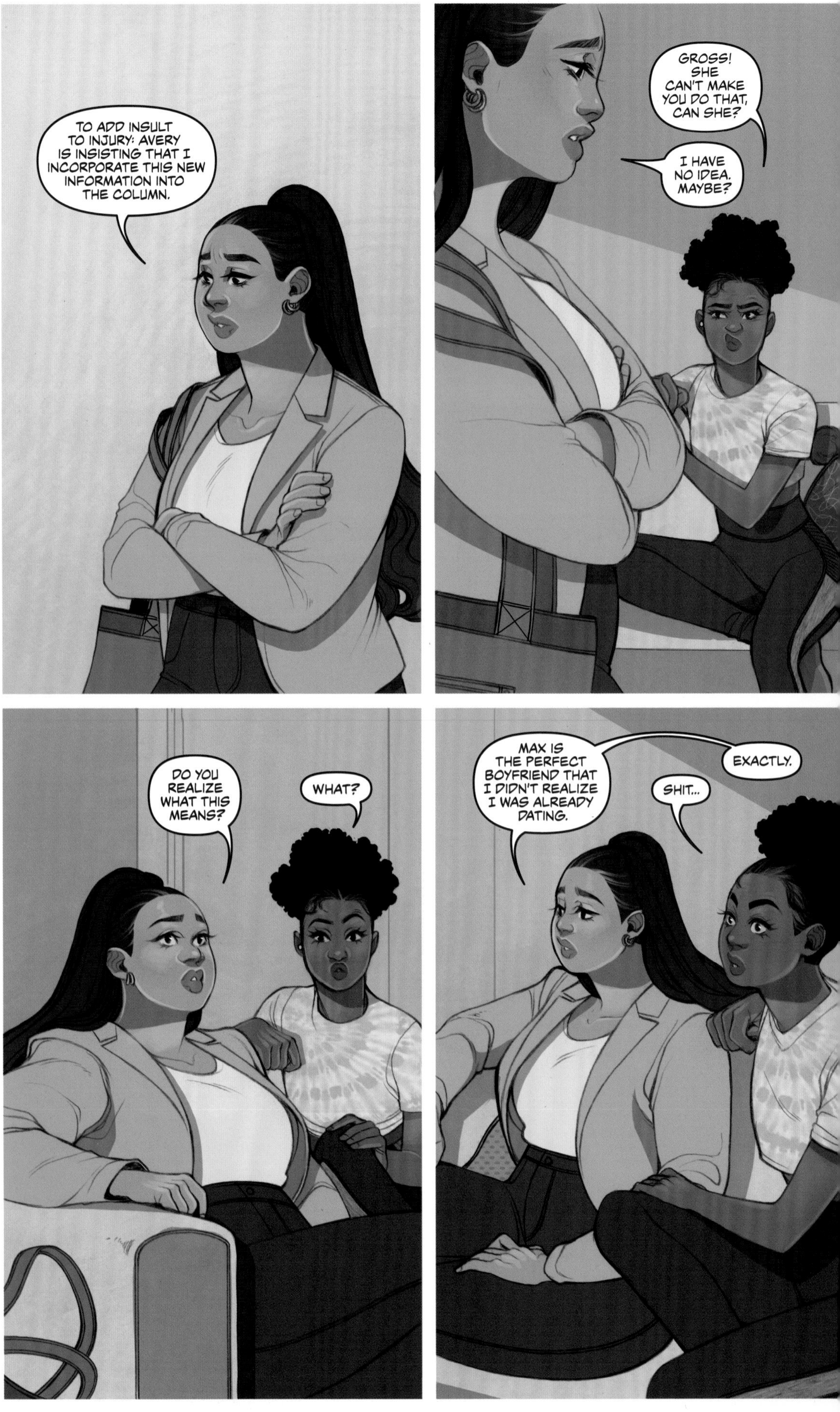
TO ADD INSULT TO INJURY: AVERY IS INSISTING THAT I INCORPORATE THIS NEW INFORMATION INTO THE COLUMN.
GROSS! SHE CAN'T MAKE YOU DO THAT, CAN SHE?
I HAVE NO IDEA. MAYBE?
DO YOU REALIZE WHAT THIS MEANS?
WHAT?
MAX IS THE PERFECT BOYFRIEND THAT I DIDN'T REALIZE I WAS ALREADY DATING.
SHIT...
EXACTLY.

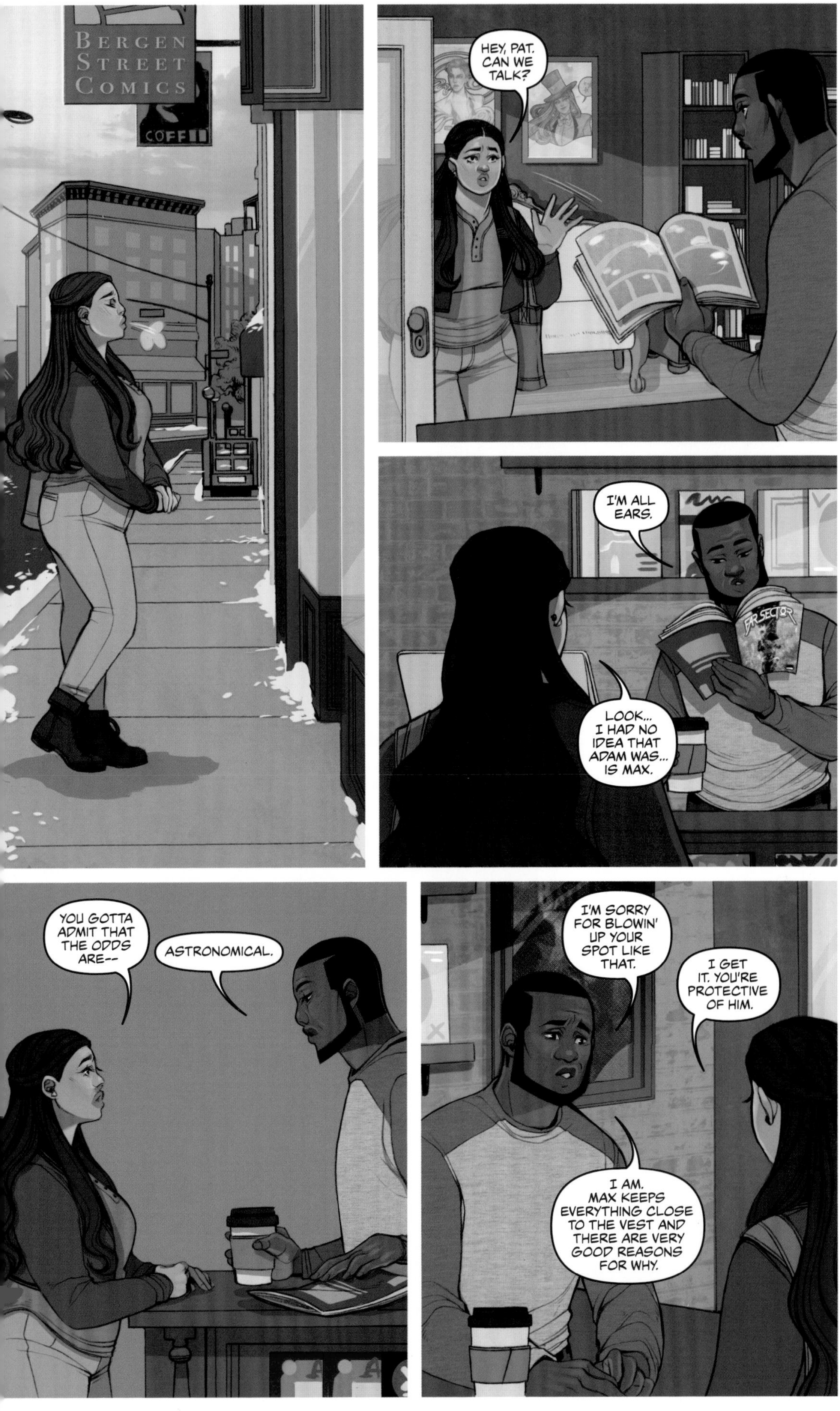
BERGEN STREET COMICS
COFF
HEY, PAT. CAN WE TALK?
I'M ALL EARS.
FAR SECTOR
LOOK... I HAD NO IDEA THAT ADAM WAS... IS MAX.
YOU GOTTA ADMIT THAT THE ODDS ARE--
ASTRONOMICAL.
I'M SORRY FOR BLOWIN' UP YOUR SPOT LIKE THAT.
I GET IT. YOU'RE PROTECTIVE OF HIM.
I AM. MAX KEEPS EVERYTHING CLOSE TO THE VEST AND THERE ARE VERY GOOD REASONS FOR WHY.

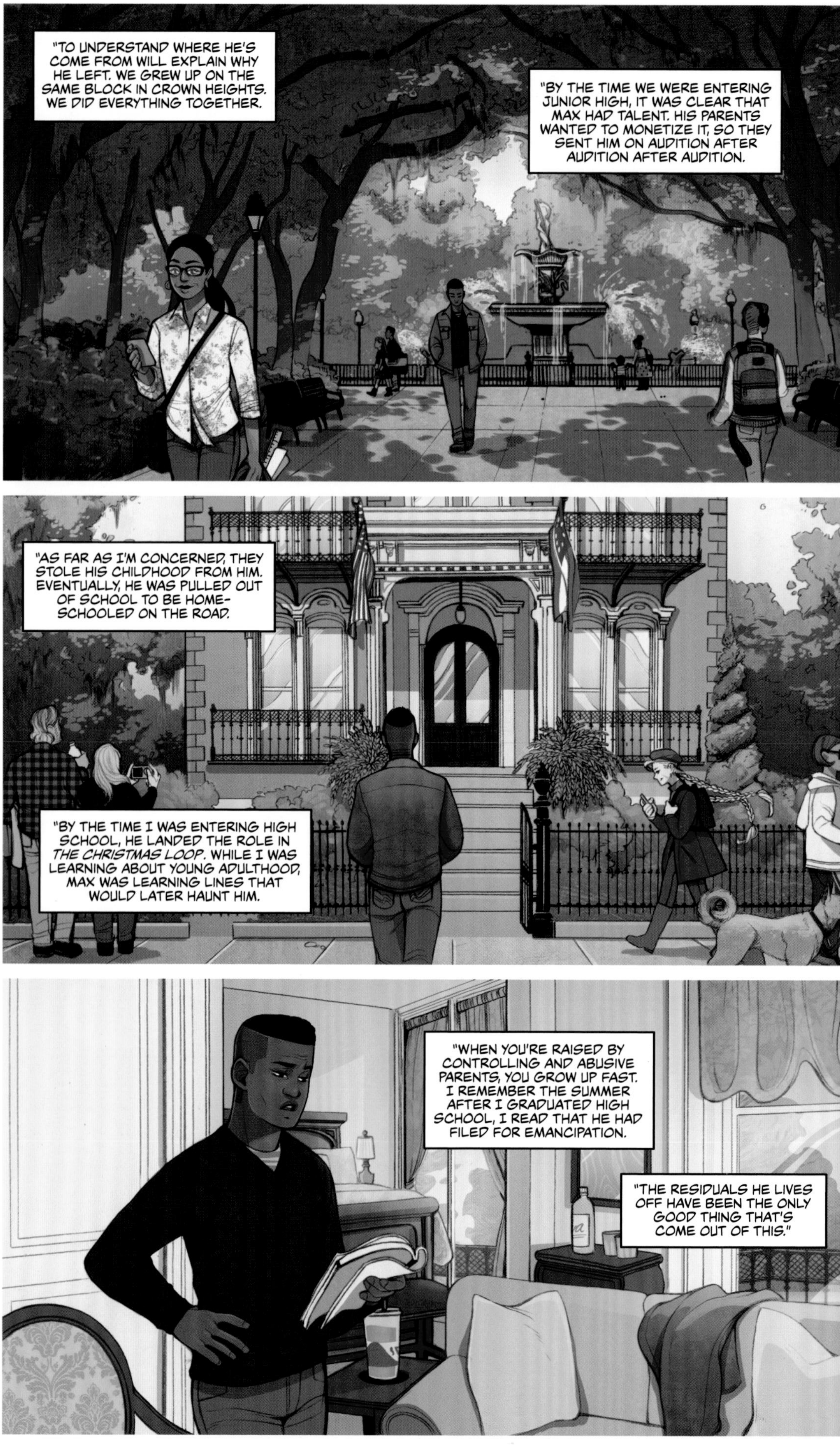
"TO UNDERSTAND WHERE HE'S COME FROM WILL EXPLAIN WHY HE LEFT. WE GREW UP ON THE SAME BLOCK IN CROWN HEIGHTS. WE DID EVERYTHING TOGETHER.
"BY THE TIME WE WERE ENTERING JUNIOR HIGH, IT WAS CLEAR THAT MAX HAD TALENT. HIS PARENTS WANTED TO MONETIZE IT, SO THEY SENT HIM ON AUDITION AFTER AUDITION AFTER AUDITION.
"AS FAR AS I'M CONCERNED, THEY STOLE HIS CHILDHOOD FROM HIM. EVENTUALLY, HE WAS PULLED OUT OF SCHOOL TO BE HOME-SCHOOLED ON THE ROAD.
"BY THE TIME I WAS ENTERING HIGH SCHOOL, HE LANDED THE ROLE IN *THE CHRISTMAS LOOP*. WHILE I WAS LEARNING ABOUT YOUNG ADULTHOOD, MAX WAS LEARNING LINES THAT WOULD LATER HAUNT HIM.
"WHEN YOU'RE RAISED BY CONTROLLING AND ABUSIVE PARENTS, YOU GROW UP FAST. I REMEMBER THE SUMMER AFTER I GRADUATED HIGH SCHOOL, I READ THAT HE HAD FILED FOR EMANCIPATION.
"THE RESIDUALS HE LIVES OFF HAVE BEEN THE ONLY GOOD THING THAT'S COME OUT OF THIS."

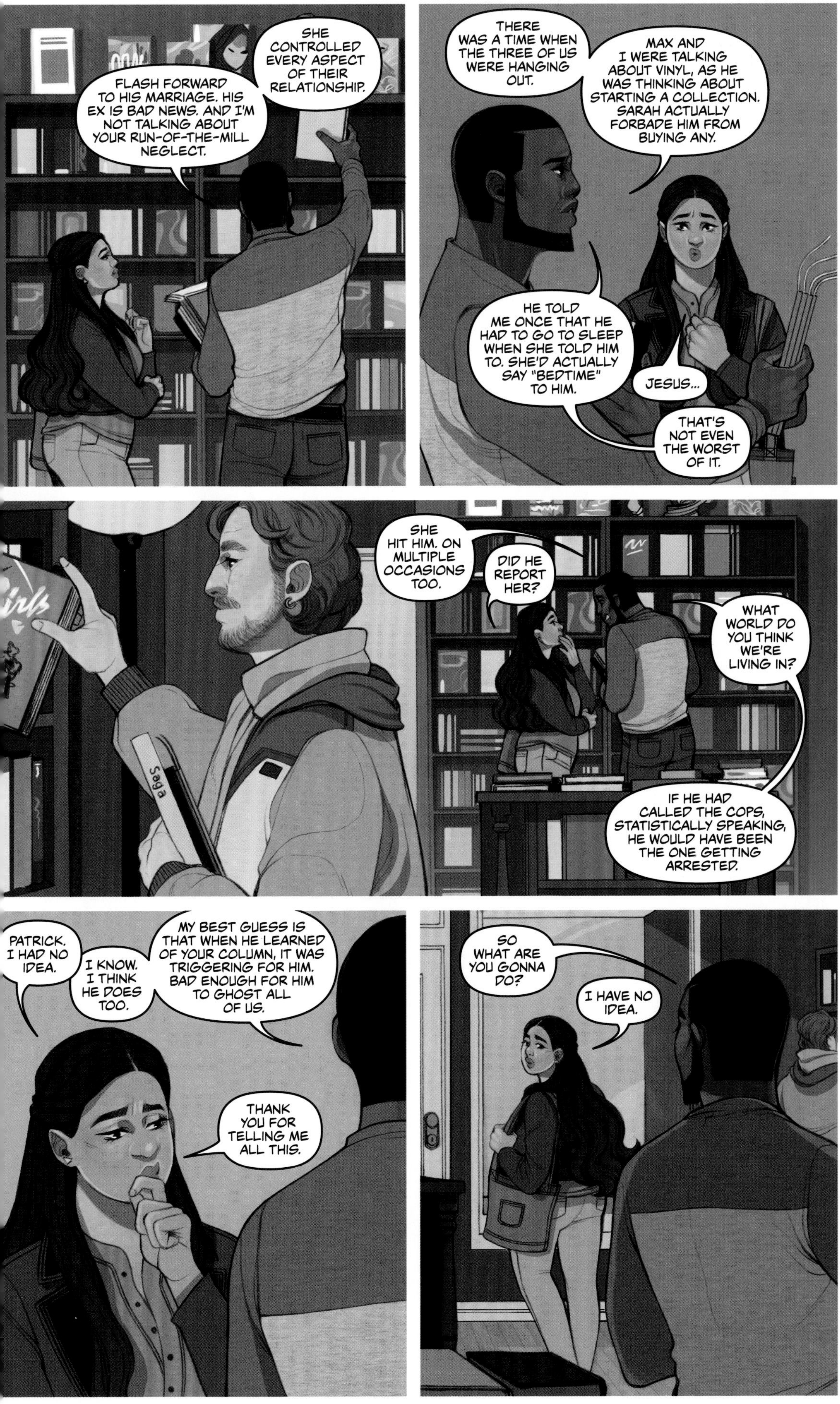
FLASH FORWARD TO HIS MARRIAGE. HIS EX IS BAD NEWS. AND I'M NOT TALKING ABOUT YOUR RUN-OF-THE-MILL NEGLECT.
SHE CONTROLLED EVERY ASPECT OF THEIR RELATIONSHIP.
THERE WAS A TIME WHEN THE THREE OF US WERE HANGING OUT.
MAX AND I WERE TALKING ABOUT VINYL, AS HE WAS THINKING ABOUT STARTING A COLLECTION. SARAH ACTUALLY FORBADE HIM FROM BUYING ANY.
HE TOLD ME ONCE THAT HE HAD TO GO TO SLEEP WHEN SHE TOLD HIM TO. SHE'D ACTUALLY SAY "BEDTIME" TO HIM.
JESUS...
THAT'S NOT EVEN THE WORST OF IT.
Saga
SHE HIT HIM. ON MULTIPLE OCCASIONS TOO.
DID HE REPORT HER?
WHAT WORLD DO YOU THINK WE'RE LIVING IN?
IF HE HAD CALLED THE COPS, STATISTICALLY SPEAKING, HE WOULD HAVE BEEN THE ONE GETTING ARRESTED.
PATRICK. I HAD NO IDEA.
I KNOW. I THINK HE DOES TOO.
MY BEST GUESS IS THAT WHEN HE LEARNED OF YOUR COLUMN, IT WAS TRIGGERING FOR HIM. BAD ENOUGH FOR HIM TO GHOST ALL OF US.
THANK YOU FOR TELLING ME ALL THIS.
SO WHAT ARE YOU GONNA DO?
I HAVE NO IDEA.

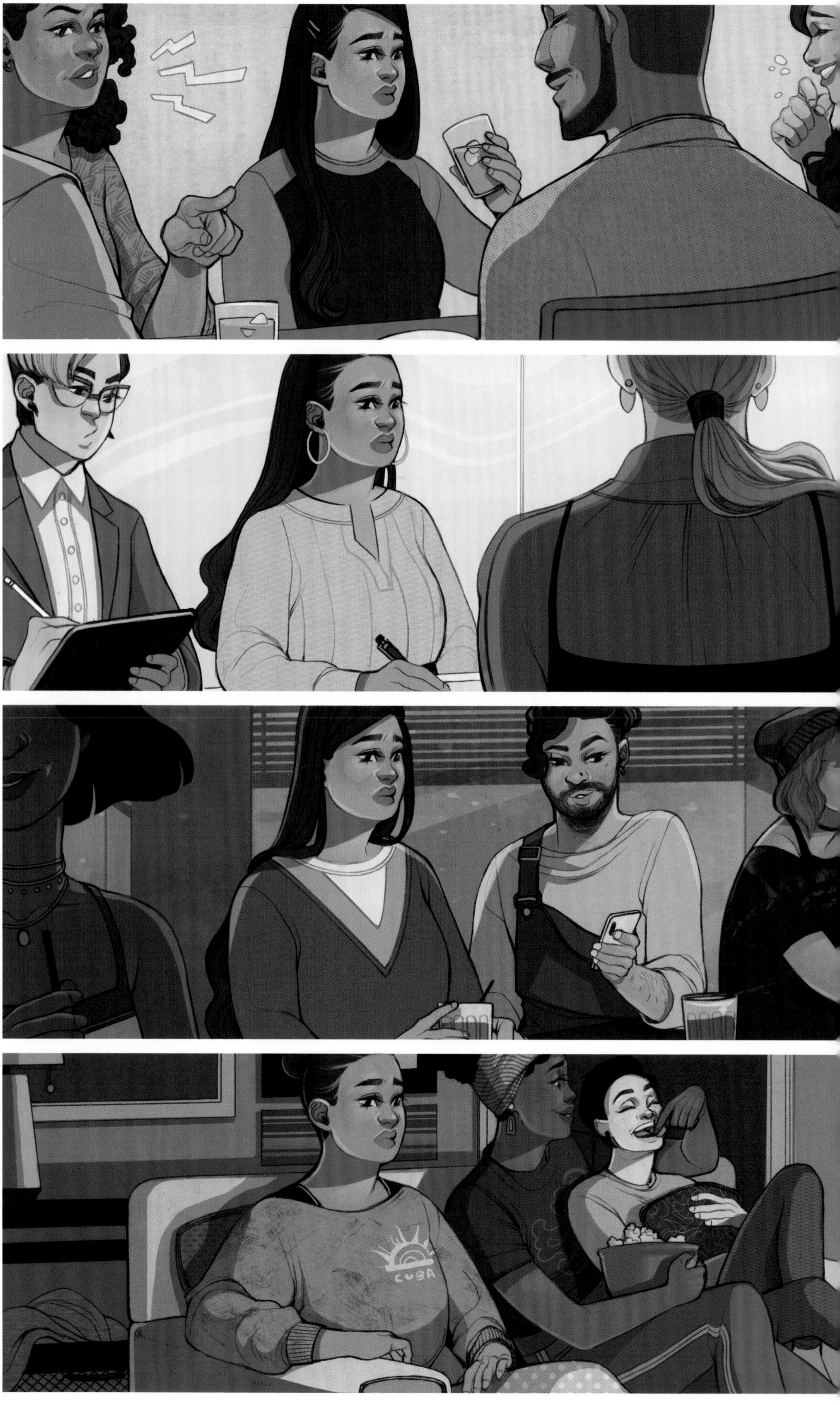
CUBA

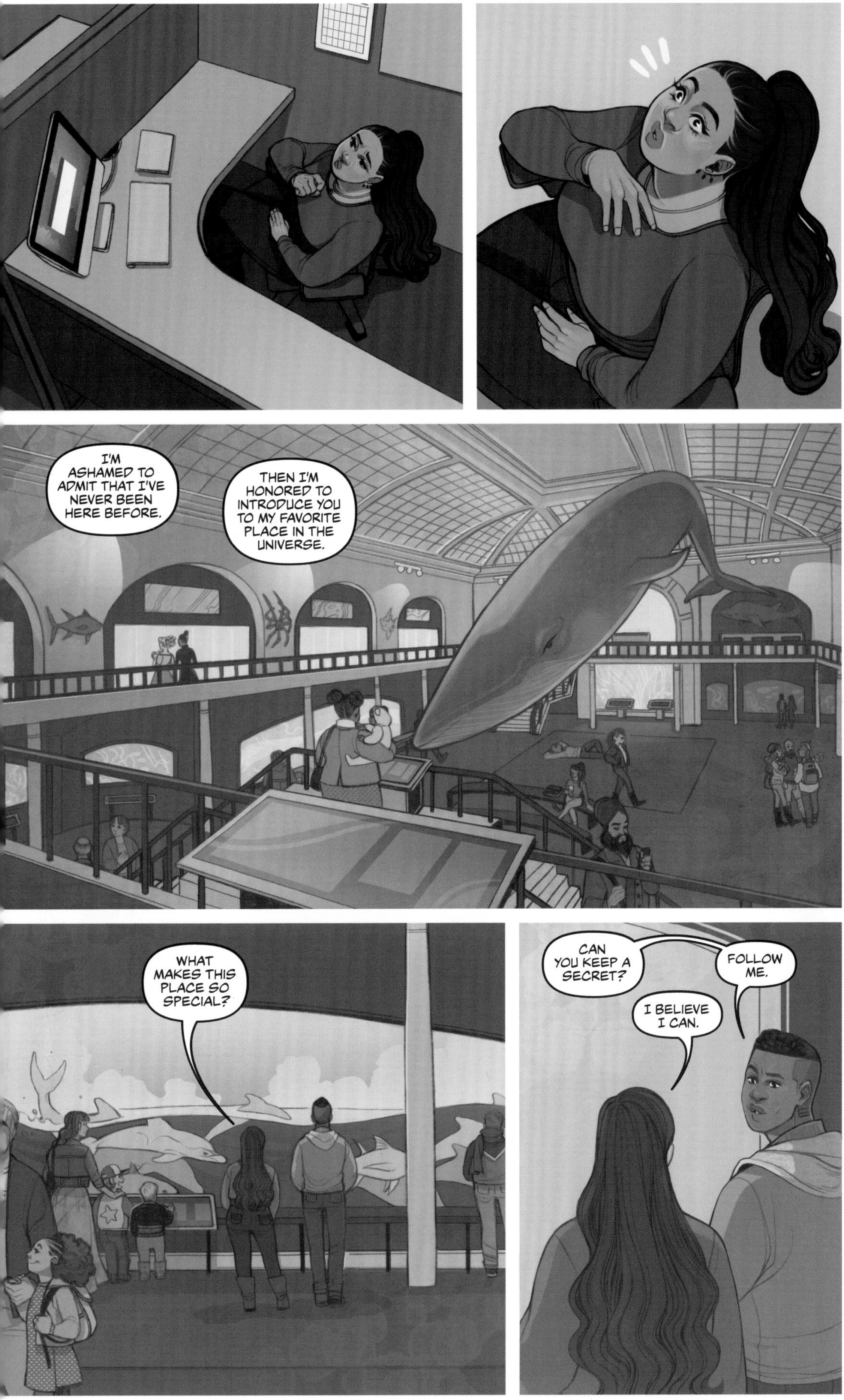
I'M ASHAMED TO ADMIT THAT I'VE NEVER BEEN HERE BEFORE.
THEN I'M HONORED TO INTRODUCE YOU TO MY FAVORITE PLACE IN THE UNIVERSE.
WHAT MAKES THIS PLACE SO SPECIAL?
CAN YOU KEEP A SECRET?
I BELIEVE I CAN.
FOLLOW ME.

THIS IS WHY. IT'S THE EARLIEST MEMORY I HAVE FROM MY CHILDHOOD.

REALLY? WHY THIS?

I DON'T KNOW. I THINK THE FEAR I FELT FROM THE GIANT SQUID LEFT ITS MARK.

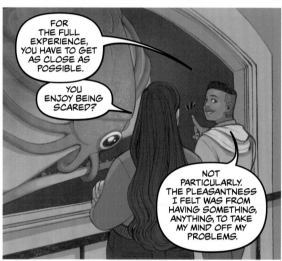

FOR THE FULL EXPERIENCE, YOU HAVE TO GET AS CLOSE AS POSSIBLE.

YOU ENJOY BEING SCARED?

NOT PARTICULARLY. THE PLEASANTNESS I FELT WAS FROM HAVING SOMETHING, ANYTHING, TO TAKE MY MIND OFF MY PROBLEMS.

AFTER MY FIRST VISIT, I PLEADED WITH MY PARENTS TO TAKE ME BACK, BUT THEY NEVER DID.

I GUESS I'VE CARRIED THE FEELING THIS GIANT SQUID GAVE ME ALL THOSE YEARS AGO.

IN A WAY, IT WAS A FRIEND WHEN I NEEDED ONE THE MOST.

WOW, SORRY. THAT TOOK A SAD TURN.

I DON'T THINK SO. I THINK IT'S A REALLY SWEET THOUGHT.

FUN FACT: THIS IS THE ONLY LARGE-SCALE DIORAMA IN THIS HALL THAT IS NOT BEHIND GLASS.

I LIKE TO THINK IT WAS DONE INTENTIONALLY TO HEIGHTEN THE TERROR OF THE GIANT SQUID REACHING OUT AT ANY MOMENT...

AND PULLING YOU DOWN WITH IT!

OH MY GOD!

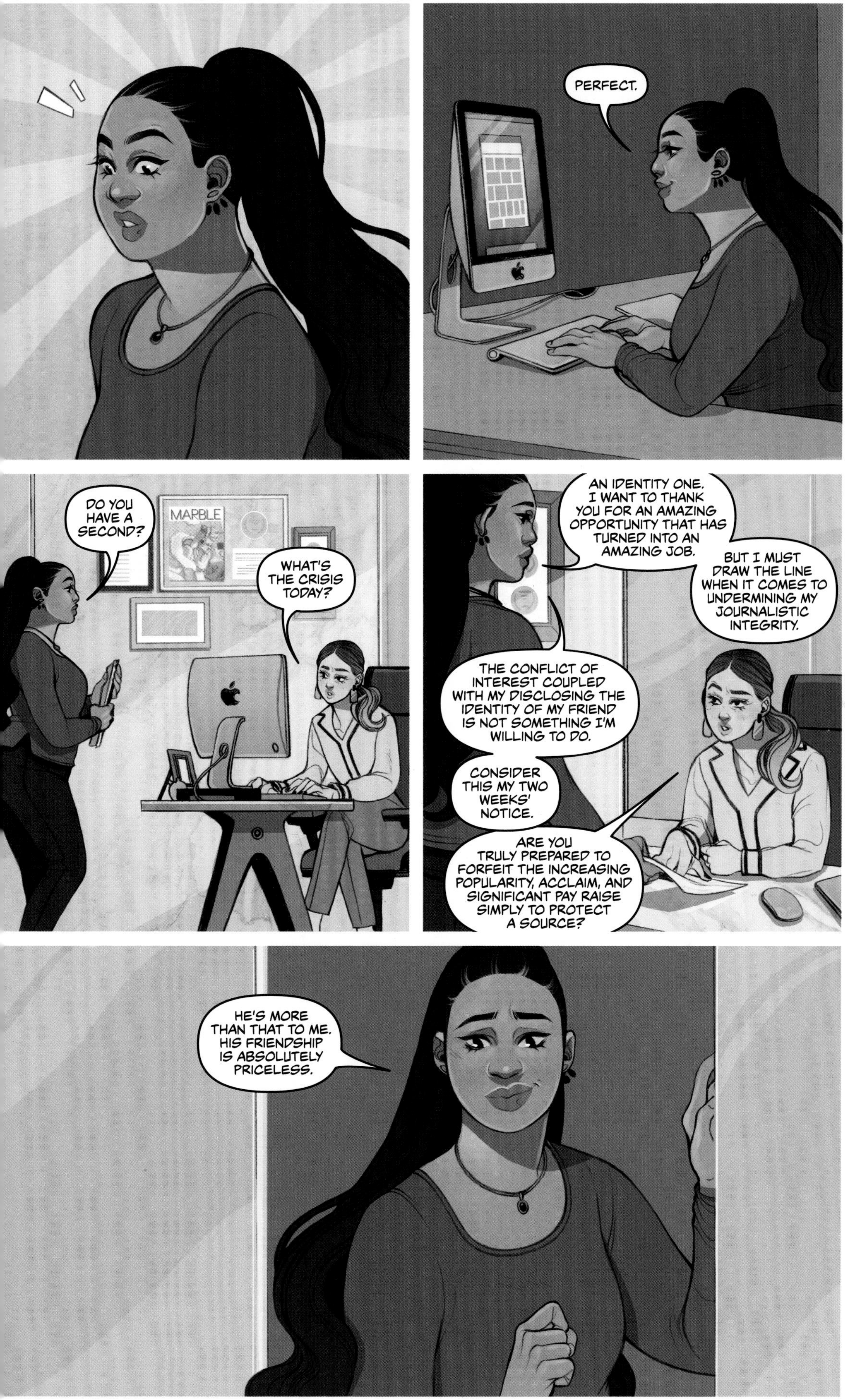
PERFECT.
DO YOU HAVE A SECOND?
WHAT'S THE CRISIS TODAY?
AN IDENTITY ONE. I WANT TO THANK YOU FOR AN AMAZING OPPORTUNITY THAT HAS TURNED INTO AN AMAZING JOB.
BUT I MUST DRAW THE LINE WHEN IT COMES TO UNDERMINING MY JOURNALISTIC INTEGRITY.
THE CONFLICT OF INTEREST COUPLED WITH MY DISCLOSING THE IDENTITY OF MY FRIEND IS NOT SOMETHING I'M WILLING TO DO.
CONSIDER THIS MY TWO WEEKS' NOTICE.
ARE YOU TRULY PREPARED TO FORFEIT THE INCREASING POPULARITY, ACCLAIM, AND SIGNIFICANT PAY RAISE SIMPLY TO PROTECT A SOURCE?
HE'S MORE THAN THAT TO ME. HIS FRIENDSHIP IS ABSOLUTELY PRICELESS.

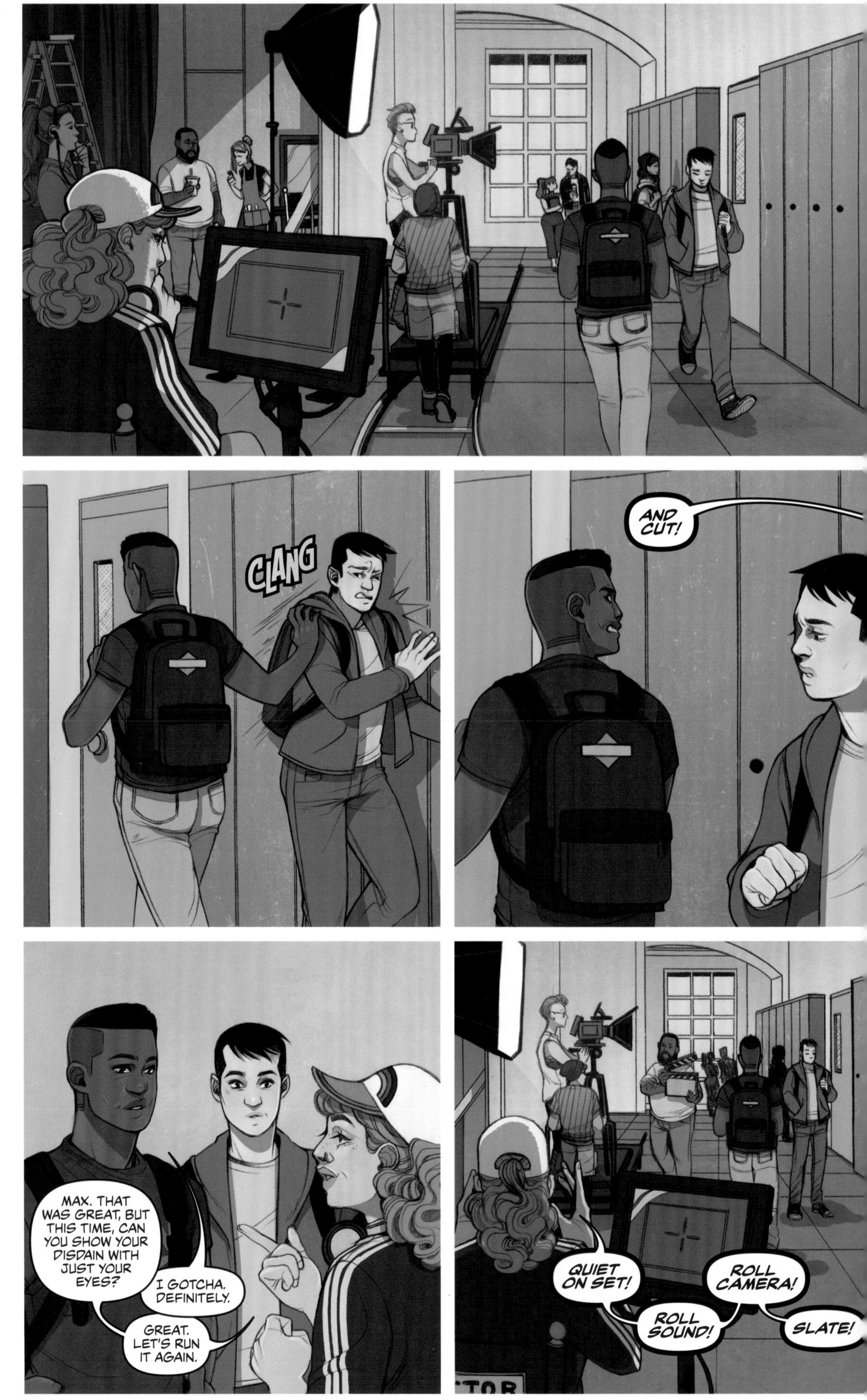
CLANG
AND CUT!
MAX. THAT WAS GREAT, BUT THIS TIME, CAN YOU SHOW YOUR DISDAIN WITH JUST YOUR EYES?
I GOTCHA. DEFINITELY.
GREAT. LET'S RUN IT AGAIN.
QUIET ON SET!
ROLL SOUND!
ROLL CAMERA!
SLATE!

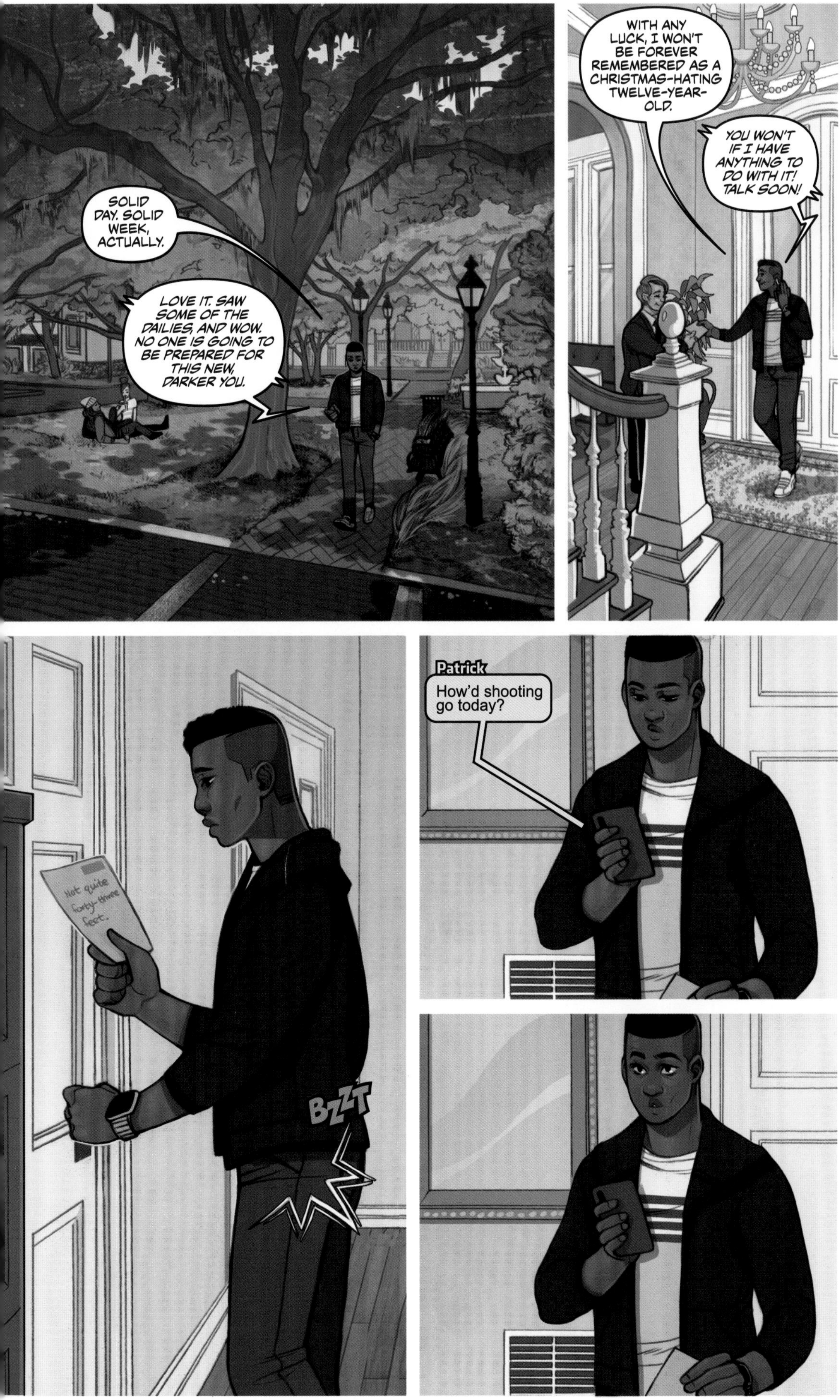
SOLID DAY. SOLID WEEK, ACTUALLY.
LOVE IT. SAW SOME OF THE DAILIES, AND WOW. NO ONE IS GOING TO BE PREPARED FOR THIS NEW, DARKER YOU.
WITH ANY LUCK, I WON'T BE FOREVER REMEMBERED AS A CHRISTMAS-HATING TWELVE-YEAR-OLD.
YOU WON'T IF I HAVE ANYTHING TO DO WITH IT! TALK SOON!
Not quite forty-three feet.
BZZT
Patrick
How'd shooting go today?

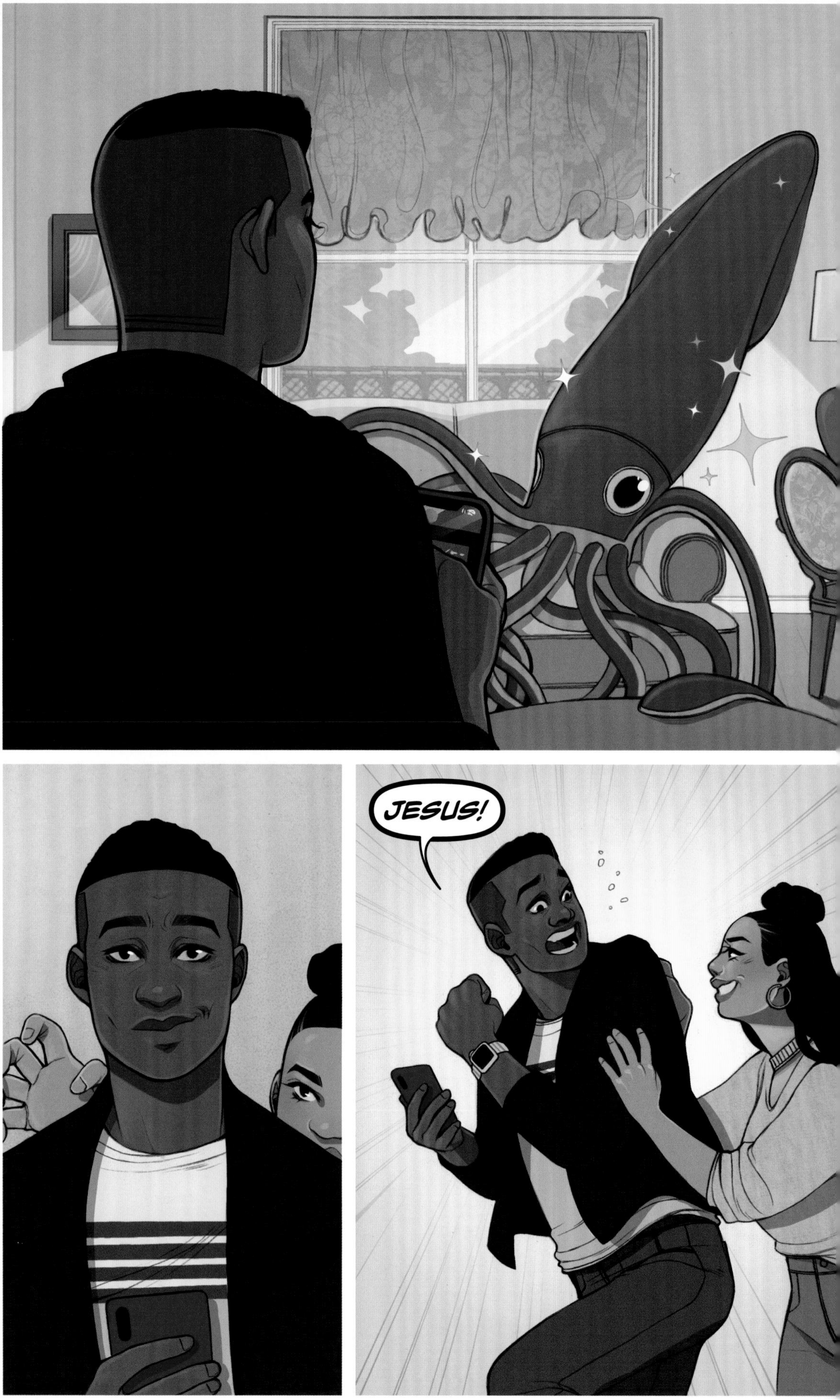
JESUS!

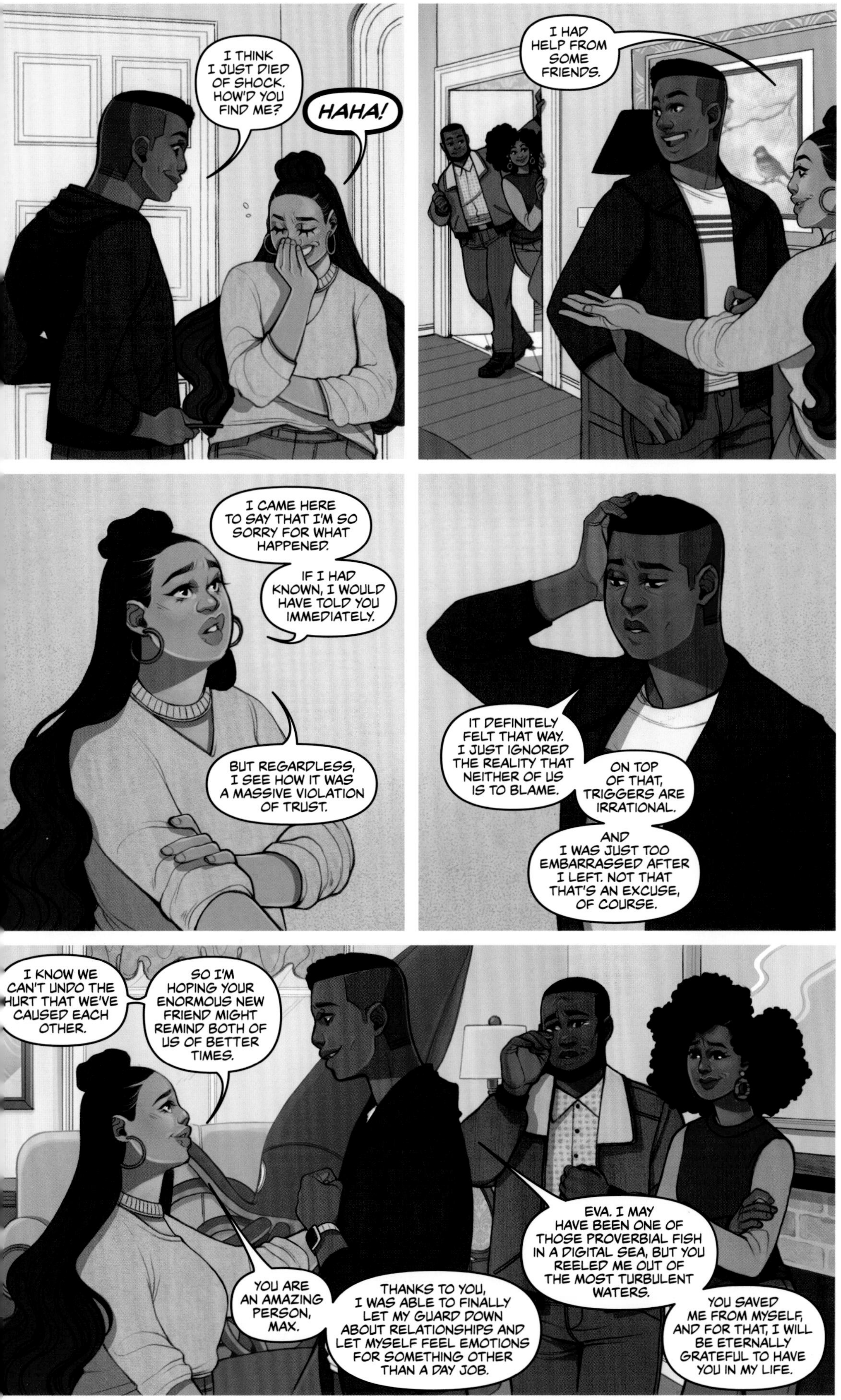
I THINK I JUST DIED OF SHOCK. HOW'D YOU FIND ME?
HAHA!
I HAD HELP FROM SOME FRIENDS.
I CAME HERE TO SAY THAT I'M SO SORRY FOR WHAT HAPPENED.
IF I HAD KNOWN, I WOULD HAVE TOLD YOU IMMEDIATELY.
BUT REGARDLESS, I SEE HOW IT WAS A MASSIVE VIOLATION OF TRUST.
IT DEFINITELY FELT THAT WAY. I JUST IGNORED THE REALITY THAT NEITHER OF US IS TO BLAME.
ON TOP OF THAT, TRIGGERS ARE IRRATIONAL.
AND I WAS JUST TOO EMBARRASSED AFTER I LEFT. NOT THAT THAT'S AN EXCUSE, OF COURSE.
I KNOW WE CAN'T UNDO THE HURT THAT WE'VE CAUSED EACH OTHER.
SO I'M HOPING YOUR ENORMOUS NEW FRIEND MIGHT REMIND BOTH OF US OF BETTER TIMES.
YOU ARE AN AMAZING PERSON, MAX.
THANKS TO YOU, I WAS ABLE TO FINALLY LET MY GUARD DOWN ABOUT RELATIONSHIPS AND LET MYSELF FEEL EMOTIONS FOR SOMETHING OTHER THAN A DAY JOB.
EVA. I MAY HAVE BEEN ONE OF THOSE PROVERBIAL FISH IN A DIGITAL SEA, BUT YOU REELED ME OUT OF THE MOST TURBULENT WATERS.
YOU SAVED ME FROM MYSELF, AND FOR THAT, I WILL BE ETERNALLY GRATEFUL TO HAVE YOU IN MY LIFE.

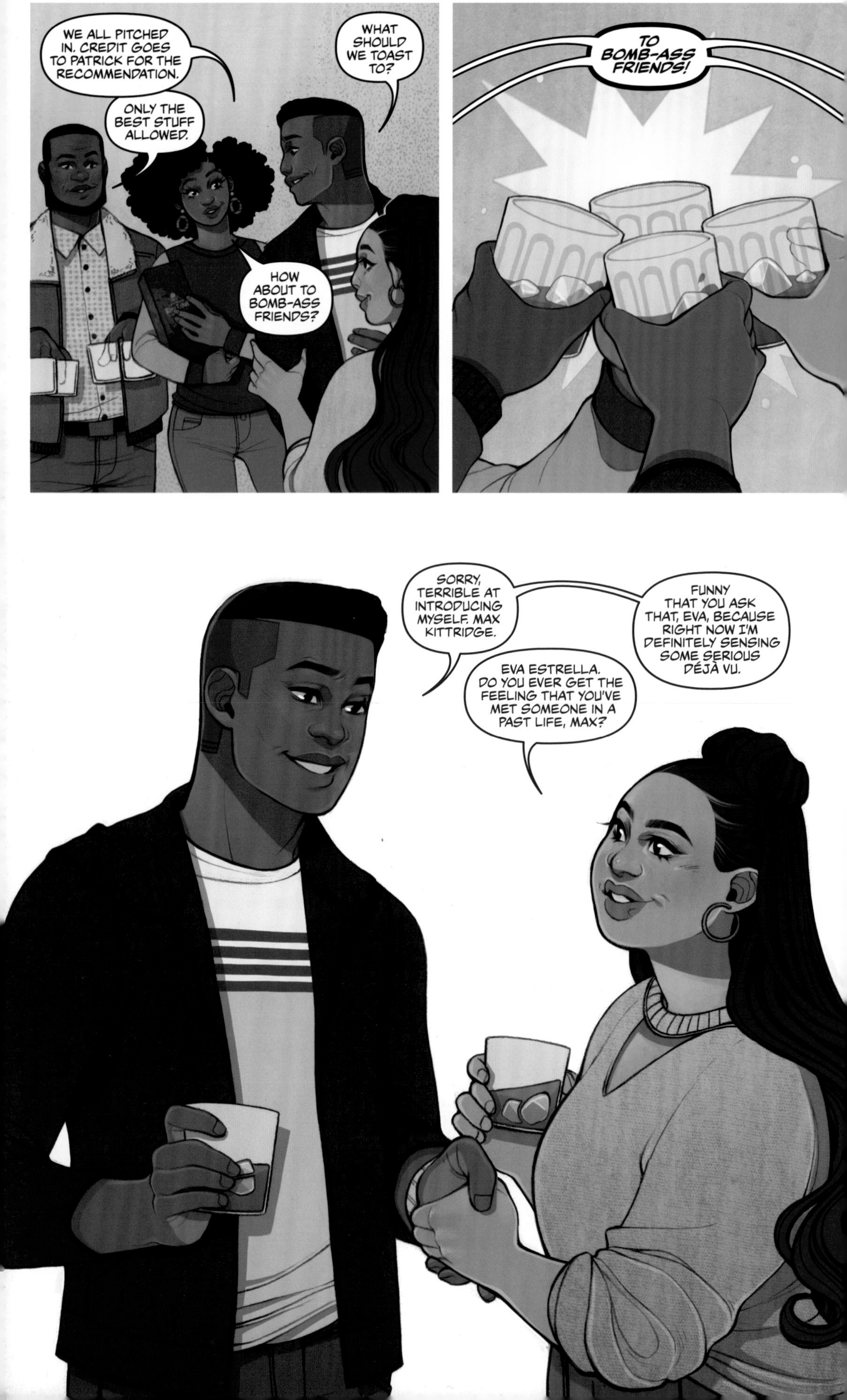

WE ALL PITCHED IN. CREDIT GOES TO PATRICK FOR THE RECOMMENDATION.
ONLY THE BEST STUFF ALLOWED.
WHAT SHOULD WE TOAST TO?
HOW ABOUT TO BOMB-ASS FRIENDS?
TO BOMB-ASS FRIENDS!
SORRY, TERRIBLE AT INTRODUCING MYSELF. MAX KITTRIDGE.
EVA ESTRELLA. DO YOU EVER GET THE FEELING THAT YOU'VE MET SOMEONE IN A PAST LIFE, MAX?
FUNNY THAT YOU ASK THAT, EVA, BECAUSE RIGHT NOW I'M DEFINITELY SENSING SOME SERIOUS DÉJÀ VU.

PAGE TWELVE
(four panels)

12.1) Without prompt, Katie starts making a rum and coke for Eva.

1. EVA: That's debatable. Oh and get this: Izzy signed me up on a dating app…

2. EVA: Sort of.

3. KATIE: And the plot thickens. Phone. Now.

12.2) While Eva sips her drink, Katie looks impressed by Virtually Yours' service. Eva remains skeptical.

4. EVA: I'd hate my sister if she wasn't so damn thoughtful all the time.

5. KATIE: Have you looked through this? It's kinda impressive.

6. EVA: It's totally pointless. What happens when my friends and family eventually want to meet this theoretical guy?

12.3) Katie shrugs. Eva contemplates her advice.

7. KATIE: Easy. Just say you two broke up. That shit happens every day.

8. KATIE: Wait a week, and select your next fake boyfriend. It's kinda brilliant actually.

12.4) Eva rests her face in one hand while she twirls the straw around her drink with the other. Katie is still looking at Eva's phone.

9. EVA: Shit…I hadn't thought of that.

10. KATIE: Of course not. You don't date.

11. KATIE: Your sister…your sexy, radiant—

12. EVA: Stop.

13. KATIE: She's right. This is your Get-Out-of-Jail-Free card.

14. KATIE: Now let's break you out of that prison you call your parent's house, and find you some theoretical strange.

LAYOUTS

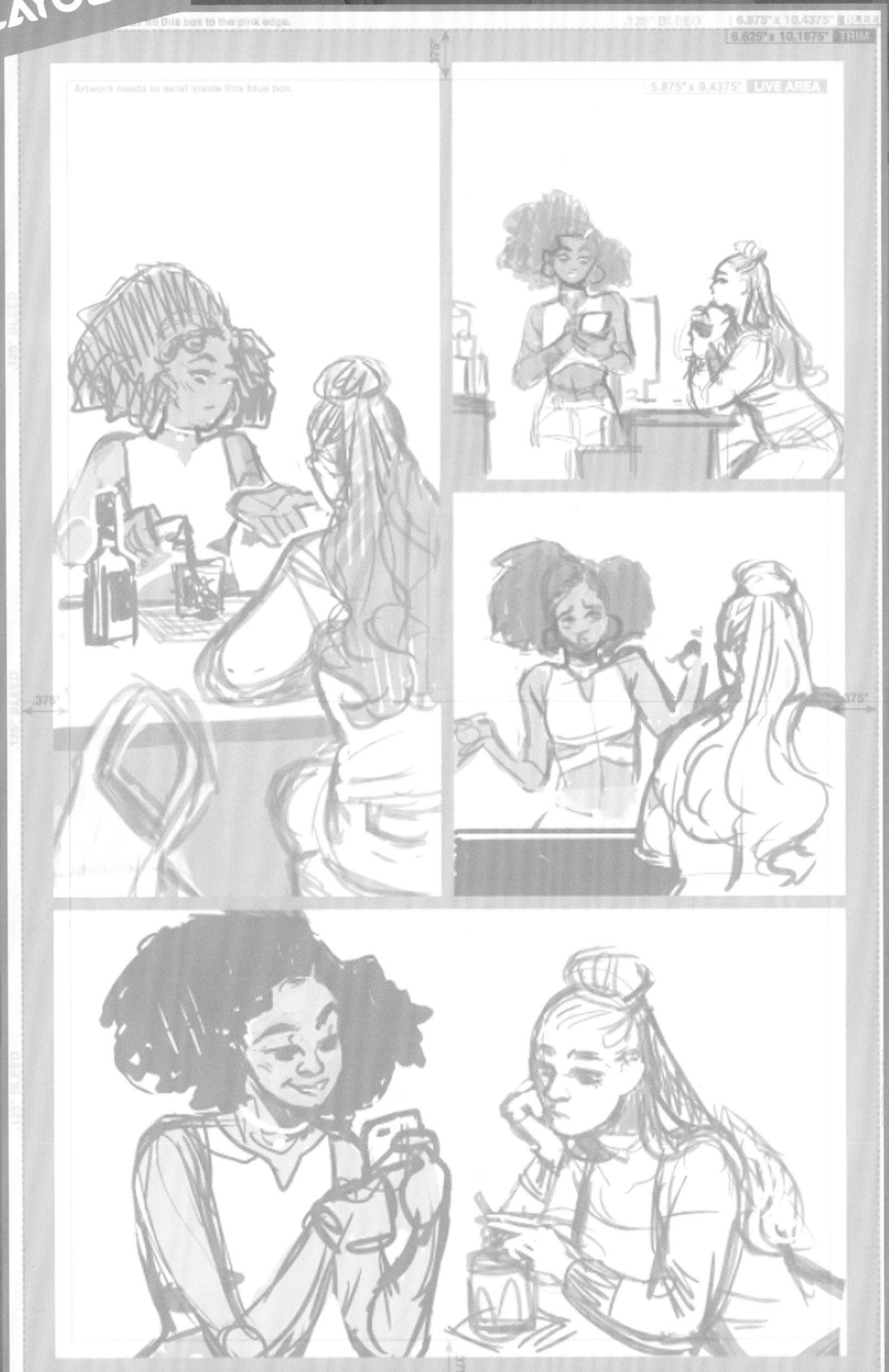

6.875" x 10.4375" BLEED
6.625" x 10.1875" TRIM
Artwork needs to exist inside this blue box.
5.875" x 9.4375" LIVE AREA
.125" BLEED
.375"

INKS

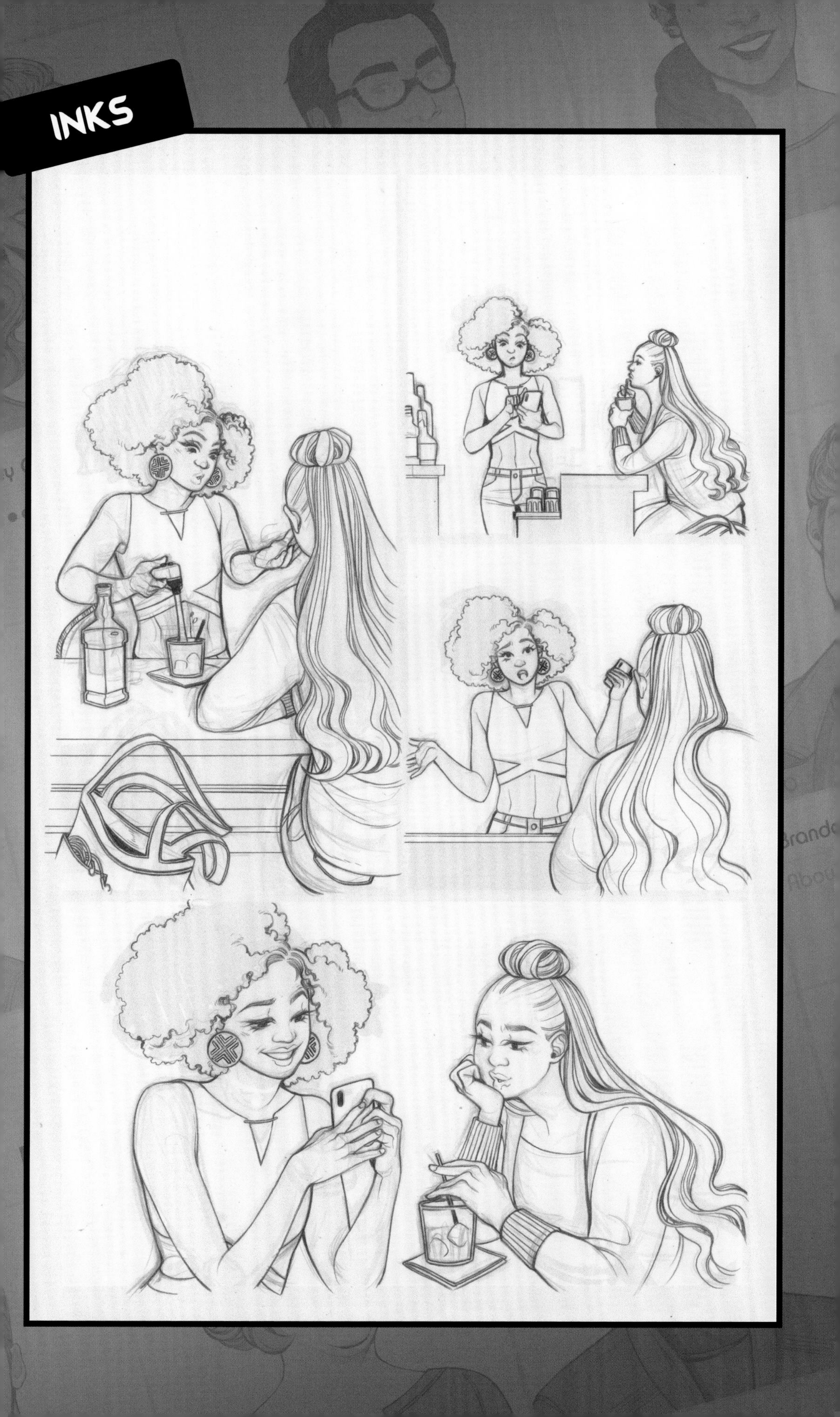

FLATS

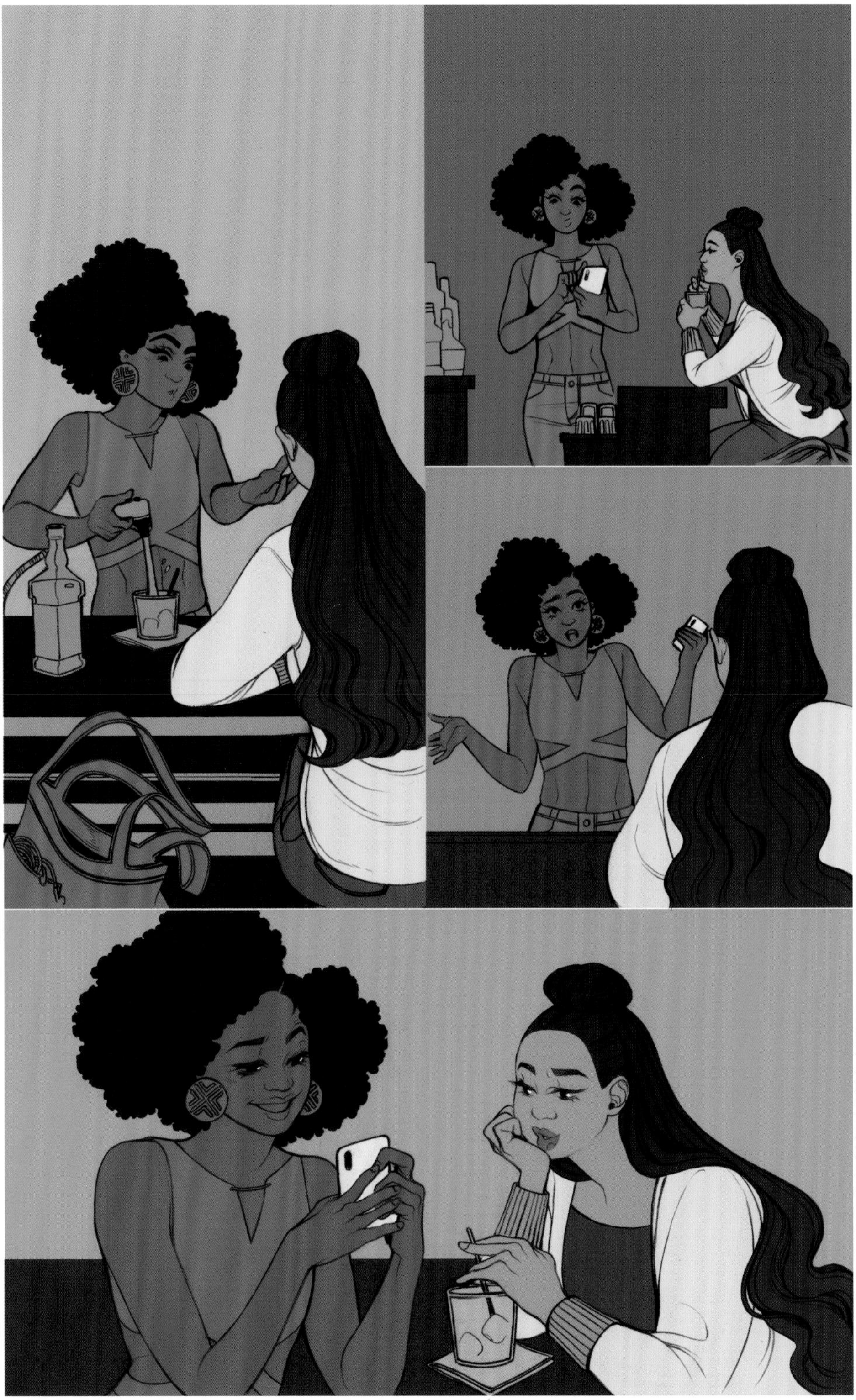

COLORS

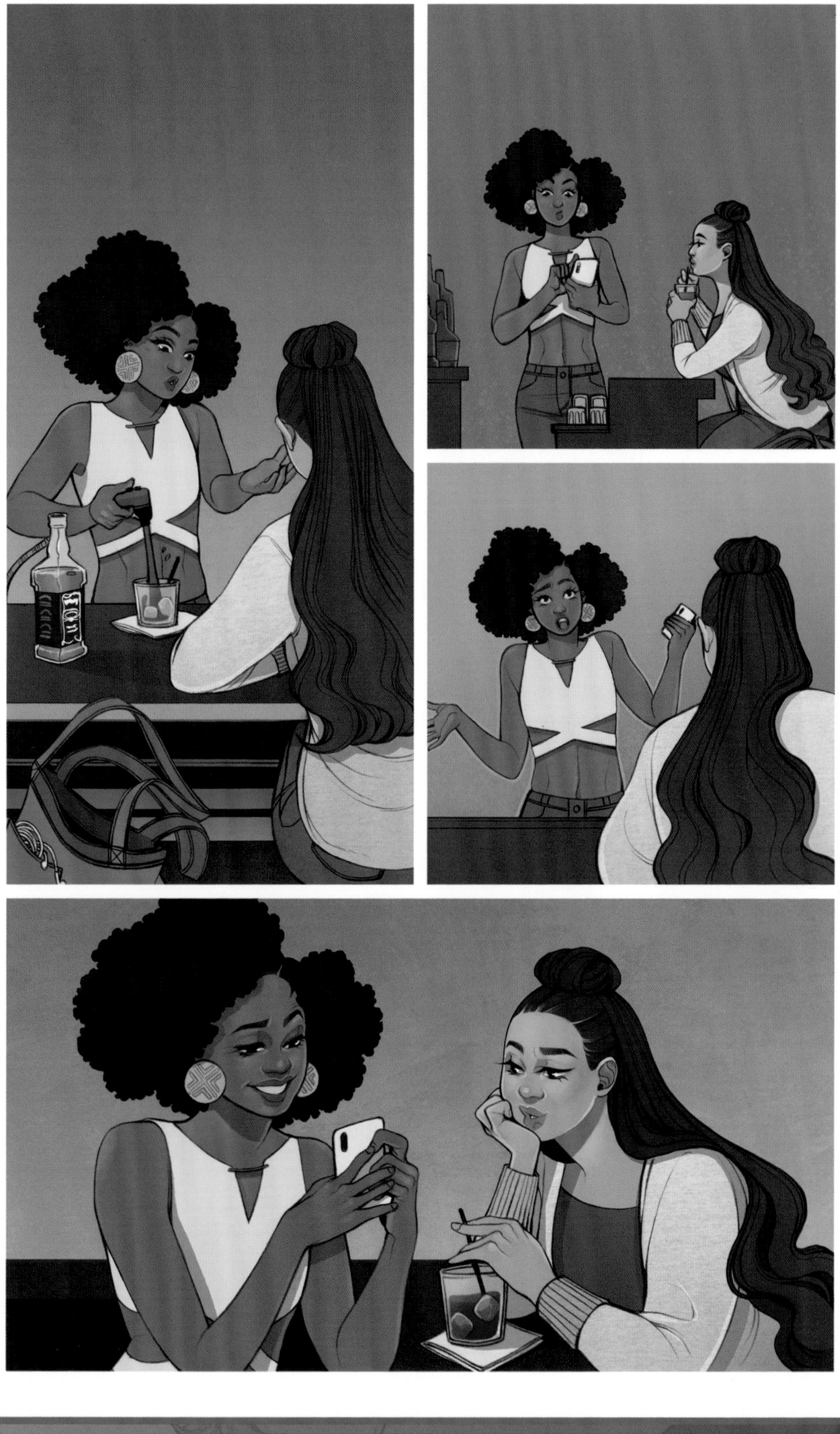

LETTERS

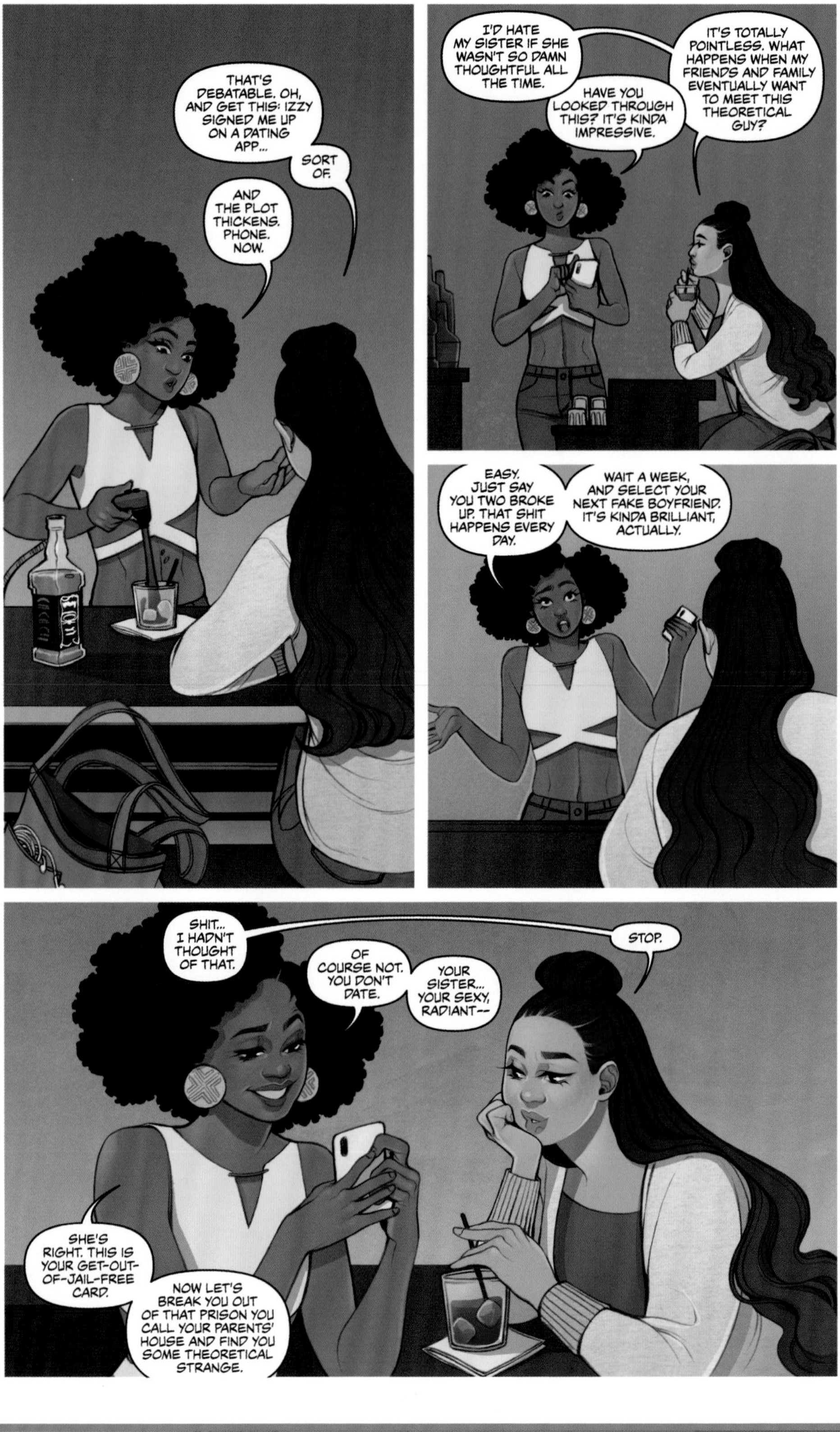
THAT'S DEBATABLE. OH, AND GET THIS: IZZY SIGNED ME UP ON A DATING APP...
SORT OF.
AND THE PLOT THICKENS. PHONE. NOW.
I'D HATE MY SISTER IF SHE WASN'T SO DAMN THOUGHTFUL ALL THE TIME.
HAVE YOU LOOKED THROUGH THIS? IT'S KINDA IMPRESSIVE.
IT'S TOTALLY POINTLESS. WHAT HAPPENS WHEN MY FRIENDS AND FAMILY EVENTUALLY WANT TO MEET THIS THEORETICAL GUY?
EASY. JUST SAY YOU TWO BROKE UP. THAT SHIT HAPPENS EVERY DAY.
WAIT A WEEK, AND SELECT YOUR NEXT FAKE BOYFRIEND. IT'S KINDA BRILLIANT, ACTUALLY.
SHIT... I HADN'T THOUGHT OF THAT.
OF COURSE NOT. YOU DON'T DATE.
YOUR SISTER... YOUR SEXY, RADIANT--
STOP.
SHE'S RIGHT. THIS IS YOUR GET-OUT-OF-JAIL-FREE CARD.
NOW LET'S BREAK YOU OUT OF THAT PRISON YOU CALL YOUR PARENTS' HOUSE AND FIND YOU SOME THEORETICAL STRANGE.

DESIGNS

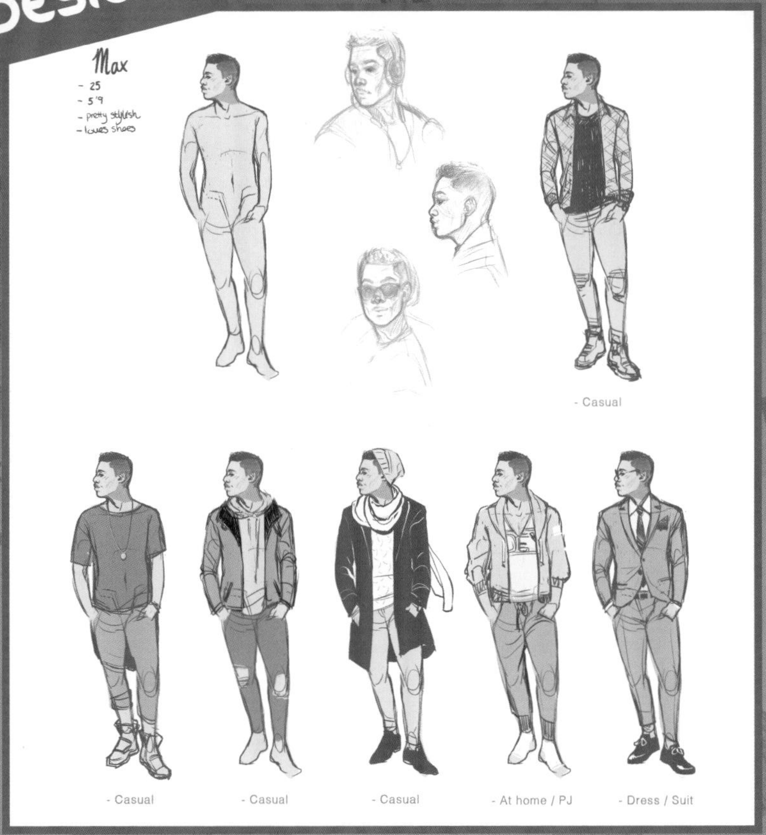

Max
- 25
- 5'9
- pretty stylish
- loves shoes
- Casual
- Casual
- Casual
- Casual
- At home / PJ
- Dress / Suit

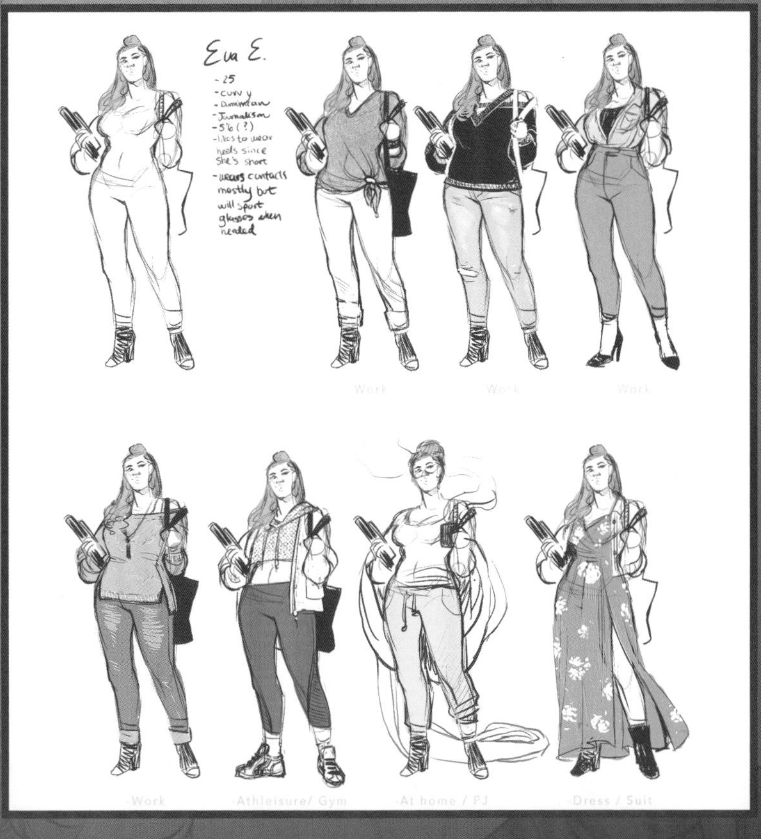

Eva E.
- 25
- curvy
- Dominican
- Journalism
- 5'6 (?)
- likes to wear heels since she's short
- wears contacts mostly but will sport glasses when needed
Work
Work
Work
-Work
-Athleisure/ Gym
-At home / PJ
-Dress / Suit

JEREMY HOLT

Jeremy Holt is a nonbinary author whose most recent works include *Made in Korea*, *Before Houdini*, and *Skip to the End*. They have received high praise from Brian K. Vaughan (*Y: The Last Man*, *Saga*, *Runaways*), as well as magician and *New York Times* crossword constructor David Kwong.

ELIZABETH BEALS

Elizabeth Beals is an Atlanta-based illustrator best known for her love of detail, geeky pinups, and cover work. She graduated from the Savannah College of Art and Design with a BFA in illlustration. When not drawing she enjoys baking, wooing the neighborhood cats, and rereading all her magical-girl mangas.

ADAM WOLLET

Adam Wollet is a writer and letterer from Jacksonville, Florida. He is the cocreator of *Kingdom Bum* (Action Lab), and his lettering work can be found in books from Image Comics, Heavy Metal, Action Lab Entertainment, and others.